the ABCs of Spellcraft

the ABCs of Spellcraft

COLLECTION
VOLUME 2

JORDAN CASTILLO PRICE

jcpbooks.com

First published in the United States in 2020 by JCP Books
www.JCPBooks.com

ISBN 978-1-944779-16-0
First Edition
Also available in audiobook

DEDICATION

The majority of my time spent writing happens in my own head without anyone else around, so I always look forward to the part where I get to collaborate with my friends.

Andy Slayde is not only a fastidious continuity editor, but one of my biggest supporters. Her suggestions always make the books so much better.

Nick Hudson, the voice of Dixon and Yuri on audiobook, is an absolute joy to work with. I'm so thrilled he was willing to narrate a new-to-him genre and bring Spellcraft to life.

Contents

LAST BUT NOT LEASE

DIXON

1

"Yuri? Do they have beaches in Russia? I mean, obviously, they must. If not on an ocean, some other body of water. A sea, maybe? At the very least, there must be a lake or two. Russia's a pretty big place, after all. Cold, though...so, there's always the possibility the water's frozen over. But frozen or not, there'd be a beach under all that snow. Right?"

Yuri flipped down the visor where the sun cut into his eyes, then glanced at me as if he wasn't sure whether or not my question was rhetorical. Traffic was sparse on this side of Pinyin Bay, out toward the waterfront by the off-season campground he called home, so he could spare a glance from the road. I offered him my most encouraging smile.

"There are beaches."

"See? I knew it. There's just nothing like a day at the shore! I'm sure Pinyin Bay—the actual bay, not the city—might not be the most inviting body of water around, what with the bacteria count and the eels. But, the memories...."

Oh, the memories.

When I was twelve and my cousin Sabina was almost ten, I was so giddy with excitement over the annual Penn family picnic, I don't think I got a wink of sleep for at least three days. I always loved it when the whole clan was together—this was back when Papa Tobar was still with us—especially if the shindig happened at the beach, even if this meant some truly irritating grains of sand crept all up into my business.

I was particularly eager to embark on a new water game I'd invented, a test of prowess and will that I stood some chance of winning, since it didn't involve any actual swimming. It hadn't occurred to me that I wasn't so hot at standing still, either. But luckily for me, neither was my cousin.

While my dad and Uncle Fonzo wrestled with the flimsy sun shelter that kept trying to blow away and my mother chased everyone around with a can of aerosol sunscreen, Sabina and I braved the water.

It was still early in the season, and though Pinyin Bay isn't very deep, it can be well into the spring before it's finally warm enough to disguise the fact that someone just peed. (Though if you're convincing, you can pass it off as a wayward current.)

The water was cool, but not too cold for a couple of intrepid young souls like us. I was probably lit from inside by the sheer eagerness of my anticipation. And Sabina was always compelled to prove that despite being the younger one, she could do anything I could do, and more.

This probably explains the sheer length of time we spent in the water.

What kid isn't up for a good game of chicken? And in the version I'd dreamt up, the rules were simple. First one out of the water loses. It wasn't the cold we were competing against, though. It was the fish.

The aquatic ecosystem of Pinyin Bay isn't exactly noteworthy. There's carp and minnows, catfish and bass, and even the occasional eel. And perch, of course, but only in the deeper parts you can only reach by boat. Seagulls own the shore, though Spellcrafters who haven't been quilled yet steer clear of them, since their feathers would make for some incredibly small writing implements.

I'm not sure what it was that nibbled on you if you stood still for any length of time. But whatever it was, there sure were a lot of them.

Sabina and I faced off several yards from shore, me up to my chest in murky green water, her up to her shoulders. Her mom had raked her dark hair into a ponytail on the top of her head, and not a very careful one at that. It canted sideways like a jaunty, avant-garde hat, while Sabina narrowed her eyes and watched me closely, daring me to move.

We stood there for what seemed like ages. In reality, it was more like half an hour, each of us watching as the other tried not to flinch while the fish accosted us with their curious nibbles. Who knows how long it might've gone on, had Mom not called for us to come get our hot dogs before the seagulls did.

Our game of bay-chicken ended in a draw, which we both acknowledged with a solemn nod as we turned to slog toward the shore.

That's when we discovered the Pinyin Bay leeches were more that just urban legend.

But, hey. How many people can actually claim their first-ever hickey wasn't from a fellow human being?

I snuggled up to Yuri once he turned down Campground Lane. The posted speed limit is only 15 miles per hour on the rutted dirt road, and given that all the connective tissue beneath his truck is suffering from corrosion, he usually takes it even slower than that.

So many memories on Pinyin Beach. And not all of them as G-rated as Leech Day.

"Yuri?" I said. "Your cabin...is it anything like Russia?"

For a few seconds, he was so quiet I almost thought he didn't hear me. But of course, he'd heard me. I'd spoken loud and clear and the radio was busted. Even so, I was just on the verge of repeating myself when he said, "Pinyin Bay is nothing like Russia."

Was that a good thing? A bad thing? A thing that was just so different it was difficult to assign a value judgement? Before I had to come right out and ask, he said, "St. Petersburg is a historic city. Palaces, cathedrals, museums. That's the part the tourists all see… but that's nothing like the parts we lived in. Square. Plain. Gray. All the buildings were Soviet-built to be solid and unpretentious. But there was no place for creativity. No artistry. No joy."

I watched Yuri's intimidating profile as he scowled through the glass with his eyes fixed on the road ahead. While he was certainly capable of doing joy, you really had to know him to spot it.

We emerged from the tree-lined road, its canopy budding with fresh green leaves, and turned down the track to Yuri's tiny vacation cabin. The place was a steal—apparently the campground owner was extremely grateful when Yuri saved him from a particularly tenacious elk that was trying to romance the guy's bicycle. Since it was off-season and the property wasn't generating any income anyway, he let Yuri move in. And yet, when Yuri looked all wistful and soft like he did just now, gazing through the windshield with that faraway look in his eyes, I suspected frugality wasn't the only reason he lived where he did.

The attic was pretty crowded now that Uncle Fonzo was home, so I slept at the cabin more often than not. Come Memorial Day, Yuri would need to find himself a new place. But until then, it was just him, and me, the smell of cedar and the hypnotic sound of the surf….

And the sheet of paper posted on the cabin door.

Yuri cut the engine and approached the cabin with long, purposeful strides. I scampered along behind him. "What is it?" I asked. "Did the Avon lady drop by? Usually she just leaves a catalog hanging off our doorknob, but sometimes there's a sample of shampoo or lip balm inside. Or glitter hand lotion that smells like candy canes…although it doesn't taste nearly much like peppermint as you might imagine—"

Yuri snatched down the paper and scowled at it hard. "It is not hand lotion. It's an eviction notice."

YURI

2

My possessions, what few there were, had been heaped into a cardboard box with a diaper logo printed on the side. A cartoon baby bared its two lower teeth at me as if to mock my situation. I turned the box with the toe of my boot so I didn't have to look at its leering face while I tried to figure out my next move, but all sides of the box bore the same unsettling image.

Intellectually, I knew it was nothing to be distressed about. The cabin had always been a temporary solution. And getting displaced in Pinyin Bay would be nowhere near as daunting as finding myself on the streets in Russia. But I'd been so sure I had at least another month.

At least.

Dixon thrust out a hand, palm up, and looked up at the sky. "It's starting to rain. We should get your stuff inside." He hoisted the box and staggered to one side, wobbled, and righted himself. It wasn't heavy. Just awkward. He strode confidently back to the truck and nearly wound up sprawled in the gravel when he banked off the passenger door. "Open that for me, wouldja?"

"It won't fit."

"You don't know that. Cardboard is flexible, after all."

It would be easier to let him prove himself wrong than to argue, so I opened the door. He shoved the box against the opening. Angled it. Tried again. Set the corner onto the seat, put his back to the box, and shoved with both legs. And only after he'd pushed and strained long enough to work up a sweat—or maybe it was the rain, coming down harder now—did he observe, "Who'da thought the door would be so small? Guess we'd better put it in back."

The box was already soggy by the time we had a tarp duct taped around it securely enough to stop the plastic sheet from flying away. A brief flash of lightning lit up the bay as I pulled away from my cabin, and the grayish sky darkened.

Dixon sighed happily. "April showers bring May flowers!"

Wordlessly, I headed toward his apartment.

Dixon lives in an attic. It would certainly make a serviceable apartment, had anyone ever managed to do more than the bare minimum of renovations. From what I pieced together, the "upstairs move" had been a hasty affair. With the help of a grateful plumber whose love life was bolstered by Spellcraft, the family had added a minimal bathroom and kitchen.

But the Penn family was not exactly handy. The attempt to wall off Sabina's bedroom consisted of a few 2x4s hammered crookedly together with a single sheet of gaping drywall screwed to one side. Once they'd realized carpentry wasn't something that could be made up as you went along, they opted to construct the rest of their "walls" with the creative arrangement of furniture.

An entire houseful of furniture.

Now with an assortment of small animals in their cages placed precariously on top.

I wasn't sure we'd be able to fit my box inside. Though maybe, thanks to the rain, it would now be flexible enough to cram it in somehow.

Dixon insisted on carrying my box, even though he couldn't see over the top of it. I allowed him to do it, since he seemed to want to so badly. But he also insisted on trooping up the stairs in front of me, which then left him standing on the narrow landing at the top with no way to open the door.

As much as I find Dixon's relatives surprisingly likable, I had hoped that his uncle and cousin would be at work, even if that meant mashing Dixon into the wall while I squeezed an arm past my wet cardboard box to open the door myself. I was still grappling with the unexpected news that I'd need to find a new place, and I would rather not have to endure anyone's helpful suggestions while I figured out my next move.

"Sabina? You home?" Dixon called out. "Can you grab the door?"

"Just a sec!"

The doorknob rattled. A man's voice: "Is it locked?"

Fonzo said, "It doesn't have a lock."

So. Unfortunately, not only were they both home…but they had company.

The doorknob rattled harder.

"The other way," Sabina called out.

The door rattled in its frame.

"Push," Fonzo said in exasperation.

And then the door swung open with such force, it nearly sent Dixon somersaulting down the stairs. Fortunately, the stairwell was narrow enough that I was able to brace against both walls, although it meant Dixon took a solid smack to the face from a wet cardboard box.

The strapping young man on the other side of the door was blond-haired, blue-eyed, and smiling. He had straight, white American teeth that were clearly the result of good nutrition, braces, and solid cosmetic dentistry. "Hi! You must be Dixon! I'm Biff, the luckiest guy in Pinyin Bay—your cousin's quite a catch." He stuck out his hand for a handshake…which Dixon obviously couldn't see, due to the huge box between them.

"Pleased to meet you, Biff." Dixon stepped forward and butted the box into Biff's chest. "Say, d'you mind? My arms are getting tired."

"Oh, right." Biff stepped aside. Dixon squeezed past him. Then I did the same. The boy smiled even more brightly and said, "You must be Dixon's significant other—I'm Biff!"

"Yes. I heard."

He thrust out his hand again. I ignored it.

Bad enough Dixon's family was there. But this cheerful stranger? I wanted nothing more than to put down my things and go somewhere I had room to think. I pushed a magazine rack out of the way with my foot and attempted to take the box from Dixon, but the Biff person was in my way, all eagerness and garish white smile. "Here! I got that."

"Leave it," I said, but Biff was determined to help me, whether I wanted him to or not. We both made a grab for it. I tried to hold on, but the plastic tarp was slick from the rain. It slipped from my grasp. Biff rotated the box at an angle to swing it around Meringue's cage. The cockatoo bobbed expectantly as she watched the unfolding action with eager eyes like two polished onyx beads.

Once he was clear of the cage, instead of righting the box, Biff turned it on its side. A shirt slid out from a gap in the tarp. Then a towel. Then a sock.

Sabina called to her new boyfriend, "Biff, gravity!"

"What? Oh, right." He rotated the box, which was useless. It just left the open top facing away from him instead of to the side. Clothing continued to slip out, leaving a trail of socks now as he strode along.

Fonzo met my gaze. We had an understanding, Fonzo and I. He saw me for who I was...and even so, he showed me more kindness than my own family ever had. But that didn't make him a pushover. In fact, he respected me more because of my edge. He gave me a subtle eye-roll, then told the boy, "Other way, kiddo."

"Ah! Gotcha!"

Biff turned it upside down. The tarp fell off and all my earthly belongings dropped to the floor. Everything I owned was drab, from my suits to my sweaters to my stiff woolen blanket. Everything but the plastic bottle of edible body glitter. Which was sparkly and pink. And which landed directly on top...for everyone to see.

Dixon dove in, scooped up the incriminating thing and swaddled it in a bath towel, but the others had already seen. His family has plenty of practice brushing things under the rug, though, and his cousin and uncle both pretended their attention had been elsewhere.

Meanwhile, Biff was still trying to figure out why the box suddenly weighed so much less.

To say Dixon had a bedroom in the attic was using the term very loosely. A bookshelf, a tall dresser and a few overstuffed racks of clothing walled off a futon on the floor covered with a polyester Wonder Woman blanket. When Fonzo saw Dixon was heading toward the "room," he moved to intercept.

"Just so you know, Dixon, since you've been staying over by Yuri's, I've availed myself of your empty bed."

Dixon paused in the "doorway"—the gap between dresser and bookshelf. "Oh."

I angled myself to peer over Dixon's shoulder. A box of Fonzo's things had been unpacked, and his clothing was draped over every available surface, while the Wonder Woman blanket was folded neatly in the corner.

"Temporarily, of course. While I get back on my feet." He brandished his mutilated right hand, which had been recovering slowly from its run-in with the dead man's quill. "Though, of course, I'd be happy to move to the davenport...."

He said it in such a way that it was clear he fully expected his nephew to demur. Instead, Dixon brightened and said, "That'd be great, Uncle Fonzo! I'd be happy to take the couch myself, but it would be a tight squeeze with Yuri, since he got kicked out of his place. Thus, the box."

The last thing I wanted was for my problems to be aired for everyone to see. But before I could fend off the family's concern, Fonzo was tutting with great vehemence while Sabina climbed over a recliner stacked with boxes to give me a hug, which I accepted stiffly.

While his daughter hugged me, Fonzo said, "Did they catch you bookmaking in your room?"

"What? No. I am not involved in any—"

"You can tell me if they did."

"I am not a gambler."

"'Cause I'm great at keeping a secret. Especially one where I'd stand to make a few bucks."

Dixon scooped up another armload of clothes, scattering socks. "No, Uncle Fonzo, Yuri didn't have any illegal gambling action going on—nothing he cut me in on, at least. We always knew the cabin was temporary. It was a vacation rental, remember?"

Sabina was affronted. "But it's not even Memorial Day."

"I know! Weird, right? And it happened without any notice at all. Just this morning we were…um…." He blushed vividly, no doubt recalling the creative uses we'd discovered for a feather. Not his Spellcrafting quill, obviously—just a goose feather we found by the water. But the roleplay was scandalous, nonetheless. "Ahem. We were *talking* earlier about the fact that we haven't seen a single tourist yet, even though the weather's been decent." He glanced at the sodden cardboard box, which Biff was still turning around in his hands. "More or less."

"I can stay at Biff's place," Sabina told her father. "Then you could take my bed."

"That's a great idea!" Biff said.

Fonzo gave a forced laugh. "What? No! I wouldn't dream of displacing you from your own bed. Not when the davenport is so comfy."

Hardly the word I would choose. There was a stray spring that seemed to find me no matter which part of the couch I sat on. "I will sleep in my truck," I announced.

But, of course, the Penns would not hear of it.

"Nonsense," Fonzo said. "My old buddy Ladin Silver is in the market for a place since his lady-friend kicked him out. We could go in on a bachelor pad together—"

Dixon was puzzled. "Isn't that the guy Aunt Rose left you for?"

"Water under the bridge," Fonzo said grandly. "That was years ago. And I've got to admit, I've always admired his moxie."

"I'll just pack an overnight bag," Sabina said, but Fonzo casually sidestepped and blocked her way. As cavalier as he may seem, he's always been protective of his daughter.

Dixon said, "I still have an office, technically. We could stay there."

"I tried that once," Fonzo said. "The pizza joint next door is up all night making dough. All that banging and clanging and mixing and kneading—I hardly slept a wink."

"What about your parents' place?" Sabina suggested to Dixon.

"Now that they've got all those animals, I'm not quite sure where we'd fit. If Dad let me sleep in his recliner, Yuri could take the sofa...."

Biff piped in, "Or you could form a hunting party."

We all ignored him, since he was having an entirely different conversation and was blissfully unaware.

Fonzo said, "There's always the Pinyin Inn. Overpriced for such a fleabag—er, budget conscious motel. But if you trade a little Craft—" Abruptly, he cut his eyes to Biff. Scriveners were loath to discuss their business in front of the Handless. Even Handless as oblivious as Biff. "Craft beer. All the rage. A couple of six-packs should do it."

Sabina said, "Sometimes you can get a deal if you book online." She poked around on her phone for a moment, then frowned. "Says here Pinyin Inn shut down last week."

"For repairs?" Fonzo asked.

"Weirdly enough, no—looks like they sold to some investors from out of state."

All three Penns assumed identical expressions of puzzlement, as if no one had invested in Pinyin Bay in the history of the city.

Biff didn't notice. "I'd form a hunting party."

"I'll call Ladin." Fonzo brushed his palms together—winced as he jostled his injured finger—then gazed out at the sea of boxes and furniture, and asked, "Has anyone seen my address book?"

I would sleep in my truck. I had done so before and could do it again. The tarp should keep out the rain where the window didn't quite seal shut. Where had the tarp gone? Stuck to Fonzo's foot and dragged halfway across the attic. This was why I was better off alone. Friends and family might mean well, but in the end, I was not cut out to be around so many people.

While I made my way toward the tarp, Biff took Sabina's phone, tapped something in, and handed it back to her. She scrolled for a moment, then brightened. "Hey, guys, look at this! Hunting Party Apartment Hunters. Not only do they guarantee the best prices in Pinyin Bay, but you can move in the same day. And no credit check!"

It seemed too good to be true. But when Dixon turned his bright, eager smile toward me, how could I refuse?

DIXON

3

Although Yuri really had his heart set on camping, it was actually kind of nippy outside—not to mention raining like all get-out—so I convinced him to stay with me until we could get his official living situation squared away. I know it was silly of me to feel guilty for sleeping in my own bed, but poor Uncle Fonzo was so uncomfortable on the davenport, we heard him snorting himself awake all night long. And while I would have happily traded places with him, I don't think Yuri would have appreciated sharing a bed with my uncle.

First thing in the morning, Yuri and I got in touch with Hunting Party Apartment Hunters and arranged to meet them in the Spellcrafter part of town, informally known as Scrivener Village. I wasn't raised there, myself. The Penn family has always maintained that it's best to live among the Handless, since they're the ones keeping Practical Penn in business...plus my mom refers to it as a "Spellcraft ghetto." But I've always been fond of that wonky old neighborhood. Nobody gives you any flak about being in the Craft. The buildings have plenty of character.

And it's incredibly affordable.

More importantly, maybe our fellow Spellcrafters really were our target customers now. If we lived among the Scriveners of Pinyin Bay, between my Uncrafting and Yuri's amazing Seens, we could drum up enough business to actually pay the rent.

"Okay, Yuri, take a right just up ahead, then a quick left…wait, you missed it. That's fine, we'll circle around. Up that alley. Watch the pothole…easy. There! I know, it looks like a driveway, but it's more of an alleyway…well, that's how we all use it, anyhow."

"Is there not a single street that goes through?"

"You'd think so, but no. We have a saying in Pinyin Bay: *crooked streets for crooked Spellcrafters*. Actually, it's more the Handless that say that…but we Scriveners have basically made it our own. The neighborhood grew up organically as the Scriveners settled here and let their friends and families know the coast was clear. And you know how Scriveners like to work with their hands. It's a lot cheaper to add on then to buy new. New York, San Francisco, Chicago—they've got awesome Scrivener Villages that even rival their Chinatowns…unless you were hoping for dim sum, in which case, Chinatown definitely wins out."

We pulled up in front of a spindly four-story walkup decked out in no less than four types of siding. Faux wood. Faux brick. Faux stucco. And peeking out at the corner that had a run-in with a vehicle, some very real asbestos.

Yuri squinted at the building. "Where is the address?"

"Sometimes in Scrivener Village you've got to extrapolate based on the addresses all around." A car pulled up and a Handless woman in her mid-thirties climbed out and wandered onto the sidewalk, repeatedly checking her phone. I rolled down my window and called over, "Are you from Hunting Party?"

She brightened. "I'm meeting them at…." she checked her phone again. "Well, I can't tell if I'm in the right place."

This woman would stick out in Scrivener Village like a blonde-haired, blue-eyed sore thumb. But, hey. If she wasn't worried about finding her car antenna stolen, more power to her.

She drifted toward the far end of the building while a car pulled up behind her little hatchback—a BMW ragtop. Very sporty—or very douchey, depending on who you talk to. A Handless man in a suit climbed out and moved to join her....

Why did he look so familiar?

"Come," Yuri said. "I don't want her getting first crack at the apartment just because she's a woman." He strode purposefully toward the newcomer. "I am Yuri Volnikov. Ten o'clock."

"Brad," the suit guy supplied. "And this is Molly."

Brad. Brad. Braaad. Had I gone to school with him? Maybe he lived near my parents. Though I think I'd remember such a fancy car in their neighborhood. It was really bugging me something fierce. Where the heck did I know him from?

Brad checked his watch. Rolex? No, Cartier. Way more cash than I'd ever wear on my wrist—and I'm really fond of my hands. "We'll just give the rest of the party a few more minutes before we set off."

Yuri scowled. "My appointment is at ten. It is ten."

"And you, clearly, are new to the Hunting Party concept. Hunting Party is an up-and-coming crowdsourced experience that really moves the needle on the traditional rental acquisition model."

Normally I'd say, *Hey, Yuri, I can hear your teeth grinding.* But this Brad guy. So stinking familiar.

"By sourcing multiple end-users across a series of properties and lowering average acquisition time, we reduce costs by minimizing the vacancy time of any given unit."

He flashed a grin at all of us to demonstrate how smart he thought he sounded—and that was when it hit me.

The thing about Brad, when he acts like a cad, it comes back to burn him...but twice as bad.

This was the creep who marked me late for my WheelMeal delivery by making me stand there outside his door! Of all people. "Funny," I said, "how chill you're acting about your last client's tardiness."

Brad gave me a blank look. Maybe it was for the best that I wasn't particularly recognizable without WheelMeal's trademark lime green visor.

A familiar voice behind me drawled, "Who's tardy? I'm right on time."

I swung around and found myself looking at none other than Vano Shirque—my childhood nemesis. Well, he would've been, had that word been in my vocabulary when we were seven. Vano was the great-grandson of Morticia Shirque, the oldest Spellcrafter in our circuit. Financially, the Shirques were no better off than any other Scriveners. But in terms of status, the entire Spellcraft community considered them a cut above the rest of us.

I'm a people person. I *like* people. But being bookended by both Brad and Vano was enough to make me break out in hives. Before I could suggest to Yuri that we go find an apartment on the other side of Scrivener Village, however, Brad said, "That's everyone. Gather 'round and prepare yourselves for a cutting edge take on the rental experience that utilizes all the latest research to streamline your transition and help you pivot into your new home."

Brad the Cad motioned for us all to follow. Yuri muttered, "I have no idea what he is talking about."

I slipped my hand through the crook of his arm. "Just your typical jerky blah-blah-blah."

"That...I understand." Yuri hung back—which I realized when I snapped back against him as if we'd been bungeed together. Once we were a few paces away from everyone else, he dropped his voice and said, "What about the Scrivener? You took one look at him and went pale."

"I'm sure it's just the lighting." As I claimed as much, of course, I noted it was shaping up to be a gorgeous spring day, bright and sunny.

Yuri adjusted his leather gloves with a tug. "Do you need me to work him over?"

"What? No! That's crazy! He's not selfishly malicious like Brad— at least, I don't think he really *means* to be a jerk. I've known Vano forever, and as far as I can tell, it's just his nature. And besides, whatever's happened between us is all water under the bridge."

"But he is your enemy?"

"Not exactly. More like...a frienemy."

Yuri narrowed his eyes, but didn't ask me to translate.

That was a relief. I wasn't sure I even could.

My relationship with Vano was complicated. I'd always thought he was the epitome of cool. Everyone did. Even the Handless could sense a certain something about him. An unflappable disregard of anyone else's approval. A confident ennui.

Did I mention we were seven?

In public school, I participated in spelling bees. But impeccable spelling is crucial in my family's line of work—just ask the Scrivener who killed himself trying to magically change the color of his hair. So, in my after-school Scrivener lessons, we did spell-offs, which took spelling to an entirely different level. Not only were we required to face off one-on-one and spell out random and obscure words, but to pen them in flawless calligraphy. In the event that both potential Scriveners spelled the word correctly, points went to the kid with the best lettering.

That year, I was to be matched up with Vano Shirque. I couldn't imagine anything cementing my reputation as a promising young Scrivener-to-be more than besting him in a trial of intelligence, artistry and skill.

Oh, who are we kidding? I wasn't hoping to best him. I wanted to mop the floor with him.

With Sabina keeping me company, I'd been up late into the night practicing a new flourish I'd recently mastered, a bold, rounded swoop off a lowercase double-f. Dad warned me not to be too fancy, but Uncle Fonzo had encouraged me with a secret smile. After my late night at the inkwell and an interminable day at public school, there I sat, waiting in that dank basement room beneath the public library that grudgingly allowed us to convene there. And sat...and sat.

Until it was clear that Vano couldn't even be bothered to show up.

I won by forfeit.

"A win is a win," my mother declared, while tacitly trying to cheer me up with a plate of store-brand Ritz Cracker knockoffs topped with genuine Velveeta.

Even so...who knew winning could be so hollow?

Now, today, as Vano slunk into the building—all easy grace and listless disdain—I was tempted to demand a re-match. Though given that he'd have no idea what I was talking about...I should probably hold my tongue.

We gathered inside the vestibule of the building, where Brad the Cad was waiting with an expectant smile and a handful of pre-printed name tags, the sort of cardstock things in a clear plastic holder with a pin on the back. He handed them out, but since Yuri was the one who'd booked the appointment, there wasn't one printed out for me. Brad dug out a blank tag and a felt-tip marker and handed them over. Writing with such inferior implements was no mean feat. But I slid out the card stock, propped it against the wall and—despite the pen's worn tip—inked my name with a stunning flourish that swooped up and over the terminating letter n and loop-de-looped through the capital D. The line might be slightly ragged, but the cartouche was spot-on.

Take that.

Vano didn't appear to notice. Not even after Molly cried out, "Wow, look at your gorgeous writing! I took a calligraphy elective at community college, but my letters were never *that* good."

While Vano ignored everyone, Molly fiddled with her own name tag, which she was struggling to open. Eventually, Brad the Cad took pity on her—or maybe he just wanted to get on with his awful spiel. He plucked the tag from her grasp, opened the pin, stuck it on her coat, and declared, "Decisiveness is key. The first party member to sign the Hunting Party rental agreement takes the lease."

"And everyone else?" Yuri asked.

"They move on to the next property, where we'll be joined with another hopeful tenant." Brad gestured toward the stairs. "Let's begin."

$$4$$

The stairs were loud. All three flights of them. Oh, they were carpeted—with the sort of indoor-outdoor carpeting that's basically the same color as dirt, and just as plush. But the staircase squeaked alarmingly with every step we took. Each person's footfalls were a bit different. Brad's felt impatient, Molly's tentative. Vano's, unhurried (naturally). Yuri's? Surprisingly soft. Mine? Embarrassingly syncopated, as I snagged my foot on nothing and managed to fall *up* the stairs.

We gathered in the vacant apartment's kitchen, with its harvest gold fridge, avocado range, and burnt orange dishwasher. I had no idea dishwashers even came in orange. Yuri narrowed his eyes. He was pickier about color than a non-Seer might be. Maybe his eyeballs have more rods and cones. At any rate, I could tell from the get-go the apartment would be a no-go.

It was so ugly that even Vano took notice. He telegraphed his displeasure with a single raised eyebrow, but Brad the Cad was unperturbed. He had a script to follow.

"You've all been pre-approved." Brad drew a sheet of paper from his breast pocket, opened it with a snap, and smoothed it out on the ugly gold countertop. He set the cruddy felt tip marker beside it. "Remember, the first one to sign is the winner."

I'm not sure "winner" was the word I'd use to describe anyone willing to linger in that apartment. Not only did the living room have red shag carpeting—but it ran halfway up the walls! Although I'd always been one to admire a bold design choice, even I had my limits.

I didn't notice Molly had come up behind us until she spoke. "Isn't it interesting how all this carpet really muffles the sound? The floor still creaks, even in here." She shifted her weight experimentally. "You can feel it if you really pay attention. But all those squeaks and creaks we heard coming up the stairs are nowhere to be found. People don't realize how important a good soundscape can be to their happiness." She sighed wistfully. "My boyfriend is especially sensitive to sounds. I asked him to move in with me, but he said he'd never be able to stand this little gurgle my radiators make. So I'm thinking I can change his mind if I find somewhere less...gurgly."

Poor Molly. Once she was out of earshot, I told Yuri, "She obviously doesn't realize that was just her boyfriend's way of telling her he had no intention of moving in together. I know the way guys think, even straight ones. And moving in is a giant step...even for the Handless—who think their relationships needed sanctioning by City Hall to be legit, never mind how easy it was to get a divorce. The official act of co-signing a lease? Just one step shy of the altar."

Yuri grunted and went back to make sure all the kitchen cabinets opened and closed. I paused just inside the bedroom to check out a rather weird combo of paneling—no less than three shades of wood. Either the decorator scooped up a bunch of rejects from the paneling sample showroom, or they were colorblind. Although even the texture was markedly different. As I tried to tally up the various textures, lost count, and started over again, Molly called out, "Wow. There's even wallpaper in the bathroom. On the ceiling!"

I heard a small laugh—scarcely a breath—and spun around to

find Vano Shirque had drifted up behind me. It's rare that I'm ever at a loss for words, but being alone with him had me second-guessing myself. Would I sound like I was trying too hard if I casually mentioned I was involved with a Seer? Maybe. But failing to mention it would hardly be the boyfriendly thing to do.

Then again, Vano probably forgot I was a Scrivener to begin with.

If he even remembered me at all.

Vano slipped past me. He opened the closet door to the clatter of a dozen wire hangers, closed it again, then said, "Congrats on your new quill." Without waiting for an answer, he wandered back into the hall.

So…was that sincere? Or was there some kind of reverse psychology in play—and by congratulating me, what he actually meant was to call attention to the way my Quilling Ceremony had crashed and burned?

I followed him out into the hall—which had a kind of funhouse effect happening, what with the different styles of vertically striped wallpaper there. But before I could probe to see whether or not he was dissing me, Brad the Cad popped out like a well-tailored Jack-in-the-box and said, "You'll note it's a very spacious unit for the price. Plenty of closet space and high ceilings."

I angled into an office that had been a porch in its original life. The far wall was hung with an old patchwork quilt. Vano was prodding at the edge. "Whoever painted last didn't take this thing down. Now the edges are sealed into the paint." True…but it really did seem to dampen the ambient noise. Which really was surprisingly pleasant. He picked more industriously at the paint job until he could slide in a finger and peer behind. "Is this whole wall made of old doors?"

"Why are you here?" I blurted out. "I mean, obviously you're looking for an apartment, and where else would a Shirque live if not Scrivener Village? But your great-grandmother has that massive Victorian out on the edge of Pinyin Beach. I thought you had a room there. In a turret."

Vano gave a disinterested shrug, as if turrets are something one encounters every day. "Nana's moving into a senior condo. They offered to waive the 60-and-up age requirement for me…but, I told them not to bother. Figured it must be a sign that it was time to leave the nest."

Was that a dig about me living in my uncle's attic? Because I was totally an adult—I'd left home years ago. I just happened to need a place to stay when I got back.

Did he even know I lived in my uncle's attic?

Discombobulated, I headed into the living room. I found Yuri there, pondering the faux marble surrounding an empty rectangle on the wall that must've had a decorative mantle on it…several remodels ago. I planted myself beside him and cocked my head to try and see whatever it is he was seeing. Planning on getting himself a TV? Or maybe planning something a little artsier? But before I could start suggesting all the interesting things he could paint inside the strange plasterboard gap, he said, "What is it?"

"Just wondering where the mantle went. Did one of the former tenants pry it off the wall and take it with them? Or did someone try to start a fire inside and end up burning it down? Though you'd think—if that happened, there'd be some residual effects from all the char."

Yuri went to rattle some windows in the hallway, while Molly joined me and cocked her head at the same angle as mine. "Look, there's an outlet. It's the perfect spot for one of those new electric fireplaces. You know the kind—with the fake fire inside? The plastic embers look so realistic."

An electric fireplace really would make the room look a lot homier.

Brad the Cad strode in and said, "This apartment building was on the short-list for Pinyin Bay's historic preservation site for nearly twenty-five years."

Vano looked up from a nearby cabinet he'd been poking around in, pushing the door shut. It popped back open. "So what you're actually saying is that it was never approved?"

Brad ignored him. "The woodwork is all original. Solid pine."

Pine was the cheapest wood you could buy. I wasn't quite sure it mattered anyhow, seeing as how most of it was hidden under at least a dozen layers of kelly green paint. All except the wedgewood blue in the master bedroom, I now saw, which had been painted to match the country-fried wallpaper border of hearts, flowers and kittens.

Molly poked her head into the room and smiled broadly. "I love cats!" Cheerful girl. "When my boyfriend moves in with me, maybe we can get a cat of our own. It'd be like having a child. But without the stinky diapers."

"Plus they're a lot quieter than dogs," I observed. And even though I didn't own a cat, I could concede that the kitten wallpaper was awfully cute.

"You're so right! I'll keep that in mind if Teddy has any misgivings."

"I take it that's your boyfriend? Teddy?"

Her cheeks pinked rather cutely. "That's just what I call him. 'Cause he's a big ol' smush-bear."

"O...kay." Hopefully the smush-bear was on the same page about moving in together. Because if he wasn't, well...my heart might kind of break for Molly. And I'd known her for less than half an hour. Aiming for a purely philosophical tone, I said, "Some people like to live with a partner. Or a family. Or a cat. But some people are really into their alone-time. And folks like that need a lot of personal space."

As I said this to Molly, Yuri paused in the doorway and furrowed his brow. At least, I think he did. Gravity often seemed to have an undue effect on the man's eyebrows. Yuri joined me and said, "You know this city better than I. What do you think? Is this the sort of place you would consider?"

The place had grown on me. Had I really thought it was garish when I first walked through the door? I took another look around. It was entirely possible there was some kind of color harmony at play that I was totally unaware of, but I didn't really trust my judgment where color was concerned. I might've been taught a dozen different ways to cross a letter-T, but the ink I used was invariably black. Yuri was the Seer, not me. "What matters is what *you* think."

The furrow between Yuri's dark brows deepened.

Molly crossed to the front window and gave the miniblinds a tug. They cascaded down from the bracket with a clatter. At least the little slats matched each other. Though when I tried the blinds on the next window over, I saw that not only were the blinds two different shades of off-white, but they were slightly different sizes. Despite the fact that she was now dealing with a pile of fallen blinds, her optimism was undeterred. "This apartment has so much potential. Not only is there a formal dining room, but a dedicated office."

Huh. When Molly put it that way, the apartment did seem to have a lot of potential. And "dedicated office" was definitely more appealing than "room made of scrap doors."

Vano had been meandering past as Molly pointed it out. He looked back toward the porch and blinked, then wandered off again. Molly picked the blinds up off the floor and set them sheepishly on the windowsill.

I went out into the hall and took yet another look around. Maybe it would be a good place for Yuri and me to settle down, I decided. Not only was my heart now set on one of those cute electric fireplaces, and not only was the kitten wallpaper border disarmingly adorable, but now that I thought about it, maybe an office would be just the thing. Wouldn't it be nicer to paint in a dedicated office than the way Yuri was doing it now? Namely, shoving aside piles of whatnot on the most convenient horizontal surface and bracing them with his right arm so they didn't fall over and wreck his Seen?

Before I could find Yuri and remark how surprisingly exciting it would be to have an office of our own, Brad the Cad announced to the apartment at large, "And the Hunting Party has its first official catch."

I felt a little twinge of pity over the thought of Molly signing a lease on an apartment her boyfriend might not even want. But then I realized she was still fiddling with a third set of blinds—one that didn't quite match either of the other two. So if it wasn't Molly…had Yuri pulled the trigger?

I dashed off to the kitchen, and there it was, lying on the countertop for all to see. The Hunting Party contract, with all its vaguely shady-sounding legalese. Inked across the bottom?

Vano Shirque.

And his signature was downright exquisite.

"Now, take a right at the next intersection, but make sure it's a hard right, not a soft right; the diagonal streets can get a little tricky. Once you see the gas station, cut through their parking lot—don't worry, everybody does it—and we should be just about there."

Cobblestone peeked through the asphalt, and as it passed beneath the wheels, the suspension shuddered. Good thing traffic in Scrivener Village obeyed the speed limit. Anything faster and we'd end up leaving half the exhaust system on the road.

If I'd signed for that apartment, we wouldn't be leaving a trail of dislodged rust behind us on the crooked street. But I hadn't. I'd held back even as I saw Dixon's "frienemy" headed for the contract. It was a good apartment. Quiet and spacious. But maybe... too spacious for just one man.

In St. Petersburg, finding an apartment was more competitive than any contrived "Hunting Party" event. Most places had entire families crammed into just a few plain rooms. True, the flat we'd just seen had been put together without even a passing nod to harmony. But the carpeting really had muted the sounds of the neighborhood. And I was capable of handling more than just the small paintbrush in my pocket.

And yet, I'd hesitated. Once Dixon asserted that what mattered was what *I* thought, I realized I had been presuming the two of us would be moving in together—in his words, one step shy of the altar—while Dixon had been thinking nothing of the sort.

Good thing I hadn't made a fool of myself by saying so out loud.

"There it is, Yuri, across the street. Ooh, and it's right above a Spellcraft shop—the one that claims to be a payday loan place? Yep, that's the one. Just don't ever refer to the financial side of that business as a 'front.' Uncle Fonzo learned the hard way how touchy someone can get if you accuse them of something so obvious."

Pinyin Bay was not St. Petersburg.

"And there's Brad the Cad in his Beamer. Clearly, it should've been a Caddy. Quick, let's make sure we're the first ones in." Dixon gave me a thumbs-up and hopped out of the cab. I lingered for just a moment—Brad would wait for the whole group regardless, to get as much as possible out of the contrived competitiveness.

As for me, I found myself reluctant to even view the next apartment. In Russia, I took great pride in having a place all to myself.

But not anymore. Now, the idea was just…lonely.

A tiny hatchback pulled up behind Brad's convertible and two women got out. Scriveners do tend to have a similar look about them, but these two more so than most. Twin sisters: Violet and Pansy Strange. We hadn't seen them since the incident at their family crypt. Thanks to social media, though, we'd been able to watch them spend the money their mother had extorted.

"He-ey!" Dixon called out gleefully as he pranced up to the twins…then stopped short of hugging when he couldn't figure out which was Violet and which was Pansy, thanks to two pairs of dark sunglasses. He gave an abrupt, cutesy wave instead. "Don't tell me the two of you are apartment hunting, too! What are the odds?"

Given that their mother was a sadistic sociopath and their old home was a former mental asylum, probably pretty good.

One of the twins tossed her hair and said, "Now that we've seen the wider world, Strangeberg is feeling a little too small for our taste. Not that Pinyin Bay is exactly a sprawling metropolis."

The other added, "But at least I won't have to listen to Dahlia accusing us of financially ruining the family." Violet found the word "mother" distasteful—I knew the feeling—so that was who this twin must be.

Dixon asked, "So you're looking for a place in Scrivener Village where you can establish yourselves professionally?"

Both women cringed, and Violet said, "Not at all. This is just the only neighborhood we can afford. I haven't touched my quill since we got on that plane."

Pansy said, "Me neither. Scribing holds no appeal to me whatsoever. There's so much more to life than Spellcraft. Ever since we were kids, that's what everyone presumed we would do."

Violet said, "But did anyone ever consider what we might want?"

Dixon looked from one to the other. "What *do* you want?"

Pansy tipped up her chin and said, "I'm exploring the field of baton twirling."

Dixon's smile went a bit forced. "Uh...professionally?"

"Well, you do need to start on the amateur circuit and work your way up."

"Wow. I hadn't realized there was money in that."

"Haven't you heard the expression, *Do what you love and the money will follow?* Things become sayings for a reason."

"A...bsolutely. How about you, Vi?"

The other Strange twin tipped down her sunglasses and gave us a look over the frames, one brown eye, one disturbingly violet. "I'm going to be a model."

"Oh...uh, right," Dixon stammered out. "I'm sure you'll find *all* kinds of modeling work. Especially since most models are so freakishly tall, no doubt there's a real niche opportunity for someone barely five-foot two soaking wet. Hey, look, here comes the final member of the Hunting Party."

Molly joined the group, looked from the twins to Dixon, and said, "Are these your sisters?"

The three Scriveners exchanged a look, and Dixon said, "Just old friends."

"Wow, I'll bet you get that a lot."

Only from the Handless. Dixon was too polite to mention it. But before he was forced to come up with yet another stilted nicety, Brad approached the group and said, "Ladies. Gentlemen. Are you ready to view one of the hottest rental properties this up-and-coming area has to offer?"

An old woman dragged a shopping trolley through the center of the group, muttering to herself. And though her wispy hair had gone white and her eyes were pale with cataracts, there was no doubt in my mind that her bent fingers fit easily around a quill. As she pushed through the group, she hawked and spat, barely missing Molly's foot.

Brad bared his teeth more fiercely and said, "Let's go upstairs."

The building was only two stories...at least, that was what it appeared from the outside. But inside? On the landing halfway up was a narrow door of the sort I'd expect to conceal an ironing board, but this door was set with a peephole and a lock. Brad produced a key and unlocked the door.

"That's unusual," Molly ventured.

Brad opened the door with a flourish and said, "This property is absolutely brimming with custom craftsmanship and old-world charm."

Not only did I need to duck to fit through the ludicrous door, but I had to turn sideways as well. And even then, it was a good thing I wasn't claustrophobic.

The inside of the "apartment" was no better. Whether the floors upstairs had been raised or the ceilings downstairs had been lowered, I could not say. Perhaps both. But judging by the accumulated patina and wear, the alterations had been made many decades ago.

I reached up and touched the ceiling...and I didn't need to stretch. It was barely more than two meters high.

Dixon had paused beside the front door, looking puzzled. "How does furniture fit through?"

Brad was prepared for the question. "That's the beauty of this property. It comes fully furnished with beautiful antiques."

More like someone walled off the rooms without realizing there was no way to get the furniture back out without a sledge-hammer. The furniture was certainly old. A strange combination of Victorian and Art Deco, all of it elaborately carved, inlaid and veneered. I am not picky about furniture, so I was sure it would suffice. Until I looked closer, and saw that the carving was not merely decorative, but figurative. Every table had claws for feet. Every finial bore a face. And every last stick of furniture was staring at me.

Molly came up beside me at the dinette and said, "Look how cute! This table's got a monkey carved into every leg. And they have tiny little people-hands!"

I shuddered and went to see where Dixon had gone off to. I followed the sound of the twins' voices and found the three of them in the bathroom. A claw-foot tub was at the far end. The floor sloped toward it, straining to bear the weight of the cast iron. I dreaded to think what would happen once the tub was filled. In fact, I wasn't so sure, structurally speaking, the four of us should all be standing in that room together.

The Scriveners didn't seem to notice.

Pansy said, "Once we got back from Europe, do you know what Mother had the gall to tell us? That we'd need to take on boarders to make ends meet—and it was all our fault."

Violet crossed her arms. "I still say she should sell the place."

Dixon chimed in, "It's a total seller's market—that's what I heard Brad mention. And, sure, he's not entirely trustworthy...but given the slim pickings in the real estate section, I'd say he might not be exaggerating much."

Pansy said, "Mother should have our family members trans-ferred from the mausoleum and just sell the place off while she can, but she never will. It's a matter of pride."

Violet rolled her eyes—one brown, one violet. "If real estate's as skewed as they say it is, maybe the whole boarder idea isn't so far-fetched after all. But what kind of weirdo would want to live in Strange Manor if they had *literally* any other choice? Look at this." She shoved a printed flyer into my hand that read, *Your Manor... Your Home.* I squinted at the photo. Dahlia had attempted to dress up the front door with a welcome mat and a pink floral wreath... and it still looked like a haunted mental institution.

"The sooner we get out of there, the better." Pansy crossed over to the sink and opened the medicine cabinet—more thoroughly than she'd intended to, as the cracked mirror came off in her hands. Gingerly, she propped it against the wall. "But I don't see why we're looking at apartments in Scrivener Village. Every one of them will be as dubious as the next."

"Sad but true," Violet murmured. "I've had it with Spellcraft, and frankly, I'd rather live anywhere but this part of town. But there were no listings in our price range other than the ones through Hunting Party. Not a one."

I ducked through the doorway and headed out to find somewhere less crowded to suffer through the remainder of the viewing. The rent might have been affordable in this place, but with all the furniture staring at me, I'd cave in my skull on a doorjamb before the week was out.

Yet, something about the place appealed to me. No doubt some deeply buried Freudian predilection. And the monkeys carved into the dinette, in a certain light, were actually somewhat...cute.

I found my way to the living room, where the ceiling was even lower. My scalp prickled as invisible cobwebs caressed my stubble. Molly was there, gazing at a mantle carved with elaborate vine work. I looked closer. Small faces of miniature carved birds looked back. Molly moved over to make room for me and said, "You don't see elaborate work like this. Not anymore. My boyfriend Teddy says handcraft is a dying art. Ever since the first car to roll off an assembly line, all people care about is how fast, cheap and uniform something can be produced."

"What is his job?"

"Teddy? He's a mortician." Molly was focused on the woodwork as I was wracked by an uncontrollable shudder, so she went on as if this were something I wished to know. "It's a dying art—and that's no pun. Caring for the remains of our loved ones is part science, part ingenuity, part artistry. But people around here aren't willing to pay what they used to for a nice funeral."

I have imagined my own funeral many times. Never has it been "nice."

"Teddy always thought he'd be able to buy out his boss at Final Slumber once the old man retired—you know the place, people always mistaking it for a mattress shop?—but then Mr. Final went and sold it to some developers from out of state. Razed that beautiful old building right to the ground." She sighed wistfully. "There was a gorgeous apartment there too, overlooking the wooded side of Pinyin Bay—just above the crematorium. Original hardwood floors. Gorgeous crown molding. Stunning flocked wallpaper. And so warm and cozy, even in the dead of winter."

Molly ran her hand along the carved mantel as she reminisced. Did she expect me to draw her out with polite questions? If so, she would be disappointed. The less I knew about the funeral home, the better.

"I always imagined that sweet little apartment would be our place, Teddy's and mine. And now there's nothing left of it but memories."

She sniffled, and I took a step back. Better to fall through the bathroom floor than be subjected to a stranger's tears. But before she could topple into her sentimental distress, something distracted her. She teased a tiny slip of paper from the twisted carvings, unrolled it, and read.

"Flames for candles and hearth-fires for bread, but beyond these red bricks, the fire will not spread."

The Spellcraft was older than everyone there put together. But still, it flickered faintly with *volshebstvo*.

"Would you look at that funny, old-timey cursive. People just don't write like that anymore. Except your boyfriend. He's got very pretty handwriting."

"I'm sure he is pleased you've noticed."

Molly rolled up the Spellcraft and tucked it back into the crevice where she'd found it, probably unaware that she was motivated to do so by anything other than a stray impulse. "If the two of you want this place, I understand. I'm not sure Teddy would be keen to live here, even with all the wonderful old-world artistry. This whole neighborhood is kind of iffy." She lowered her voice and said, "He's not too fond of Spellcrafters."

I was intrigued, though I made sure not to appear too interested. "Oh?"

"Well, you know how it is." Molly laughed nervously. "Have one bad experience with a certain type of person and it colors your perception of the whole bunch."

"If his problem is a bad Crafting…I may know someone who can fix it."

"No, no, nothing like that. It's just some raucous neighbors of his. Apparently Spellcrafters are an…*exuberant*…bunch."

Scriveners had their ways and traditions, and true, they shared some common characteristics—but exuberance was not one of them. If anything, they tended toward caution. Though compared to cooling corpses this man was accustomed to, no doubt most people would annoy him.

"This is such a beautiful apartment," Molly said. "But if you and your man have your hearts set on it, I won't hold it against you for signing on that dotted line before I have a chance to send Teddy some pictures."

Of course I didn't want the place. Not only did "my man" have no intention of joining me here, but I could barely stand up straight—and, besides, now that I shifted my focus, I felt the telltale tickle of Spellcraft emanating from all around me. I followed the sensation to a fire escape, though the landing didn't quite align with the window, and the sash was sealed shut with a century's worth of varnish and paint. Poking out from a gap in the molding was a bit of paper. I pulled it from its hiding place. Cotton rag—hardly yellowed with time. The Seen was a neat brick building, quite obviously the one in which I now stood. The cars out front were absent. And the Scrivening?

The building inspector and fire marshal too
see everything here is tickety boo

I did not know exactly the meaning of this "tickety boo," but as Dixon often said, I had the gist. And this long-gone fire marshal would have to be blind not to recognize the place for the baffling death trap it was. I left Molly snapping photographs of the creepy mantle and went to rejoin Dixon.

Conversation drifted out from the bathroom. I couldn't tell which twin was talking without seeing her. "Vinnie and Vito are getting their travel visas together, but they should be here in a few weeks. I'd hardly compare Pinyin Bay to the canals of Venice, but the guys are pretty eager to see America."

Dixon said, "Your new boyfriends are Italian? Ooh—I'll bet those are some sexy accents."

"Yeah, it's pretty much like living out a spaghetti sauce commercial. Good thing I don't mind chest hair."

"That's always important. But even more important...how tall are they?"

"I dunno. Normal-tall."

"You should take that into consideration."

"No doubt. And even if these weren't the lowest ceilings in Pinyin Bay...the last place my sister or I want to settle down is Scrivener Village."

Dixon strode from the bathroom with a small slip of paper in his hand. He was so focused on the paper, he nearly collided with me. He gave a little start and backed up a step. "Oh, hey, Yuri! Guess what I found! Actually, given the neighborhood—and given that it's all sparkly—you can pretty much assume. But listen to this: *Whether swell or undertow, ample waters always flow.*"

"This place is stupid with Spellcraft," Violet said. "I'll bet it's the only thing holding the walls up. And I'm so sick of it all—the fussy calligraphy, the careful wording, the scorn of all the Handless. I just want to be me…and be a highly paid fashion model. Is that too much to ask?"

Dixon chortled to himself. "Flow and undertow. Some rhyme! It's so *awesome* when Scrivenings rhyme."

Molly joined us in the hallway. "Did you notice that the building next door blocks the east wall of the bedroom? No annoying early-morning sun waking you up. Heck, I'll bet you could get away with regular shades instead of room-darkener shades. I haven't heard back from Teddy, but I don't know…this place might be too good to pass up."

Violet might claim that she wanted to just be "herself" (and also a model) but the look she exchanged with Dixon was pure Scrivener through and through. It declared, *the Handless see only what they want to see*.

Scriveners are a proud people.

Molly looked to me, but I had no advice to offer. But before I could even say as much, Brad strode out into the hallway and announced, "Another hunter takes the trophy! Better luck next time."

The four of us looked at one another, then trooped into the dining room to see with our own eyes. Pansy stood beside the dinette looking dazed. The contract on the table bore her signature, with the "y" so heavily flourished it looped across the entire width of the paper. The streaky felt-tipped marker hung absently in her hand.

Violet pushed past me, stomped up to her sister, tore the pen from her hand and threw it on the floor. "Pansy—how could you? No way can you twirl a baton in here without punching holes in the ceiling."

Pansy blinked as if waking from a dream. She pointed at the table and said, "But the carved monkeys have tiny little people-hands."

I should consider myself lucky that Dixon had no particular fondness for monkeys. And yet…part of me wondered if I would regret failing to pen my signature on that lease.

DIXON

6

I had no idea just how exhausting looking for an apartment would turn out to be. By the time Brad got Pansy squared away (and by the time Pansy got Violet onboard with Pinyin Bay's lowest ceiling) it was dark outside and well past suppertime. Brad the Cad collected everyone's name badges, said he'd text us the address of the next Hunting Party quarry in the morning, hopped in his dumb Beamer, and drove away.

Once Molly headed off to join her smush-bear of a mortician, I asked Yuri, "You don't think Brad literally means a quarry, do you? Like with rocks and stone and boulders and ore? Because as far as I know, the only quarry in Pinyin Bay was closed long before I was born. Too much natural gas escaping from mysterious underground channels. Total fire hazard."

"I would put nothing past him," Yuri said. And I couldn't be positively sure, but I think he sounded just a tiny bit hangry.

I joined him in the truck and said, "Why don't we head back to the attic?" Because there'd be all kinds of take-and-bake pizza there. Best of all, it would be free. And free makes anything taste just a little bit better. "Now, I know we've revisited the discussion on pineapple topping umpteen times, but it's worth mentioning that I had an initial aversion to it, too. But if you get drunk enough, pretty much anything can seem palatable...."

Try as I might, I was unable to get Yuri to weigh in on the merits of any particular pizza topping. And by the time we pulled up by Uncle Fonzo's house, I was pretty darn peckish, myself.

We climbed out and headed for the door, with me doing my best to squeeze in a few more toppings before I had to clam up. Our tenant, Edward Greaves, took particular umbrage if he could hear us walking up the stairs. Double-strike if we were actually speaking as we did so. And since his car was out front taking up its usual spot-and-a-half, our sojourn up the stairs would need to occur in silence.

There's a squeaky board just inside the doorway that I habitually step around. It just so happens to align with my natural gait, so I always need to remind myself as I open the door to veer to one side. If I plant my foot just right, I can avoid the board without knocking any of the pictures off the walls. But when I swung the door open and found someone sitting on the steps, I was so startled, my foot came down right on the loudest part of the board. It let out a reverberating squawk—followed immediately by vigorous pounding on the other side of the wall.

Uncle Fonzo looked up at us and gave his head a sad shake as picture frames rattled against the wallboard. "Six months left on this guy's lease?" Mr. Greaves wouldn't hear him above all that pounding. Probably. "I dunno if I can take it."

Yuri slid into the tiny hall behind me and eased the door shut. The floor didn't creak for him—he walks with uncanny silence. He pitched his voice low and said, "I can offer him something else to punch...something which will gladly punch back."

Uncle Fonzo sighed fondly. "And I'd just as gladly take a ringside seat. But we can't afford to lose him—not just yet, at least. Not until my finger heals and I can start earning for the family again." He skootched over and patted the stair beside him. I sat, while Yuri crossed his arms and settled back against the closed door. Uncle

Fonzo gestured vaguely at the rattling pictures. "Forget about the tenant. At least he's got an expiration date. I'm more worried about this Biff guy."

I'm sure Biff was plenty of things...but *concerning* was not at the top of the list. "He seems pretty harmless to me."

Uncle Fonzo gave his head another rueful shake, then settled against the wainscoting and gazed up at the portrait just above my head. I craned my neck to see. It was a Christmas card photo from the year Sabina was seven or eight, judging by the way her new front tooth had come in gigantic and screwy—whew, thank our lucky stars for braces.

"Every Scrivener hopes and dreams their daughter—er, *child*—will settle down with a Seer." Uncle Fonzo shot a glimpse at Yuri, as if he was still pinching himself over my good luck. "But I never really held out much hope. Finding an eligible Seer is like getting struck by lightning...while you're winning the lottery. And I didn't necessarily expect Sabina to find herself a Scrivener either, what with all the interfamily politics."

My eyes returned to the portrait. Aunt Rose was Handless when she and Uncle Fonzo met, that fateful night when her station wagon broke down outside the gentleman's club—the one he claimed made the best Brandy Old Fashioneds. (Happy Jack's no longer has topless waitresses—at least, I hope not. Nowadays, it's a pancake house.) My aunt and uncle had a whirlwind romance, though they didn't marry. Most Scriveners never do. But when Sabina came along, as far as the Spellcraft community was concerned, Aunt Rose became one of us.

Even if she left Uncle Fonzo ten years later for Ladin Silver—though as far as I knew, the two of them never produced any step-siblings for Sabina.

"I always told my daughter to make sure she didn't pick anyone who could beat her in an argument. But I tell her lots of things. Who knew, of all my advice, that would be the piece she'd take to heart?"

Laughter carried down the stairs from the attic apartment.

Sabina's...and Biff's. Followed by a volley of ceiling-pounding.

"It's not that he's Handless," Fonzo said. "It's that he's as dense as your mother's angel food cake, and the thought of him laying his hands on my little girl...."

Sabina's a grown woman, and I'd hardly wish her a life of abstinence. But certain mental images I could definitely do without. "Maybe it's best to not think about it. Especially when you could be telling me what kind of leftover take-and-bake pizza she brought home from work tonight—"

"Maybe I can't hold my quill again. Not yet. But, Dixon? We need to nip this thing in the bud. And we need to do it now." His gaze flicked to Yuri. "With all the tools at our disposal."

The legality of Crafting to break up a relationship wasn't in question—*super* illegal—but I wasn't exactly shocked my uncle suggested it. When all you've got is a hammer, everything looks like a thumb.

But Yuri disagreed. "The *volshebstvo* will not take kindly to you meddling in the affairs of another Spellcrafter. And when your daughter finds out what we did—not *if*, but *when*—she will only cling to this man more tightly."

Uncle Fonzo deflated. "Then, that's it. I'd better keep my eye out for a bumper sticker that says, *My Grandchild is Dumber than Yours*."

"No one's having any babies," I said, though now that he'd mentioned it, I could totally picture a bunch of little Biffs scampering through the attic, all blond and smiling and earnestly blank. "There's got to be another way to, ah, encourage him to leave."

Yuri muttered, "Lead him to a revolving door—he may never find his way out."

Uncle Fonzo cocked his head to consider whether or not this might actually be a feasible plan.

I thought back to the day Yuri and I spent with the Handless in Scrivener Village—*crooked streets for crooked Spellcrafters*—which gave me an idea. "Has anyone filled this guy in on the family business?"

"Not yet," Uncle Fonzo said. "That's always a delicate...

conversation." The wheels were already turning. He began to brighten. "One that can go so disappointingly sour."

By the time he stood up and brushed off his knees, he was smiling.

"Dixon, my boy, you're more clever than people give you credit for. Let's go see how our buddy up there takes the news."

We found the big blond quarry upstairs—hey, wait, *now* I got it… *that* kind of quarry. Not rocks and drills and mysterious underground gases escaping. Anyway—Biff was sitting on the davenport with an arm slung around my cousin while the two of them watched videos on her phone.

"How'd the apartment hunting go?" she asked us.

Yuri gave a disgruntled grunt, waded over to his box, and started digging through it. We all paused to see if any further explanation was forthcoming. When it wasn't, I figured it couldn't hurt to seize the opportunity to set up the conversation so Uncle Fonzo could bring up his topic.

"Oh, you know how the neighborhood is up around Cursive Court. Twists and turns and dubious carpentry, all of it barely held together by…." I cut my eyes to my uncle. "Uh, sorry. I shouldn't have said anything."

Smooth as you please, he gave a convincingly regretful sigh—probably because he truly did regret our current situation—and said, "It's okay, Dixon. The truth was bound to come out sooner or later."

Sabina and Biff looked up from the phone. Biff with vacant curiosity, Sabina with mild alarm.

Uncle Fonzo moved aside a crate of old National Geographic magazines, planted himself gingerly on the coffee table, and said, "I think it's time we have *the talk*."

"Now?" Sabina squeaked.

"Now." Fonzo settled in despite the creaking protests of the table. "Biff, there's something you need to know about my family."

Biff looked up from the phone and blinked. "Are you in witness protection—and that's why you're hiding in this attic?"

"We're not hiding, we're economizing. And, no, nothing quite as exciting as that. It's the family business. What has my daughter told you about her job?"

"That she works in an office?"

It was the standard line we gave anyone who didn't need to be privy to the details—and people always seemed eager to change the conversation to a less mind-numbing topic.

Uncle Fonzo shifted into storyteller mode and fixed him with a dramatic look. "An office. That's exactly right. But it's what we do there that's so special. You see, for generations, the Penn family has been part of the fabric of the Pinyin Bay community. People turn to us in their hour of need—and we respond. Using the talent we were born with and the time-honored skills we've honed, we're there for people when they need help. Biff, this might be hard to hear. But Sabina, me, Dixon, even Yuri...we...are Spellcrafters."

"Sure, I've heard of you! The one-hour opticians out by the Interstate."

"No," I said, "that's Lenscrafters."

Uncle Fonzo hunkered down and tried again. "Those who practice Spellcraft work with pen and ink to harness the unknown forces of the universe and condense them down to a single potent creation that's both deceptively simple and stunningly complex."

"Oh! Right! I got a Spellcraft set for Christmas one year, but then I lost most of the little plastic wheels, and it wasn't much fun after that."

We all stared at him for a long moment—even Yuri, who'd unearthed an electric kettle from his belongings and was now attempting to plug it in somewhere.

Silence hung there between us all for a long moment...and then I realized what Biff was talking about.

"That's not Spellcraft...it's a Spirograph."

Uncle Fonzo decided to give it one more shot. "We don't draw designs, Biff—at least, the Scriveners don't. We write. Complex phraseology that weaves together what is, and what we hope will be, in a powerful web of words. Our mystical art is shrouded in secrecy, and no one would blame you if you were unsettled by Spellcraft."

Biff had been listening really, really hard. And then he brightened. "Don't worry, Mr. Fonzo. I've read those stories before and they hardly ever give me nightmares."

Over by the kitchenette, Yuri gave a long-suffering sigh. "Lovecraft. The author is Lovecraft."

Finally, Sabina couldn't take it anymore. "Biff, we don't make glasses or graph spiros or publish creepy novels. We write spells. Magic spells. Practical Penn. That's our shop. That's where we do Spellcraft."

As Mr. Greaves pounded on the ceiling—Sabina's voice really cut through the floorboards when she got excited—Biff processed the revelation. If it were possible to see a cartoon cutaway of Biff's brain, I imagined it would be powered by a fat little hamster running on a wheel. One that was half asleep, had its cheeks stuffed full of Cheerios, and was constantly falling off.

"Wait a minute," Biff said, and the rest of us all braced ourselves for another doozy. "You're saying you guys are Scriveners?"

Sabina threw her hands in the air. "Yes! That's what we're saying."

"Oh! Cool!"

Aaand…apparently, that was the totality of his opinion on the matter.

Uncle Fonzo wasn't quite buying it. "You're sure it doesn't bother you? Spellcrafters keep our cards close to our chest, and most Handless…er, *handsome* young guys like you are bound to have certain misgivings."

"Can't imagine why. My next-door neighbor dated a Scrivener and everyone loved her. She even helped my sister address all her wedding invitations. Best handwriting we'd ever seen. Even after they demolished three packs of wine coolers."

Sabina stood up from the couch so suddenly, she knocked over a box of handweights. They were more for toning than sculpting—we're talking three-to-six-pound range. Even so, it made a pretty big impact. Followed by even more impact, as Mr.

Greaves pummeled the bedroom ceiling with his complaints. "Dad? Can I talk to you in the hall?" She snagged me by the arm. "You too, Dixon."

The three of us crowded out onto the landing and closed the door behind us. Dozens of smiling family photos surrounded us on either side, reminding us that we truly were a close-knit bunch. But Sabina wasn't smiling now.

In an agitated whisper, she said, "Why are the two of you trying to scare Biff? He's never been anything but nice to either of you."

My Uncle puffed up like does when he gets all affronted...which generally means he's been caught massaging the truth. "Scare? I meant nothing of the sort. He's obviously led a very sheltered life. I just wanted to *prepare* him."

"You don't approve of him because he's Handless."

"Come on, kiddo. We both know I've got nothing against them."

"*Them*? You're prejudiced. That's what you are."

"If I were prejudiced, would I have ended up with your mother?"

Sabina poked him in the shoulder. "You're still mad about mom leaving you for Ladin Silver, aren't you? And now that we reminded you of your humiliation—"

"I wasn't humiliated! The relationship had run its course!"

"—you're taking it all out on poor Biff. Let me tell you both something. Biff is a nice guy. He's agreeable. He's optimistic. And he has never mansplained a single thing to me. Not even once."

Probably because he didn't understand anything well enough to even attempt it—but I knew better than to fan the flames when Sabina was on a tear.

"Look, kiddo, you can't blame your old man for wanting to make sure Biff was worthy of you."

"Sometimes the Handless can be kind of mean about our livelihood," I said in all sincerity.

Uncle Fonzo said, "If breaking the news about Spellcraft was a test, then he passed with flying colors. How can you possibly be upset about that?"

Sabina might have been mollified, but when she turned to head back into the attic, my uncle caught my eye and gave me a look that conveyed he'd be asking us for that Scrivening again just as soon as the coast was clear.

Once my cousin was out of range, I whispered, "You'll need to be more subtle, Uncle Fonzo. Yuri was right—the more Sabina needs to defend Biff, the harder she'll dig in her heels." Which would then, no doubt, be followed up with a vigorous volley of thumps on the ceiling of the room below. "You've gotta be chill."

"Chill? When my daughter's shacking up with that…guy?"

"No one's shacking up. There will be no bouncing Biff babies. Sabina's pretty smart—give her some credit. There's only so long she'll put up with a boyfriend who can't figure out how to open a door."

Uncle Fonzo gave a grudging harrumph. "What about you and Yuri? Sign any leases?"

"I'm thinking we should limit ourselves to one. But, no. Nothing yet."

"The boys down at the coffee shop say properties in Pinyin Bay are getting snapped up left and right."

I considered this as I headed back inside to make sure Sabina wasn't still fuming. "Maybe so. But sometimes it's best to keep your options open.

I found Sabina wedged onto the davenport between Yuri and Biff. The old couch was listing toward Yuri's end, though they probably couldn't redistribute their weight without someone sitting directly on top of the wayward spring. Yuri and Sabina each held a bowl, and a couple of spent packets of instant oatmeal were tossed on top of the boxes on top of the coffee table.

Sabina was stirring angrily. Yuri's stirring actually looked a lot like Sabina's. But since Yuri always looks at least mildly perturbed, I didn't read anything into it.

Biff didn't seem to notice, even as Sabina practically drove the first spoonful directly down his throat. He spluttered a bit, then chewed happily. "For the longest time," he said around the mush, "I used to think it was called goatmeal. Which is pretty silly, since everyone knows goats only eat tin cans."

Sabina shot us a withering look, then shut him up with another heaping spoon of goatmeal.

7

I've never considered myself the type of guy to hold a grudge, but I'll be honest...I wasn't too keen on finding an apartment via Brad, since I didn't trust that guy any farther than I can throw him. Which is a weird expression, when you think about it. But since I doubted I'd be able to chuck him more than a couple of feet, maybe the saying was pretty apt. Anyway, since the whole Hunting Party thing seemed just a little too slick, I even resorted to looking for listings in a good, old-fashioned newspaper. (There just so happened to be one on the porch—what luck!) There were only a dozen ads, and I called them all. Every one of them who answered said the exact same thing: the place was already taken.

Which left us meeting up with Brad—yet again—bright and early, on a crooked old street in Scrivener Village. Now *there* was a guy who knew how to exploit his loopholes. How could I possibly trust any kind of legal document knowing Brad the Cad was involved? Unfortunately, unless a magical apartment complex sprouted up out of the ground, it was Hunting Party or nothing.

Molly was back again for another round of apartment hunting, looking painfully chipper. Or maybe she just had resting cringe-face that she thought would pass for a smile. "Hi, guys! Today's gonna be our lucky day, I just know it. I've been sending us all kinds of positive apartment-finding vibes."

"How useful," Yuri murmured.

"My Teddy was just beside himself last night. His inconsiderate neighbors were in rare form—stomping, screaming, throwing things around. I don't know how much longer he can take it. Ohh, look—popcorn!"

We all turned toward a storefront with the smell of margarine wafting out the ventilation system. The Colonel's Kernels was a mainstay of Pinyin Bay snacking. The shop did brisk business during the tourist season, selling popcorn and caramel corn and cheesy corn and, in a stroke of very creative upwelling, sunglasses. But we weren't in tourist season, and their main product had a pretty ephemeral shelf life. Denizens of Pinyin Bay knew better than to shop at Colonel's Kernels between November and May, unless they liked their popcorn chewy...or unless they misplaced their shades.

Yuri scrunched his face. "Something is burning. Between that and the fake butter...this smell is turning my stomach."

"Are you hangry again?"

"What is this *hangry?*"

"'Cause I can go grab you a popcorn. Once that buttery chemical hits your system, you'll hardly smell a thing."

I was just about to sell Yuri on the virtues of traditional American artificial flavorings when the shop door swung open with a jingle of perky little bells, and a portly guy strode out with a family-sized bag of popcorn in his hands. It was the infamous Colonel's Kernels "mixed bag," an offering bigger than a small child, filled with popcorn of every flavor—basically whatever they wanted to get rid of, up to and including whatever they scraped off the bottom when they cleaned out the hoppers.

As the bag shifted, a familiar face was revealed—a face belonging to the guy who'd swept Aunt Rose off her feet once her relationship with Uncle Fonzo had "run its course." There was a lot of the man to take in—let's just say he could polish off the "mixed bag" without any help from anyone's former aunt. I hadn't remembered Ladin Silver being quite so rotund. Then again, I'd never spent much time with him, since whenever Aunt Rose stopped by for a visit, he'd stay out in the car studying the off-track betting forms.

He ground his way through the handful of popcorn, then announced, "Chewy!" And then he took note of me and said, "Dixon Penn? Well! It's been a few years. How's your little ragamuffin of a cousin?"

"Sabina? Er...all grown up."

"Glad to hear it. I was always pretty fond of the kid. Park her at the kitchen table with a few plastic dinosaurs and she could entertain herself for hours—and she didn't ask any awkward questions. Now my last Handless lady-friend—you wouldn't believe the doozies her rugrats come up with."

"You dated a woman with no hands?" Molly said with dismay.

Ladin blinked, not having realized he was in mixed company, then recovered. "Industrial accident. Resilient girl, though, never let it keep her down. As long as you left all the doors slightly ajar, she did just fine."

Luckily, before his story got out of control, Brad the Cad butted in. "So good of you to join us, Mr. Silver. Now, before we get started, name tags." He passed out the pins, which were the same ones from yesterday, given that mine was still the one I'd hand-written.

Again, Molly had trouble with her pin, and again, Brad pinned it to her lapel, then herded us all toward the door. "Everybody brace yourselves for the apartment of a lifetime. This building was one of the first constructed in Pinyin Bay—back in the 1800's, when it was known as Eel Harbor—and it served as a boarding house for pioneers working on the railroad."

Molly said, "But there is no railroad in Pinyin Bay."

"And you can thank Des Moines for that. But in the age of steam, there was a man with a dream. And that man built the stately structure that stands before you. Let's head inside."

I'm not sure if the Scriveners of yore had any particular feelings about handcrafted goods. After all, back before the Industrial Revolution and the printing press, everything was done by hand. But nowadays, with most everything standardized and mass produced, it's a novelty to find something individually crafted. And as a people who take pride in writing things by hand when a fancy font will do, we Spellcrafters tend to appreciate anything handmade.

Apparently, we weren't the only ones. "What a beautiful railing," Molly exclaimed.

The handrail leading up the stairs was hewn from a tree that was felled long before any of us were born. The wood was worn smooth from more than a century of hands gliding up and down, and it glowed with a gentle patina that could never be replicated by synthetic stain and polish. Most people are too caught up in their busy, day-to-day lives to notice those kinds of details. Heck, I might have missed it myself, had Molly not pointed it out. And that would've been a real shame. It truly was one handsome railing.

At the top of the stairs, we found ourselves in a long, narrow hall with so many doors up and down each side that when I tilted my head, the perspective swam. Brad the Cad paused beside the first door and said, "If you're looking for convenience, look no further. This unit is the epitome of time-saving ergonomics, with everything in reach."

"Unless you're like that poor amputee," Molly murmured with a shudder.

As Brad searched through his keyring, I took the opportunity to get the scoop on Ladin's current living situation. "I heard you were in the market for a place. How come?"

"I'd been calling Bayview Park my home for as long as you've been alive."

"That trailer park out by defunct strip mall?"

"That's the one. Cheap rent and a stunning view of the Bay... when you could manage to crane your neck around the county detention center. But a few days ago, every trailer in the park had an eviction notice tacked to the door."

"Couldn't you just take your trailer and go somewhere else?" I wondered.

"It's not as easy as you'd think—it's a mobile home, not a winnebago. And, unfortunately, when I tried to pry it off the foundation, the whole darn thing fell in on itself. Probably should've hired professionals instead of a group of panhandlers willing to work for five bucks apiece. Anyway, what's done is done, and once the trailer collapsed, I figured it was a sign for me to move on."

He sucked a few popcorn kernels out of his teeth, then said, "I had no idea it would be so hard to find a rental. I called every ad in the paper and came up empty-handed. I've got to find my own place. Living with my new lady-friend is getting old, fast. How can we keep the magic alive if I'm depending on her to keep a roof over my head? A man needs a place to hang his hat. A place to claim as his own. Otherwise, the next thing you know, he's standing outside a fitting room holding someone's purse."

Brad unlocked the door and the five of us piled in, Ladin Silver chomping contentedly on another handful of popcorn, Yuri walking silently on the creaky floors. The apartment door let into the kitchen—at least, that's what I thought.

"Where's the rest of it?" Ladin asked.

I wasn't sure there even was a "rest." With a bathtub slotted into the corner between a two-burner stove and the world's smallest cafe table, this room took multi-functioning to an entirely new level.

"Oh, it's just like those old-time efficiencies in New York City!" Molly exclaimed.

"That's right," Brad said. "Every inch of space is maximized so there's zero waste. It's the perfect milieu for the new minimalism."

Ladin strolled over to the tub and shot a dubious look inside. "In other words, it's smaller than a wool sweater that went through a hot wash."

Unruffled, Brad strode to a low cabinet and swung it open. The space beyond was tucked beneath the stairs to the third floor, which made for a diagonal ceiling and a triangle of a space...with a toilet wedged inside. "Back when this property was built, it was a luxury to have your own water closet."

Yeesh, "closet" was right. I wasn't sure I could squeeze myself in there, let alone Yuri. He'd have to go easy on the resistance training if he was hoping to fit on the commode. And no way would Ladin be able to cram his bulky self in there, especially with a popcorn shop at the foot of the stairs.

Frankly, I couldn't imagine anyone in this day and age who'd want to live in such a cramped apartment, minimalist or not.

In the main room—the *only* actual room—Brad was giving a demonstration of how a murphy bed folded down from the wall. "Tiny houses are all the rage these days. So are historic homes. This tidy unit combines the best of both worlds."

Brad would say anything to unload the apartment. That much was obvious.

"Isn't it romantic?" Molly asked me.

That hadn't exactly been the way I would describe it. "Romantic, how?"

Molly took in the tiny room with a sweep of her hand. "Wanting your own place, like Mr. Silver says, has nothing to do with gender roles. Showing your loved ones you care is universal. The setup here—the tub, the stove, both in the same room—it's the perfect place to luxuriate in a bubble bath while your main squeeze cooks you a romantic dinner. And then, when things get interesting, a bed folds right out of the wall."

When she put it that way, it almost sounded fun—and, frankly, until Uncle Fonzo went back to work, my chances of scoring some alone-time in the attic with Yuri were slim. When I took another look at the bed, I couldn't help but imagine how much fun it would be to see just how much pummeling it could take. Yuri and I hadn't had any privacy since we'd found his cardboard box sitting outside the cabin door. And the more I thought about that, the more eager I was to try out that foldaway bed.

Hold on a sec, what was I thinking? Neither Yuri nor I could cook worth a darn, and it was highly unlikely he'd woo me from the stove while I was scrubbing down my nether regions. Besides, was that a little sparkle I glimpsed over by Molly? I thought it might be. But where?

There's an old Scrivener game called "Spot the Splot," where the first one to pinpoint the stray ink spatter in a big sheet of elaborate calligraphy wins a shiny new pen knife. Finding a Crafting is a lot harder. Because while it's most likely a tiny slip of paper, there was nothing preventing a Scrivener and a Seer from working their magic on any surface capable of holding paint and ink. And looking for basically anything in a room that might or might not contain a Crafting is a pretty big challenge.

Why bother? Obviously, apartments in Scrivener Village were more than likely to house at least a few bits of Spellcraft. But the question was, what were those spells meant to do? After the whole Precious Greetings debacle, I was a heck of a lot less cavalier these days around other people's Craftings.

On a narrow set of shelves beside the stove—barely enough for salt, pepper and a single place setting—I reached overhead and ran my hand along the highest shelf to see if any telltale slips of paper fluttered down. All I got were a few stray pieces of very old popcorn.

Had I felt Spellcraft at work or just imagined it? I scanned each of the four walls in turn, looking for the telltale sparkle, which can be pretty darned subtle.

Nothing.

Since the five of us were shoehorned into a space barely big enough for one, it was hard not to overhear Ladin chatting with Yuri. While Ladin tried the taps—apparently, they worked—Yuri frowned down at the bathtub. "Of course, my lady-friend has a pretty nice setup in those senior condos out by the box factory. But a man needs his own space if he wants to be taken seriously. Know what I mean?"

Molly tipped up her chin. "It's not about being some kind of provider. It's about making space for someone you love."

Yuri was looking at her very closely, and I was truly curious what he had to say on the matter. But before he could explicitly agree nor disagree, Brad the Cad whipped out a familiar-looking sheet of paper.

He slapped the lease down on the countertop and said, "Don't deliberate too long, because a place like this won't stay on the market forev—oof!"

One minute he was spouting his trumped up sales pitch, and the next he was flying aside like a skinny girl in a roller derby as Ladin Silver made a grab for the lease in a burst of stale popcorn. Brad bounced off the Murphy bed and the springs squealed like a banshee in a car crusher. But before I could conjure up any mental images of the spring symphony I'd be subjected to if I ever got up to any sexytimes on it, I realized that Ladin wasn't the only one going after that contract.

Ladin had one side of the lease, but Yuri had the other. They each paused just long enough to size one another up...and then they both pulled. Yuri ended up with only the top corner of the document, while Ladin got the rest, which he immediately yanked out of the way, then turned to shield it with his bulky body.

Yuri grabbed the big red marker. If he couldn't snag the lease himself, he could at least stop Ladin from signing. But Ladin is a Scrivener—and we never go anywhere without a good pen. Smiling triumphantly, he whipped out a heavy silver fountain pen, pulled off the cap with his teeth, slapped the contract on the rim of the tub and signed on the dotted line. The signature was crooked, smeared, and practically indecipherable. But unattractive or not, it was still a legally binding document.

Brad levered himself up off the squeaky mattress and plucked the lease from Ladin's grasp. "Now *there* is a man who knows how to get what he wants! I'm sure your lady-friend will be very pleased."

Ladin hoisted his massive bag of scrap popcorn. "I'm sure she will." He a took good look around, somewhat dazed. "It's so... romantic."

You'd think I'd find it a relief that Yuri didn't manage to grab that lease. He was no stranger to living in a cramped space, what with the cabin being barely large enough to hold a bed. But for such a fearless guy, he's easily squicked. I knew that eventually, the smell of fake butter would get to him. Especially whenever the popcorn downstairs burned. Was I disappointed he couldn't cook me a romantic breakfast while I lounged in the tub? And, more importantly, would I need to break into the building to get another look at that gorgeous railing in the stairwell? It seemed like I should be more devastated...and yet, once I'd mentally conceded the apartment had gone to Ladin Silver, the appeal of kitchen-tub and the handcrafted railing began to fade.

Brad handed us an address on the opposite end of Scrivener Village with a triumphant little smirk and said, "The spoils go to the victor. Maybe next time you'll be a little quicker on the draw."

Yuri and I headed downstairs and climbed into the truck. "I'd love to wipe that smug look off Brad's face," I muttered.

Yuri pulled on his driving gloves. "It's better to show your displeasure with something that doesn't leave a mark."

I was about to clarify that I didn't mean *physically* when my phone rang. It was Uncle Fonzo. And he sounded pretty frazzled.

"We should have known Biff wouldn't have the good sense to feel the same aversion to Scriveners that every other Handless in Pinyin Bay seems to. In fact, I think the whole confession only brought him and Sabina closer together. After the two of you left this morning, they rolled out of the bedroom together. And on top of spending the night, he stayed for breakfast."

"The toaster pastries with the little frosting packets?"

"That's right. Not only did he finish off every last one, but he oohed and ahhed over the way Sabina swirled on the frosting."

Sabina always was pretty snazzy with her freeform cartouches.

"Don't worry, Uncle Fonzo. We'll think of something."

"I sure hope so, kiddo." And muttering something about *world's dumbest grandkids*, he hung up.

I turned to Yuri. He was deep in thought, with a stark frown line etched between his brows and an intense squint that had nothing to do with the sun slanting through the windshield. "I'm sure there's nothing to be worried about," I said. "Biff seems basically harmless."

Yuri made a dismissive gesture. I love it when he gestures. He always makes it look so European. "I care nothing about Biff, so long as he does not interfere with us. Your cousin is a strong woman and she can make her own decisions." He frowned even more fiercely, drummed his fingers on the steering wheel, then said, "Here's what I cannot fathom. Somehow, even Biff has a home to call his own."

Had Brad the Cad managed to get inside Yuri's head? Maybe I did want to treat him to a comeuppance after all—right in the nose. But my mother always says, "Punching something might feel good—but you know what feels even better? Not breaking your Scrivening hand."

I pried Yuri's fingers off the steering wheel and squeezed them in mine, then drew a little swirl on the inside of his wrist with my forefinger to get his attention. Yuri looked down at our hands, and his gaze softened. I said, "The hunt's not over yet. And frankly, in retrospect, I'm relieved you didn't pull the trigger on any of the places we've seen so far. Maybe the housing market is a little wonky right now—I'm sure it hasn't helped that both Pinyin Inn and Bayview Park closed down—but there's bound to be a place where you can stand up straight *and* turn around without running into a hot stove or tripping over the bathtub."

Yuri scrunched his face even harder. He does that when he's feeling emotional, while I act like I don't notice.

I said, "Let's just ditch the Hunting Party. After all, it was Biff's idea, so what does that tell you?"

"I need to find a place," he said. I would have recognized that tone even if he wasn't squeezing my hand hard enough to crack my knuckles—let's just say it's a good thing it was my non-dominant hand in reach. "It is important...." He trailed off and shrugged— which also manages to look European when he does it—then said, "It's important I make space...for us. At least, if you were planning to spend any time there."

What on earth? "*If*? What do you mean, if?"

Another shrug, this one less European, more pensive.

"Yuri." Gingerly, I extricated my hand from his vise-grip and cupped his jaw, running my thumb along the corner of his frowny mouth. Something was screwy. And if Spellcraft was at the root of the problem, someone was going to discover the business end… of my left fist. Which probably wouldn't make very good contact, given how right-handed I am, but it would certainly prove a point. "Why would you think otherwise?"

"I heard what you said to Molly. About people needing their 'alone-time.'"

"*People*, Yuri. Not me. I was just trying to soften the blow for when her smush-bear leaves her high and dry in the apartment he's never had any intention of moving into. Heck, I was so sure of my welcome, I didn't even question whether or not you wanted to move in together. Not that you should actually put me on the lease. If they ran a credit check on me, let's just say my record might leave something to be desired."

Yuri wouldn't look me in the eye. But his shoulders did unhitch. Marginally.

"You are not worried about 'keeping the magic alive?'"

"Pretty sure the magic's as vigorous as the victim of a regrettable spray tan with a rough washcloth."

Yuri grunted something that could be construed as agreement.

"Everything will work out," I reassured him. "So long as we stick together, how can it not?"

I must have expected him to shrug me off for seeing him get so *verklempt*, so I was surprised when, instead, he turned and breathed a kiss into my palm. A shiver raced all the way up my arm and settled in my molars. It almost felt like Spellcraft…but wrong arm. And a thousand percent sexier. I knew full well what that mouth was capable of. And I was eager to see if there were any other intriguing tricks it might yet reveal. My voice was a little breathy when I said, "Let's head over to the next apartment so Brad the Cad doesn't start without us. We've seen apartments too ugly, too short and too small. With any luck, this next place will be just right."

YURI

I once suspected Dixon's relentless optimism was a charade. Who could possibly maintain a positive attitude in the face of such adversity? But he is nothing if not sincere. Whenever he said everything would work out, I might not quite believe it...but he believed enough for both of us.

What a relief.

We would find a place. For the both of us. And while I have never had much use for hope, determination would suffice.

Dixon slipped on a new pair of sunglasses, pointed toward a narrow driveway and said, "Hang a left up there, we'll save a few minutes while the Handless are stuck at the four-way stop sign no one pays any attention to. But watch out for the potholes. There's a real doozy up behind the mechanic's shop. I almost lost the Buick to it last spring. Say, d'you think the grease monkeys keep the hole there on purpose? And do you even call them grease monkeys in Russia? Speaking of monkeys, I wonder what that stinky little guy we liberated from Precious Greetings would have thought about that table. I hope he's happy at the zoo...."

I found the address and pulled up in front of a tall, narrow building just as old as the rest of the neighborhood. This one had a florist on the ground floor. They should make for reasonable neighbors, unless the florists took to pounding on the ceilings like the intrusive tenant back at Fonzo's house.

The building itself was understated—pale brick with sedate, neutral blues and greens for the window casings and shutters. Scriveners tend to gravitate toward vibrant color and pattern, so the subtle decoration made the building visually recede among the garish paint jobs on either side. I did not share the same aesthetic as those born into the Spellcraft, so to me, the building looked reasonably appointed.

Every property we'd seen had been so unsuitable—albeit strangely compelling—I presumed there must be something horribly wrong inside. Slanting floors. Crumbling walls. A total lack of stairs or a hole in the ceiling that looked up into the apartment above. Still, I was running out of options. No matter what the place looked like, if it even remotely resembled a dwelling, I was determined to claim it for Dixon and me.

As I put together my plan of attack—keep one eye on Brad to snatch the lease from him as soon as he pulled it out—Dixon looped an arm through mine, took a deep breath, and exhaled. "It really is for the best you didn't end up above the popcorn shop, Yuri. I think the smell of fake butter is still clinging to the inside of my nostrils. It's just too bad Ladin was the one who got it. No way would Uncle Fonzo think about moving in with him now. The two of them would never fit! Unless they slept in shifts—I've heard the sailors do that in submarines. Do you have submarines in Russia, Yuri? Or are they called U-boats? Actually, I'm pretty sure that's—"

He sucked in a breath and nearly choked on it, and I doubt it had anything to do with marine vessels.

I turned to see what was going on. A massive white Rolls Royce had pulled up to the curb. It must have been grand once—maybe twenty years ago—but there were hints of rust around the undercarriage now. An old woman climbed out, dressed in finery that was even older than her car. Some eighties fashions have made a comeback, but not this wool coat with padded shoulders, or the sagging, floppy hat...all in purple.

Her single long braid was the gray of Pinyin Bay on a winter's morning, but I strongly suspected it had once been black. She had the bone structure of a Scrivener. "Who is it?" I asked.

"Morticia Shirque—the head of the whole circuit. I haven't seen her since—" he broke off mid-sentence, huffed into his palm to check his breath, then smoothed his eyebrows. "Do I look okay? I should have shaved."

"You look fine." Actually, he looked adorable when he was flustered—and when he did shave, his five o'clock shadow came back in before he finished breakfast. But I doubted the old woman would notice. "Some relation to Vano?"

"His great-grandmother."

That explained Vano's status—and Dixon's nervousness around both of them. Many words don't quite translate from my native tongue to my adopted land, and many customs, too. But this so-called "pecking order," I understood. Scriveners come into power not because they have bribed or blackmailed the right person, but because they are better than others at bending the *volshebstvo* to their will. Those who are born with such talent only get better with age.

Anyone who knew the place of this Morticia Shirque in the local circuit would be a fool to underestimate her.

If the old woman was Vano's great-grandmother, she must be at least eighty. She looked closer to a hundred. But she still drove (although she parked nearly a meter from the curb) so her mind must be intact. When she climbed from the car, she walked with a strange, scuttling gait, as though her joints might complain, but she wouldn't let that keep her from getting where she needed to be.

Most importantly, her eyesight was still sharp—perhaps because the *volshebstvo* required that she be able to see the words. Even from a distance, she zeroed in on us and called out, "Dixon Penn! I need to speak with you."

I would have thought Dixon might drop my arm under the

scrutiny of his elder, but he clutched tighter instead. I might have been holding him up, I realized, as his knees began to shake. I gave his hand a surreptitious pat, though it didn't seem to help.

Morticia toddled over with great purpose, then squinted up at him. Her dark eyes were still canny. She cleared her throat elaborately, then said, "Is it true what they say? You found your quill after all?"

A deer in headlights…yet another useful American expression. I jostled him with my elbow, and he said, "Y-y-y-yes?"

"I'm relieved, for you and for your family—what with your uncle out gallivanting around—that the quill business is settled and done. Have you managed to figure out why the quilling failed?"

Dixon's mouth worked helplessly. No one could know Fonzo had lost his quill to a Handless. Not without ruining the Penn family.

"Bird was in captivity," I said. Not only was that explanation plausible, but it was true. And if there was any Spellcraft on the woman to alert her to a falsehood, it should have no issue with that statement.

"The quill chooses the Scrivener," Dixon said brightly. "Says so right in the ceremony."

She narrowed her eyes. "I see. Then the ceremony itself was not at fault."

"Circumstances being what they were, there was no good way the quill could have found me. I'm sure it's for the best that the laws of nature conspired to leave the poor bird intact."

Morticia turned her sharp eyes to me. "And you are?"

"Yuri. I am Seer. From Russia."

Obviously.

Dixon's nerves must be contagious.

"What an interesting development." The old woman sized us both up, missing nothing. Her gaze settled on Dixon's hand wedged into the crook of my elbow. "Very interesting, indeed."

Dixon said, "Were you looking for Vano? He won't be here—at least, he shouldn't be, unless he tours random vacant apartments for fun. He signed a lease yesterday."

Morticia gave a rattling sigh. "No, I'm looking for a place myself. Moving into that senior condo was the worst decision I ever made—all those old Handless men trying to seduce me with their Aqua Velva and their dentures and their tedious descriptions of their aches and pains. I never should have sold my house, but what's done is done. At the very least, I need to live among my own tribe."

We were saved from making any more "small talk" with the old Scrivener by the arrival of Molly. She said, "The driving around here sure is aggressive. I never thought I'd get through that stop sign, but it's a relief to be here now. Oh, what a charming old building!"

Brad was right behind her. He swept past us all and said, "Listen up, folks, enough lollygagging. It's time to hunt." He led us up a narrow set of stairs that were old and slightly shabby. "You'll notice the rent in this particular unit is unusually low..." he unlocked the front door and pushed it open. "But I'm required to disclose that this block has the highest concentration of Spellcraft shops in Pinyin Bay, which always drives down the property value."

What a relief. I'd been worried he was about to say that someone had been killed there...unless murders were just something he wasn't required to disclose. More Scriveners meant more potential income for me. But I did not want to get my hopes up without seeing the place—Brad was still blocking the doorway. And for all I knew, we'd find the floors were missing...and he had no obligation to disclose that, either.

I had steeled myself for something truly awful. I realized this when the door swung open to reveal a sitting room. Smallish. Plain. With hand-plastered walls and hardwood floors. And nothing collapsing, disintegrating or disturbing in any way.

Brad strode to the window and yanked open the blinds. Not only did they not fall down...they opened smoothly. "The walls are thick, so noise isn't an issue. Pets will be considered on a case-by-case basis. And there's off-street parking available just off the alley."

Strange. The features Brad was talking about sounded like actual features, and not contrived benefits to camouflage the fact that the apartment was practically unlivable. Unless there was Spellcraft at play, and I was only seeing what I wanted to see and hearing what I wanted to hear. But as Brad walked us from room to room, I searched hard for that subtle bending of the light around him that revealed the *volshebstvo*, and I saw none.

The bedroom was large enough for a double bed. The bathroom contained all the fixtures you would expect…and nothing you wouldn't. Since boiling water was the extent of my cooking skill, the galley kitchen would suffice. When Brad opened a door in the far wall, I presumed it would be a pantry, and was surprised to be led into yet another room…a room that was all windows, flooded with natural light. "This three-season porch gets the afternoon sun, so it's reasonably comfortable on all but the coldest days of the year."

The florist downstairs must have been using the space to keep their greenery green. Several big potted plants were stationed around the room, which made it look lived-in and inviting. But most appealing of all was the huge potting bench that stretched across the far side of the room. The perfect place to paint.

The apartment was on the small side and slightly shabby, with chipped woodwork, worn carpets, and windows beaded with condensation. It would not be to everyone's taste. But to me—it actually seemed rather…charming.

I took in the room and tried to see myself living there. The image came readily enough. And then Dixon crossed the floor and stood at my side, matching my gaze. The view was nothing special, what little we could see through the haze of moisture, just the alley and backs of the apartment buildings across the way. It was not the view that made my heart swell with dangerous hope, but the light. And the imagining of Dixon sitting beside me at that old potting bench, practicing his calligraphy while I daubed my paintings.

Dixon leaned forward and squeaked away some condensation with the side of his palm. I peered through and said, "Is that Vano?"

"Sure looks like it." Across the alley on a fire escape two floors up, Vano lounged on a stack of plastic milk crates, in corduroy slacks, a woolen scarf and a heavy sweater, looking surprisingly comfortable with a drink in his hand and his feet propped on the railing. "One of the doors in his office wall must've still been functional. But… is that fire escape made from old doors, too? That doesn't seem altogether safe…."

I hadn't realized we had circled round so close to that first apartment, but I wasn't surprised. Scrivener Village was not that big.

At the sound of her great-grandson's name, Morticia Shirque hobbled over and joined us at the window. Dixon, who treated her with the utmost respect, sidled over to make room. "Why, it is Vano. Of all my family—five great-grandkids—he's got a special place in my heart." She cut her eyes to the Handless, who were too close to miss our conversation. "Even if he hadn't inherited the talent for the *family business*, he'd still be my favorite. Young people these days don't respect their elders like they used to. But not my Vano. He's always been sweet to his Nana."

We all watched as he sipped his drink and thumbed around idly on his phone, oblivious to the fact that he was being gawked at by a roomful of apartment hunters across the way, or possibly just not caring.

"Still," the old woman said, "it was time for him to spread his wings and leave the nest. Have a life of his own. Maybe even allow me to meet a great-great-grandchild before my name is written in the stars. Even so. I do miss that boy something fierce."

And even though the two of them no longer lived under the same roof, if Morticia took the apartment, at least she could still see him from her porch, and they'd only be a short walk apart.

Brad noticed the three of us gathered at the window and presumed we'd discovered some flaw. "The condensation is just a result of all the humidifiers and plant sprayers downstairs. Most people consider the moisture to be an asset, what with static electricity and the drying effect of winter heating systems on the sinuses."

Again, I searched for *volshebstvo* as he spoke. And again, I saw none.

Molly joined us at the window, where she drew a heart in the condensation with the tip of her finger. "I think this sunroom is absolutely wonderful. It's the perfect place for an early morning cup of coffee with your loved one. And look how the potted plants are thriving! I've always felt guilty about throwing out poinsettias after New Year's, once all their leaves start dropping. But here, I'll bet I could keep them alive all the way through to the next Christmas. If only it weren't for all those Spellcraft shops. Don't get me wrong—I have no problem with those people myself. They're only trying to earn a living, and they provide a real service. But Teddy's just convinced they're all bad news."

"It *is* a wonderful room." Dixon said this mainly to himself. "And with the way real estate is being snapped up left and right, a place like this might never come along again. And I'll bet you can score poinsettias dirt cheap after Christmas."

As he said this, Brad reached into his jacket. When he pulled out a folded sheet of paper—its shape now familiar to most of us—everyone in the group turned to face him, and all of us tensed in anticipation. Molly was the farthest, and would need to shove past everyone else to get to the paper. I could stop her from reaching it without even trying. Dixon was in front of me. But closest of all was Morticia Shirque. And while she might not have been privy to the whole competitive nature of the lease signing, if she wanted that paper, all she had to do was take a few steps forward and grab it.

I glanced down at her orthopedic shoes...which was why I noticed Dixon's foot shooting out to trip her. It was tempting to let him have his way—and the image of a sunroom filled with poinsettias nearly blotted out every other conscious thought—but word of his successful quilling was just now getting around. I simply couldn't let him demolish his precarious reputation. It was no easy task. But somehow, I managed to resist the urge to fight for the apartment so I could stop him from making a terrible mistake.

I hauled him to one side before he sent the head of the Pinyin Bay circuit sprawling, which would seal his family's fate just as surely as revealing their secrets to Emery Flint. Dixon staggered, righted himself, then swung around to give me a look of affronted dismay.

Unaware that she'd nearly been knocked to the floor, Morticia took the lease from Brad and toddled over to the windows to look it over.

Dixon strained toward her, but I had a good grip on his arm. He snapped back against me and said, "Hey—what gives? Can't you see this apartment is perfect?"

I pitched my voice so that only he could hear. "I see that you are about to create a bigger scene than you did with your quilling ceremony. One which will be much harder to recover from."

He shook his head, confused. "But it's such a *wonderful* room. And...poinsettias! Yuri, you need to sign this lease."

So very tempting. Still.... "There will be other rooms," I said firmly.

Though given the current rental climate, I could not be sure those rooms existed in Pinyin Bay.

DIXON

9

When Yuri shoved me into a booth at the Pinyin Vittles diner, it took me a few seconds to realize that we were no longer standing there in the world's most *wonderful* three-season porch watching the head of our circuit pen her name on the lease. "You let that place get away?" I demanded. "Yuri—did you not see the natural light?"

Yuri crammed into the seat across from me, grabbed both my hands, and dragged me forward across the tabletop to face him. "You almost broke that old woman's hip. Think for a moment, Dixon. You might be enthusiastic, but you're not a violent man. And no apartment is worth hurting someone over. Not in front of all those witnesses."

It was almost as if my mind was just as steamed up as those windows, and slowly, as I focused on Yuri and reoriented myself to my surroundings, the haze began to clear. My breath caught as I realized that I'd almost sent Morticia Shirque sprawling. And I would've done it, too, if Yuri hadn't held me back.

"Brad is using Spellcraft," he murmured. "I am sure of it." He let go of my hands, laced his fingers, and flipped his hands inside out.

His knuckles gave off a muffled crack inside his leather gloves. "We need to expose him. But to do that, we must find the Crafting first."

"I thought the very same thing. In fact, I was looking for sparkles—at least until I found myself mesmerized by that wonderful room with all those windows—and I didn't see the little telltale glitters that usually give it away."

"And I did not see the light bending around the *volshebstvo*. But that only means he was clever when he hid the Spellcraft."

Or...that it really was a *wonderful* apartment. Or...was it? Because now that I really thought about it, the place was okay, and the light was nice, but it wasn't worth tackling someone's great-grandma over it. "We could just ditch the whole Hunting Party plan and move on to plan B."

"What is plan B?"

"No idea. But we're bound to come up with one sooner or later."

"True, we could walk away." Yuri steepled his fingers, looking vaguely sinister and intriguingly butch. "But I do not appreciate being manipulated."

"Then it's settled!" I squirmed against the booth in anticipation, because Brad the Cad's comeuppance was long overdue. "The Crafting is probably in his jacket, so if we admire the tailoring, maybe we can get him to show us the lining. Or, even better, maybe I mess up his hair and you go through the pockets like you're looking for a comb. Or—ooh, I know—we find a roach and plant it in the apartment, and then...well, I'm not sure. But it works in the movies when people sneak them into a restaurant to scam free food."

When I paused to take a breath, Yuri fixed me with a meaningful look and said, "Or...we Craft."

"Are you sure?" I asked playfully—because Yuri wouldn't have said it if he didn't mean it. "Countering Spellcraft with Spellcraft is tricky business."

The corner of his mouth curved into a secret smile. Because if harnessing the Spellcraft together has taught us anything, it's that while loopholes can definitely trip you up, they can also be turned to your advantage.

It gets me so incredibly fired up when Yuri looks at me like that. We're living proof that opposites attract, especially when we've got the same goal in mind. Uncrafting was my specialty, but without the spell in hand, there was nothing to Uncraft. And Scribing something to try and counter the effects of the magic already in play would only make things worse.

But I could deal specifically with Brad.

I mashed myself into the table so hard, the edge dug into my diaphragm. Yuri leaned in, too. When we were practically close enough to kiss, I said, "What did you have in mind?"

Yuri gave another delightfully European shrug. "The trick to Seeing is to let the *volshebstvo* do what it will." And with that pronouncement, he pulled out his paintbox and settled his water glass within reach. But he looked pretty annoyed when he patted down his pockets. "My paper is back at the attic. I put it in my box under the plastic to keep it from getting wet."

My eyes went to the chrome napkin dispenser. Those napkins always felt tough as nails when I wiped my mouth with them. But as I spread one open on the formica tabletop, I could see there was no way it would survive me writing on it. Especially not once it was all moist from Yuri painting his Seen.

I glanced around to see if our waitress had a notepad. Unfortunately, Ethel had been schlepping burgers and hash since I was just a gleam in my father's eye, and she kept all her orders in her head. Maybe the cash register could spare some receipt tape... but when I craned my neck to see if someone friendly was working the till, where the big old cash register used to be was now just a little tablet on a stand.

Seriously? The diner picked *now* to go digital?

"There must be something. Maybe in the truck."

Yuri shook his head. "I found the paper I kept in the glovebox covered in the urine of a squirrel, so I threw it away. There is nothing."

I could see where the rodent pee wouldn't make for a very good Crafting, but seriously, you'd think the two of us would be better prepared. I could tell Yuri thought so too, but he patted himself down again, and brightened when something in the jacket's inner pocket gave off a papery crinkle. He drew it out and placed it next to the open napkin.

Your manor... Your home.

"Wow," I said. "That's one very pink wreath." I opened the brochure, which was clearly a home desktop publishing job, and found a gap about the size of a business card between the weird photos of Strange Manor. "What do you think, Yuri—is this enough space to Craft something?"

He rolled a kink out of his neck and flexed his left arm as if it had fallen asleep. "It had better be."

I pulled out my pen knife to trim the square from the rest of the paper, but Yuri stopped me before I could pry the thing open. "Any ragged edges you create will warp the *volshebstvo*. We must leave the paper whole."

"O-kay. You're the Seer." I carefully tucked my pen knife away, worried that I'd manage to cut the air around the magic and wreck our only sheet of paper.

Yuri checked to make sure no one was paying us any attention, but we were in an out-of-the-way corner, and everyone in the diner was focused on their lunch. He scowled even deeper than usual—his glasses were back at the attic, too—and focused in on the blank spot as he tugged off his gloves, then swirled his brush in his water. Ice tinkled gently against the glass. I watched, fascinated, feeling a tug of recognition at the gesture created by his stirring, like it echoed the sort of flourish that would flow from my pen.

He drew his wet paintbrush through the gouache. The colors were close together, and Yuri will capture the mixed and melded shades between the pans as often as he takes the pure colors themselves. In a hand less skilled, the paint would look muddy. But not Yuri's. Instead, he achieved a subtlety of tone you just can't find in a premade color, and a range you'd never find without carting around a paint set ten times as big.

He painted something that was soft in tone, but angular in shape. Pale and abstract...at least until he turned it to face me, and I saw it was actually a windowpane with light streaming through.

It would be easier to achieve the tones he'd created with lots of water, but that's not what Yuri'd done. He'd used very little water, in fact, but the most delicate touch. The paint was practically dry before I even blew across the surface.

And the whole thing was crackling with Spellcraft potential.

Brad the Cad deserved a taste of his own medicine, and I was more than eager to dish it up. I cast around for just the right words—things like *boomerang* and *retribution* and *vendetta*. But none of them made for very good rhymes. Rhythms, either. And more importantly, anything I could think of that would allow my glorious dreams of vengeance to play out? It simply didn't sit right on Yuri's delicate Seen.

I wanted to stick it to Brad so badly I could taste it—figuratively speaking, of course, since mostly I was tasting the chocolate malt Ethel'd brought over—but Yuri was right. If Spellcraft were a dance partner, it was best to let it have the lead.

With no little amount of regret, I released my notion of Brad getting his just desserts and opened myself up to the painting instead. It wasn't actually moving, but in my mind's eye I could picture the light. The same light shone through windows all across Pinyin Bay. And, surely, one of those places would be one we could call home.

The cockatoo quill was capable of very fine lines, and the letterforms flowed from its nib just as I envisioned them.

No more quarry
No more chase
Instead we find
Our perfect place

I went easy on the flourishes, since there was hardly enough room to ink the words themselves. But the way that special tingle shivered all through me and out onto the page, the flourishes must not have been necessary.

There was a rightness to the words. Just like there was a rightness to the painting beneath them, the simple translucent strokes that evoked the feeling of light. "We're right on the brink of finding our perfect place, Yuri. I just know it. Though after all this time crowded into the attic, it'll be weird waking up all by ourselves without Sabina and Uncle...Fonzo?"

Even before I got his name out, the Buick pulled up behind Yuri's pickup truck and my uncle slipped out from behind the wheel. Sabina hopped out of the passenger seat, and the two of them headed right for the diner. Until Sabina looked like she'd forgotten something, turned around, and went back to the car.

Apparently, Biff was no better with car doors than he was with door doors.

Uncle Fonzo brightened when he saw the two of us, ambled over and plunked down into the booth beside me. "I thought I'd find you boys here—I tell you, this whole Biff situation is driving me nuts. He came to work with us, and now he's been looking at her with goo-goo eyes all morning."

Yuri said, "Maybe this is how he always looks."

"I'd like to think so, really, I would. But telling him about the family business didn't do a darn thing to get rid of him...so we need to pull out the heavy artillery."

While it was no fun seeing Uncle Fonzo beside himself over Sabina's choice in men, the idea of Crafting her love life—at least without her permission—didn't sit well with me at all. "We'll talk about it later," I said, as Sabina and her beau got tangled up in the entryway both trying to get through the door together. "In the meanwhile, let's see if we can get Biff to put his money where his mouth is."

Uncle Fonzo went a little green. I probably shouldn't have picked such a loaded saying.

I hastened to add, "Make it sound like dating Sabina will hit him where it counts: right in the wallet. Tell him Scriveners are super traditional, and it's bad luck if the guy doesn't pay for the meal."

"Not bad." Uncle Fonzo cut a look across the diner to Biff brushing off Sabina's jacket and tweaking her fauxhawk into place. "Since he obviously doesn't have a job—I mean, who would hire the guy?—he can't play the gravy train for long. Order yourself another malted, kiddo. Let's see if we can break the bank."

My cousin and her boyfriend joined us, holding hands, and crammed into the booth beside Yuri with Sabina squashed in the middle. "How goes the apartment hunt?" she asked as she reached across Yuri and yanked a dozen napkins out of the dispenser like a stage magician performing some kind of trick.

I made a hands-empty gesture. "We lost the last place to Morticia Shirque."

"I thought she lived with her creep of a grandson, Vano."

"Great-grandson," I said, still marveling over the fact that I nearly trampled an old lady to get to that contract. "And, no. He grabbed a place of his own yesterday—surprisingly quick on the draw for someone who could barely be bothered to show up."

Ethel swung by to take the newcomers' orders. My uncle's always had a prodigious appetite, but today he ordered enough to feed not only himself, but every tapeworm in the city. Sabina's eyebrows twisted up—she knew her dad well enough to know he wasn't just especially hungry—but other than a little side-eye, she didn't question the order.

While we waited, Sabina and Biff sure did seem to get along. And he was a nice enough guy, even if he did need to ask three times how they managed to refill the salt shakers through those tiny little holes.

Once the food came, Uncle Fonzo dug into his chicken-fried steak (and a side of fried chicken) with great relish—I always get a kick out of it when someone eats "with relish," especially if there's no actual relish involved—while I indulged in a second malt and Yuri embarked on yet another plate of dry toast. Sabina and Biff split an enchilada platter. The enchiladas in Scrivener Village are about as Mexican as I am, but melt enough cheese on top and nobody complains.

While Sabina picked up her cutlery from the table, Biff whipped out a fork from the inner pocket of his jacket. Plenty of folks think it's weird that I carry around a quill, but you never know when you're going to need an emergency crafting. But...a fork? He didn't strike me as a germophobe—not if he was willing to split a big, sloppy plate of pseudo-Mexican cheesiness with Sabina.

Weird enough that Biff brought his own fork. Even weirder when he sliced into the enchilada with it...and a blade shot out from one of the tines.

"What's with your fork?" I asked.

"It's not a fork. It's a f'knife."

"A...f'knife?"

"You've heard of a spork—a spoon and a fork. It's like that, but with a fork and a knife—which is way more useful, if you ask me. Because there's so many things you need to eat with a knife and fork, and nearly nothing you eat with fork and spoon."

Huh. He had a point. And not just the one jutting out from his fork tine.

He speared a hunk of enchilada and the knife tucked itself away. "It's a great conversation starter. Plus, it's a lot more convenient. No more trips to the emergency room to get my tongue sewed up."

My second malt did a little flip flop in my stomach over the thought of Biff mixing up his silverware and assaulting himself in the mouth, but I managed to keep the gag reflex in check. Whoever invented the f'knife might not have a large customer base, but undoubtedly the ones they had were very loyal.

We finished our food. Uncle Fonzo somehow packed in the last morsel, and said, "What a delightful meal." Then he gave Biff a conspiratorial look and added, almost reluctantly, "My daughter's told you about the Scrivener restaurant etiquette, hasn't she?"

"I don't...think so."

Sabina's eyes narrowed, but she didn't challenge her father.

"Well—she probably didn't want to intimidate you, and really, it's such an old-fashioned tradition. Time-honored and endearing...

but totally archaic, really, in this day and age."

He couldn't have reeled in Biff any harder if he'd done it with a harpoon. "I'm all ears. What is it?"

"When a man's courting a young Scrivener lady, he picks up the check. The whole check. For the whole family. A quaint custom, no doubt—"

Sabina couldn't hold it in any longer. "What the heck, Dad? That's not a thing!"

"—and no doubt you kids these days might even find it a bit silly...."

But before Sabina could protest, Biff was on his feet, scooping up the check. "Not silly at all! I wouldn't dream of going Dutch... unless that was what Sabina wanted."

She rolled her eyes and gave an exasperated flap of her hand, and he trotted off to the cash register, humming to himself.

As for me, I wasn't sure how to feel. On one hand, Uncle Fonzo's plan hadn't gone so well, which meant he'd undoubtedly hit me up for some Spellcraft later. On the other...I did get two free malts out of the deal.

While Biff was occupied, Sabina leaned in and whispered, "Scrivener tradition, my eye! What on earth was that little stunt supposed to accomplish? Are you trying to scare Biff away?"

"*Scare* is such a strong word." Uncle Fonzo laughed nervously. "I just don't want my little girl dating a cheapskate, is all. And if he is a tightwad, better to find out sooner rather than later."

"What reason could he possibly have to be a cheapskate? He doesn't just eat with that crazy f'knife thing, he invented it. He's got *all kinds* of cash. He's loaded! And thanks to some shopping network licensing deal, more money rolls in every single month."

There's nothing Sabina likes better than to whisk off imperiously after she's rendered someone speechless, and she wasted no time in flouncing away. She strode over to the counter, grabbed Biff by the arm, and hauled him out the door. He turned and gave us a bright wave goodbye as she hailed a cab.

Once they were gone, Yuri said, "Your daughter landed rich man who adores her, who is also too stupid to take advantage of her. Do yourself a favor and leave well enough alone."

Uncle Fonzo gave a gusty sigh. "You're right—I know you're right. On paper, he's not a bad catch. But he's just so stunningly dumb."

"Listen, Uncle Fonzo. I take back my idea of making up new Scrivener traditions to get rid of Biff. If he isn't the right guy for Sabina, she needs to figure it out on her own."

My uncle gazed down at the salt shaker with its tiny little holes. "Well, you can't blame her old man for trying." He pried himself out of the booth, let his belt out two notches, said goodbye to Ethel and headed back home.

Hopefully, they'd all work things out somehow—the attic wasn't exactly big on privacy, what with its lack of actual walls. But with any luck, Yuri and I could turn the tables on Brad the Cad, expose whatever Spellcraft he had going on, score a decent apartment, and create a little breathing room back at Uncle Fonzo's house. It was all a matter of getting that douchey realtor in the vicinity of the Crafting we'd just made....

I glanced around the table. There was a mostly-eaten enchilada platter, a plate with a few crumbs of rye toast, a heaping pile of dishes Uncle Fonzo had cleaned admirably, a bunch of paper napkins, half of them unused...but the Spellcraft?

Gone.

When Biff had jumped up and grabbed the check to pay it, there was no check to pay. It was all electronic. So the thing he swept off the table while Sabina was arguing with her dad?

It could only have been the Spellcraft.

YURI

10

Finding another slip of paper somewhere to try and Craft again should not be too difficult, but harnessing the *volshebstvo* is draining. It would take time for me to gather the strength to create another Seen—time we did not have.

Dixon was nervous. I can tell when he gets pensive—he tenses up all over and he pats the quill in his pocket to make sure nothing has happened to it.

"We can walk away," I told him. "Head back to the attic, forget about Brad, and let the next apartment go to Molly."

Even as I suggested it, I knew Dixon would refuse. "I wouldn't feel right about it, leaving an innocent like her to the wolves. No, we need to expose Brad for the true cad he is. And then, if the apartment's anywhere near as decent as the last one...you and Molly can draw straws."

Brad and Molly were waiting for us on the sidewalk. The block was a typical Scrivener Village block—which is to say, the architecture was cobbled together, the traffic signal was blinking randomly, and the street numbers made no sense. Brad checked his watch pointedly, then shot us the look of a man with something to hold over our heads.

Being cognizant of the fact that he must be using Spellcraft to his advantage wouldn't do us much good. Simply knowing the *volshebstvo* was in play was no defense against it. We could only hope that the Crafting we'd created at the diner would pull us in a more advantageous direction, despite the fact that it was no longer in our possession.

"So good of you to join us." Brad oozed superiority. "The apartment nearly went to Molly by default. And as it's the last available listing in your price range, it would've been a real shame if you didn't get a crack at it."

I knew exactly what he was doing—trying to stir up an inflated sense of competition between us. But when I cocked my head and looked for the telltale bending of the light around him, I saw none.

Molly fell into step with us and whispered, "I wouldn't have let him start without you. It wouldn't be fair."

No one expected fairness but the gullible and the weak. The thought of this Brad person preying on someone as vulnerable as Molly made me twice as angry.

The building was covered in vines from top to bottom. Half as many vines might look picturesque. But we could literally not see the building for all the strangling greenery.

"I've always wanted to live in a vine-covered building," Molly told me. "It seems like something out of a fairytale."

One in which we ended up hanging in the larder of a crone with a taste for human flesh, perhaps. Still...if this was the last place I could afford, I should keep an open mind. And once we exposed Brad's illegal tactics, we could really play hardball, as they say, in our negotiations.

We filed into the hallway and up the stairs, which all seemed slightly out of plumb, as though over the years, the vines had pulled the very framework of the building out of alignment. The apartment itself was small and worn, with old carpeting and older linoleum. It was dark inside like a cave. I pushed aside the curtains and found the window completely covered over by vines. Brad saw me noticing this and said, "Just think of all the money you'll save on shades—a good night's sleep, every night. And the natural awning keeps the place nice and cool all summer long."

Molly peered out a second window and said, "So much better than sleeping with the air conditioner running. Not only are those things loud, but they can really dry out your sinuses."

Maybe she had a point. And so what if it was dark inside? That's what lamps were for. When it came down to it, I have lived in worse conditions. I would survive. And, really, were the vines not at least somewhat picturesque? I glanced at Dixon, who was circling the perimeter, searching for Spellcraft. As long as Dixon and I were together—what did the look of the place matter?

Dixon was in the dining room now, scoping out a hutch built into the wall. He struggled to open one of the doors, gave up, then tried to close another, which simply popped back open.

I checked the single bedroom. Small and dark. The closet door stood open. I tried to close it, but the latch would not catch. I have always been leery of bedroom closets—who knows what might lurk inside—but if I couldn't force the door shut, I could always drag my bed out into the living room.

I rejoined Molly and Brad. He gave us both a predatory smile and said, "Anyone would be crazy to pass up the opportunity to live in such a conveniently located property...the very last one either of you can afford."

As he reached into his jacket for the lease, I scrutinized him closely, certain I would see the telltale signs of *volshebstvo*. But I saw none. Too dark to tell? Perhaps. And as for me? Part of me was eager to snatch the lease from him and tear it up so no one would be able to sign it...but another part was calculating exactly what angle it would take to drive my elbow directly into Molly's face to stop her from getting to that paper so I could sign the lease on my *fairytale* apartment.

Good thing Dixon chose that moment to shove between us all. "Everyone hold your horses!" he said, overly loud—and I saw his ears were stopped up with paper napkins from the diner. "I see the way you're both so eager for him to whip out that lease, and something hinky is definitely going on here. No way would anyone pay good money to live here."

"Wait!" Brad called out.

Dixon slammed the front door shut, then leaned back into it with his arms crossed triumphantly. "I don't know where you're keeping it, but there's definitely Spellcraft in the vicinity. And no one here is signing anything under the influence of a Crafting."

"You weren't supposed to close that door. Now we're stuck here till someone lets us out."

We all pulled out our phones—except Dixon, who hadn't quite heard Brad through all the napkins. No signal. I motioned for Dixon to move aside and tried to open the door myself. The frame creaked, but it held firm. I had a good grip with my leather gloves, though, so I pulled harder, until I felt something shift. One more good tug....

And the doorknob came off in my hands.

"So butch," Dixon said with delight, then turned to Brad and shouted, "Now we've got you exactly where we want you. And unless you want Yuri to strip-search you in front of everyone, you'll come clean with whatever Spellcraft you've got up your sleeve."

Molly looked from Dixon to Brad and back again with alarm. "Spellcraft? Are you sure? Maybe it's just a really great apartment."

"What?" Dixon said, "I can't hear you."

A really great apartment.

It *was* a great apartment. Perfect, in fact. Fairytale perfect. And I couldn't allow Molly to get to that lease before I did. I flung the doorknob to the floor and made a lunge for Brad, but Dixon was quick on his feet. He squeezed between us and said, "You'd better come clean, Brad. You can see how vehement Yuri is about this whole thing. I don't know how long I can manage to hold him back."

Brad held up his hands in exaggerated-surrender. "I have no idea what you're talking about."

It took Dixon an extra moment to respond—I think he was lip-reading—but he got the gist. "Then let me take a good look at that lease. Without all the high-pressure tactics and manipulation."

Brad handed the lease to Dixon with a careless shrug. My hands flexed within their gloves as I fought back the urge to snatch the paper away from Dixon.

He unfolded the lease and held it up sideways to peer at it. Sometimes I think the *volshebstvo* must exist in some other dimension we can only see when we reduce the Spellcraft to a single plane. He scrutinized the paper hard, as did I. No distortion.

Undeterred, Dixon held the paper up to the light. I would not be surprised if some Scrivener was capable of inking very small letters which could blend into a printed page, but the ink itself would give away the Crafting. Hand-lettering ink is too different from that of a computer printer, and the lines would show some contrast, however subtle.

But the page was completely uniform.

Dixon wears his emotions on his sleeve—and all over his face. The moment he second-guessed his convictions was plain. But he had played his cards and would have to see his accusation through. "Fine. The Crafting's not on the lease. But I know it's here somewhere. And obviously we're not going anywhere in a good, long while. So why don't you just do yourself a favor and tell us where it is?"

"There's not a single slip of Spellcraft on me."

"What?"

Brad rolled his eyes, pitched his voice louder, and declared, "I. Have. No. Spellcraft!"

I didn't believe him, and neither did Molly. She said, "I can't sign a lease if there's Spellcraft involved—if I did, my Teddy would never even consider moving in together. We need to make sure this guy's telling the truth!"

We absolutely did.

I shouldered Dixon out of the way, grabbed Brad by his lapels, and stripped off his jacket. I went through all the pockets while he looked on with a smug little smile on his face. And then he turned out the pockets in his trousers, too, then hitched up his pant legs to show there was nothing in his socks. Molly and Dixon turned to searching the apartment itself, but there weren't many places to look. Stove, refrigerator, toilet tank, medicine cabinet. They pried open the built-in buffet and found that empty too.

Meanwhile Brad, in his shirtsleeves, gave the occasional pound on the front door, calling out, "Hello-o? Is anybody out there?" But he seemed more amused than threatened. He watched. We searched. Long minutes passed. Minutes that stretched into hours. Eventually, every square inch of the apartment had been scoured. Short of prying up the floorboards or cramming a hand down Brad's underwear, there was nowhere left to look. And still, we found no Spellcraft.

Eventually, a neighbor responded to the knocking and came to our rescue. The old Scrivener had to remove the door's hinges to set us all free. As we spilled out from our confinement onto the sidewalk, frustrated and dazed, Brad said, "Given that fruitless little show of distrust in there, I'm making an executive decision to forego the competition and offer the lease directly to the one member of the Hunting Party who wasn't threatening me. Namely... Molly."

But his pronouncement was interrupted as our phones all registered that they were receiving signals from the cell tower again. Everyone's pockets or purse began to ping and vibrate with the incoming calls and texts which had built up all afternoon.

Dixon pulled a wad of napkin from his ear and said, "Uncle Fonzo called me half a dozen times."

I glanced at my phone. He'd called me as well, but hadn't left any messages. This was for the best. I was in no mood to hear more complaints about Biff.

Brad had the lease in one hand and a pen in the other, extending both of them toward Molly. But all of Molly's attention was focused on her phone, and her blue eyes went wide. With a delighted squeal, she said, "My sweet Teddy-bear texted me. He says he found a wonderful new home—and he wants me to move in with him!"

I may never be sure what compels certain strangers to fling their arms around me—perhaps giddiness due to a lack of oxygen in the brain. Or too much air, if that were possible, since Molly was now hyperventilating with glee. She squeezed herself against me, added a heartfelt snuggle, then, thankfully, released. "You guys are such an adorable couple! I sure hope everything works out for you two—just like it has for my Teddy and me!"

DIXON

11

I'm not sure whose expression was more priceless: Brad, as he realized we were the last people in the "party," and no way could he could offload that terrible apartment on us—or Yuri, as Molly hugged the living daylights out of him.

We might not have found the Crafting, but thanks to the fact that I couldn't really hear Brad's obnoxious spiel back at the apartment, I saw the place for the hovel it was. It might take some time for us to find some new digs, but I'd rather be crammed into the attic with my uncle (and all his furniture) until something suitable came along than to try and make the best of such an awful hole in the wall.

With a bright wave, Molly let go of Yuri, whirled around, and skipped away. But it seemed she'd left a little something behind. Her name tag. Which was stuck to Yuri's lapel. I wriggled the pin free, and as I did, I realized the paper tag had slid partway out of the holder. And there was writing on the flipside.

No, not just writing. A painting of a bunch of green dashes that looked like a swirl of cash money, too.

Spellcraft.

Create a sense of
scarcity
SELL
SELL
SELL

No *wonder* we hadn't been able to find a Crafting on Brad the Cad! He'd stuck it to Molly and made her an unwitting shill.

Yuri and I both turned toward Brad—who naturally tried to deny what we all knew it to be.

"A positive affirmation," Brad claimed. "Silly, I know. But setting a helpful intention can be such a motivational boost."

Of all the nerve, trying to pass off a Crafting as an affirmation. To a pair of Spellcrafters, no less! I knew I should have Scribed a good comeuppance for him back when he'd bilked me out of my prompt WheelMeal delivery. Then again, at the time, I hadn't been quilled just yet, so maybe the point was moot. Did the word *moot* have a Russian equivalent? I'd have to ask when I wasn't so darn angry.

And I wasn't the only one who was angry. Yuri's leather gloves gave off an audible creak as his hands curled into fists...but before he did anything in broad daylight that might end up with him getting deported, Brad's phone dinged again, and he glanced down at his messages.

I noted with no little satisfaction that it looked like unwelcome news.

He jabbed his phone's call-button and turned away from us—as if that ever stopped anyone from eavesdropping on a conversation—and said, "What's this about an eviction?"

Not one of the renters he'd placed. But him.

Yuri met my eyes and bit back a rare smile.

The person at the other end of the line said something, lost to the ambient street sounds of Scrivener Village, but hearing Brad's side of the conversation was more than enough. "No, I mailed my rent three days ago. You can even check the postmark for yourself...when it shows up."

While Brad tried to convince his landlord that his payment was on its way, I smiled back at Yuri, caught his left hand in my right, and gave it an affectionate squeeze. If Brad mailed his check from Scrivener Village, who knows when it would show up, if ever. "Yuri, do you think he has anything to do with the whole apartment shortage?"

"A man like him? No. A truly powerful man does not need to play up his own importance. He is just a vulture circling for scraps."

"I hope he does get evicted," I decided. "Maybe that's petty of me."

Yuri cut his eyes to Brad, who was gesticulating at his phone. "It would serve him right. Besides, he wouldn't be on the streets for long. Not with such an affordable apartment just waiting for a new tenant."

We both turned to the crazy mass of strangling vines that engulfed the building. Hard to say if it was Spellcraft sparkling among the leaves, or just the sunlight catching on a bit of dew. But if Spellcraft was as sentient as Yuri made it out to be, I'd like to think it favored those of us who treated it with respect.

We left Brad on the sidewalk arguing with his landlord and climbed into the pickup truck. "This is the disturbing part," Yuri said. "Even though I know I was under the influence of the *volshebstvo*, part of me still longs for that apartment."

"The one we've been trapped in all afternoon?"

"The very one."

"So whatever Molly said about it really made an impression. And she was such an upbeat person, she couldn't help but play up every last feature...even if it was really a stretch. I thought it was Brad I was blocking out with those napkins, but it was actually Molly."

Yuri nodded. "I can see this. Why else did I not turn around and leave when I noticed those carved monkeys? And why else would I have thought the place over the popcorn shop was romantic? When I think back on it now, all I remember was how the carvings made my skin crawl. And how nauseating was the stench of fake butter."

"It must be the way the Crafting was phrased: sell, sell, sell. Maybe once it was sold—or at least signed for—the compulsion wore off."

"Until we entered the next apartment. And the cycle started all over again." He glanced at the viney building. "The awareness that I was under the influence of the *volshebstvo* is not enough. If you put that lease in front of me and thrust a pen into my hand, even knowing what I know, I would still sign it. Even now."

I watched Yuri gazing longingly at the vines, and decided that any amount of time he spent pining over that dark, dingy death-trap of an apartment was far too long.

Molly's name tag was in my pocket. I pulled it out and looked at the back. I didn't recognize the penmanship or the Seen, not that it mattered. It was a real bear of a Crafting, and not just because it was on such a tiny slip of paper. I couldn't think of many words that started, ended with or contained the word *sell*. And it appeared not once, but three times.

Undersell that weaselly chiseller came to mind…but I'd become pretty good at reading the furrows in Yuri's brow, and the current furrow was troubling. As much as I wanted Brad the Cad to get his just desserts, I was more worried about releasing Yuri from the compulsion to sign the lousy lease. My yen for the other wonky apartments we'd seen had faded once someone else signed the lease—once they were sold. But without Molly to convince them, I don't think anyone would actually want a pitch dark, vine-covered apartment they might never be able to leave. No, it was up to me to unravel this Crafting.

Was *unsell* a word? Even if it was, what good would it do? Ditto with *sellout*. And *tinselly*.

Yuri tugged off his leather glove and placed his big, warm hand on my shoulder. "You can fix this. I have faith in you."

Gah. Leave it to Yuri to make my heart feel too darn big for my body. I looked even harder at those words, really focused in, and suddenly realized that the way the word SELL had been written—in block capital letters—I could alter the letter Ls to be some other letter. A capital E? Easily. A capital Y? If I played fast and loose with the descender, then yes. And could I cram a pair of letter Ts between those blocky letters? It would take a lot of creative license and a really delicate touch...but I'd give it my best shot.

The Crafting was tiny, and what I was attempting to do was dubious at best. But my cockatoo quill was phenomenally precise. And when the new Scrivening formed in my mind's eye, the words began to flow.

I held the tiny card against the dash, and I Scribed. In and around the existing Craft, I changed letters and added words. Until eventually, the following Spellcraft took shape. I fit much nicer words in and around *create a sense of scarcity*.

Create a sense of Calm.
No Scarcity.

And the SELL, SELL, SELL part? I tweaked it to read:

IMMENSELY
SELECTIVE
and SETTLED

Something shifted in the air. Maybe it was the *vol-shep-shi-bo*...or maybe it was Yuri's tense shoulders unhitching. He gave me a small nod, then put the truck in gear and headed back toward the attic.

I could have offered some word of encouragement about how I was sure we'd find the perfect place anytime now, but somehow, it didn't seem like I needed to. I squeezed Yuri's knee instead, and he answered by settling his hand over mine and squeezing back.

And maybe it was a good thing that I didn't offer any platitudes. Because when we pulled up in front of Uncle Fonzo's house, we found the curb piled so high with garbage bags we could barely see the porch. The whole house was lit up like a beacon and the front door was open.

I crept up to it and peeked around the doorjamb, expecting to find that Mr. Greaves had pounded on the ceiling one too many times, my uncle had stomped downstairs and done away with him, and now we were dealing with the fallout. But instead of a bunch of crime scene investigators snapping photos, I saw the davenport was back in its proper place. In the living room. Where it belonged. With all the rest of Uncle Fonzo's furniture.

My cousin called out, "Look who's here!" She edged around me with her favorite pink and purple throw rug slung over one shoulder and her toaster dangling by its power cord. As she passed, she leaned in and said, "Whatever convinced you to make Greaves take a hike—especially after you stopped me so many times from doing it myself—I have no idea. I'm just glad someone finally got rid of that nasty ceiling-pounder once and for all."

"But I didn't do anything."

Sabina gave me a sly smile and said, "*No more quarry, no more chase, instead we find our perfect place.* Even if I didn't know your handwriting, the rhyme would be a dead giveaway." She walked me inside and pointed to a familiar brochure stuck to the fridge with a Niagara Falls magnet, then plucked it off the fridge and handed it to me. "I don't know where you came up with this pamphlet or how you talked Biff into passing it along, but Greaves took one look at it and fell in love with Strange Manor. He couldn't break the lease with us fast enough. Before I knew it, the movers were here—and the best part is, we don't even need to give him his security deposit back! By the time we have another mortgage payment due, Dad should be back at work and we won't need his stinkin' rent money. Good riddance!"

It takes a lot to render me speechless. Like, a *lot*. But it has been known to happen. "Um...wow."

"But here's what I wanna know, Cuz. In your Crafting, you wrote, *we find our perfect place.* That's *we*, plural—not *I*, singular. How on earth did you figure out Ed Greaves was angling to move in with his girlfriend? Frankly, I can't picture anyone in her right mind letting that nasty ol' undertaker stick it to her—"

"Hold on. Mr. Greaves is a *mortician*?"

Beside me, Yuri made a weird noise and shuddered.

"I thought you knew!" Sabina said. "Creepy job for a creepy guy.

But his little blonde chickadee looked surprisingly normal—and weirdly ecstatic. Guess it just goes to show there's someone for everyone."

Speaking of which...evidently, Biff had proven himself phenomenally helpful in hauling furniture downstairs. Once they propped the doors open, it was smooth sailing.

Yuri and I headed up to the attic. The walls in the stairwell were still stacked all the way up to the ceiling with family photos, but I no longer felt a twist of anxiety seize my gut every time I placed my foot on a creaky step.

I paused at the top landing to take it all in. Without my uncle's furniture packed inside, the attic looked huge. My futon over in the corner, surrounded by bookshelf and clothing-rack walls, seemed very far away. Other than mismatched salt and pepper shakers, the folding card table that served as the kitchenette was empty. Yuri's box sat in the middle the floor. And beside it, Meringue dozed in her cage with her head tucked under her snowy wing.

I tore the Crafting in half and shivered as a breath of magic played down my spine. "This might not be as nice as the apartment with the sunroom," I ventured. "The one that Morticia Shirque ended up with. But I'm guessing my Uncle will be more than reasonable with the rent. Especially since we recovered his quill."

The corner of Yuri's mouth quirked. "Are you officially asking me to move in with you?" he asked, as if it wasn't obvious.

"Were you hoping for an engraved invitation?" I said playfully. "Or do you need me to perform a strip-o-gram? Because I totally will."

Yuri snagged me by the jacket and pulled me up against him. The spent Spellcraft fluttered to the floor. When he pressed his lips to mine, I caught the faint scent of cedar in his coat. I would miss the days (and especially the nights) we'd hunkered down in that snug little cabin together. But we'd always share those memories, and now we could make some more.

He scrunched up my lapels in his hands, and he kissed me. Tenderly. But intense.

When we work our Spellcraft together—when the tip of my quill touches his enchanted painting—I get an inside scoop as to what's going on in his head. But when we connected like this, just two guys making our way through the world, I'd have to extrapolate.

His kiss tasted like relief. That we hadn't ended up in a sketchy apartment. That Brad the Cad's Spellcraft hadn't snared either of us for long. And most of all...that the two of us were actually making our living arrangement official.

Awww.

As we lingered over each other's mouths, Meringue stirred. We came up for air, and Yuri stooped down to hand her a peanut from his pocket.

I rounded the cage and dropped, cross-legged, to the floor. Yuri folded himself down beside me and I snugged up against him. We both looked on, smiling softly, as Meringue prodded the nut from the shell with her funny black bird-tongue, clucking happily to herself.

The next few weeks were a flurry of activity—loud activity that involved lots of hammering and even a few power tools. Not because Uncle Fonzo was fixing the ceiling in the master bedroom, which bore the marks of constant pummeling with a broom handle—he just stapled a sun-and-moon tapestry from a nearby head shop over it and said he'd deal with it later. Maybe he would, maybe he wouldn't. The tapestry did lend his room a certain exotic flair.

No, the activity was mostly in the attic. I might have been the kid who flunked out of shop class—mainly because my mother gave so many dire warnings about getting my hands anywhere near the bandsaw—but Yuri could really rock a tool belt. And when I offered a nearby hardware store a Crafting to help them move their leftover stock of last year's topsoil, they expressed their appreciation with a pretty nice discount.

Sabina had moved back into her bedroom downstairs, and the half-finished walls that framed her old room in the attic were fully finished now. Not just with drywall, but actual paint. Yuri's a lot better at painting paintings than he is at painting walls—but he looked so sexy doing it, I had no complaints. There was a lot of work to do, but we tackled it a bit at a time, tucking extra insulation between the joists and drywalling the ceiling. The space looked a lot more clean and inviting.

It looked like a home.

"Knock knock," Sabina called from the top of the stairs. It was midmorning on a Saturday, and Yuri and I were ensconced at the kitchen table. Mr. Greaves hadn't cancelled his subscription to the Pinyin Bay Journal, so Yuri had made a habit of immersing himself in the local news every morning. He looked absolutely adorable in his glasses, reading his paper and sipping his strong black tea, tattooed muscles bulging everywhere and a crease between his brows—but I didn't comment on it. Wouldn't want him to feel self-conscious.

Sabina poured herself into the plastic folding chair we all thought of as "hers," namely because it was so rickety it wouldn't have held anyone else without collapsing, and Yuri set a cup of tea in front of her. She claims he boils water better than anyone else in the house. I suspect she may be right.

"Did you hear Morticia Shirque is in the hospital?" she asked.

"Really? Huh. I always thought she was pretty spry for her age, but I guess she's not getting any younger."

"It's not old age that got her—it's black mold. Apparently her new apartment was crawling with it."

Yuri met my eyes over the top of the newspaper. We exchanged a meaningful look. Maybe I'd been lenient about serving Brad the Cad his comeuppance, but I doubted the head of the Pinyin Bay circuit would be quite so merciful.

Sabina propped her feet on my knee and began scrolling through her phone...with a sort of left-swiping pattern I knew all too well. "Are you on a dating app?" I asked her.

"Same old, same old."

"But...what about Biff?"

"We decided to just be friends."

Clearly, there was more to the story. Even Yuri thought so. I could tell by the way the corner of the newspaper drooped ever so slightly so he could keep an eye on my cousin. I stopped what I was doing and waited expectantly. Eventually, she caved in to the stare of scrutiny and said, "Okay. Fine. Remember that warm snap last week? Guess who came strutting out of the house in a pair of freaking sandals? And you *know* how I feel about gnarly manfoot."

Big time. Whenever she caught me with my shoes off, she'd force me to shave my toes.

"Too bad," I said. "He did seem like a genuinely nice guy."

"Flip-flop weather is coming," she said ominously, and got back to rejecting a swath of potential suitors on her phone.

Flip-flop weather *was* coming. And that meant sharing all those beachy things with Yuri I'd always loved—things we could only dream about when we'd snuggled together in his cedar-scented cabin on those frosty spring nights. Cooking hot dogs over an open fire and eating them before the seagulls dove in. Picking sand out from between our toes. Finding rare coins and jewels washed up on the beach. Okay, that was something I'd never actually done— yet—but I was still open to the possibility. "Say, Yuri, why don't we head back to your old digs today and have ourselves a nice picnic on the beach? You do have picnics in Russia, don't you?"

"No picnic."

"Then you're in for a real treat! I'll call Mom—she'll make us some sandwiches. If we drive really fast, they won't be too soggy by the time we get there—"

"Dixon—yes, we have picnic in Russia. But you and I will not be picnicking at Pinyin Beach."

"You're not still mad about that eviction notice, are you? Because you've gotta admit, everything did work out in the end."

Yuri moved aside his mug and flattened the newspaper on the card table. As a Scrivener, I'm not bad at reading upside down. But my eyes were more drawn to the accompanying photo of a bunch of big, heavy equipment—massive trucks and bulldozers and diggers. In the very corner of the shot was a line of vulnerable-looking cabins that I knew all too well. One even had an eviction notice still tacked to the door.

And the headline?

Historic Pinyin Beach Is History.

DON'T ROCK THE BOARDWALK

DIXON

1

Practical Penn is not a fancy shop. It's situated between a take-and-bake pizza place and a dollar store. The floors are linoleum (worn), the walls are paneling (fake wood), and the acoustic drop ceiling tiles are vaguely discolored. But Practical Penn is more than just a store in some seventies strip mall, it's my family's livelihood. And for that reason, it's the best shop ever.

Unfortunately, businesses come with regulations.

While I did still have an office in the shop, it was just an out-of-the-way little closet of a room. To save on our liability insurance, my mother had taken me off the books several years ago while I was trying out every youth hostel in Europe. That move turned out to be to everyone's advantage. Because not being officially employed there meant I didn't have to go to the annual Spellcraft rules and regulations training that was required of every Scrivener in a small-to-midsized shop. With me unofficially manning the helm at the store, Practical Penn could stay open while every other shop in the city had to shut its doors.

Win-win.

Technically, I didn't need Yuri to come along and keep me

company. Chances were, I'd just be sitting around all afternoon watching adorable chipmunk videos on my phone. But he insisted that if Rufus Clahd was the only one I had for backup, some intrepid robber would clean us out for sure. And so, he came along, parked himself at my cousin Sabina's desk, and shot apprehensive looks at Rufus's door when he thought no one was watching.

Poor Yuri. I think Rufus freaked him out because he'd never met another Seer before. And Seers tend to be...unusual. Whether it's because they possess a talent that's basically a genetic mutation, or because every Scrivener they meet treats them like the next Messiah? Hard to say.

As long as you don't mess with his things, Rufus can be fairly easygoing. But though he's got a normal-sized ego, he's also got extremely large hair. My cousin and I have speculated over the years as to whether or not it's a white-guy perm. She thinks it must be, whereas I'm not so sure. While some days it looks more tightly coiled than others, I think the discrepancy could be due to a change in shampoo, or humidity...or maybe the occasional trim.

I hadn't yet determined what Yuri thought of the hair, but I'd wager he had an opinion. It was Yuri's desire to keep an eye on everything that landed him front and center when the mime walked in.

I often ponder what Yuri's nightmares must be like—no doubt, they're in Russian. Yuri's got a thing about clowns. And while a mime isn't technically a clown...I guess it's close enough. He stood up so fast, the office chair spun out behind him and crashed into the wood paneling with a giant clatter. It made enough noise to wake our Seer from his current nap. Rufus's door cracked open just as I made it over to Yuri's side to catch him in case he fainted. He'd probably squash me. But, heck, I was used to him squashing me. I might even kind of like it.

The mime walked up to the service counter and started swatting at a bug on the Formica surface. We keep the place well-fumigated, but I supposed it was possible that some of the feeder crickets had escaped their stinky little tank. The office was now home to a variety of nocturnal creatures—apparently, toads get really loud around one a.m. And crickets were a lot less icky to handle than mealworms. Still, those little suckers could really hop. I picked up an empty coffee mug and a pizza menu, and came over to rehome the poor cricket, who'd probably enjoy getting squashed a heck of a lot less than I did. But when I got up to the counter, there was no cricket. And the mime was still swatting away...at nothing. I picked up the edge of a phone directory to see if the little escape artist got away.

"Mime is ringing service bell," Yuri supplied, from a safe distance away, with an accent gone thick.

Oh. Right. The mime brightened and nodded vigorously.

I could've sworn he was swatting a bug.

You wouldn't think a little greasepaint would make all that big a difference, but I couldn't really get a bead on the man behind the makeup. Was he older or younger than me? Dark or fair? And, most importantly, was he better-looking? Between the whiteface and the eyeliner, it was really hard to say. The only thing I knew for sure was that his drawn-on eyebrows made him look perpetually startled.

He gestured at the counter. I looked at it. Back in the day, when smoking was in vogue, a lit cigarette had fallen from an ashtray and left a nicotine-yellow burn on the surface. The mime shook his head and gestured for me to stop looking at the burn mark and pay attention to him instead.

He pinched his fingers together on both hands and raised them in an arc. "You're typing," I ventured. "You're reading the newspaper. You're folding laundry."

At the sound of all my excited guesses, Rufus Clahd ambled out of his office. Practical Penn's official Seer was my parents' age, and he still dressed like it was 1979. He'd been working here for years... if you counted napping in his office as working. He joined in the guessing game, sounding half-asleep. "You're eating corn on the cob. With lots of butter. And a sprinkle of Himalayan sea salt."

Yuri snapped, "He is opening briefcase."

The mime touched the tip of his nose, winked, and pointed at Yuri.

Yuri shuddered.

Rufus squinted at the mime. "You sure it's not corn?"

The mime pointed at Yuri again.

"I'm really pretty good at charades," I said. It wasn't my fault this mime was so ambiguous.

Once the "briefcase" was open and all three of us Spellcrafters were watching, the mime pulled something out of the case. Except the thing wasn't imaginary, like the purported briefcase. And it was really obvious he'd just pulled it out of his pocket.

And…it looked a heck of a lot like Spellcraft.

He placed it importantly on the counter and indicated it with both hands, then started making frantic little looping motions.

"You're cranking a pepper grinder?" I guessed. "No? Crocheting an afghan. Wait, I know—you're playing Yahtzee."

Rufus shook his head. "No way, man, he's definitely waving a sparkler on the Fourth of July, just after sundown, throwing white-hot sparks against the night sky."

Huh. I'd really never figured Rufus was that imaginative. Then again, it made a lot of sense, given that the weird watercolor blobs he painted (the ones that never looked like anything to anybody) still managed to fix the Spellcraft mojo onto the paper.

Unfortunately, judging by the frustrated huff that came out of the mime, Rufus was also wrong.

Yuri matched it with a huff of his own, though he made no move to come any closer, as if mimeness might be catching. "He is drawing—from right to left and bottom to top. He wishes you to Uncraft spell."

The mime made a really big deal out of gesturing toward Yuri. Yuri backed up another few steps, until the wood paneling creaked against his back.

Rufus and I both leaned in to get a better look.

I might not have figured out the pantomime for "Uncrafting a spell," but the Spellcraft itself? That, I recognized right away…

even though I really wished I hadn't. Not because of the Seen—it wouldn't be the first Rufus Clahd creation I'd unmade—but because of the Scrivening.

The mime waved his hands in a flurry of inexplicable gestures. Rufus scratched his chin and said, "You went for a swim, but the water was colder than you thought, so instead you focused on your Tai Chi."

While even the mime looked befuddled over that guess, Yuri said from across the room, "He is disturbed by Crafting and hopes we can help him."

Either Yuri had a better view from where he was standing way over there, pantomime was a flourishing art in Russia (which gave him an unfair advantage), or learning a second language had just made him pretty darn perceptive. The mime hopped up and down in excitement and gave Yuri an eager thumbs-up.

I took a better look at the Crafting. The Seen, predictably, was a messy blue-gray blob that could have been anything—but the Scrivening was pretty darn specific. *Go-getters get their goal.* I was big on rhyming, and Uncle Fonzo liked to Craft fortune-cookie type sayings. The alliteration, though?

It couldn't have come from anyone but my father.

No one likes to be the source of a bum Crafting, so naturally, I considered claiming it must've come from some other shop. But before I could, Rufus said, "Oh, I remember that one."

"Really?" I said. "Because it's awfully, uh...abstract."

"Nope. That's Pinyin Bay. See the dip over here? That's where the power plant sits. And the flat side over here is where they shored up the coastline, so the inmates at the county detention center couldn't swim away anymore. And the tiny flecks of black inside the water—those are leeches."

Well...now that he pointed out all those details, I *supposed* I could see it.

Yuri said to the mime, "I read article that said South Dock Boardwalk is threatened by developers. Is that where you have come from?"

The mime nodded with great purpose.

"The South Dock Boardwalk can't be sold off," I declared. "It's a Pinyin Bay institution!"

Rufus agreed. "That's where everyone loses their virginity on a full moon under the pier to the sound of off-key buskers yodeling in the distance."

"Um…not everyone," I said. "But it's bad enough some out-of-state corporation bought up the rental cabins on Pinyin Beach. Are they gunning for the Boardwalk, too?"

The mime made an exaggerated frown and nodded.

Yuri said, "If same buyer also has Morticia Shirque's estate as well as the cabins, when they take the Boardwalk, this entire coastline of the bay will be theirs."

That couldn't be. "*All* of Pinyin Beach?" Even as I said it, landmark after landmark cropped up in my mind's eye as if I was cruising past on Old Bay Road. The trailer park. Pinyin Inn. The cabins. The Shirque Mansion. From the power plant on one side of the bay to the crumbling bluffs that separated Pinyin Bay city limits from the road to Strangeberg on the other, the only property that hadn't recently changed hands was the Boardwalk.

The mime knuckled away a fake tear.

I snagged the Crafting by the corner and pulled it across the counter to get a better look at it, but as I did, Yuri caught me by the back of the collar and dragged me into my office. Since I hardly ever used it, tanks filled with toads and lizards and whatever else ate all those escaping crickets took up a lot of the meager real estate. But Yuri crowding me into a gap between my desk and a coatrack was something I could hardly complain about—even though I was pretty sure no kissing would be involved. Not this time, anyhow.

"You would Craft for *mime*?"

Obviously, Yuri was none too keen on the situation. Even if I didn't know he had a thing about clowns, he'd been dropping articles left and right ever since the guy gestured his way across the threshold. I said, "Pinyin Beach means a lot to me. But even if it didn't, that's not just a Practical Penn Crafting out there...it's my dad's."

Yuri understood. He answered with the sort of slow-blink he reserved for those moments when a long-suffering sigh simply wasn't enough.

I patted him on the chest. And then added a few more pats for good measure. And then trailed a fingertip along his neck tattoo in a way that made him shiver. "Think about it this way, Yuri. Pinyin Bay is riddled with Spellcrafters. The mime could've brought this Crafting to any one of them. But, as luck would have it, we were the only shop open. It's as if it was meant to be."

"Nothing is ever a coincidence with the *volshebstvo*." Yuri pulled me against him roughly, smoothed my hair back, and paused to cup my face in his palm. Gazing down into my eyes with exquisite tenderness, he said, "You are always taking on problems that are not yours to solve—so, how could I expect you to leave this Crafting to the wind? I know you must do it...but I do not have to like it. Especially when Uncrafting involves no Seen, and can only be done by you, and you alone."

I brushed a kiss across his frowny lips. "I just *knew* I could count on your support! Now, let's get back to the mime before any more Spellcraft shops open up and he can start comparison-shopping."

We headed back out to the lobby, where Rufus was regaling the mime with a rambling tale about...well, frankly, it's just as hard to follow Rufus's stories as it is to figure out which end of his Seens is up. But whatever the narrative might be, it involved a trashcan, a used harmonica and some shaving cream. Just as Rufus wrapped it up by saying, "...and then all of us broke into a half-hearted rendition of Auld Lang Syne!" my cousin shouldered her way through the front door with a teetering stack of pizza boxes in her hands from the take-and-bake joint next door.

"Who holds a meeting in this day and age and doesn't supply any donuts?" she demanded with all the vehemence with which she demands...well, everything. "I swear I could hardly hear the presenter over the groaning of all the empty Scrivener stomachs."

Sabina had dressed "professionally" for the mandatory meeting—which was to say, she didn't have any holes in her black jeans, her Doc Martens were polished, and her bra straps weren't showing. Fortunately, Spellcraft is one of those professions that doesn't require you to dress to the same standards as a banker or a politician or a high school principal.

I, myself, might be fond of sharp tailored suits and natty bowties, but Sabina balked at the notion of wearing anything even remotely conservative. My cousin has crammed herself into a pair of pantyhose exactly once in all her twenty-five years. And by the time she was done clawing them off again ten minutes later, everyone up and down the street knew exactly what she thought of them.

Yuri relieved her of the pizza boxes and steered them into the break room, where three toaster ovens we'd found at various garage sales and thrift stores awaited. And with no stack of boxes blocking his view, the mime did an exaggerated double-take at my cousin.

Sabina looked equally as startled—and knowing that she can be just a teensy bit acerbic if you rub her the wrong way, I quickly attempted to steer the mime's attention back to the matter of the Uncrafting. I slid a contract from a pile of legalese, slapped it down in front of him, and said, "I'd be happy to see to the matter at hand. All I'll need is your signature on the dotted line and five hundred dollars. We take all the major credit cards, but there's a five percent discount if you pay cash."

The mime pretended to be pulling down his pants.

Even if I were single, trading sexual favors for Spellcraft was a line I was simply not willing to cross. "I'll have you know this is a respectable family business."

Yuri said, "He is showing you his pockets are empty."

"Oh. Fine. Well, there may be some wiggle-room." We didn't need a Seen painted, after all. "It's a real stretch, but I can go down to $399."

The mime repeated the gesture.

"Looks like he's frying up some bacon and eggs," Rufus observed. Was that a euphemism? Hard to say.

"$299?" I tried. No dice. "$250, and that's really the best I can do."

Unfortunately, it turned out that if I didn't want my dad's Crafting to fall into the hands of another Spellcraft shop, I'd have to settle for twenty bucks. I'm usually a lot better at negotiation, but frankly, it's unsettling when the other party is constantly pretending to disrobe.

The mime handed over a crumpled bill, then pretended to sign the contract with his fingertip.

Sabina rolled her eyes and handed him an actual pen. He brightened and plucked a tiny paper flower from his sleeve, then offered it to her in return with a grand, courtly bow. Until Yuri swatted it out of his hand, anyhow. "Stop dawdling and sign. There is much work to do."

The mime made a big deal of signing with a flourish. Spellcrafters always get a big kick out of what passes for a flourish among the Handless. But as I spun the contract around to face me, it wasn't to critique his penmanship, but to figure out what in the heck I should call him. Because it hardly seemed fitting to keep referring to my new customer as "the mime."

His signature was a vague squiggle.

"Look," I said. "If we're going to be working together, I need to know what to call you."

The mime smiled, spread his arms wide as if to say *get a load of this*, then bent his knees and straightened them again.

"What the heck is that supposed to mean?" Sabina demanded.

The smile went a bit pained. He repeated the motion.

"You're jumping rope," I said. "Are you a boxer? Is your name Muhammed Ali? Ooh, I know, it's Rocky."

The mime shook his head and did it again.

"A bunny hop," I guessed. "A pogo stick."

Rufus nodded sagely. "That's exactly how the slow-motion dismount of a gymnast from a pommel horse would look. He's trying to tell you his name is Trigger."

Sabina was running out of patience. "How long have you guys been at this?"

"Too long," Yuri said.

Dang it, I had to get *something* right. It was a matter of principle now. "You're looking for something on a low bookshelf. You're doing squats at the gym. Wait a minute—I know! You're crouching." The mime shook his head emphatically...but if he wasn't willing to speak up for himself, it was his problem, not mine. "That settles it. *Crouch* it is."

Either Crouch was incapable of speech...or he was just phenomenally stubborn. And since I have encountered more stubborn men in my life than mute ones, I was betting on stubbornness. Twisting a flailing arm around his back and giving it a good, stiff upward yank should elicit a word or two. Lucky for him I had a policy against making physical contact with anyone in greasepaint.

While Crouch performed a stilted "glass box" routine for Sabina, Rufus wandered off. I joined Dixon in his office to figure out our next move.

Dixon brushed away a stray cricket and set the Crafting in the center of his desk. He crossed his arms and considered it. "*Go-getters get their goal.* Innocent enough."

"Until it falls into the wrong hands. Is there room on the paper to Uncraft it?"

"Maybe...but there aren't many words that end with *go*. Dingo? Virgo? Ooh, wait, maybe *bongo* has some promise...."

"And then Pinyin Bay will be crawling with Beatniks. If anyone can turn the Crafting around, it is you. But whoever is behind the push to buy the Boardwalk must have money. If you do not first root out the source, they can simply go to a different shop and buy another piece of Spellcraft."

Dixon rubbed his hands together in delight. "I've always been curious about the South Dock Boardwalk—and, for the record, I most certainly did not lose my virginity there. Boardwalk folk aren't exactly my type. They're insular and clannish and play by their own set of rules."

Should I state the obvious correlation? No. Too easy.

Dixon went on. "Plus, they generally don't take too kindly to strangers."

"The fact that we are preserving their livelihood should be enough of an inroad."

"You'd think so. But Boardwalkers are leery of outsiders poking around in their business. If we hope to get to the bottom of this, we'll need to fit in."

I very much disliked where the conversation was headed. "I can just force Crouch to talk."

"No, Crouch must be just as much in the dark about whoever commissioned the Crafting as we are. I'll bet one of their own is selling them all out. And we'll need to get in there ourselves and expose the traitor."

"Or we could simply ask your father who bought the spell."

"We...could." It was obvious Dixon wished to do no such thing. "But what if he *did* lose his virginity under the pier? He'll be devastated to learn his Crafting was part of some scheme to sell off the whole shoreline. I can hardly let him bear that burden. It would be un-son-like of me."

"You just want to wear a disguise."

"Okay—you got me. When else would I have the chance to dress up like some kind of kooky street performer? Except Halloween. Or a costume party. Or, really, any day of the week I wanted to make a bold fashion choice...."

It was not the things he said as he rambled on about costumes—those were all one-hundred percent Dixon—but the way he said them. He'd agreed with me far too quickly.

"...and, of course, there's always the hand-eye coordination it takes to create a plausible suit of armor from a bunch of industrial-sized tin cans without cutting off your own finger—"

"Dixon." He stopped mid-stream. "What is the real reason you won't ask your father?"

He sighed, then went serious. "It's a funny thing, Yuri. Uncrafting. I have no problem dismantling the work of strangers. And it goes without saying that I would at least try to fix the one-word wonders Uncle Fonzo penned with Hawthorn Strange's quill. But...this is my dad's Crafting. I don't want to be the one to tell him it needs to be reversed. What if he tries it himself and only ends up setting the magic like a stubborn stain? Or what if he does leave the job to me, and I fail? Or even worse, what if I succeed?"

I would love nothing more than to best my own father at something—and then to rub his nose in it once he was defeated. But Johnny Penn was nothing at all like the sullen, angry man who'd raised me. In fact, Johnny Penn had shown me more kindness than my own father. When I needed a work visa, he signed off on the forms without hesitation. But more than that, when I needed a kind word, he was ready with a joke that was so bad, it was almost good.

"Fine," I said. "Before we hurt anyone's feelings, we check out the Boardwalk ourselves. That does not mean we concoct some sort of ludicrous story about who we are and why we are there—"

As I attempted to set a few "boundaries," the Practical Penn Seer paused in the doorway. I have not yet determined if the man's stream-of-consciousness was sincere, or if it was all some sort of persona designed to keep everyone off-balance. Rufus bared his teeth at us, held up a book, and said, "Check this out, guys—I found a copy in my art reference library." He ambled over and opened the book on the desk beside the Spellcraft. "*I've Been in Pinyin* by Mildred Merriweather Block. Some name!"

The book? Or the author? I did not suppose it mattered.

"Back in the day," Rufus explained, "you could hardly turn around without tripping over this book. The resale shop has so many copies, they've stopped accepting them. But there's lots of nice pictures inside." The book was a few decades old. It was a cloth-bound hardback, the sort of coffee table book most people just bought, flipped through once, then left to molder in some corner of the living room. Rufus paged through. The photographs inside were clearly dated, but there were plenty of them. "Get a gander at the living statue. He holds the world's record for most defecated on by birds."

Dixon scrutinized the photo. "Huh. I did not know such a record existed."

"He must've lobbied for the category himself…then went and sat under the eaves of the municipal garage where the seagulls all roost. I guess he'd be dead by now—unless he lived to be a hundred and twenty…in which case, there's another record he could add to his portfolio." He closed the book and slid it across to Dixon. "Maybe this will help you keep the Boardwalk safe and sound."

"Wow. Really? Are you sure you don't mind?"

"By all means, take it. I'd hate to lose such a quintessential piece of Pinyin Bay to so-called development."

It was the most coherent thought he had ever uttered in my presence.

Rufus drifted away—no doubt to fit in another nap before closing time—while Dixon flipped open the book, whispering, "Rufus might seem easygoing, but he's weirdly territorial about his stuff. The Boardwalk must really mean a lot to him if he's giving us his book." He paged through the book, growing more and more animated all the while. "Hey, check this out! The Boardwalk is a haven for performers. There's a sword-swallower. And a juggler. And a sword juggler. Boy, they really know how to specialize. Anyway, this is the perfect opportunity to learn a new skill we've always dreamed of."

I have certainly never dreamed of making a spectacle of myself in front of mobs of hostile strangers. "We should pose as tourists."

"Just think. I could be a unicycle rider. Or a one-man-band. Or a contortionist." Given the things he insisted we try in the bedroom, the contortionist might actually have some promise. Then again, I've lost count of the number of times he has nearly thrown out his back. "Ooh, I know, I can take up the mantle of the living statue, minus the bird poop. You can paint me gold...even in the places no one else will see."

"You are unable to sit still for more than two minutes, at most."

"Maybe I just need to practice."

"Be wary of whatever claims you make. Street performers are good at reading people. They will know if you are just putting on an act."

"And you can be the Strong Man." He fluttered his long eyelashes and dropped his voice. "Do they have that in Russia, Yuri? All bulging with muscles, barely covered with the skimpiest of faux-fur loincloths, with just a tantalizing little strip of furry fuzz crossing that broad, yummy chest?"

I narrowed my eyes at him.

"I'll bet they do. And I'll bet you'd look phenomenally hot...."

"Maybe later. But for now we must focus on a plausible identity." Ideally, one from the current century. "The Boardwalk is not far away. We will go check it out—from a distance—and determine how to approach."

"That sounded just like something out of a movie full of car-chases and explosions." Dixon surreptitiously hugged himself. "Okay, I'm sold."

When we returned to the lobby, Crouch was gone. On one hand, I was relieved I would not have to drive him anywhere. On the other...maybe I would have felt better knowing exactly where he was so he couldn't sneak up on me. "Where is mime?" I demanded.

Sabina glanced up from her pizza. "Beats me. He swung his arms around until finally I nodded like I understood, and then he took off down the street."

"Come on," I told Dixon, hoping we could make it to the truck before Crouch came back. "Let's go."

The South Dock Boardwalk was just down the road from the cabin I'd once called home. Not a long drive from the office...but long enough for Dixon to regale me with facts from the old history book.

"Say, Yuri, listen to this. In old-timey days, Pinyin Beach used to be known as Coral Beach."

"On a fresh-water lake?"

"Turns out the 'coral' was actually an old pile of bricks that got submerged after a heavy rainfall. Still, too bad the name didn't stick. It sounds nice and beachy." He flipped through the book some more, then said, "And another fun fact: back in the fifties, a ship carrying lab animals to a testing facility sank in a freak storm. The crew didn't make it, but they think the animals survived. To this day, most of the wild mice in Strangeberg are white."

I pulled off the road where an unofficial parking lot existed. The grass was patchy and the earth packed from the accumulated weight of all the vehicles compressing the soil. As I searched for a spot that wasn't too muddy, Dixon said, "Now, here's something I didn't know. Pinyin Bay was in the running to be the fire hydrant capital of the world...until a town in Alabama stole the title. Which was totally not fair, since they had a fire hydrant factory, whereas Pinyin Bay just had an enthusiastic fire chief who lobbied for lots and lots of hydrants."

"I'm sure the architecture in Scrivener Village had nothing to do with it."

"Well, that and the fact that our water pressure is so good. It's just common sense to use that feature to its best advantage."

As I climbed out of the truck, it was hard to say if it was the *volshebstvo* which played across my scalp, or just a breeze coming off the bay. Despite living just down the shore, I had never had a reason to visit the Boardwalk. In the winter, the only thing open was the tourism office with their ungainly slogan, *You're in Pinyin Bay! (The city, not the body of water. Otherwise, you'd be wet.)* And I had no need of an outdated map or a coupon for a rental car upgrade.

From where we stood, the Boardwalk looked much as I expected: garish, somewhat shabby, and entirely underwhelming. An ancient yellow Ferris wheel creaked as it made a slow circle. Tourist shops lined the wooden walkway, selling souvenirs made halfway around the globe. The street performers outnumbered the tourists nearly two-to-one, and throngs of seagulls lurked nearby—waiting for a french fry to drop, or perhaps calculating whether they could get away with stealing a small child.

Hardly the spot where we could hope to lose ourselves in a crowd and blend in, I thought. Until a massive tour bus rounded the bend and pulled up alongside my truck. It was a deep maroon, with Big Burgundy Bus Tours painted in a swoosh down the side. The door swung open and a throng of middle-aged humanity in matching, hot pink *Back to Nature* T-shirts piled out. Every seat on the bus must have been full. And every person in the group turned an expectant eye toward the Boardwalk.

Last off the bus was the driver. He wore a burgundy uniform which matched the bus—and an expression of stupefied bewilderment. He was maybe forty, though given the dishwater blond dreadlocks and the braided beard, it appeared he hadn't outgrown his twenties. Either that or he had never heard of a barber. "Wassup?" he said to me. "Are we in Strangeberg yet?"

Dixon popped up beside me. "Strangeberg is on the other side of Pinyin Bay...the body of water. This is Pinyin Bay, the city."

The bus driver glanced down at a map on his phone, then turned it upside down. The map reorientated itself to the same direction it faced before. He shrugged and introduced himself as Isaac. Dixon introduced himself and then me—as his *grown man friend*—then said, "What's with the bus?"

"A bunch of nature lovers on their way to some annual shindig. At least they're pretty chill. Not like that busload of auditors I had to cart around last week. Their idea of fun was doing math, and at every darn rest stop, it took 'em forever to split the check."

"Do you have any extra T-shirts?" Dixon asked.

Reflexively, I said, "I do not want pink shirt."

"Because we're huge fans of...random T-shirts. With slogans on them. From groups we know nothing about."

Isaac scratched his beard. I shuddered at the thought of what sort of mites were probably living in it. "The tour group did bring one for me, but it says in my contract I'm supposed to wear this uniform at all times for the duration of the trip—unless I'm asleep. Then I can wear my own clothes." He looked back through the door of the bus and scratched his beard some more. "I'm not sure what I did with the shirt, but I'll let you know if it turns up. Speaking of sleep...if you don't mind, I'm gonna catch a few z's."

Was everyone in America so fond of napping? Dixon did not fall unconscious in the middle of the day. But I strongly suspected he produced enough adrenaline for the whole of Pinyin Bay.

"Come on," I told Dixon. "We do not need pink shirts to blend in. All those bodies are camouflage enough."

"I can't disagree. That's more action than the Boardwalk's seen all year." Dixon looped an arm through mine. "Let's go eavesdrop and find out the scuttlebutt."

"Scuttle...butt?"

"It's one of those words that means what it sounds like."

"It sounds like nothing."

"Hey, look, there's a gap in the crowd. Let's go."

DIXON

3

Apparently, the South Dock Boardwalk already had a new living statue. At least I figured that out before I painted myself gold and did anything to provoke an unintentional rivalry. But given that he just sat there on a park bench (well away from the seagulls), we probably wouldn't learn much from spying on him.

And so, Yuri and I scoped out the rest of the Boardwalk. One thing Isaac was right about: the Back to Nature crowd sure was a happy bunch. Unfortunately, while the tourists were numerous enough to hide behind, they kept the Boardwalkers so busy, the buskers and salespeople had zero time to talk among themselves. The ukulele player didn't stop strumming for a second. The trained poodle jumped through the hula hoop until it was too full of treat-kibbles to move. And the yodeler yodeled himself hoarse.

Yuri and I threaded through the crowd from one end of the Boardwalk to the other and back again. "I'd thought the crowd would settle by now," I said, "but they only seem to be getting more rambunctious."

"And the performers are all occupied. We need to figure out

the best way to infiltrate." Yuri gave the paintbox in his pocket a meaningful pat.

Spellcrafting with Yuri is not so different from our bedroom antics—fun and thrilling and ever so slightly risqué. So, it goes without saying, I'm totally up for it, anytime, anywhere. If he was in the mood, then I was on board. We squeezed through the pink-shirted crowd until we found an unoccupied picnic table. The way the sun was glaring off the bay, it was easy to see why no one had settled at that particular spot. But Yuri put his back to the water and made his own shade—enough for both him and me.

"What do you have in mind?" he asked me. "Is the *volshebstvo* plucking at your Scribing hand yet?"

I wouldn't exactly say I was overstimulated, but between the press of the crowd, the smell of the corn dogs and the shrieks of the seagulls, I couldn't quite separate my own edgy anticipation from the feel of nascent Spellcraft tickling around the edges of my creativity. "Hard to say. You take the reins and I'll follow your lead."

Yuri got the faraway look in his eyes he gets when he searches through the ethers for his inspiration. Like me, he was born with the gift. But while I'd prepared my whole life to be a Scrivener, Yuri had a crash course in Spellcraft as an adult. In Russia. Where, I gather from the occasional stray comment, his teacher wasn't someone you'd invite to your potluck...and not just because she'd bring something unappetizing, like borscht.

Yuri pulled out his notepad and opened up his pocket paint set. I pulled my water bottle out of my bag and tipped a few drops of water into the lid. His expression went grim. Okay, grimmer than usual. Yuri's not a big fan of crowds, especially crowds that're really enjoying themselves, so this press of pink-shirted humanity definitely wasn't helping him focus, either. I drew a circle around one of his knuckles with the tip of my forefinger and said, "The world is full of Handless, Yuri, but the Spellcraft doesn't take any notice of them. Not until we tell it to. You got this."

He looked at me, hard. I often think he sees more than the rest of us, even when he's not officially Seeing. Normally, I'd be a little nervous about what he saw when he stared at me like that. But that look has never once been followed by an admonition to lower my voice, or calm down, or man up. Okay, once in a while he might suggest I stop talking. But only when something objectively dangerous is going on.

With his eyes fixed on me, Yuri wet his brush, then dabbed it along the traces of paint that had settled into the cracks between the compartments, where the hues had mixed into something more subtle. But just as he set brush to paper, a man burst through the crowd.

A very loud man.

In a very colorful apron.

Covered in sequins.

Spelling out the words, *Drew Draws*.

"As I live and breathe!" he cried out, rushing the picnic table. "Never in my life did I think I'd be so happy to have competition encroaching on my territory!"

I always figured I was familiar with every Seer in Pinyin Bay, though the way I met Yuri clearly demonstrates that you never know when a new Seer might surface. This one was a middle-aged guy in a sparkly beret. I'm pretty sure I would've remembered him. "Are you new to the area?" I asked.

"Lived here long enough to stake my claim on this very Boardwalk. I'll have you know you can't just set up shop wherever you please. There are rules. Paperwork. Permits. And that's not even counting the unwritten rule of the Boardwalk. I was here first. I have dibs."

"No doubt dibs are sacrosanct," I said. "But you've lost me."

He gave me an exasperated look and framed his sparkly apron with jazz hands. "Drew Draws. I'm the official portraiture artist of the South Dock Boardwalk." Oh. Not a Seer after all. He turned to Yuri. "And you, my large friend, are in my spot."

"I was not painting portrait," Yuri said.

Drew looked pointedly at the paintbox. And the paintbrush. And the way Yuri was seated across from me, gazing at my face...and I supposed I could see where the artist had come to that conclusion.

Drew told Yuri, "I will let the infraction slide, if you agree to collaborate on this latest bunch of tourists. Fifty percent kickback and you can officially hang out your shingle right beside mine."

"I will do no such thing."

"Forty percent," Drew said. Yuri glared at him. "Fine—thirty percent, and that's my final offer. Either take me up on it, or I send a portrait of you to the Pinyin Bay Journal with the word *buttinski* scrawled across your forehead. A very unflattering portrait. You choose."

I won't say I can read Yuri's mind—and if I could, chances are he wouldn't be thinking in English—but I'd bet my last cricket that he was about to tell Drew to go right ahead. I tugged at Yuri's hand. Wow, his fist was really clenched tight. "Weren't you just telling me how eager you were to brush shoulders with all the fine talent on the South Dock Boardwalk?" Yuri looked at me as if I was certifiable, but hopefully Drew would just think that's how his face always was. "Remember? Like the living statue in the book of world records? And the hot dog vendors? And the sword jugglers? Now's your big chance!"

Yuri grimaced. "I am sure there is another way."

"You know what they say. Don't look a gift coral in the mouth. It might turn out to be an old pile of bricks."

As awesome as it would be to draw portraits of tourists, obviously Yuri was overqualified for the job. But it was a better inroad than either of us could have hoped for. So, I batted my eyelashes and did my best to convey that I'd really shower him with appreciation later. Not that I ever needed an excuse to do that. Sometimes even in the shower.

Yuri scrunched his eyebrows together. "Fine." He grabbed a wad of napkins and swabbed the wet paint out of his paintbox lid. "Let us hope I am not the only one who finds what he is looking for."

"Russian sayings. So cryptic. Best not to read anything into them." I waved as Drew Draws drew Yuri away, momentarily stunned by the alarmingly skimpy short-shorts revealed when Drew turned around. I stood up myself and found a young woman had snuck up behind me, standing so close I nearly sprawled backward over the picnic table to keep from tripping over her.

The close-stander was around my cousin's age, but worry had already etched a sharp line between her thin eyebrows. She had hair as dark as any Spellcrafter's, but skin that was milk-pale, and eyes as blue as Pinyin Bay (the water) on a crisp fall morning. In a conspiratorial voice, she asked, "You know about the bricks?"

"Well, sure." I have no clue what possessed me to imply that I hadn't, in fact, just learned about them on the way over. But whatever it might've been...I went with it. "Doesn't everybody?"

The woman with the worry-line edged even closer. "You'd be surprised how people tend to see only what they want to see. And anything that might challenge their worldview gets swept conveniently under the carpet. As far as your average person is concerned, Pinyin Beach never had any other name. And the pile of fresh-water coral never existed. But what's even worse than that, the ones who do know about the bricks...think they just ended up where they were by accident."

"They...didn't?"

"Not at all. Clearly, the bricks were a result of a failed dam."

"What would anyone have to gain by damming off the bay?"

The woman fixed me with a meaningful look. "Now you're asking the right questions. People around here are complacent. They don't ask enough questions, and even when they do wonder about something, they're willing to accept the first explanation they find. You've heard of fake news? How about fake history?"

I had a feeling our little chat was about to turn political—Spellcrafters are even less fond of Handless politics than we are sports or religion—but there was a pretty solid picnic table cutting off my escape. "Say, look at the time."

"Take the first person to write about those bricks...the author of *I've Been in Pinyin,* Mildred Merriweather Block. She could have delved deeper into the origins of the bricks. But instead she just wrote it all off as some sort of accident. A coincidence. Nothing to see here, folks. Nothing to see here."

While I love a good paranoid rant as much as the next guy, I had a Boardwalk to spy on. Plus, my new friend was brushing up against my suit in too many places for such a recent acquaintance. But luckily, as I struggled to come up with a plausible exit line, a matronly Handless woman with steely eyes and a tiny, pursed mouth peeled out of the Historical Society and saved me the trouble. "Charlotte?" she called over.

Charlotte leaned in closer yet and said, "Geez. You'd think I could get away from Pearl for two minutes."

Pearl said, "Why are you lollygagging around with just one tourist? You can see the next Barge on the Bay tour is all sold out."

It was then that I realized Charlotte had on a nautical-themed blue polyester blazer that no one in their right mind would willingly wear unless they were freezing to death. And even then, they'd probably think twice. As someone who once delivered food in a lime green visor, I could definitely sympathize. Pearl wore a similar blazer—but with sparkly gold epaulets that ranked her higher than Charlotte.

As I pondered whether the addition of lamé epaulets was enough to raise the garment from unfortunate to tackily charming, Pearl said, "With a crowd this big, we'll need to run the tour together."

"No," Charlotte answered quickly. "Really, that's okay. I can handle it myself."

"Safely regulations. We need one staff member aboard for every twelve people. I don't make the rules."

Charlotte squeezed herself behind me as if to use me for a human shield. "Then, good thing the community college sent over a new intern!"

The manager narrowed her eyes. I highly doubted a random fact from an old book would impress her, but how many chances would I feasibly get to parrot a little Pinyin Bay history to someone who might actually appreciate it? And besides, it was flattering to think I still looked young enough to be in community college. I squared my shoulders and said, "Pinyin Bay has the most fire hydrants per capita. Outside Alabama, that is."

Pearl looked surprised, then grudgingly pleased. "Oh. Well, then. It's about time you showed up. You get one fifteen-minute break for every four hours you work. And the glare off the bay is no small matter. I suggest you wear sunscreen—though you'll have to provide your own. The Barge of the Bay runs on very slim margins." And with that proclamation, she turned on her heel and went to wrangle the T-shirted tourists.

Charlotte leaned in closer yet and whispered, "Talk about a close call! That woman drives me bonkers. If I get stuck with her on the barge one more time, I can't be responsible for my own actions."

My excitement over scoring my first official internship wilted at the thought of riding on the Barge of the Bay. I don't know much about nautical terms—aside from *seamen*—but I really couldn't think of a more unappealing name for a ship than *barge*. Except *scow*. Or maybe *dinghy*.

"Well," I said briskly, "glad I could spare you from an afternoon of alone-time with your boss, but I've gotta be going—"

"What? You can't leave now, I'll be in big trouble when the barge offloads and I'm the only tour guide on it." Charlotte grabbed me unceremoniously by the arm and hauled me off to a nearby shanty. The inside was covered with photos of Pinyin Bay—the sesquicentennial, the annual four-legged race, and even the Pinyin Bay Perch cutting the ribbon at the opening of a new car wash. I was so busy taking in all the history that I didn't notice Charlotte sneaking up behind me with a blue polyester blazer until she thrust it into my hands...along with a bright yellow tie.

"Bold fashion choice," I said, figuring a little flattery might help me weasel out of putting the appalling getup on my body. "But synthetics make me break out in hives."

"If you want to pass yourself off as an intern, you'll need to look the part."

I shook out the blazer. It had yellow piping that matched the tie. And sparkly stars on the cuffs. You'd think I'd jump at the chance to wear lamé...but not like this. "Are you positive there's no other way? I'm sure a jaunty name tag would suffice." Heck, even a lime green visor was preferable.

"The key to fitting in is looking like you belong." Charlotte shoved the blazer at me more insistently, and quelling a wince, I accepted it. Because she was right. And what better way to keep an eye on the Boardwalk than from the Barge of the Bay? So, even though it involved swallowing my pride and wishing I was colorblind, I looped the tie around my neck and slipped on the jacket.

But that didn't mean I had to like it.

YURI

4

D rew Draws—if that even was his real name—had opinions. About everything. And he had no qualms about making them known.

"It kills me to give away my trade secrets, but since forty percent of nothing is nothing, I'll give you an important tip."

"Thirty percent," I grumbled.

"Tourists are eager to spend their money, but they expect something in return. Plus, you're competing with the keychain kiosk and the magnet shack. Getting your bayside portrait drawn might be all about the experience—because, let's face it, the silly things all look the same—but you've gotta give 'em a keepsake, even if they just end up sticking it in a scrapbook and forgetting about it the second they get home. There's no way you can charge twenty bucks for a tiny little slip of paper like the ones you've got there. You'll need to go bigger."

We approached a purple sun shelter with "Drew Draws" painted across it in big, cartoony letters. It was an impressive stretch of canvas, many meters wide. The structure was set parallel to the air currents so as not to fall in on itself, though the surface had bowed and distorted into a permanent curve from the wind coming off the bay. Beside the huge purple sail, Drew opened a small locker and pulled out a drawing board, which he brandished self-importantly and waved under my nose. His paper was cheap. Not the sort I usually painted on, unless I was desperate. But I wasn't painting a Seen, I reminded myself. I was insinuating myself among the so-called Boardwalkers.

"Lucky for you, I have an extra pad. And that teeny-tiny paint set of yours? Precious. But it'll take you forever to fill the page with that dinky little brush." He thrust a fat marker into my hand. "Do yourself a favor. Broad strokes. Work fast. And compliment the tourists while you're drawing. Works like a charm."

When I painted a Seen and the *volshebstvo* flowed through me, my left arm felt like it had a life of its own. A separate being… though I felt every last stroke of the brush down to my core. Sometimes, even touching the brush brought back a shiver of memory. But when Drew shoved that marker into my hand? I felt nothing at all.

Could I even render an image without the help of the *volshebstvo*? I would soon find out.

"You know the basics of composition?" Drew asked me. "The golden ratio? The rule of thirds?" I narrowed my eyes, though whether he took that for affirmation or ignorance, I could not say. "Doesn't matter. Throw it out the window. Can you draw an oval?" I nodded cautiously. "Good. Then here's all you need to remember." He swept open the tent, and I saw the back wall was lined with example portraits.

None of which looked like anyone in particular.

"Oval head. Big smile. Tiny little vestigial body. That way, you don't need to worry about offending any plus-sized folks by drawing an accurate portrait. And unless someone's got a shaved head, like you, make sure you give them plenty of hair. People like to think they have hair."

He gestured toward the water.

"A brown boardwalk, a few blue waves, and a sketchy

approximation of the Strangeberg bluffs across the way, and you're good to go. Any questions?"

Only existential ones. Was this actually happening to me? And how did I manage to get myself into these situations? But since I would trust no answer coming from a man in a sequined apron, I merely shook my head.

"Good. Because every moment I waste getting you up to speed is a handful of tourist dollars getting away."

Drew turned to the crowd, and abruptly, his annoyance turned off. His public demeanor was expansive. Welcoming. Even jovial.

"Welcome to the South Dock Boardwalk, my fine folks! Enjoy the water! Enjoy the scenery! Enjoy the sun! And when you're done riding the rides and sampling our delicious fried perch, be sure to stop by for a portrait to commemorate your stay! Or, better yet, grab that portrait now—while there's no waiting!"

Drew's patter did draw people in. I cringed inside as a few individuals peeled off from the crowd and came over to inspect the gallery of smiling, oval-faced portraits. Surely no one would pay twenty dollars for a simple, generic cartoon that took all of five minutes to create. But then a frumpy woman in a pink T-shirt marched up to me, thrust a twenty-dollar bill into my hand, and said, "Which do you think is my best side—the right, or the left?"

"They are same. I will paint from front, anyway."

She pawed at her neck. "Just be sure you don't accentuate my double chin. And don't make my nose look too big. And not too many freckles, either."

Oval head. Big smile. Tiny body. I was beginning to see the wisdom in this advice.

Still, one cannot simply forget thousands upon thousands of hours of practice. Although my Seens came from my internal landscape—gestural things which found uncanny counterparts in the real world, but only once they were Scribed upon—originally, I had taught myself to paint by observing the world around me. Could I capture the particular expectant angle of this woman's head with an oval? Could I render the distant Strange Manor in a few jagged strokes? Could I do justice to the bay, and all it meant to me, with a few wavy blue lines? Unlikely. But I must have felt compelled to at least try.

I was so focused on capturing the woman's likeness in a few simple shapes and gestures that I belatedly realized I heard the murmur of someone talking behind the tent—and I most definitely caught the phrase "buy up another lot." But when I rounded the canvas wall, the person was already gone. I made a mental note to quit losing myself in the drawing. After all, I was not here to appease the tourists. I was here to see what Crouch was so upset about.

As cartoon portraits went, that first portrait I did was...passable. But though I mimicked the smile from Drew's portraits, there was something almost melancholy in the way I'd canted the mouth. With only the simplest of facial features, I'd rendered something elusive, even poignant, in the oval's expression.

I kept my expression carefully neutral as I turned the drawing to face the woman. She was clearly unimpressed. I could hardly blame her. Who would wish to be reminded that happiness was fleeting? That the face we show the world is so often a facade? That even within pleasure, it is so easy to experience disappointment?

The woman said, "My hair looks a little flat."

I scribbled an extra few lines around her head then showed it to her again.

"Great! Now can you tell me where to buy sunscreen without paying an arm and a leg?"

Soon, another tourist took her seat—this one a man who insisted on removing his shirt. I couldn't imagine why. His flabby physique had me itching to drop to the Boardwalk and do a few sets of crunches to stave off a similar fate. I assured him I did not have to shade it pink, that he could choose any color he wanted—so he could put his shirt back on anytime. He insisted the open air felt good on his skin.

I scribbled plenty of hair on his head and quickly moved on to the next customer.

DIXON

5

"You take the back of the barge," Charlotte told me, and pressed a laminated cheat-sheet into my hand. "Tell everyone it's your first day and they'll go easy on you. Heck, I claimed it was my first day all last summer and no one knew the difference. It's not as if anyone would take the Barge of the Bay cruise twice in the same year."

The barge was a broad, flat vessel with no propulsion of its own. A tugboat at the front dragged it back and forth across the bay. A quick glance at my cheat-sheet informed me that a century ago, the barge was used for hauling lumber from the forested regions of Pinyin Bay (the city) across Pinyin Bay (the water) to Strangeberg, which was then known as Cliffton. And in return, Cliffton sent loads of gravel from their infamous bluffs.

I was already so bored I practically fell asleep standing up. And when the wind pulled the cheat sheet out of my hand…I may not have tried all that hard to catch it.

I boarded the barge behind the tourists, doing my best not to feel mortified about the blue polyester blazer with bright yellow piping. After all, the tourists were here to look at the bay. Not my unfortunate wardrobe.

And in their hot pink *Back to Nature* T-shirts, frankly, they didn't look much better.

Still, given that I tend to be a bit of a clothes-horse, presenting myself to a large group of people in such a ridiculous outfit was bound to leave me feeling self-conscious.

And when I'm nervous...I talk.

A chubby guy hanging off his seat snagged me as I was going up the aisle and said, "I forgot to bring my motion-sickness pills. Is this going to be a rough ride?"

"Not at all," I reassured him. "The barge only rocks when the Pinyin Eels are spawning." Though I had no actual knowledge of the mating rituals of eels—let alone whether or not they'd get busy enough to churn up a barge—the answer seemed to satisfy the tourist. And that's what customer service is all about. Keeping everyone happy.

But then the woman behind him asked, "Are those eels a native species, or were they introduced to the area?"

"I'm sure whatever introductions occurred were entirely proper," I said confidently. Judging by the titter that rippled through the crowd, it was the answer they'd all been hoping for.

Being a tour guide was a lot easier than I thought it would be.

I took up my station at the back of the barge while the crowd got settled. Up front, Charlotte appeared to be giving me a very concerned look—but given that I now shared an attic with someone who also had resting grim-face, I didn't take it personally. After all, that deep crease between her eyebrows wouldn't have simply disappeared unless she'd had Botox on her way up the gangplank.

An elderly man directly in front of me was so eager to feel the sun on his wrinkly skin that he took off his shirt. But when the breeze picked up and skittered across the water, he thought better of it and put it back on, and the folks with sweatshirts tied around their shoulders or waists girded themselves against the wind. I probably should have been thankful for the polyester blazer. Let's face it, though. That was never gonna happen.

The tugboat tooted its whistle, and we were off. Once the barge got going, it was a pretty smooth ride, though the guy who forgot his pills was looking a little green around the gills. I said, "In old-timey days, the Barge of the Bay hauled gravel and lumber." I figured that factoid should either distract him from his nausea or bore him to sleep. But my strategy didn't exactly pan out—the tourists all decided the single fact I knew about the barge meant it was open season for Q&A.

"Why is the Ferris wheel yellow?" one of the nature lovers asked, pointing to the shore where the ride in question embarked on a slow rotation.

The answer was most likely that yellow paint was on sale when the caretakers were looking to spruce it up, but people don't like hearing about the practicalities of running a tourist attraction. "The yellow paint commemorates the golden hair of the mistress of the man who created the ride—Joe Wheeler."

"I could've sworn Ferris was the inventor's name," someone murmured.

"Of course, Mr. Ferris himself didn't build this particular instance—Joe Wheeler did. That's obviously what I meant. And then he painted it yellow. Next question?"

"How deep is Pinyin Bay?" someone asked.

I hadn't the faintest idea, though I suspected if I couched my reply in nautical terms, it would sound pretty official. "Several leagues."

A few of the naturalists went puzzled. Since "nature" was their area of expertise, it was possible they actually did know how long a league was. Should I have said two? Twenty? Two hundred? No clue.

"Next question."

A woman with binoculars pointed toward the far end of the Boardwalk. "What's that fence for?"

I shielded my eyes and followed her gaze. Maybe thirty feet from the spot where the plank walkway ended, a tall wooden fence marked the outer edge of the beach. It had been there as long as I could remember. Sabina and I had always just called it The

Fence when we raced each other to reach it. And dry sand can be surprisingly hard to run on.

With the authority befitting an official tour guide, I said, "It keeps wolverines off the Boardwalk."

The naturalists looked even more puzzled.

The guy who'd been unsuccessful in his de-shirting said, "You mean, the animal?"

"We'd hardly need to protect the area from comic book characters, would we?"

As the tourists all craned their necks to get a better look at The Fence, which I'd just rendered infinitely more entertaining, Charlotte stomped up the aisle, snagged me by the blue polyester sleeve, and hauled me over to the farthest corner of the barge. "What on earth are you telling these people?" she whispered—very assertively, I might add.

I reassured myself that the wetness I felt against the side of my cheek could very well have been the spume coming off the bay. But the barge wasn't really going fast enough to cause any spume. And it smelled of butterscotch candy.

She hissed, "Watch what you say! You never know who will be listening. There are no wolverines in Pinyin Bay. The mean depth of the water is seventy-five feet. And the Ferris wheel was painted yellow after voters chose the color in a local referendum."

Huh. Now the festive *Better Dead than Red* lawn signs that cropped up a few years back made way more sense.

"What about The Fence?" I asked.

"Who cares about some old fence? Stick to the script." She shoved a new copy of the laminated page into my hand, turned to the cluster of curious tourists, and said apologetically, "You'll need to cut Dixon a little slack—it's his first day."

6

꒳

Being a tour guide on a slow-moving barge is hard. A lot more difficult than I'd originally thought. Good thing I was just posing as an intern and not relying on the Pinyin Bay Historical Society for my actual employment. It turned out to be a long day with three separate batches of tourists. And Charlotte had been wrong. Some of them did ride more than once. Luckily, though, not the one who was seasick.

On our way home, I looked up exactly how long a league was. Five and a half kilometers...which meant nothing whatsoever to me, either. More than seventy-five feet, though? Possibly.

Once Yuri got a good look at me upstairs in our apartment—he uses these pricy, full-spectrum light bulbs that really help him see what he's painting—he said, "You look very tan."

"And you look very annoyed."

He huffed out a sigh. "I got so caught up in drawing those ridiculous portraits that I learned nothing about who is buying the land. What about you?"

"Unfortunately, I didn't fare much better. I managed to get a job on the Barge of the Bay, which seemed like a great idea at the time. But the only locals on the barge were the other tour guide and the captain—and he was all the way over on the tugboat. It was all tourists, fresh off the bus. So, I didn't pick up any juicy gossip. Not about the developers, anyway...but I'm told nobody likes Marla Pitt's ambrosia surprise, and at every potluck they take the smallest scoop possible and just stir it around their plates. Say, do you have marshmallows in Russia?"

Before Yuri could answer, Sabina called from the top of the stairs, "I know one thing for sure, I've got more marshmallows than you can shake a stick at."

Sabina was holding such a massive cookie bouquet, I wouldn't have even known it was her if she hadn't spoken up. Except that it would either be her or Uncle Fonzo, since they were the only other ones who lived here. And Uncle Fonzo is the best uncle in the whole world...but he'd think twice about sharing a cookie bouquet. Especially since they have a relatively long shelf life.

Yuri relieved her of the ginormous arrangement, and I cleared a spot for it on the card table.

It wasn't unusual for happy Spellcraft customers to express their thanks via food. Sometimes the gifts were small tokens of appreciation like a pan of homemade brownies, which left us all battling one another for the gooey middle pieces. But once in a while, someone went over and above. Like the customer who sent us an entire side of beef...which left us all dumbfounded. My mother speculated that it might even be some sort of threat. I ended up helping my father and Uncle Fonzo dump it off in an alley at the far side of Scrivener Village. Which is where you'd leave anything that needs to disappear.

Meringue seemed pretty excited about the whole undertaking. As Yuri gingerly lowered the arrangement to the table, she started flapping her wings and doing her best impression of the smoke alarm. Which, honestly, I'd only set off maybe three times burning candles. Four, tops. She must have mistaken the arrangement for a big red parrot—one that was honing in on her territory.

As cookie bouquets went, it was truly startling. A lot cuter than the side of beef…but no less puzzling. I won't say the sort of baked goods we usually receive are boring, but they're definitely a lot more platonic than the one Sabina brought upstairs. There were cookie pops shaped like roses, with enough red frosting to make my molars tingle in anticipation. There was a jumble of big pink cookie hearts. There were sprigs of white chocolate-dipped pretzels covered in pink and red sprinkles. And there were pink chocolate-coated marshmallows studded with silver bb's, all jammed into a heart-shaped vase and tied up in a sparkly red bow. It looked incredibly sweet…in more ways than one.

As Yuri clucked a gentle Russian reassurance to the cockatoo, Sabina's phone rang.

"Hello? Hello??? Look, I know it's you. If you're trying to butter me up, it won't work. Like I said, I'm not dating someone who can't hold up their end of a conversation. So, the cookies are great and all. But I'm just not interested."

Once she hung up, I said, "Spill the tea, Cuz. Who was that? Do I know him?"

She glared at the cookies and planted her hands on her hips. "Sure you do. It was that Crouch guy."

Yuri, who'd been poking through the bouquet to strategize his first cookie-pilfer, yanked his hand back as if the goodies were electrified.

Yeah. I could see him not being too keen on the whole mime thing. Me, though? I'd never dallied with a mime—so, I was intrigued. "What did he say?"

"Nothing. That's how I knew it was him."

Yuri shuddered.

I pulled a chocolate-coated pretzel out of the arrangement and took a bite—one of my favorite flavor combos, sweet and salty—while Sabina broke the edge off a cookie and handed it to Meringue. While the bird clucked eagerly and hopped to one side of the perch so none of us could steal her cookie fragment, Sabina said, "Do you guys think I'm being too picky?"

"No," Yuri said—very decisively. "Never think that, Sabinochka.

You have your family, so you are never alone."

I added, "Not to mention the fact that you don't owe anything to anyone just because they bought you a gift." I said this around a mouthful of pretzel. But I'm sure she got the gist.

Sabina gathered up all the cookies decorated with hot cinnamon heart candies and left the rest of the bouquet for us.

I've dated guys before who were really into resistance training, including one who ate nothing but canned tuna until he actually tested alarmingly high for mercury—but Yuri didn't exercise so he could show off a set of washboard abs. He wanted to be strong, simple as that. Actually, he didn't want to be—he *needed* to be. Because even though I doubted he'd be called upon to physically defend himself in Pinyin Bay, he felt more secure knowing that if it came down to throwing punches, the last guy standing would be him.

All of which was to say he didn't deny himself a treat. And also that he had a little something to hold onto here and there—though I'd never be so gauche as to utter the phrase "love handles." Even though they were adorable.

Yuri might be leery about the wordless origin of the cookie bouquet, but eventually he gave in and tried a cake pop himself... though I suspected they might not have cake pops in Russia. The cake-and-frosting-mashup middles are kind of an acquired texture. Yuri took a bite, cringed, and slipped the half-eaten rose back in with the others.

When his hand was free, I caught it in mine and confessed, "I might not have learned anything we can use today about the Boardwalk...but seeing it like I did from out on the bay, I'm more determined than ever that we can't let developers buy it up. From the deck of the barge, I could see all up and down the coastline, from the trailer park to the cabins to the Shirque Mansion. There's big, heavy machinery creeping in all up and down the shore, and I even caught the sound of drilling out past the correctional facility. I know Pinyin Bay isn't the most metropolitan city. Half of Scrivener Village is held together with duct tape, and its biggest claim to fame is its fire hydrants, which may or may not even work. It's nothing like St. Petersburg with its historic palaces and cathedrals—"

"Dixon." Yuri squeezed my hand and stood up from the table so he could see me without needing to crane his neck around the cookie bouquet. He folded down to one knee in front of me where I sat, cupped my chin, and looked earnestly into my eyes. "A city is more than titles and architecture. Just as a home is more than four walls and a roof." He gathered up both of my hands in both of his and drew them to his lips. His longish stubble whispered across the backs of my fingers as he pressed kisses to my knuckles. Maybe my right hand tingled with Spellcraft at the touch of his left—but frankly, when I felt his lips brushing against my skin…I lost track of where the tingles were coming from.

He squeezed my hands again for emphasis and said, "It matters nothing to me what records Pinyin Bay holds, or which buildings are within its borders, or what the rest of the world might think of it. For you, Pinyin Bay is where you grew up, and you've made many good memories here. And for me…" his voice went thick with emotion, "it is the first place I have ever been happy."

The thing about Yuri—not that I would let on that I was privy—is that he's a lot like the cake pops in the outlandish cookie bouquet. There's a thick shell where he's been dipped over and over in the bittersweet chocolate of adversity. Once you crack through that protective coating, though…the inside is surprisingly soft…and delectably sweet.

I leaned in, slipped my arms around his broad shoulders, and kissed him. Tender and slow—and deep. Not because I was overcome with passion, but to spare him the vulnerability of sharing his feelings. I've never been with anyone quite like him, it's true. But my gut was telling me it would be a lot easier on him if the candy coating melted away in layers instead of cracking off all at once.

The taste of the cake pop was a surprise. Not the metaphorical one that stood for Yuri, but the real one he'd just bitten into. If the frosting had any flavoring beyond pure sugar, I would expect it to be spiked with vanilla—or, since it was tinted red, maybe cherry.

Whoever had assembled this particular cookie bouquet had a real flair for the dramatic, though, and they'd flavored the icing with rosewater. A gentle hint of roses blossomed in our kiss. It was delicate...and it was delightful.

Since I met Yuri, I'd been leaning into the unexpected a lot. And it hadn't let me down yet.

We stripped off one another's clothes. While my old futon, now serving as our sofa, was only mere feet away, we resisted the urge to adjourn to it. Meringue could see us. We had no qualms about walking around in the buff in front of the bird—not only was nudity entirely natural, but it wasn't as if *she* was wearing anything. But we drew the line at engaging in sexytimes within eyeshot. Studies have shown that cockatoos are capable of using tools, and they have the mental equivalent of a kindergartener. So, although Meringue might not be the same species as either of us, there were certain activities she really didn't need to witness.

Especially since she had a tendency to repeat things.

Meringue had an uncanny knack for vocal impersonations. She'd nailed Sabina's distant laugh, just like it sounded through the floorboards, and she had the *hmph* Yuri makes when he reads the newspaper down pat. That meant that not only did we need to retreat to the bedroom when things turned steamy, but we had to be quiet, too.

No complaints on my end. All the secrecy just made our love life seem clandestine and thrilling. Even if we only were, in essence, hiding from a bird.

Our bedroom—I still loved saying that, *our*—had four full walls, each of them fully painted, and a door that both shut securely, and opened again when you wanted to leave the room. Given how hard it was to get everything level and plumb when you're not an actual carpenter, this was no minor accomplishment. The inside of the room was fairly spartan. Yuri had gone with off-white paint for the walls, claiming we didn't have money to throw away on a fancy paint job. But I suspected it was more that he preferred to surround himself with clean neutrals. Boring? Sure. But less competition for the potential Seens that must be constantly flitting past his mind's eye.

And my Wonder Woman quilt did make a spiffy focal point amidst the plain walls.

White chocolate on my lips mingled with rosewater frosting on his tongue as I tipped him back onto that blanket and luxuriated in his Yuriness. Yes, I'd squandered a whole day on the Barge of the Bay with nothing to show for it. And yes, the sound of those massive drills was most definitely not encouraging. But Yuri and I were the left and right hands of Spellcraft. Between the two of us, we would keep Pinyin Bay intact.

When I scrunched myself under the Wonder Woman blanket and worked some magic that had nothing to do with Spellcraft, Yuri managed to stifle the noises I was doing my best to elicit—barely. And while the origins of the cookie bouquet were somewhat dubious, I definitely enjoyed the contrast of the lingering sweetness in my mouth against the earthy salt of his skin. You know. Down *there*.

As we spooned together afterwards—I was the big spoon, wrapped around his back like a too-small cardigan—I was considering going back for another pretzel when I felt Yuri sigh, then heard him murmur something in Russian.

"Ya tebya lyublyu."

He spoke softly...as if to sneak the words past Meringue. Or me. Or himself. But I'd heard him quite plainly. And while I may not speak a lick of Russian, I'd not only looked up that particular phrase, but memorized it in hopes of someday having it directed at me. It sounds a lot like *Yahtzee Blah You-Blue*, and it translates to those three little words any lovesick guy would be thrilled to hear.

Not-saying something is always a heck of a lot harder for me than saying it...but I could tell this was another one of those moments I'd need to be careful not to break the protective candy shell. So instead of blurting out my undying love—it really was a challenge—I eased myself away from Yuri's back just enough to slip a hand between us. In big, easy letters, I wrote with my forefinger, "I love you too." And instead of a flourish, I sealed the top of the letter-o with a kiss.

YURI

7

Love is full of contradictions. On one hand, it makes you strong. On the other...it leaves you falling asleep, naked and vulnerable, with nothing in your belly but a bite of rose-flavored frosting. The bedroom I shared with Dixon had no natural light, and I woke feeling disoriented and confused as to whether we'd slept for just a few moments or the entire night.

I exited the bedroom and squinted against the pale gray light illuminating the single louvered window. Voices drifted up from downstairs. To this day, I still clenched my fists whenever I overheard Dixon's family, thinking some irate tenant would pound on the walls or ceiling, leaving me quelling the urge to go pound *him*. And then I reminded myself that the *volshebstvo* had handled the man *for* me. Edward Greaves lived in a defunct insane asylum now, where undoubtedly the walls were thick enough to suit even him.

Although I took care not to step on any of the squeaky floorboards, Meringue heard me nonetheless. How a creature without visible ears managed this, I had no idea. I could tell by the way she ruffled her feathers she would soon wake Dixon with her morning food-begging routine, which consisted of an obnoxious jingle for a competing Spellcraft shop. Just the first few notes, but we all knew it for what it was. I filled her pellet bowl and distracted her before she started singing, then scrounged her a stick of celery from the small refrigerator, which would keep her occupied with the business of de-stringing before she actually ate it.

We were always conscientious about having food for the bird. Not so for ourselves. There was no coffee. Which was a problem, since the flower-shaped sugar cookies were surprisingly dry.

Fonzo and Sabina had not run out of coffee since I'd known them, so I pulled on some clothes and headed downstairs. There was a time when I would not go into the main house without an express invitation—and then, only with Dixon at my side. Until one day the handle broke off my screwdriver right in the middle of installing a new towel rack while Dixon was out getting his hair cut. I tapped sheepishly at the door to see if I could borrow another, and Sabina snapped, "Do I look like your butler? For crying out loud, Yuri. We're not going to wait on you hand and foot forever. Just come in and help yourself!"

It was the most heartwarming rebuke I'd ever experienced.

Living with the Penn family was unlike living with my own in more ways than I could count. For instance, the sound of laughter coming from the kitchen—men's. My father's laugh was nothing like this. A cruel thing, filled with scorn. The sound I heard now was inviting. Even as it made my throat catch...and not just from those dry cookies.

"Well, look who's here," Dixon's father called out as my shadow fell across the kitchen counter. "Did you hear about the Scrivener who walked into a bar and asked the bartender to draw him a beer? Hold on, he says when he gets his drink—you mean you're not a Seer?"

Fonzo shook his head. "Pull up a seat, Yuri, and take a gander at this."

Johnny Penn sat with his brother at the kitchen table, each with a mug of coffee placed far off to the side as they studied a bit of Spellcraft. The Crafting was between them inside a plastic sandwich bag. The *volshebstvo* was unhampered by this precaution, but the paper was protected from dampness or grease.

Chortling to himself, Johnny said, "Fonzo just had his first return since he's come back to work at the shop...and it's a doozy."

Fonzo looked unduly affronted—exaggerating for show. "I still say if they'd just let the darn thing play out, everything would fall into place."

I poured a cup of coffee and had a look for myself.

You find every shortcut
On the road to success

The Seen—a brown squiggle—looked as much like a road as it did anything else. "What is the problem?"

"Apparently," Fonzo grumbled, "three hours south of here, there's a little podunk town called Success."

Ah. The *volshebstvo* could be annoyingly literal.

Johnny said, "And the customer knows about eight ways through the surrounding cornfields by now—all found while he was just trying to get to MallMart. So, you can understand why he'd like it Uncrafted." He clapped Fonzo on the shoulder. "Growing up, this guy gave me all kinds of grief for my alliteration. But who's laughing now?"

I was baffled that either of them seemed amused by the Crafting's failure to please the customer. So many of the family's interactions were harder to figure out than an elusive American idiom that no interpreter could precisely explain.

Fonzo sighed expansively. "Johnny just likes to gloat about his track record."

"And what would that be?" I asked.

"Over thirty years of Crafting and never once been asked for a re-do." Johnny buffed his nails on his corduroy jacket. "Not bad, if I do say so, myself. I'll bet I can even make it to retirement without a single Uncrafting."

"You *did* bet that," Fonzo said. "After a few too many Mai Tais, you bet the Monte Carlo to Ladin Silver."

"And with any luck, my spotless record will hold up at least as long as that old car. Miss a few measly payments on your business loan and the bank is none too eager to finance an automobile."

"Bank, schmank," Fonzo said. "That car will outlast all of us. Your Craftings might be a little stilted, but they always work like a charm. No one's gonna tarnish your winning streak—and Ladin's never gonna get his hands on that old jalopy."

I swallowed my coffee quickly, hardly tasting it, then poured a cup for Dixon and said my goodbyes. I was more convinced than ever that the problematic Spellcraft had contrived to present itself to us at the shop while the rest of the family was gone. Of course, it could also have been coincidence…but if one is willing to draw a long enough line between one event and another, eventually they can all be connected.

Upstairs, I found Dixon now awake and tackling his morning routine. While he shaved, Meringue stood beside him at the bathroom mirror, bobbing happily at the sight of her reflection beside his and making a sound like a bicycle horn. "Maybe we should just let Sabina take a stab at this problem," Dixon said as he dabbed off the shaving foam. "Since she's got an inroad with Crouch."

I trusted Sabina to handle herself, but I was still leery of the randy young men around her. Especially the mime. Besides, the fewer people we involved in dismantling Johnny's spell, the better. But at the very least, I supposed, I could be grateful that Crouch was unlikely to spread any gossip. "The *volshebstvo* has placed itself in our hands. We will deal with it ourselves."

I caught a glimpse of Dixon's secret smile in the mirror. He had never wanted to hand off responsibility to his cousin at all. Despite the fact that I knew I was being nudged into Crafting, I pulled out my paintbox gladly. I was as eager as Dixon to ensure his father's good name, such as it was, remained intact.

And it was more than just his car at stake.

It came as no surprise that Meringue's continual background chatter went quiet whenever the paintbox came out. Birds can sense the *volshebstvo*. Maybe even more so than humans. A storm was brewing. Far on the horizon—perhaps little more than a quick cloudburst that would be over and gone soon enough. But something in my gut told me it would be wise to take every possible precaution.

Especially now that so much of the waterfront was in an outsider's hands.

I calmed myself. I closed my eyes. I cleared my mind. And I entered that receptive state by which I approached my Seens.

Nothing happened.

I opened my eyes and glared at the paper, the paints, the brush. They were all as they should be. In fact, I required no particular tool, not like Dixon and his quill. It was not the tools at fault...but me.

Dixon had finished in the bathroom and now busied himself tidying up the lounge. There were no walls between us, and he did his best to act as if he was not simply hovering nearby in case I needed him, though without looking at me, so as not to distract me from my Seeing. But the mere fact that he wasn't waxing eloquent about some random and meandering topic was evidence enough that he knew what I was doing.

Or...make that *trying* to do.

Annoyed with myself, I wet my brush and looked at my paint.

I could not choose a color.

When drawing a mundane image, it is always possible to alter one's artistic impulse to fit the situation—to add more hair to make the customer happy. But Seens are different. They are more than mere images. They are some fundamental truth.

And to have this truth elude me...was disturbing.

I made a sound of displeasure—which Meringue immediately repeated, twice as loud. Dixon seated himself across from me and said, "Yesterday, you spent the whole afternoon drawing. Maybe you just need more rest."

Seers were notorious for magically depleting themselves as they Crafted, but not only had I enjoyed an entire night's rest, but it was not Seeing I had done out on the Boardwalk. Only drawing.

I didn't realize I'd been clenching my fists until Dixon reached across the card table and pried at the seams of my fingers with his fingertips. He took a hand of mine in each of his and said, "You always say the *vol-shi-bol-sha's* got a mind of its own, and there's no forcing it to do what it doesn't want to do. If you don't have a Seen in you at this very minute, then put your paints away—at least for now. We'll go back to the Boardwalk and try again...though I'm going to pose as a tourist this time." He gave a theatrical shudder. "I've reached my limit of polyester."

DIXON

I dug a couple pairs of sunglasses out of a box marked "Beachwear."

"*That* is your disguise?" Yuri said.

"I've got this awesome straw fedora, too. Tourists love hats."

Yuri made a doubtful noise.

"No one really looks at anyone else too hard unless they're cruising," I told him. "And even then, they're mostly looking at your package. Anyway, I'm sure that to a Boardwalker, a tourist is a tourist—and the tourists themselves turn over like crowds in a restaurant."

Yuri gave me *the look*—the one that only makes me that much more eager to prove I'm right—but he took a pair of shades from me and put them on. He looked like he was ready to rappel off a helicopter in an action movie and beat up some bad guys. Or maybe good guys. Or whoever the director pointed him at.

We headed over to the Boardwalk and took in the expanse of it. Not exactly the world's biggest boardwalk, but we'd cover more ground if we split up. It was still early by Boardwalk standards, but the vendors were all prepping for the day's crowd with purpose and focus. "I'll take the right side and you take the left," I said, since these were obviously our lucky sides. Yuri, who was facing me at the time, seemed to know exactly which *left* I meant and headed off toward the food vendors to see what he could find out.

I love a good gossip session, but hearing stories about what people in the distant past have said and done was not my idea of fun—which means history's not exactly my best subject. My memory is fine, but I tend to learn by experience. I can tell you all about the places I've traveled and the folks I've met along the way. I wasn't so sure of the Boardwalk, though, since I hadn't seen much of it since I was a teenager. Hopefully immersing myself in the South Dock Boardwalk as a full-fledged adult would yield a clue as to why someone was scarfing up the waterfront.

The centerpiece of the Boardwalk is a big bronze bell called the Wishing Bell. Kind of like the Liberty Bell...but without the crack. But with wishes! It stood at the nexus of the Historical Society, the piers, and the Ferris wheel, under the watchful eye of the living statue. They say the Wishing Bell has never chimed—not for any particularly ominous reason, but because the clapper was stolen before anyone got a chance to ring it. As to why Pinyin Bay's founders then mounted it at the center of the Boardwalk instead of just buying a new clapper? That reason is lost to history. But whatever it might've been, the city's population ran with it. Wishes made on the Bell were said to have a better-than-average chance of coming true, so long as you weren't too greedy about it. There was a slot in the tall base. Once you wrote down your wish and slipped it inside, you'd get up on your tippytoes and pat the Bell three times while chanting, "The Bell brings great things." The old-timers of Pinyin Bay would then turn their heads, hawk and spit.

Thankfully, that part of the ritual has mostly fallen out of favor.

Once I determined I wasn't standing in anyone's loogies, I rubbed the Bell for luck, then took stock of the Boardwalk. I was pondering exactly which pier Rufus might have lost his virginity under when someone accosted me and dragged me toward The Fence—the tall, mysterious fence that was purportedly *not* protection from wolverines, though the jury was still out on that. I never saw the guy coming. But in my defense, it was an overcast day and my sunglasses were really dark.

I slipped off my shades, and my attacker gesticulated at me urgently.

"Crouch?"

He scrunched his eyebrows and shook his head vigorously, made an exasperated "forget it" gesture...and then began to pantomime something.

"You're singing karaoke. You're lighting a cigar. Hold on—you're not propositioning me, are you?"

He looked alarmed and shook his head.

"Good—because if I re-lose my virginity under the Boardwalk, it won't be with anyone but Yuri."

Crouch sketched an hourglass shape in the air and then repeated the gesture, now eating the microphone. Or cigar. Or...you know. "That's way too kinky for me," I said firmly. "And I'm incredibly open-minded."

The mime crossed his arms and glared.

"Wait, I know. You're annoyed."

He rolled his eyes.

"Anyway," I said, "there's no time for guessing games. We spent all day out here yesterday and came up with a big, fat nothing. Where was it exactly that you found the Crafting?"

Crouch pointed across the Boardwalk at the Pinyin Bay Historical Society. Ugh, polyester. I shuddered. He spun out something that I'm sure would be an absolutely fascinating story—if he'd used actual words. As it was, I didn't understand a single thing he was trying to convey. Mostly it looked like him waving his arms around. I could see now why my cousin acted like she understood him just to make the flailing stop.

The wind was up, the gulls were screaming, and the water made the watery sounds it makes when it laps against the beach. It reminded me of Yuri's cabin—which now starred in my favorite memories of the beach. Ones that made me especially sad to see all that machinery rolling in.

I was gazing off down the shore when I heard Yuri say, "I am not here to draw," from somewhere behind the wolverine fencing. It was soft and semi-disguised by the ambient shoreline sounds, but I'd know his voice and his accent anywhere. I figured he must have come to get me and ended up talking to Crouch. But when I peeked through the slats of The Fence, there was no one on the other side. Just a big hole with a metal gate set into it and a bunch of *caution* signs. And the mime was still behind me, alone, pretending to sit and think. Which must have been really hard on his thigh muscles.

"Did you just throw your voice?" I demanded. "That's the best Yuri imitation I ever heard." Seriously, Crouch should have been a ventriloquist, not a mime. He didn't even realize that the crazy head-shaking he was now doing looked more like a denial than a gracious acceptance of my compliment.

He cupped his ear, gestured at The Fence, then pointed at the opposite end of the Boardwalk, and back at The Fence again. I said, "I've already looked behind it. Honestly, you've really gotta learn to get a feel for when a joke has run its course."

If there was nothing to learn from the buskers, maybe I could find some historical clues to point me in the right direction. Although Crouch was still gesticulating, I decided that with my awesome tourist disguise, I could get away with scoping out the Historical Society without anyone being any the wiser, and headed off toward the building.

The new living statue was set up right in front, shielding his eyes and gazing off into the distance like he was keeping an eye out for seagulls with overzealous digestive systems. As makeup went, I realized, this getup was actually nowhere near as time-consuming as I'd originally thought. Yes, he was painted metallic from head to toe, but most of that was clothing. His hair was a wig, and the amount of actual skin he'd need to paint was minimal. Since I was the only one around, I couldn't exactly scrutinize him too hard without being obvious. I'd have to sneak a better look at him later to see exactly how he'd put his costume together. Not that I actually wanted to be a living statue—keeping still and quiet wasn't really in my repertoire of skills. But if Yuri and I did decide to tryst under the pier, a little role-play could really spice things up.

I circled the statue as slowly as I could without looking suspicious, took in what details I could about his costume, then slipped through the Historical Society doors. The air inside was cool and slightly stale. Once my eyes adjusted, I noted the interior was the height of fashion—fifty years ago. Dark wood predominated, with parquet floors, chunky shelving, and informational posters featuring models who looked like they'd stepped off the set of the Mod Squad. It was such a time capsule it was practically retro. I surmised the right person would pay a lot of money to reproduce the look—until I saw that everything was subtly worn, as if it had been cleaned so many times, the finish was coming off. And then it pretty much looked old.

"Dixon?" someone whispered—surprisingly loudly. "What are you doing here?" I spun around and found Pearl, the manager, standing in the doorway of a section marked *Reading Room—Quiet, Please*. Her graying hair was slicked back in a severe updo, and her polyester blazer was cinched tight with a gold lamé belt that matched her epaulets.

I'd had no idea how intimidating epaulets could be.

Before I could demand to know how she'd recognized me not only in sunglasses, but with *a hat*, she hissed, "Why aren't you outside helping Charlotte?"

"I wasn't sure I was on duty today. Because I never got a schedule. Or a timecard. Or an official Pinyin Bay ballpoint pen."

Was a reading room the same thing as a library? I've never been welcome at my neighborhood branch—the head librarian referred to me as "motormouth," imagine that. Hopefully my chatterbox reputation hadn't preceded me all the way to the Boardwalk.

Pearl didn't shush me, but she did whip out a stack of index cards and rap them against her palm. In the quiet of the building, the sound was like a miniature paper spanking. I flinched. She whispered, "These are comment cards from the Barge of the Bay.

And I'll have you know, I take customer feedback very seriously."

Uh oh.

"Say, is that Charlotte calling me, off in the distance? Pretty sure it is. I'd better go see what she wants."

"Just a moment, Dixon," Pearl said sternly. I've always had a thing about pleasing authority figures, even though I'm not particularly good at it. She whapped the index cards against her palm a few times, then said, "The Back to Nature group must have really enjoyed their historical cruise yesterday. They gave you a very high rating. Not perfect, mind you. But, still, surprisingly good, especially for your first day."

"Really? Wow." I was actually starting to warm up to Pearl. Did I mention how fond I am of praise? "Say, listen, as someone with unfettered access to the Historical Society, I'll bet you know a lot about Pinyin Bay."

Pearl preened at the generous words. "I suppose I am quite the authority."

There were so many things I wanted to know. What was The Fence all about? Was it entirely impossible wolverines might be involved? But most importantly—who the heck was buying up the shoreline? But before I could ask, the Historical Society door swished open on silent hinges. It was opened with some urgency, but it made only a gentle sigh—though the pages of a few open books nearby fluttered. "There you are," Charlotte whispered to me—very loudly. She snagged me by the sleeve and said, "Hurry up—the barge is waiting."

YURI

9

Perhaps Dixon was right, and no one truly looks at anyone else. Or if they do, they don't see. The Boardwalk was bustling, but at this early hour, only with the people who worked there. The shopkeepers cleaned windows, the maintenance crew swept sand from the planks, and the deliverymen dropped off more cheap souvenirs to sell. I stood on a section that had been recently swept, and gazed off in the direction of the cabins where I had wintered. I could not see the beach. But the top of a massive auger was visible above the treetops, and it saddened me.

How strange to be sentimental about the city where I had lived less than a year, when St. Petersburg could collapse and I would accept the news with a shrug. I had no use for this sentimentality. But since I could think of no particular remedy, there was nothing else to do but determine who was buying the shore.

The prospect of stopping them—by whatever means necessary—was a much more encouraging thought to dwell on.

I paused outside a "gallery" selling cheap jewelry and mass-produced ceramic trinkets. My reflection in the plate glass window greeted me, shielded behind the sunglasses. I was both resident and outsider. Knowing without being known. And it was a comfort to be able to operate outside the system, to be just an observer, with no claims to my time—

"Yoo hoo!" called a familiar voice—one which had been grating on my very last nerve, to the point where it intruded in my dreams. Drew Draws was already outfitted with his rhinestone apron and ridiculous glittery beret. "Buttinski!"

"That is not my name."

"Oh please," he said dramatically. "You should be *thanking* me for giving you a moniker. Really. You should. Everyone knows that a memorable presence is the best marketing."

I took another glance at myself in the shop window and wondered how I ever thought a pair of sunglasses would be adequate disguise. "I am not here to draw," I said.

"Nonsense." Drew plucked at my sleeve. "Now stop admiring your large, strapping self and come over to the tent before the tourists get here." As he marched off toward the corner of the Boardwalk he'd carved out for himself, I got a good look at what he was wearing beneath that apron. Shorts. Satin shorts. Extremely short satin shorts.

Shorts I would never un-see.

Had he been wearing such things yesterday as I stood beside him all day drawing tourists with exaggerated amounts of hair?

Well. Now it was not just his voice that would haunt my nightmares.

Ignoring his request, I turned and power-walked out to the parking lot as a new idea formed in my mind. Dixon might look enough like any other Spellcrafter to make the Handless second-guess whether they had seen him before or not. In my suit, though, with my shaved head, I was too easy to recognize. But I had been offered something which would make a much more effective disguise—something that would ensure none of the Boardwalkers (except Drew) could possibly take me for anything but a tourist.

Unfortunately, that item was pink.

But the sight of the auger convinced me to do what needed to be done.

I was relieved to find the Big Burgundy Bus had not yet departed. I rapped on the door, and Isaac the bus driver greeted me with his uniform askew and his dreadlocks tied up in a paisley bandanna. He appeared to be the only one on the bus. "Where are tourists?" I asked.

"They took one look at the sand dunes and decided it was the perfect place to camp. Makes no difference to me, since I sleep on the bus to protect everyone's luggage, but that's cool. I'm not big on the great outdoors." He scratched at his braided beard. "Too many bugs."

"Will this not throw off your whole tour?"

"What can I say, man? If the customers are happy, I'm happy."

And if the busload of nature enthusiasts was staying an extra day, it was especially fortunate for me. "Did you find the extra T-shirt?"

Isaac looked up from where he was picking something out from beneath his fingernail. "Dude! It totally slipped my mind." What a shock. "Come on up and take a load off while I have a look. The seats are pretty cushy."

Although the bus bore evidence of being in use, with various bags and towels and articles of clothing here and there, every-thing was plush and new. And burgundy. And pervaded with the so-called "new car smell" which was strange to me, but surprisingly apt. There was a sign hanging behind the driver's seat that read, *For your safety, remain seated while the bus is in motion.* A dull and forget-table sign, to be sure. And yet, my eyes kept returning to the words.

"You feel it, don't you?"

Isaac's voice came from right over my shoulder, and I flinched away. How had I possibly allowed him to sneak up so close behind me? He had ample opportunity to attack while I stared at the forgettable sign. Luckily, his body language was not aggressive in the slightest. He slipped past me, walked up to the sign, and said, "Check this out, man—it's trippy. I was hanging out in the bus one day and, for some reason, I felt like I needed to know what was on the back of the sign. If it was blank. Or the same as the front. Or maybe a mirror image of the front, like you'd actually see if you were looking through the paper. Or whether the paper actually existed. Okay, I might've ingested a gummy or two before I had this thought." He smiled wistfully at the memory. "But you won't believe what I found."

Oh, I was pretty sure I would.

He slipped the sign from its holder and turned it around. The back of the sign held a meticulous photorealistic painting of the bus, an image which must have taken days to create. And over the top, in dramatic calligraphy, had been Scribed:

Daytime
Nighttime
Rain or Sun
Big Burgundy Bus
Is Always Fun

Dixon would have been tickled over the fact that it rhymed.

Isaac said, "You can guess what this is, can't you?"

I hardly needed to agree. Spellcrafters might think the Handless are all ignorant, but of course, they are not. Once someone commissions a Crafting for themselves, they often realize many stray bits of verse around them are more than just positive affirmations. Many mass-produced graphics with sayings looked so much like Spellcraft...enough of them that I wouldn't be surprised if an enterprising Spellcraft family had begun printing them as a smokescreen for what was really going on.

It is one thing to spot Spellcraft out in the open.

It is another to notice it hidden.

When I was a younger man, a gay activist group in Moscow covered the slogan of the United Russia party in protest with a rainbow. It did no good, of course. The "homosexual propaganda" had been successfully linked to pedophilia by the government—as if the older generation needed any more reason to condemn us. But the activists...I could hardly imagine being so fearless. Even so, whenever I passed graffiti on the streets of my own city that had not yet been painted over or scrubbed away, I often sought out glimpses of rebellion to reassure myself I was not alone—even if I was not, myself, brave enough to stand up for my cause.

A particular spot behind a small row of shops never failed to catch my eye when I saw it on my way to and from my miserable work, even though I walked nearly half a kilometer out of my way to pass by.

The walls themselves were always painted over within a week… but no one bothered with the trash bins.

I presumed I had been looking for a hint of a rainbow among the graffiti, and had not even realized I'd been staring at the painted wall behind the bins. Not until an old woman paused beside me and said, "What is it you see?"

Don't talk to strangers is a phrase repeated often to every American child—but children know empty words when they hear them. In America, strangers are always remarking upon the weather, complaining about the traffic, or randomly greeting people they have never seen before and may never see again. In the grim St. Petersburg neighborhood that had spawned me…speaking with strangers was simply not done.

Either the old woman had mistaken me for someone she knew, or she was senile. I ignored her, thinking she would surely go away.

She did not. Instead, she stared at me until, finally, I could not help but look back at her. I had expected her eyes to be filmy and pale. But instead they were as black and sharp as obsidian shards. When I met her gaze, she asked again, "What do you see?"

"Nothing," I snapped, and walked away.

I sometimes wonder what would have happened if I later avoided that spot. I often wished I had. But, no. Despite the fact that someone had noticed me searching—for what, I hardly knew—I returned the very next day.

The shrewd old woman—Ulyana—was waiting for me.

I would say she smiled, but there was no joy in her. Only a grim satisfaction. "You do not need to see," she crooned, "in order to See." She set a different inflection on each word, so that somehow I knew, deep in my bones, they were different. She hobbled over to the wall behind the bins and scratched away some cheap, thickly applied latex with her thumbnail. Beneath it, I expected to see graffiti. But while the paint below the cover-up was not especially colorful, it shimmered. Not like metallic flecks were added to the paint—but like heat rising from the surface of the brick as though it were a hotplate.

"It is as I thought," Ulyana said. "The *volshebstvo* is visible to you."

I shook off the memory I would just as soon forget and peered at Isaac, mostly in my peripheral vision. He was obviously no Scrivener. He lacked all the characteristic features. And yet, he'd noticed the Spellcraft face down against the wall. Many Seers must have no clue about their own potential, but I was unsure if it was my place to break the news.

It might only be a burden. There were many times I myself considered the *volshebstvo* a curse.

Though...not lately.

"What do you know of Spellcraft?" I asked him.

"If you'd asked me that a few months ago, I woulda said it's mainly wishful thinking. I mean, a positive attitude can't hurt, right? But I've driven for other bus lines, and I'll tell you what. The passengers on the Big Burgundy Bus are waaay cooler than anywhere else. And they can't even see the poem."

He slipped the Spellcraft back into its holder, Crafting hidden, then peered up into an overhead compartment.

"No T-shirt." He looked perplexed, scratching the whiskers on his neck, and then he brightened and snapped his fingers. "Hey, I know, why don't you talk to Husky Lou? You're just about the same size, and maybe he's got an extra."

As much as I hated to ask anyone for anything, let alone a stranger named *Husky Lou*, I had little desire to squeeze into anything Isaac might have worn and end up with some sort of parasite or fungus. In fact, the thought of something crawling from him to me brought a quick end to my indecision about what I should or shouldn't tell him. I backed off the bus and headed out to find that T-shirt.

While the Strangerberg side of the bay is rocky and home to many dramatic bluffs, our coast is sandy. There are dunes just beyond the Boardwalk, though with its stunning view of the power plant, the area has never been much of a tourist destination.

But today, it was.

Tents formed a ring around the top of the largest dune, and the nature group was gathered within their shelter. A bonfire smoked. People sang to the accompaniment of an out-of-tune guitar. There was camaraderie and laughter—hearty enough that I wondered if they were still under the influence of the *volshebstvo*, and how I, with my grim nature, would possibly be mistaken for one of their group.

I trudged up the dune. For each step I took, the sand sent me back another half-step. Jogging the hill would make for a good workout, but I had no time to indulge. When I was close enough to the tents to be heard, I called out, "I am looking for Husky Lou."

"That's me!" a man's voice called back. "What can I do ya for?"

His head popped up over the top of a tent. His face was round, his neck was thick, and his complexion was ruddy, framed by a full, graying, reddish-brown beard. Judging by the height of the tent and the fact that I could only see the tops of the other tourists' heads, he looked to be at least six feet tall. And he wasn't scratching himself—not that I could see. That was a good sign.

"I was told you might let me borrow a T-shirt."

"Absolutely. Long-sleeve? Short-sleeve? Tank top? UV protection? Rashguard?"

He was going to make me say it. I bit back a sigh. "The T-shirt... from your group. The pink shirt."

Husky Lou brightened. "You're interested in Back to Nature? Why didn't you say so?" He ducked back behind the tents and rummaged through one of them. I watched the progress of his head above the tent line as he made his way around to an opening. And then he stepped through the gap.

Without a stitch of clothing…other than the pink T-shirt wadded in his hand.

"So, are you already familiar with naturism, or is it something you're just beginning to explore?"

I could hardly admit it was yet another case of *this word does not mean what I thought it did*. Not if I wanted that shirt. And so, I defaulted to the response that always painted me in the best possible light. "I knew this thing only in Russia. It may be different here."

"I'm not surprised. Attitudes about naturism really vary from place to place. You need to get all your ducks in a row. We were thrilled Pinyin Bay granted us a camping permit on such short notice."

I would not be surprised if whoever issued the permit made the same assumption I had: that they were hosting a group of wildlife enthusiasts.

Husky Lou held out the shirt…but when I took hold of it, he did not let go. "Just so we're clear—this isn't a swingers' shindig. People who join our club to hook up are sorely disappointed. And there's an application you need to fill out. A vetting process before you can strip down to your birthday suit and join in the festivities."

"I am not looking for sex," I said, with surprising conviction. "I would be grateful if I could just see what it is like to be among your group—not here, naked, but out on the Boardwalk—and get to know more about this…naturism."

The answer pleased him, and with a nod, he released the T-shirt. "What a relief. You'd be surprised how many folks want to jump right in and whip off their clothes without learning all the ins and outs. I'm right in the middle of brunch, so I'll meet you over by the Ferris wheel in an hour for a one-on-one orientation."

Hopefully by that time I'd figure out who was trying to buy the Boardwalk, and could simply return the ludicrous pink shirt without needing to hear about the "ins and outs" of naturism.

DIXON

10

"Listen," I told Charlotte. "Don't get me wrong—I'm grateful you rescued me from your boss. Frankly, the thought of her frowning at me makes me a little nervous. Add to that the chance that she might actually *tut* her disapproval—"

"Forget about Pearl. There's something you need to know about the Boardwalk."

I'd been trying to figure out how to disengage from the tour guide before I ended up stuck on the barge again...but I'm such a sucker for a juicy bit of gossip. "Is it a scandal? Because I love a good scandal. They're so scandalous."

Charlotte narrowed her eyes and sized me up. The furrow between her brows deepened. "I hope I don't regret this." I gave her my winningest smile, and she relented. She cocked her head toward the parking lot and said, "I'll tell you—but not out in the open where just anyone can overhear."

We headed off toward a hatchback parked at the far end of the lot. Pinyin Bay gets pretty hot at the height of summer, to the point where you could toast a bagel on the seat of a closed car parked in the sun. Those hot days were still a few weeks away. Even so, the single car at the edge of the lot had collapsible foil sunscreens covering the interior of every window.

"Air conditioning on the fritz?" I asked sympathetically.

"Why do you ask? Have you been spying on my car?"

"I wouldn't have even known it was yours." Awkward. "Say, why are you confiding in me, anyway?"

"To open your eyes."

Clearly, this was now the point at which I should start determining my escape route. "Okey dokey, then. Eyes open. Mission accomplished."

"Not so fast. First of all, you need to promise me you won't tell anyone what I'm about to reveal. As far as They're concerned, for all we know, the Wishing Bell is just a place to make a wish and spit."

I could practically hear the capital-T in the word *They*. "Who are *They*?" I wondered aloud.

"Shh! No specifics. Not until it's safe to talk." Charlotte beeped open her car, rummaged a roll of aluminum foil out of the back seat, tore off a sheet, and handed it to me. Then she pulled out a baseball cap and showed me the inside was lined with foil. "Good thing you have a hat. Otherwise the foil tends to blow away."

"You want me to—?"

"Shh!" She put her cap on, then pointed at me.

My mom always says, don't mess with someone who's not playing with a full deck—but Uncle Fonzo says it's all a matter of working the game. I glanced around to make sure no one was around—luckily, we were alone—and tried my best to look like I thought it was perfectly normal to drape a sheet of foil over my head.

Charlotte reached over and mashed my straw fedora on top of it, then nodded with satisfaction. "We can't let Them know about the foil trick. If we do, They'll just change the frequency of their devices."

"Um. Wow."

"Don't tell me you can't hear the voices."

"I'd hate to jump to any rash conclusions—so many tourists

around. So many voices."

"That's true. The South Dock Boardwalk isn't usually so busy. When it's less crowded, the voices are way more obvious. I can't even tell you the number of times I've been standing around shilling barge tickets, had someone ask me a question—and realize I was the only one there. And it stands to reason, if I can hear them, They can hear me."

"Ri-i-ight. Good thinking."

"But even though it's safest to just play along and act like we don't know about Them, I can't in good conscience force you to parrot their lies without letting you in on the big secret." She whipped out a tattered edition of Pinyin Bay Journal from the mounds of stuff in her back seat. "Check out this headline: Local Referendum is In! Yellow Wins - by a Landslide."

"The Ferris wheel?"

Charlotte leveled a knowing look. "No one likes yellow *that* much. Obviously, this was the work of a small handful of people."

For all that I was itching to shuck the tinfoil and run away, I had to admit—I'd been hoping to get an inside scoop on the Boardwalk. Hopefully the scoop I was about to receive wouldn't be too nutty.

Charlotte took back the paper and carefully tucked it among all the other stuff stashed in her car. "Everyone thinks the elected officials are in charge of Pinyin Bay, but between the parking lot and the water, it's a different story. All the decisions here are made by a secret society: the Boardwalk Board."

"Wow. Who's on it?"

"They wouldn't be a secret society if they went around announcing their members. Even they don't know who their fellow members are. Whenever there's an issue they need to vote on, they cast anonymous ballots at the Wishing Bell. Whoever's on it, they're old. Really old. Because they've been running this Boardwalk behind the scenes for decades."

Given the overall state of the Boardwalk, maybe some of them should consider retiring. In fact, maybe some of them already had. "You don't think they'll decide to sell, do you?"

"I hope not." Charlotte glanced skyward as if she felt the free-floating microwaves pinging against the foil lining of her hat. "But from the whispers I've heard, it sounds like most of them are on board with selling out. All of them but one."

"Who's the holdout?"

"What part of 'secret' don't you understand?"

Well, how about that? A secret society. Right here in Pinyin Bay!

I could hardly wait to tell Yuri.

But before I could head off to fill him in, Charlotte grabbed me by the Scribing arm and hauled me back to the barge.

Husky Lou was a gregarious man. Normally, this would annoy me. But there was something—dare I say it—*wholesome* about him which made him bearable.

"I can't emphasize enough the importance of sunscreen." He then launched into a story of nakedness which was surprisingly easy to ignore.

Striding up and down the Boardwalk beside another large man in a matching pink shirt was a much better disguise than the sunglasses alone. The only one who would recognize me as a local should be Drew, so I steered Husky Lou toward the opposite end of the walkway, where the boards underfoot were lost to sand, ending with a curve of stout fencing.

"Anything that protrudes is particularly vulnerable to sunburn." Lou squirted a blob of sunscreen into my hand. "And I mean *any-thing*. Not just your nose. A baseball cap is always a good idea—I never go anywhere without one. And this is where having a belly can really come in handy...."

As the nudist blathered on and I swiped lotion over the back of my neck, I realized we were not alone. Behind the fence, another conversation was taking place. One in which I was extremely interested. "It's nine to one in our favor—look, I don't know why they need a unanimous vote, they just do. Now it's only a matter of figuring out how to make the last one give in."

Where had I heard that voice before? Difficult to say, with him whispering and Lou droning on over top of it. I prodded Lou and put my finger to my lips, then gestured to the other conversation with a nod. He shrugged and bent his head to listen in, too.

"But don't worry, even if the holdout is too stubborn to see common sense, it's just a matter of figuring out who they are. They might think they're anonymous, but I'm watching that ballot box like a hawk. Soon as I figure out who's blocking the deal, we can apply some direct pressure." A pause, then a whisper. "Someone's here, gotta go."

I hurried around the fence, thinking to catch this person in the act—but when I rounded the far side, there was nothing there but a tunnel sealed with a security gate—a gate which appeared to be rusted shut.

"Some trick," Husky Lou said.

"And what would that be?"

"The way sound bounces right here—almost makes it seem as if voices are coming from that old hole. But obviously, the gate hasn't been disturbed in ages, and what you're hearing is actually more like an echo." He sketched the shape of the fence with a meaty hand. "See the way the wind has bent this fence into a parabola? It's forming something called a whispering gallery with another structure on the other side of the Boardwalk. And whoever was just talking...." He shielded his eyes and gazed down the shore. "I'd say he's over by the tents."

I wondered briefly if this Lou person had been planted by the investors to throw us off their trail. But if that were the case, it would have involved hiring the whole tour group to perpetrate the deception, and setting them in motion days before Dixon and I decided to investigate. But just to be sure, I called up the dictionary on my phone and looked up the word *parabola*. The definition was a symmetrical curve. I supposed the fence did indeed form such a thing. And if I listened very hard, I could hear Drew Draws calling out, "Anyone can take a selfie! Commemorate your trip to Pinyin Bay with a custom cartoon!"

And, with that, I realized his tent formed a very similar curve.

"I know exactly where the sound came from," I said, and set off with Husky Lou to check out the very spot I'd been taking such care to avoid. We headed toward the other side of the Boardwalk at a jog. When Lou got winded I let him fall behind, hoping to spot someone looking suspicious in the vicinity of Drew's tent. I was positive I'd heard the voice before, and hopefully once I saw the man, it would all click into place.

I ran right up to the purple tent, where Drew was sketching an elaborate mound of hair on the portrait he was currently completing. "Well," he said to me loftily, "look who finally decided to show up. Do you know how many customers decided to go to the old-time photo gallery instead?"

I strode past him and circled the tent...and discovered *the mime* standing behind it with a phone to his ear.

"I have you now," I said with great satisfaction, and snatched the phone from his hand.

"Yuri?" said a woman's voice on the other end of the line. "Is that you?"

"Sabinochka?"

"Did you just butt-dial me? And did you get a new number? What a relief, I thought it must've been Crouch bugging me again."

I cut my eyes to the mime, who made a hopeful cookie-eating gesture.

"It *was* mime. How long have you been talking with him?"

"Talking *at* him was more like it. I dunno—ten minutes?"

It had taken me fewer than five to get there from the fence. I checked the mime's phone. The current call had been running eleven minutes, thirty-two seconds and counting. I put the phone back to my ear. "I can persuade him to stop bothering you," I told Sabina, looking Crouch in the eye as I spoke.

"Aw, how sweet of you to offer! But no, don't worry about it. I can handle him myself. Plus, now I'm curious to see if he's gonna keep sending me random stuff."

Curiosity can be a dangerous thing—and it sounded like the mime was wearing her down. But Sabina's love life was none of my business. And his charades would prove overwhelmingly annoying soon enough.

I ended the call and shoved the phone into the mime's hands. "Who else was back here making a phone call?" I demanded.

He curled his hand beneath his chin and pretended to think about it.

Sabina might not want me to work him over on her behalf...but maybe I had another, equally valid reason to do so: to see if his voice was the one I heard in the whispering gallery. "Stop with the pantomime and say something," I warned him. "Or I will demon-strate a more painful way to make you talk."

But before I ended up scrubbing greasepaint off my knuckles, Husky Lou staggered around the corner, dropped his hands to his knees, and struggled to catch his breath. "Did you find the shady character?" Lou eventually managed, between breaths.

Maybe so. Because it was entirely possible the mime could have put Sabina on hold during the call and made another. Since he wasn't speaking, she might not know the difference.

I cut my eyes to Crouch again.

He shrugged helplessly, eased behind Lou to put himself safely out of my reach...then turned tail and ran off.

He was disturbingly quick.

"Say, listen," Lou said. "Since we're so close to the pier, let's see if there's any room on the Barge of the Bay history tour. I really wanted to go yesterday, but they were all sold out. It'll be fun! My treat."

I hardly wanted to be stuck on some boat...but then I saw the mime sneaking up the gangplank and decided that while I couldn't manhandle him in front of too many witnesses, just the threat of harm would seem more serious if he couldn't get away.

"Fine. We will ride boat. Lend me your hat. Sunburn."

Husky Lou was happy to oblige. And though his baseball cap was damp with sweat, it concealed my shaved head. I was thankful for the pink shirt as we got in line for the barge. If I hunched down and positioned myself strategically, I blended in with the other Back to Nature tourists. I only needed to trick the mime for a moment—enough time to trap him between myself and the bulkhead, and force him to finally speak.

I was well-hidden as I boarded the boat—or so I thought. "Yuri?" Dixon called over. I shook my head and hunched even more...but it was no use. "Yuri! Hey, Yuri! Come sit in my section!"

I cast around to see where Crouch was sitting, but could not find him. "Take your seats, everyone," called the tour guide at the front of the boat. "And stay seated. The water is a little choppy today."

The deck lurched under my feet as the barge set off. I staggered to the nearest seat, and sat. I scanned the crowd. No mime.

Not on the barge, at least.

Back on the pier, Crouch bowed his farewell to me with a grand flourish.

I muttered a few choice curses in Russian as a hand fell on my shoulder. "That phrase is starting to sound kind of familiar," Dixon observed brightly, "though I've had zero luck finding it in a translator. Cyrillic is really unfathomable. And you look a-*dorable* in pink. Whoops, did I say that out loud?" He lowered his voice conspiratorially. "Anyhow, you'll be pleased to know I've turned up an awesome lead: a secret society."

He shimmied his shoulders in his eagerness to explain. Even I was forced to admit...it was intriguing. "Go on."

"Apparently, the Boardwalk is controlled by an enclave of anonymous of people called the Boardwalk Board. It's super-secret—as in, even they don't know who else is on it. And one of them is refusing to sell."

That jibed with the phone call I'd overheard. I told Dixon about the whispering gallery—he mouthed the word *parabola* and squinted at the fence on the distant shore with no little amount of skepticism. "That doesn't necessarily preclude wolverines," he said, mostly to himself. "Though it explains why I thought I heard you talking over there when the only one around was Crouch."

"We had better figure out who the holdout is before the buyer does. It sounded to me as though things are about to turn ugly."

"The votes are cast at the Wishing Bell." Dixon pointed to the clapperless bell mounted in the center of the Boardwalk. "And we can totally see it from here."

"Many people are sliding notes into that bell. How will we ever figure out which ones—? Hold on...is that Vano Shirque?"

DIXON

12

I've known Vano Shirque ever since I was old enough to hold a crayon—and been saddled with his presence ever since. Freshman year of high school, we were assigned to partner up for a biology class project that involved dipping some water out of the bay, testing its pH for a week, and comparing our findings. Not only did he fail to take any readings—he left his water in a sunny window, and half our project evaporated. The worst part? He didn't even have the decency to act chagrined!

If Vano was inscrutable as a gawky teenager, his sangfroid was off the charts now that he'd grown up. Not only did his heavy-lidded bedroom eyes and chiseled cheekbones leave random onlookers swooning in his wake, but he moved with the careless grace of someone who had zero figs to give. If James Dean and The Fonz had a baby—if they were both Scriveners, at any rate—that lovechild would be Vano Shirque.

Vano slunk down the Boardwalk like it was a catwalk in Milan. He paused at the Wishing Bell, leaned against the base, and pulled out his phone—probably scrolling through the eight bajillion thumbs-up his picture of today's cappuccino got on Friendlike. Not that I'm jealous. Or annoyed. Or fixated.

Not *too* fixated, anyhow.

I belatedly realized the big guy in pink next to Yuri was trying to get my attention. "Excuse me—sir? How deep is the water?"

"Seventy-five leagues," I said abstractedly—because once the crowd near Vano thinned, he stole a quick look around, then slipped a bit of paper out of his jeans pocket and crammed it into the base of the Wishing Bell—and not to make a wish, either. Whoever'd lost my father's spell had clearly just found another Spellcrafter. I'd never seen Vano move so purposefully...other than the time he snatched that terrible apartment out from under our noses. And even then, I don't suppose I actually *saw* him do it. Just the aftermath of his stupid, perfectly-formed signature on the lease.

"How deep is a league?" the guy was asking Yuri as he thumbed around on his phone to try and look it up. "I don't have any bars out here."

Yuri, too, was distracted by Vano, and said the first thing that popped into his head. "Deep enough to sink ship."

Which...apparently got Charlotte's attention. She really wasn't very good at staying on her half of the deck. She hurried over and declared, "The mean depth is twenty-five yards. And the Barge of the Bay is *very* stable."

If there was one consolation, it was that at least we knew where Vano lived. Plenty of professions have client confidentiality—psychiatry, law, wart removal. But Spellcrafters? Hardly. If Vano wouldn't tell us who hired him to influence the Boardwalk Board, it wouldn't be to protect the customer...it would be to stop us from poaching his business.

Once the Barge of the Bay finally completed its loop around the water and pulled up to the dock, I was practically ready to hop overboard and swim to shore. But Yuri, as usual, was the voice of reason. As Charlotte and the tourists disembarked, he took me to one side and said, "Forget about your 'frienemy,' Dixon."

"But I know he wasn't just making a wish. He didn't pat the Bell."

"Even if he is Crafting for the developers—it is no different from what your own family has done. You cannot implicate him without exposing your father as well."

Well...when he put it *that* way. "So, what can we do?"

He stroked his chin and gazed at the Wishing Bell. The lowering sun made it look cheerful and pink. "These shops all close in just a couple of hours. We should come back and retrieve whatever Spellcraft Vano has made. Between the two of us, you and I can duplicate the work—but without the *volshebstvo*—and Uncraft whatever it was they were using to sway the vote."

"Lemme get this straight. My idea is to go confront Vano face-to-face, while yours is to wait until nightfall, sneak back to the Boardwalk, break into the Bell, steal the Spellcraft and replace it with a counterfeit?" Yuri looked slightly alarmed at that summary, so I hastened to add, "Genius! Let's go change into something black."

I was eager to don a slinky turtleneck like a cat burglar, but unfortunately it was no longer turtleneck weather—plus, I didn't actually own one. I had to settle for a black T-shirt and jeans, and Yuri's suit was more of a dark brown.

Close enough.

There were a few random cars in the parking lot when we got back to the Boardwalk. People tended to park their second cars there when they ran out of room in their garages, since the Pinyin Bay Tourism Council couldn't be bothered to have them towed. The Big Burgundy Bus was still parked there too, but it looked empty. Yuri said, "If anyone is still there, it is only Isaac the driver, guarding the luggage."

I took a good look at the bus. "Awfully suspicious how that bus came into town right when all this Boardwalk stuff started going down. What if Isaac is the buyer's agent—and he's the one you heard making the phone calls?"

"Completely different voice."

"Okay...but if you put a little makeup on him...could he be

Crouch? After all, we've never seen the two of them at the same time."

Yuri shuddered at the mere thought, then said, "Crouch is clean-shaven and Isaac is not. And then there are the dreadlocks."

I was a little bit surprised Yuri would stick up for a guy with so much lint in his hair—Yuri tends to be a lot more conservative than the Scriveners I was accustomed to rubbing elbows with, and even just a tad bit judgy—but if he was willing to vouch for the bus driver, that was good enough for me.

Normally, at night, the Boardwalk was a riot of colored light. Not only were plenty of fairy lights strung between the shops and wound around the potted decorative trees, but when you angled your head just right, they reflected off the water, too. But as late as it was, with the shops closed for the night and the decorative lights turned off, it not only looked different, but sounded different. The water lapping against the pilings out at the end of the pier was loud. And the wind howling across the bay.

And the sound of a single man talking.

"Hello? No, don't put me on speakerphone, I can hardly hear you over all this wind."

Yuri and I melted back into the shadow of the keychain pagoda.

"Your theory about the voters didn't pan out. I watched that ballot box all afternoon, and not a single geriatric local came by. I don't care what your records say. Either the board members aren't the old coots you think they are, or they're voting somewhere else." Yuri was so right—that voice was totally familiar! I craned my neck around the side to get a look, but couldn't make out anything but a generic man-shaped silhouette. "Fine, I'll stay until midnight—and even that's pushing it. You know how early old folks go to bed. And speaking of beds, the sheets at this so-called Pinyin Inn have an abysmal thread count. That would never fly in Wichita."

Yuri and I exchanged a look, wide-eyed with surprise, and then simultaneously mouthed the name *Quint*.

Pinyin Bay was the last place I'd expected to see the obnoxious businessman we'd met back at the Spring Falls Hot Spring Spa.

Shouldn't he be off somewhere demanding an upgrade and bragging about his masseur? I was all ready to charge out there, grab him by his businessman shoulders, and pester some answers out of him—but Yuri caught me by the sleeve and gave his head a subtle shake. He put his lips to my ear and said, "He does not know we are onto him, so we have the advantage. Perhaps Vano's Crafting will shed some light on the situation."

It was really tough to restrain myself from going after Quint and giving him the what-for. But Yuri was right. We knew where he was staying—he'd be the only one at Pinyin Inn since it was no longer open for business, thanks to the developers who were pulling his businessman strings. And it really would be smart to retain the advantage of surprise.

Yuri and I both watched our watches. (Was that confusing for Yuri, I wondered, when two English words meant something different, yet tangentially related? I'd have to ask.) At the stroke of midnight, the silhouette stomped off to the parking lot, making no effort whatsoever to sneak. Yuri put his finger to his lips, and we both waited there, feeling extremely stealthy, until we heard the distant sound of a car pulling out of the gravel lot and driving off.

"Is the coast clear?" I whispered, then realized there was an actual coast in our immediate proximity. I checked the water, too. "I wonder if the first person to ask that question was literally standing right beside a pier, just like us!"

"We are alone," Yuri said decisively—I just love it when he's so commanding. "Let us have a look at what Vano has Crafted."

YURI

13

Like everything else on the South Dock Boardwalk, the Wishing Bell looked as though it had been there for generations. The shoreline atmosphere was humid, causing metal to oxidize and paint to peel. The base of the bell was the size of an especially wide coffin. There was a simple slot in the side bearing a metal plaque that read *Make Your Wish!*

And I could see no way to get in.

I rapped on each side and felt for seams. It appeared as though the face of the box which contained the slot could be opened, but there were no buttons or latches or anything to allow access. But there must be some way for the wishes to be collected—and, more importantly, the ballots.

I pushed and I pried. Nothing. But when I backed up to deliver a good, solid kick, Dixon caught my sleeve and stopped me. "Hold on, Yuri. It's the Wishing Bell. If breaking a mirror is seven years' bad luck—do they say that in Russia?—then I can't even imagine how unlucky it would be to kick down the Bell."

"Well, then? What do you suggest?"

Dixon went back over the seams with nimble fingers. And when he came to the slot at the front, he eased his fingertips in.

A small click sounded. A door at the front of the base swung out. But when Dixon let go to come around and take a look, an interior door popped up from below and sealed the hollow again. Try as he might, he could not open the interior failsafe without standing behind the door with his fingers on the latch. I was more than willing to trade places with him, but my fingers were too thick to fit into the slot. We scanned the area for a bit of driftwood or trash to take the place of his fingers, but it was no good. As much as Dixon was eager to see inside that base, he was stuck behind the door.

I shone light from my flashlight app inside. No papers. But the bottom of the small, coffin-like space was obviously hinged. I got down on my hands and knees to push and pull and pry, but the floor held firm. "There must be a second latch," Dixon said. "We went over the outside of base with a fine-toothed comb, so it's gotta be inside."

Of course it was.

I felt around for another latch from where I stood, but eventually was forced to admit it would be a lot easier if I simply got in and looked. I prodded the floor experimentally to see if it would bear my weight. It was solid. Gingerly, I squeezed inside and shone my light up into the corners.

I saw nothing—not inside the base, anyhow. But outside?

Crouch—or should I say, *Quint?*—was tramping up the beach, carrying a sack filled with who-knows-what. Come back to sabotage the vote, no doubt. And not only did I see him, but thanks to the light in my hand, he clearly saw me. "Dixon—it's Quint!"

Dixon spun around. "Where?"

"He is Crouch! Quint is mime!"

Dixon was quick on his feet, more than I could hope to be. Especially in the soft sand where my weight held me at a disadvantage for anything but a tug-o-war. He was off like a shot in pursuit of Quint. But when he released the latch, not only did the failsafe door shoot up and trap me inside....

With another click, the floor swung out from under my feet.

It was not quite a free-fall, more of a chute, rough-hewn and narrow. I scrabbled for handholds and footholds as I slid through like I was being digested by the Bell. But my momentum was too great, my fingers were slippery with old sunscreen and new sweat, and I stood more risk of breaking my hands than breaking my fall. And so, I decided to furl my left hand against my chest and make peace with wherever I might end up.

I landed hard, though thankfully, something broke my fall—a large mound of paper. I found myself in a sandstone cavern shaped by water and time. Not only was this cavern lit...it was filled with people.

Naked people.

"Yuri?" Husky Lou called out. "What're you doing here?"

Another nudist added, "And how'd you manage to fall out of the ceiling?"

"I hardly know where to begin." I rolled off the mound of papers, decided I was bruised but not broken, and asked, "What is this place?"

Lou said, "We're under the pier."

A woman with a rose tattoo on her shoulder said, "It's a natural hollow formed by the bay. And check out the graffiti on the walls. It goes back decades."

"We're all keen on street art and obscure local attractions," Lou explained. "And when we had our unexpected detour in Pinyin Bay, we did a little digging online and found out about this cave. You never know what hidden gems you'll turn up in these out-of-the-way small towns!"

I took stock of the hollow, which was lit by a camping lantern. The space was perhaps ten meters deep, with an undulating, uneven ceiling two or three meters overhead. Drier than I would have expected, with a sandy floor and gritty walls.

Those walls were covered in graffiti.

Some was skillful. Some was naive. Some vulgar, but more of it sweet.

Some of the painting was fresh. And some had clearly been there for ages. Heart shapes predominated the scheme, with names or initials inside. Layer had been painted upon layer, coalescing as a vast, communal, abstract expressionist mural. And though it was hard to see in the low light of the battery powered lantern, if I angled myself to view the sentiments at an oblique angle, I could see that some of the scrawlings were more than just graffiti.

As the naked crowd watched me scrutinize the riot of color and form, I backed up a few steps to take it all in. Only once I was practically on the other side of the hollow did I see that behind all the random doodles and drawings was a large blob. Somewhat bell-shaped. And pulsing faintly with *volshebstvo*.

Rufus Clahd had indeed spent time beneath the Boardwalk… experiencing more than one rite of passage.

I drew closer to the Seen, now looking specifically for the Scrivenings within. The painted bell was so huge, I would have expected it to contain numerous Craftings—though whether it was possible for one Seen to power them all, I had no idea. But I was not the only one to know the Seen for what it was. A decade or two of Pinyin Bay Scriveners had also recognized it. And none of the stray bits of Scrivenings impinged on the bell. None but the two lines of Crafting directly in its center.

They were old and faded, little more than scratches in the sandstone now. But once I spotted the faint *volshebstvo*, I found I could make out the words.

All goes well
When you wish on The Bell

It rhymed. Dixon would be so pleased….

"Yuri?" As if on cue, Dixon's voice carried from the mouth of the cave.

"In here," I called back.

"Are you o…kay?" He paused at the entrance and blinked at the naturists. Who stared back. Naked. And then he shrugged and began peeling off his T-shirt.

"What are you doing?" I demanded.

"When in Rome…. Say, Yuri, do they have that expression in Russia?"

"Whoa," Husky Lou said, "keep your pants on, buddy. You haven't been through the application process."

Dixon paused with his shirt rucked up to his armpits. "And how does one go about applying?"

"Dixon!" I gestured toward the pile of papers. "We have more pressing matters."

Lou said, "And it's getting a mite chilly out here, anyhow, so we'd better get back to our bonfire. I don't have a brochure on me right now, but if you're serious about joining up, just stop by the campsite."

Some nudists slipped into their shorts and pink T-shirts, and some just looped towels around their waists. But it only took them a few minutes to gather themselves, wave goodbye, and troop out of the hollow, leaving us in the cave with only the light of our phones to see by.

Dixon frowned. "Level with me, Yuri—why did my showing up end the orgy?"

"There was no orgy."

"I need to know. Was it something I said?"

"There was no orgy," I repeated. "And apparently a naturist does not promote nature—only nakedness. Non-sexual nakedness."

"Well, that's a relief. No one wants to be the guy who killed the orgy. And now that I think about it, those folks seemed a little too old to *all* be virgins looking to score under the pier. One or two, I could see. But the entire group of them? And now I get why they kept trying to take off their shirts during the barge tours. Even the women."

"How did you get here?" I asked.

"Well, I took off to go grab Quint, but he was too fast for me. He veered off the Boardwalk into the sand—apparently, there was a stepping-stone path to the parking lot. But I couldn't find it in the dark and kept sliding backwards. By the time I was on solid ground again, he was long gone. But think about it this way—if he came back to the Boardwalk, it means there's still something here for us to find." He turned toward the pile of paperwork I'd landed on and said, "We'd better get digging."

If I had not landed on the pile, maybe we could have skimmed off the top layer of envelopes and papers and taken them home. But unfortunately, everything was now scattered. Though I supposed I should be grateful I had not broken my hand. Or my neck.

Still....

I searched for Vano's Crafting by sight and by feel, but it was no good. "We will never be able to find anything by the light of our phones. There is too much paper."

"I can think of a really good way of finding things."

And the *volshebstvo* was indeed very good at revealing other instances of itself. There was certainly no lack of paper with which to Craft. My hand dropped to my trouser pocket where I kept my paintbox—and found nothing. I sighed in exasperation. "My paints are somewhere in this mess."

"Then we'd better get looking!"

It seemed like a straightforward task. Find the small metal box among the papers. But there was too much ground to cover, and soon, Dixon's phone went dark as the battery drained. "It is no use," I said.

"Chin up, Yuri—we just need a plan B. You do have a plan B, don't you?"

I muttered a curse in Russian—but then realized there was already an active Seen in the hollow. "Behind you, on wall, there is Crafting. Bend the *volshebstvo* to your will."

"Wow. You make it sound so action-hero." Dixon waggled his eyebrows eagerly. "Let's see what I can do."

DIXON

14

All goes well
When you wish on the Bell

Clearly I had my work cut out for me. Although there was plenty of space to add a few more lines, a certain H-E-double-hockey-sticks kept insisting it was the only possible rhyme to fit what was currently there—and I don't even believe the infernal destination literally exists!

I could add another couplet, a pair of lines with an entirely different rhyme, but the word *Vano* had even fewer possibilities than *bell*. Maybe the word *Crafting*...but that only rhymed with *rafting*.

Then again, if I went with an A-A-B-A scheme, my third line could end on anything, so long as it fit into the rhythm. As this realization came to me, the phone Yuri held to light my Recrafting began to dim. He was practically vibrating with the urge to hurry me along—hopefully he wasn't scared of the dark, not that I would call him on it—but even though I didn't have the specific lines in mind, I could tell by the way things were clicking into place....

"I got this, Yuri." It wasn't a brag, not at all. Just a statement of fact. I cupped his cheek briefly and stroked his stubble with my thumb. "I got this."

The surface of the wall was not exactly conducive to calligraphy. Not only was it vertical—it had the texture of those pumice stones you'd use to buff a stubborn callus off your heel. And I was none too keen to grind off the tip of my cockatoo quill on a gritty wall. Don't get me wrong, I adore my quill. But calling it dainty? That's being generous. Yet, when I skimmed my fingertips over the old Rufus Clahd image—when I encountered the relief of the Crafting that had watched over this cave however many years—I felt a rightness. Very faint. But it was there.

"Save the battery," I told Yuri. "I can see it with my heart."

Yuri didn't like it—I could tell by the sound of his breathing—but he trusted me. He turned off the flashlight app and everything went dark. At least until my eyes adjusted, and the lights from the parking lot reflecting off the water bathed the cavern in the faintest wash of light.

I ran my fingers over the old Crafting again.

A-A-B-A rhyme scheme? Yes. Definitely.

All goes well
When you wish on The Bell

I steeled myself, set my quill to the wall without even inking it, and etched two more lines into the sandstone.

The votes are apparent
And so is the Spell

I'd have to trust the Spellcraft to know I was referring to the Spell that Vano dropped in, and not any other stray bits of Spellcraft that had accumulated in that big, crazy pile. But given that the tip of my quill felt the same as always once I was done scratching in my words—no dulling, no splits—and given that I'd experienced the telltale tingle I associate with Scribing, I was confident the Spellcraft was in our corner.

I read Yuri the Scrivening in its entirety, then put away my quill and turned to the mound of paper. Spellcraft has a special affinity for paper. While it wouldn't do something as obvious as levitating the pertinent document or lighting it up like a party lantern, I wouldn't be surprised if a breeze came in off the bay and separated whatever we were looking for from the rest.

That expression, don't hold your breath? I must have been holding mine. And my lung capacity was evidently nothing to brag about. Because eventually, I couldn't hold it any longer...and I sucked in a loud gulp of air.

And even *that* didn't cause the papers to stir. But I told myself not to worry. We'd sense the Crafting just as soon as we laid our hands on it.

Unfortunately, several hours later, the only tingle I felt was in the leg that fell asleep from me sitting on it wrong while I sifted through a gazillion pieces of paper.

The way Yuri talks about Spellcraft, he makes it out to be an almost sentient thing—a capricious friend who more-or-less had your back...though they might subject you to a tasteless practical joke now and then, and their sense of humor left a lot to be desired. But even the least reliable of friends should really know how much the Boardwalk meant to me.

Maybe it just hadn't heard my cry for help. "Should I add some ink?"

In the dim, reflected light, Yuri was reduced to a faint outline. He skimmed his fingers across the wall as he considered his answer, then decided, "No. Ink is not the problem. This is not an entirely new Crafting—and it is made not only of the two lines you added, but the lines which came before. Think. The sentence you created in the middle of the crafting could read as: *When you wish on the Bell, the votes are apparent.*"

"How did I not see it? Wait right here, Yuri, I'll be back in a jiffy." I hardly stumbled at all on my pins-and-needles as I dashed outside and scrambled up the embankment. Once I was at the Wishing Bell, I rummaged through my bag for a pad of yellow sticky notes and a mundane pen. The moon had set, but my eyes were sensitized to the dark—and the halogen lights over by the parking lot were *really* bright. But more importantly, I'd spent my whole life training to take strokes of the pen and use them to create words. And meaning. And magic.

Writing the words in the dark was no problem. But finding the right words was another story.

Wishing, I realized, was not as much like Spellcraft as one might think. When I Scribe, it's with the certainty that something will happen. The mechanism of Spellcraft might not be fully understood. But, heck, I couldn't tell you how electricity got from the power plant to my electrical outlets, either.

Wishing, though? Not only did it lack the collaborative aspect of Spellcraft—a quality which I'd apparently taken for granted up until now—but it lacked all the constraints, as well. Like a genie with a chip on its shoulder, my capricious friend Spellcraft was always on the lookout for a careless loophole to bung up the works. But making a wish, here and now...I felt I should just say what I wanted. Straight from the heart.

Save Pinyin Beach

As statements went, it was plain. Not only was there no rhyme scheme—and no attempt to plug potential loopholes—but I'd written the words plainly too, with only the most restrained flourish on the descender of the letter y.

I pushed the paper through the slot and waited for the mystical shimmer of Spellcraft to play across my nerve endings. But the wish was not Spellcraft. And I felt nothing. Even after I reached up to pat The Bell.

I'd really been hoping for some definitive good news to tell Yuri, but no...wishing really wasn't much like Spellcraft at all.

I slipped and slid down the embankment and ducked into the dark hollow beneath the pier. "Anything?" I asked Yuri.

He held out his arms like he was dowsing for water. He

concentrated for a long moment, then shook his head. "Nothing."

"It's not fair," I said—and this was a position I did *not* take lightly, since I'd always been taught that fairness favors those who create their own luck. "Not only have we been playing by all of Spellcraft's rules—and, mind you, the rulebook is constantly shifting—but we always treat it with respect. Pinyin Bay is our home. How can Spellcraft just sit back and let some outsider buy our entire shoreline right out from under our noses?"

Yuri didn't do comfort. Not deliberately, at least. But he did pat my shoulder stiffly and say, "If the *volshebstvo* will not help us, then we must help ourselves. Fill your bag with papers. We will take them back to the truck, where there is light, and start searching."

Brave words. Slips of paper had been piling up beneath the Wishing Bell for ages—and Yuri's fall had mixed them all up, so we couldn't tell the old from the new. But we couldn't just sit back and do nothing, not like the miserly Spellcraft. And so, I waded in, opened my bag, and bent down to start shoveling things in....

And realized that I could see my yellow sticky note was on top of the pile.

Stuck to a small envelope.

A small envelope with a precise X marked across the seal.

I leaned across the precarious pile of paper and snagged the envelope's corner. I must have been sure I'd expose Vano's Crafting, because I felt vaguely disappointed that the telltale tingle was absent. Still, I thumbed open the seal as I walked the envelope toward the mouth of the hollow. On my way, I kicked aside a small metal object that skittered toward Yuri's feet—his paintbox. But there was no time to be self-congratulatory about that. I was too eager to expose Vano for the traitor to Pinyin Bay he obviously was.

Once the envelope was open, I drew out a small card, and read it by the parking lot lights reflected off the water.

No Spellcraft. There was a date—today's date—and a single word. *No.*

"Dixon?"

"These are some fancy serifs on the capital N. I'd recognize them anywhere. The handwriting belongs to the head of my Spellcraft circuit. This must be what Vano was dropping off. Not a Crafting. A vote from his great-grandmother."

And now we knew the single holdout keeping the Boardwalk buyers at bay.

I said, "Morticia Shirque sold off her mansion to those developers and immediately regretted her decision. I doubt any offer will change her mind."

Yuri considered the ballot. "Should we worry that the only thing standing between these people and the Boardwalk is a sick, elderly woman?"

"If the black mold didn't kill Morticia, I think she can handle that slimeball, Quint." After all, what was he gonna do? Bore her to death bragging about dumb businessman things? Morticia was nothing if not shrewd, with decades of experience under her belt. No way would she let someone like Quint cloud her better judgement.

Just as I had that thought, another notion occurred to me.

Morticia might be immune to Quint's dubious powers of persuasion.

But my cousin was a sitting duck.

"I'm sure Sabina's okay," I said hopefully. "Right?"

Yuri blanched.

"No? Then we've gotta warn her before she subjects herself to businessman tongue—or worse!" I pulled out my phone. It was dead.

Yuri was already making the call. He listened, scowled, and said, "She is not answering. Too early?"

Hopefully so...and not too late.

15

We hurried back home. The sun was just edging up over the horizon as we pulled up, and the kitchen lights were on downstairs. The chance of Uncle Fonzo being up at this hour was slim. But if Sabina was opening the shop today, she could very well be awake. I burst in as quietly as I could (meaning, I kicked off my shoes as I ran and let Yuri catch the door before it banged shut behind me) and headed straight for the kitchen.

Sabina was, thankfully, alone, sitting at the table in a ratty tank top and a pair of my discarded boxers.

She squinted at me over her coffee. "What's with you? Did you just get home? And why are you all jacked up? You didn't let someone talk you into testing their diet pills again, did you?"

Yuri came in behind me and planted his hands on his hips. As he seethed with disapproval, I realized the actual reason for my hasty visit might not go over too well. "Just stopping by to say hello to my favorite cousin."

"Uh huh." She slurped her coffee. "There's no leftover pizza, Dixon. We ate it all last night."

I assumed "we" meant her and Uncle Fonzo—my uncle can pack away a *lot* of leftovers. But then I heard the shower in the first-floor bathroom turn on...while a snore that was definitely my uncle's drifted down from his bedroom upstairs.

And I realized there was a white smudge on Sabina's collarbone that could only be greasepaint.

I have never been overprotective of my cousin. In fact, despite her being younger, it's always been the other way around: me blubbering all over Sabina every time my heart's been broken, and her pragmatically reassuring me that a pint of ice cream can fix anything—and if anyone needed the air let out of their tires, I should just let her know where the car was parked.

Then again, my cousin had never been romantically duped by a shifty businessman looking to trade our fond childhood memories for profit.

Sabina's bedroom was a small, dark first-floor room that was intended either as a minimal home office or an expansive linen closet. None too fancy, but it was right across the hall from a bathroom. A bathroom with a door that hadn't locked properly since the time we locked our young selves in, then sat and cried until Uncle Fonzo took apart the doorknob with a screwdriver. Okay, technically, I cried while Sabina tried to Spellcraft us out of there with Aunt Rose's lipstick and a whole roll of toilet paper.

Why bother replacing a perfectly good doorknob if it was just as easy to yell out, "Someone's in here!" when it rattled?

But Quint wouldn't know that.

I banged open the bathroom door, filled with adrenaline and righteous indignation. "How dare you?" I said dramatically, and whisked open the shower curtain....

Only to find the man standing in the bathtub was a stranger.

A total stranger.

A wet, naked total stranger. And not a bad-looking one, either.

Luckily, the tub had rubber treads stuck to the bottom, and when the stranger backpedaled, he didn't fall down. But he did snatch the shower curtain out of my hands. Plastic rings ricocheted off walls, ceiling and floor as the curtain snapped off the rod.

Sabina dashed into the bathroom. "What in the heck are you doing?" she cried.

"Well, I—ah, that is, he—uh...."

"Obviously, you've got a thing against mimes, but this is extreme. Even for you."

Yuri crammed himself into the bathroom behind Sabina. "Where is mime?"

I took another look at the guy in the tub. He was currently attempting to swaddle himself in the shower curtain, though it was one of those frosted plastic deals that didn't leave much to the imagination. Especially the parts pressing right up against the vinyl.

"Hold on a minute!" I said. "That's Crouch?"

"Stop calling me that!" Naked Guy bent his knees. The shower curtain rustled. "How is this a crouch? My back is straight and my knees are together. Obviously, I'm not crouching. I'm bobbing."

"I'm not entirely convinced the knee position matters," I said.

Sabina muttered, "Just let it go, Bob," and squeezed out past Yuri to go back to her coffee.

The plastic slipped as Bob made a shooing motion. "Do you *mind*?"

"Oh. Right. Sorry. My mistake."

I gathered up Yuri and walked him back out to the kitchen. He sagged into a chair next to my cousin and shook his head. "Sabinochka, seriously. A mime?"

"At least he's kinda cute," I offered.

Sabina grimaced. "What can I say? He came by to drop off a bag of seashells and one thing led to another."

"So," I said. "That's what I saw him lugging up the beach last night. Did he know how much you adore them?"

"I think it was just a lucky guess. Plus, they're free. I don't think miming is a very lucrative business, and he blew a big chunk of change on the cookie bouquet."

Yuri looked around. "I have never seen you decorate with seashells."

"I don't *decorate* with them," Sabina said, as if it was the most obvious thing in the world. "I pitch 'em into other people's yards. Like that mean old Mrs. Mangold across the street who's always giving us the stink-eye. Fresh seashells—especially the ones with little bits of sea creatures stuck inside—reek something fierce once they start going rancid."

Bob-not-Crouch strode into the kitchen in yesterday's mime-wear, sans the greasepaint, and said, "Well? Did the two of you ever figure out what that interloper was up to? Or did you fool around playing tour guide all day?"

Yuri gave him a dangerous look. "I did not see you helping."

"Unbelievable! Not only did I pickpocket his Spellcraft so you could fix it, I told each of you exactly who to watch out for."

"You told us nothing," Yuri said.

Bob struck a pose with his hand under his chin.

"You're tired from lugging all those seashells?" I guessed. "No, you're bored. No, wait—you're stumped. So, our answer is in a tree."

"For crying out loud," Sabina said to Bob. "This is ridiculous. Use your words."

"He is thinking," Yuri said. "Like the Rodin sculpture—The Thinker."

Bob pointed excitedly at Yuri with both forefingers.

Yuri nodded grimly. "Quint was not mime. He was living statue."

"I'd better get going," Bob said. "If I don't stake out my spot early, the yodeler sets up in the shade of the only decent tree." When he leaned in to give my cousin a kiss goodbye, she turned her mouth aside and offered her cheek.

Hopefully not on my account. Her love life really was none of my business.

Once Bob was gone, I said, "Sabina, you've always supported me—whether it was warranted or not. If you want to date a mime, I'm one hundred percent behind you." Plus, I had to admit, the whole pickpocket side hustle was kind of intriguing. And at least it would mean he was good with his hands.

"I'm not so sure there'll be a repeat performance," Sabina mumbled into her coffee. "That guy was *way* too chatty in bed."

YURI

16

I have stayed at the Pinyin Inn once, and only once, back when I was originally drawn to the city. The place was decrepit and smelled of old men, and even the fact that the rooms were cheap and a fairly edible breakfast was included could not keep me there any longer than it took to find my cabin. It was awful then. But now—shuttered, and practically abandoned? It was wretched.

At least I enjoyed some satisfaction knowing that Quint must loathe every moment of it.

I banged on the door so hard the entire front of the old hotel shook. I would have been perfectly willing to kick it down—but the businessman had more arrogance than common sense, and he yanked open the door to see who had the gall to disturb him at such an early hour.

He looked from me to Dixon and back again, and his eyes lit up with recognition. "Oh! It's you guys. What a relief."

Not the reaction I had expected. At all.

"Come on in." He pulled the door open wide. "Some creepy mime has been absolutely fixated on me. I was worried he might have tracked me down."

The lobby of the Pinyin Inn was even dingier than I remembered it—probably because the windows were shuttered and the television that normally played fishing reports and infomercials was off. The room had been remodeled in the early seventies, so its original plaster walls were covered in horrid gold wallpaper that drooped in some places and clung fast in others. The owners had made another attempt to freshen things up—this one in the mid-nineties—and the furniture had not been updated since. Everything was Wedgewood blue, from the carpet to the upholstery to the trim around the windows. Or it had been, once—before cigarette smoke, sunlight and time had dulled everything to a washed out bluish gray.

Quint crossed over to the check-in desk where a conspicuously new coffee pot was plugged in.

"Help yourself to some java," Quint said. "It's nowhere near as good as the organic bulletproof pour-over I would do at home, but it's fresh."

"We are not here for coffee," I said.

"And if you're making house calls, there's a terrible hitch in my shoulder that could definitely use your attention."

"We are not here for massage."

Quint eyed me over the rim of his mug. "Okay, then, I'll bite. What *do* you want?"

"We are here about the Boardwalk."

"Ah. Now I see. You want to get in on the action." He strode over to a chessboard which was set up between two Wedgewood blue wing chairs, and considered the pieces. "Unfortunately, my employer doesn't need additional investors."

Dixon said, "And who might that employer be?"

"Sorry." Quint sounded exactly the opposite. "Confidentiality agreement."

I had ways of making men talk. I only realized I was preemptively cracking my knuckles when Dixon laid a hand over mine. He said, "And what happens when the Boardwalk Board votes against your acquisition?"

Quint picked up a chess piece—the queen. He twirled it meaningfully between thumb and forefinger. "If there's one thing I've learned in all my years as a high-powered businessman, it's that everyone has their price. Besides, it's not as if they're going to get a better offer. I mean, look at this dump." He stretched his arms wide, waving the chess piece to indicate the hotel. "I handled the purchase, and believe you me, the owner got a pretty sweet deal. The Boardwalk Board is playing hardball, no doubt about it, but at some point they've gotta ask themselves what, exactly, they're trying to preserve. A broken down Ferris wheel? A few planks in the sand? A bell with no clapper? If anyone understands tradition, it's me—committees with more money than sense will pay big bucks for ugly memorials and pretentious statuary. But what has Pinyin Bay actually lost? A squalid trailer park, a crappy hotel, a falling-down mansion, a few shacks on the beach, and a funeral home. Ask yourself: were these things really worth all the fuss?"

Quint was not wrong. Pinyin Bay was only a destination for people who could afford no better vacation, and the main reason I cared about the city was that it mattered so much to Dixon. And as Dixon took in the shabby surroundings, it seemed that he had only now realized what Pinyin Bay must look like to an outsider.

Dixon ran a fingertip along the dusty countertop. "The Boardwalk is a little run down. And the city's done itself no favors keeping the wolverines all fenced off where no one can enjoy them. Maybe the shoreline really could use a little sprucing up. What's going to be built in its place? A fancy waterpark? A posh resort? Ooh, I know—go-carts. Everyone loves go-carts."

Quint scoffed. "Who said anything about building? I represent a *mining* company—and they can hardly wait to start digging."

Dixon batted the queen out of Quint's hand, startling us all. "The South Dock Boardwalk is not for sale—not at any price. Tell your boss to go dig somewhere else!"

Startled, Quint backed up a few steps. "Just you wait and see. The Boardwalk Board called a special referendum. That must mean they're ready to sell." He gave a taunting finger-wave and crooned, "Bye bye, Boardwalk."

Dixon turned on his heel and stomped out. As I treated Quint to a parting glare, he gave his own shoulder a squeeze, made a phone shape with his hand, put it to his ear...and mouthed the words, *Call me.*

In the truck, I found Dixon studying the envelope we found under the pier. "We need to get this vote back to the pile before Morticia's *NO* vote is missed. These envelopes are common; we've got some at the office. And I can duplicate the X on the seal, no problem."

No doubt. I had never met a Scrivener who did not excel at forgery.

As we headed for Practical Penn, I glanced at Dixon appreciatively and said, "It was very forceful of you to knock the chess piece out of Quint's hand."

"Maybe. But then it rolled into a mouse hole in the baseboard, which didn't exactly help me underscore the point that Pinyin Bay is worth saving."

I shrugged. "Even so. Quint does not have the sense to be afraid of me. I am glad he finds at least one of us intimidating."

Once we had the old Scrivener's vote looking as it should, we hurried back to the Boardwalk and slipped it into the Wishing Bell. There was no way of knowing whether or not the votes had already been collected, so we planted ourselves at a nearby picnic table where we could keep an eye on both the Bell and the trail leading down the embankment. And to make ourselves look as though we were not on a stakeout, I retrieved pencil and paper from the truck and set about drawing Dixon's portrait.

It was difficult to capture the set of his mouth. I was unaccustomed to seeing him frown.

"Maybe we should have dealt with the vote before we confronted Quint," he said. "What if the votes were already picked up? What if we're too late?"

A few of the shop owners had trickled in to prepare for the day while we waited. Awnings were rolled out. Sand was swept away. Bob was doing warm-up exercises under his tree. I wanted to comfort Dixon, but even as he spoke, a darker thought occurred to me. What if our timing had been compromised because the developers were at an advantage…due to a Crafting that, for sentimental reasons, we had failed to Uncraft?

I strengthened the contour of his silhouette. Even his hair looked dejected and flat.

Drawing should have distracted me from considering all the ramifications of our failure…but apparently, I was very good at multitasking, if one of those tasks was worry. Pinyin Bay had precious little going for it. With the bayside attractions all razed to the ground, the city might never recover.

I was about to suggest we stop what we were doing and Uncraft Johnny's Spell here and now, when a turquoise VW Bus pulled up at the edge of the Boardwalk—Rufus Clahd. The historian, Pearl, climbed out from the passenger seat wearing the same outfit she'd had on the day before—and her graying hair was now freed from its severe twist, loose around her shoulders. Pearl and Rufus gave each other a giddy little wave, and she drifted toward the Historical Society like she was walking on air.

Well. At least a good night was had by someone. I supposed they should enjoy their fun while it lasted—because Pinyin Bay was about to get distinctly unpleasant.

Pearl waved again, then watched as Rufus drove out of sight. But once he was gone, instead of unlocking the Historical Society, she stole a quick look around and then hurried toward the embankment. Dixon's eyes went huge, but only for a moment. As Pearl climbed down, he made a valiant effort at looking as though he was totally engrossed in having his portrait drawn. And I did the same in drawing it. Even so, it was clear that when Pearl made her way back up to the Boardwalk, she had several envelopes in her hand.

Once she'd gone inside, a smile broke over Dixon's face. "Thanks to Rufus Clahd, we weren't too late after all! And Morticia's vote was right on top of the pile. Best Boardwalk save, ever!"

"Perhaps we should see to your father's Spellcraft before our luck turns sour."

"But think about it, Yuri. *Go-getters get their goals.* It doesn't specify who the 'go-getters' are. And Quint is no longer in possession of the Spellcraft—we are."

Part of me was concerned that he simply didn't want to Uncraft his father's Scrivening.

But part of me was willing to hope he was right.

Pinyin Bay was hardly a sprawling metropolis, but the place more than made up for the lack of tourist appeal in sheer character. From Scrivener Village to the tacky Boardwalk, Pinyin Bay was a city where Spellcrafters could eke out a living, and one which Dixon and I were fortunate to call home.

"Comfortable" was not a word I would have initially chosen for the place—especially given the way I'd been lured in with Spellcraft—but now? Being introduced around town as Dixon's "grown man friend" with hardly anyone batting an eyelash? Being accepted by his insular family as one of their own? I cared fiercely for Pinyin Bay. And I would do whatever I could to preserve what was ours.

Dixon slipped a hand through the crook of my elbow as we headed for the parking lot. "Yuri? When can I see the portrait?"

"It is no good." I squeezed his hand with my biceps and lowered my voice. "I must draw another."

"Is that so?" Dixon caught my eye and grinned flirtatiously. And though I had certainly seen more than my share of nakedness these past few days, it would be no great hardship to have him strip down and pose for me. If we could manage to actually get to the portrait, that was, and not be distracted by more pressing matters.

Speaking of nakedness....

"Look, Yuri, there's your chunky buddy with the pink T-shirt! The Big Burgundy Bus is getting ready to roll out. Did you want to go say goodbye?"

I did, actually. But not to Husky Lou.

The luggage compartment beneath the bus was open, and Isaac

was just about done stowing the group's camping gear inside. He had left the biggest tents for last, and was pleased when I offered to help him with the lifting. "Before you go," I said, "I have a question for you. How good are you at...painting?"

He paused between tents and scratched his beard. "You mean painting pictures, right, and not houses? 'Cause you can't pay me enough to climb a scaffolding. I've got a thing about heights."

"Yes. Pictures."

"Funny. I haven't thought about it in years. But when I was just a little sprog, gimme a pad of paper and a crayon and I'd keep myself busy for hours."

"How come you're a bus driver," Dixon asked, "and not an artist?"

"I suppose I blame kindergarten. See, I used to be ambidextrous. But my teacher forced me to pick a lane—I guess you're less likely to smudge your handwriting with your right hand—and after that, I must have lost interest."

It was forbidden to let the Handless know the pictures behind the Craftings they bought were anything more than decorative. But Seers were so few and far between, it hardly seemed right to let the talent go to waste. "A Spellcraft shop would pay a lot of money for a good painting," I told him. "But Spellcrafters are a superstitious bunch—and they insist it must be painted left-handed."

Isaac seemed intrigued by that notion, and promised to give it more thought. He attempted to shake my hand, but I was saved from having to touch him by the distant mechanical whine of an auger. We all turned toward the noise. Judging by the direction of the sound, it was over by the cabins now. I couldn't imagine how fruitful it would be to drill so close to the bay—wouldn't the hole just fill with water? Then again, I was hardly an authority on mining. And I presumed the surveyors had some clue what they were doing.

At least, I thought they did—until a blinding flash lit the sky. A split second later, a deafening boom shook the ground so hard it flattened us all against the bus...as Pinyin Beach exploded.

Sand rained down on our heads. Dixon shook it from his hair. His mouth worked as if trying on words, but he ended up choosing none of them. For once, he was speechless.

As for me, there was nothing I needed to say. What must be done was clear. I took his hand in mine and squeezed it, more determined than ever to defend my new home.

WHAT the FRACK?

DIXON

1

At the cusp of summer, Pinyin Bay should have been packed to the gills with people. Once the north end of the beach blew up, however, it was practically a ghost town. The snowbirds who summered here fled back to Florida. Year-round residents with relatives nearby decided it was a great time to visit family. And a lot of folks just loaded their valuables into their cars, picked a direction, and drove.

It was the day after the explosion shook the Boardwalk. Up in the attic Yuri and I called home, I was batting some pesky cobwebs off the ceiling joists—with our cockatoo, Meringue, supervising loudly from above—when my mom texted, COME DOWNSTAIRS. I've shown her how to release the caps-lock I don't know how many times. Clearly, her phone was defective.

My father drops by all the time, but Mom says she's not big on "visiting" anybody but the bakery. I peeked out the louvered window and saw Dad parked out front in the Monte Carlo, with Mom standing on the sidewalk, glaring at her phone. *On my way,* I texted back, before she climbed any more stairs than she needed to and started her day on a less-than-chipper note.

I greeted her with a hug and a kiss and another big hug. She's especially fun to hug because she's so squishy, though I no longer came right out and said so like I did when I was little. "Did you want to see some photos of our latest project?" I asked. "That lighting fixture we found out behind the store looks pretty spiffy in our reading nook. Not that we do any reading there—the folding chair isn't exactly the type you'd want to sit in. But there's nothing to perch on nearby and Meringue hasn't pooped on it." Yet. Though now that there was a convenient light fixture right above it….

Mom looked me up and down, then spoke as if we were having an entirely different conversation. "You know we have plenty of room, for you and Yuri both."

"The car looks pretty full to me. Great packing job, by the way."

"Not in the car. In the motel. Your father Crafted for them when they had that huge bedbug scare a few years back—apparently some folks can't tell a carpet beetle from a bedbug—and they upgraded us to a suite free of charge."

"That's awfully generous of you guys—"

"A *suite*."

"—but Yuri and I have talked about it, and we think it's important to stay." After all, drilling was currently banned in Pinyin Bay, so how dangerous could it be?

"Those out-of-own people are working hard to get the drilling ban lifted." Mom said the word *people* as if it meant something offensive. "They have lawyers. Fancy lawyers."

All the more reason to stay and make sure the city council of Pinyin Bay didn't cave in to the pressure, what with Mayor Dunce being the first one to skip town. But Yuri, as a freelance Seer, had way more latitude than the Seers affiliated with specific shops, so if any Seens needed painting on the spot, he could paint them. And if we discovered any Spellcraft to be undone, I was the best guy for the job. Plus, Sabina had an irrational aversion to motel rooms. We didn't want her to get lonely while Uncle Fonzo was off on a romantic getaway with his current lady friend.

"It'll be fine," I told my mother. "We're not even that close to the shore. In fact, we only lost one windowpane to the last blowup."

"I don't like it, Dixon. You know who shut their doors? Pack in the Day. And they'll work through anything. Even dumpster fires."

The shipping shop at the end of the strip mall Practical Penn called home was nothing if not persistent. "They probably needed to recoup all the business they lost when their stingy owner used all those torn-up magazines as packing material." *Girly* magazines. And not the kind that gave advice on lipstick and dieting, either.

Mom was not to be deterred. "What if there's another explosion?"

"Nobody's drilling."

"Maybe not right this very minute. But mark my words. You don't just haul in all that heavy equipment for decoration. At some point, the drilling will start up again. And when you least expect it—*kaboom!*"

Mom has always had a good, strong pair of lungs, and at this point in the conversation, both Yuri and Sabina came outside to see what the enthusiastic chatter was all about. "Did something else blow up?" my cousin asked. "Why didn't we hear it?"

My mother attempted to recruit Sabina. "Nothing's blown up… yet. You kids need to get out of here while you can."

"I'm not willing to drop everything and go live in a room where the bathroom drains are full of stranger-hair! Besides, we're at least a mile from the beach."

"And if your cousin decided to run *toward* the explosion? You wouldn't just follow—you'd race him there. The two of you have always been more dangerous together than apart."

Yuri settled a hand on my shoulder. "I will keep an eye on them."

My mother looked only slightly mollified as Dad rolled down the window and called over, "Come on, Florica, we'd better check in before they give away our room!"

"It's a *suite*," Mom muttered, then subjected each one of us in turn to her trademark head-grab and forehead kiss. She climbed back in the car, Dad gave a jaunty honk, and the two of them drove off.

Once Yuri was done blushing, he said, "Your parents are right to be cautious. The only reason no one was killed in that explosion was that the cabins were empty. Now all the heavy machinery is so close to the Boardwalk, people are mistaking it for a new carnival ride. We should stay clear of the shore until all of those machines are—"

A van with a satellite mounted up top squealed around the corner. "Hey!" I said. "Is that the Pinyin Bay Journal?"

As the news van hurtled down the street, Sabina and I both ran toward the pickup truck.

"C'mon, Yuri." I popped open the locks and climbed in. "Whatever's going on, we won't want to miss it!"

Yuri paused.

"Hurry up!" Sabina punched me in the arm so hard I nearly dropped my keys. "We're gonna lose 'em!"

And with a resigned shake of his head, Yuri shoved me over to the middle of the bench and got behind the wheel.

Yuri can be the textbook definition of stoic when he wants to be, and despite Sabina exclaiming at him all the way to the beach, he took no creative license with the speed limit. Good thing. As we took the final turn that headed toward the beach, we saw a halfhearted demonstration that was well attended...by Pinyin Bay's "finest."

The demonstration took place in the scrubby area between the Boardwalk and the dunes, in a crunchy asphalt lot where Streets and Sanitation stored its leftover road salt. The lot was also the only way onto this particular stretch of shoreline, one where the earthmovers and cranes and augers hulked on the beach. The area was crisscrossed with sawhorses and bright yellow caution tape, though given how many people were milling around behind the tape, it was no big challenge to simply walk around it.

Now the cops were all standing around the sawhorses, sweating in their navy blue polyester, eyeing both the activists and the construction crew. They looked like they were daydreaming about leaving town. All but one, who was standing over a guy picking torn up paper out of the grass.

"Oh no," Sabina said. "It's Officer Hotti."

I gave the cop a more interested once-over. "I guess he's pretty cute, if you go for the stalwart superhero type."

"No, that's his real name—Hotti! Remember the bachelorette party I crashed a few weeks ago?"

"The one with the chocolate fountain? How can I forget?"

"When he showed up to warn us to keep the noise down, we mistook him for a stripper and started stuffing dollar bills down his shirt." Sabina glared in his general direction as he tore a citation off his pad and handed it to the paper-picker. "Served him right for parading around with the boombox. Anyway, he's got zero sense of humor, and he's a total stickler for the rules, and he absolutely lives to write tickets. Whatever you do, don't land on his radar."

Yuri eased the truck around to the other end of the lot, giving Officer Hotti a wide berth, and slipped into a spot on the other side of the news van. We spilled out of the truck. A few parking spots away, a tall, good-looking Handless man in a very official lab coat and a hardhat was passing out protest signs from the back of a van marked Nature World. He wore glasses—so, of course, he must be very smart.

"That guy looks important," Sabina said.

Yuri scanned the crowd. "Agreed. And the reporters think so too—they are heading right for him."

"Perfect!" I said. "Let's listen in."

We slipped into the crowd, and someone shoved a sign into my hand that read Kill the Drill. A rhyming slogan? I was warming up to the activists already. But despite the catchy rhyme, I passed the sign on to the next guy so I could edge my way closer to the reporter.

The Pinyin Bay Journal was a local institution primarily known for its fastidious reporting of high school basketball games—and the Pinyin East Pelicans hadn't made state playoffs in over forty years. Still, Pinyin Bay was proud of its one and only newspaper, even if its main function was to line bird cages and help insomniacs fall asleep.

Pinyin Bay isn't large enough to have its own TV station, but thanks to the internet, the PBJ recently decided to add live video coverage to its strange mishmash of online offerings and social media. Tiffany Tennant was the face of the Journal's new spot, "Pinyin Minute"—a show that has not yet clocked in at less than a minute, even once, in the months it had been airing. If folks were being generous, they'd claim that Tiffany had a knack for asking the questions everyone else was wondering about. Otherwise, they'd say, "That woman sure ain't the sharpest rock in the box." I'm no journalist, but it seemed to me that the reporter was chosen primarily for her looks. Then again, she had very expensive shoes— and you don't usually see a reporter's shoes—so it was possible her wealthy parents had something to do with her big journalistic opportunity.

While Tiffany primped her hair and the lab-coated nature guy looked impatient, the cameraman framed the shot of a big drilling machine behind them. The cameraman counted down, and Tiffany brightened just as he got to number one. "In the aftermath of an alarming boom, while some residents flee, others have gathered here on the dunes of Pinyin Bay to protest the drilling some surmise is the cause of the explosion. I'm reporting live with traveling geologist Dr. Skip Stone. Dr. Stone, what can you tell us about the blast?"

"It's not *surmised* that the drilling is the cause of the explosion. It's...pretty clear."

"What's not clear is the reason for the drilling, as no representatives of the new property owners have stepped forward. Why would anyone drill into the shores of Pinyin Bay?"

"In all likelihood, Tiffany, they're fracking."

Tiffany did a startled double-take, and whispered, "Language, please! This is live."

The geologist refrained from rolling his eyes. "Fracking is a process that fractures the bedrock so natural resources can be extracted. It's very controversial."

Tiffany looked like she didn't quite believe him, but the cameraman was making a go-ahead motion for her to continue, so she blithely carried on. "How is it that drilling could cause an explosion?"

"Any number of ways. There could be a pyrophoric mineral that ignites from contact with the air. There could be an inflammable gas that was exposed by the drilling."

"Don't you mean flammable?" Tiffany asked.

"Er...no. The term is *inflammable*."

"But wouldn't inflammable be the opposite of flammable? And what are your qualifications, anyway?"

"I hold the Arena Rock Award for ground-breaking advancements in my field."

"And how do we know that's a real thing? You seem awfully young to be a doctor."

Maybe Tiffany really did ask the key questions everyone was wondering. As the scientist rattled off a list of degrees he held and then explained the vocabulary in greater detail—an explanation that went in one ear and out the other—I scanned the horizon, spooked by the thought of flammably inflammable pockets of gas lurking around below us, just waiting for a wayward spark. But the earthmovers were at rest.

For now.

"This has been Tiffany Tennant reporting for Pinyin Bay Journal Online. And if you enjoyed this post, don't forget to like, share— and visit our sponsor, Happy Jack's, home of Pinyin Bay's hottest griddle."

"They're closed," someone called out. "Left town yesterday."

Undeterred, Tiffany and the cameraman headed off to get a few more shots of the protesting crowd. Meanwhile, I took the opportunity to see if the scientist might know more about who was blowing up the beach. "Excuse me, Dr. Stone? I was wondering if you could tell me more about who's drilling?"

He swung around and regarded me with hands on hips, looking more like an actor playing a scientist at the box office than an actual, real-life person. "Who? More like a *what*. The Loveland Development Corp is just a bunch of nameless, faceless bureaucrats.

You can't reason with them. I've tried. The minute one backs down, another one steps up to take their place."

I've never been one to take no for an answer...not until I've done a *lot* of pestering. "Then what can we do?"

"We need to convince the mayor to hold an emergency land use hearing and permanently revoke their drilling permit."

Sabina was incensed. "Well? What's Dunce waiting for—the whole darn city to blow up?"

The geologist shook his head sadly. "Apparently there was an unprecedented loophole in their current permit. The mayor can't stop them until he finds out what they're drilling for. They can keep on drilling until they locate something."

If only we had a dollar for every unprecedented loophole we encountered. Yuri stroked his chin thoughtfully. "What is it they are searching for?"

Dr. Stone said, "That's what I'm hoping to figure out before anyone gets hurt."

I got up on my tiptoes, hitched myself up even higher on Yuri's shoulder, and whispered in his ear, "Loophole?"

He nodded grimly. "*Volshebstvo.*"

And if we didn't do something about it, who would? "Now what, Yuri? We can't know for sure that the Crafting is in Pinyin Bay."

Even if it was, the Loveland Corporation had bought so many properties, the sheer number of places they might have stashed a small slip of paper was beyond daunting. And while Yuri and I prided ourselves on spotting Craftings in the wild, that didn't mean we could do it from a mile away.

It was overwhelming. Maybe Mom had been right, and the smart thing to do was pack everyone up and head out of town until the dust settled.

I was about to float the idea past Yuri—just in case he wanted to get out while the getting was good and he was only sticking around to humor me. But when I turned to ask him, the strangest expression crossed his face. Something vulnerable, between hurt and dismay. Just a flicker, and then his trademark don't-mess-with-me, tough-guy frown slammed back home.

I followed his gaze and saw some debris from the previous day's explosion poking out from the municipal salt pile. Rocks. Bricks. Planks of wood. I was about to reassure him that the chance of getting hit by flying rebar at this point was pretty slim, when he marched up to the salt pile, grabbed hold of something, and hauled it out.

A hunk of...plywood?

It was roughly the size of a card table, with three smooth sides and one jagged edge where it had broken away from a stud. I caught another flash of that pained expression, and when I did, I realized what we were seeing. I caught up with Yuri, snapped off a tiny, frayed bit from the broken edge, and held it to my nose.

Cedar.

I thought back to the cabin where we'd spent so many idyllic (if crowded) nights falling asleep in each other's arms to the gentle murmur of the water lapping the shore. Maybe we'd always known our time there wouldn't last forever...but we must've presumed the cabin itself would at least make it through another summer.

"We'll figure this out," I said. "Somehow."

If there's one thing I know about Yuri, it's that he'd much rather *do* something than feel his feelings, so he was all over the chance to take action. "The *volshebstvo* is powerful, no question, but it is also lazy. Its power diminishes over distance. The corporate headquarters may be elsewhere. But if there is a Crafting which will allow them to keep drilling, it will be hidden somewhere in Pinyin Bay. And you and I will find it."

YURI

2

We left Sabina at the protest to see what else she could dig up on the geologist. That was the reason we gave her, at least. I knew Dixon. And the probability was high that we'd wind up somewhere inflammable by the end of the day. Or maybe the word was *flammable*. I didn't really see the difference. English is notoriously confusing.

I flung the cedar panel into the back of the truck, then climbed behind the wheel. Dixon was waiting for me in the cab. "I've been thinking, Yuri. Loveland might be a nameless, faceless corporation, but they're still made up of people. And we just so happen to know the one who's been doing their dirty work in Pinyin Bay." How could I forget? In Spring Falls, I'd spent an hour massaging the man while doing my best not to make physical contact. "Though I'm not so sure how to search him for the loophole Crafting now that he knows we're onto him."

"Quint will see us. He is eager for another massage." Of all the men whose naked bodies I'd ever touched, his was the most repulsive—though not because of his looks. Everything about the man disgusted me, so it would feel particularly satisfying to thwart him.

We headed to the Pinyin Inn, which was locked up tight...but my crowbar made short work of the back door. Inside, the atmosphere was dark and stale, and utterly quiet. We trod carefully anyway, in case Quint was still lurking around. But a check of the first floor revealed nothing. "His car's not here." Dixon opened the coffee maker and prodded the grounds. "And the coffee maker is stone cold, so he hasn't used it this morning. I think we might be too late."

I was angry. Searching the old hotel for a piece of Spellcraft was bad enough. Searching the whole city would be impossible.

When there is no one upon which to take out my anger, I do my best to swallow it down. Anger makes a good crucible. One which hardens the heart to disappointment and loss.

But Dixon did not cope with such things by hardening himself. Instead, he fostered resilience. "Well, you never know. Maybe he bought his coffee this morning at the cafe. We'd better check around and make sure he's really gone. There are how many rooms here?"

"Two dozen, at least."

"Then, we'd better get started!" Dixon dashed halfway up the staircase, then turned and gestured eagerly for me to follow. "Come on, Yuri — who knows what kind of oddball stuff we might find?"

I had little desire to paw through the leavings of whatever derelicts once lived at Pinyin Inn. Their belongings were doubtless of little value to begin with, and they would have removed anything worthwhile when they were evicted. Still, we could hardly squander the opportunity to be sure Quint was well and truly gone.

We headed up to the second floor. The carpeting was not simply dingy and worn. It was threadbare, with a trail worn through the center that went all the way down to the floorboards. The windows on either end of the hall were thick with grime, and what little light pushed through was stained sepia. I am not a sentimental man. But the sight of this squalid hotel brought back the memory of my life before Dixon in such a vivid and tactile way, I could not help but relive that feeling of coming to this foreign land and feeling so utterly alone.

Until, that is, a hand slipped into mine.… And squeezed. "You okay, Yuri?"

"Fine."

Dixon squeezed again. "Let's check these rooms and get out of here."

Many of the doors stood open, and most of the rooms were thoroughly stripped. Peeling wallpaper, stained mattresses, and in one room, a collection of glass jars filled with what appeared to be urine. We made quick work of checking each room, closet and bathroom. If Quint had been using one of them, he had removed all traces of his stay. And the likelihood that he had ensconced himself on the third floor was slim, since it would have involved climbing so many stairs. But it would be lax to leave any stone unturned.

We checked the first room at the top of the stairs, which was crammed with outdated newspapers and thick with dust. I said, "The farther up we go, the less likely it is we will find anything. Even the long-term residents didn't want to drag themselves all the way up here."

"It does feel awfully deserted," Dixon agreed. "Just a quick check, and we can—" Something plinked against the baseboard. Dixon crouched down and picked it up. "Huh. An airplane bottle of vodka. Empty, unfortunately."

As he held it up to the light and considered it, a clink sounded from a distant hallway. He cut his eyes to me. I made a series of gestures, motioning for him to take the right-hand branch of the hallway while I took the left. He tried, but failed, to suppress an eager grin. He often claims I look like I am starring in my own action film. Silly. But I wanted to ensure Quint did not know we were onto him.

I took the hallway I'd presumed the noise came from, but after a careful check, found the rooms not only empty, but long disused. I rejoined Dixon back where we'd first heard the sound. I was about to suggest the possibility of rodents when Dixon flashed three more tiny vodka bottles, each clamped between two fingers of his right hand, one beside the other. He waved them all in greeting. "I guess coffee wasn't cutting it anymore," he whispered. "He's been up here on the third floor recently. These are fresh—the little dregs of booze haven't had a chance to evaporate. But if he was in any of the rooms I checked, he's a lot better at hide-and-seek than I've ever been. If he was up here before, he's not anymore." He smiled at his own rhyme. "I think Quint's given us the slip."

I was about to agree when another clink sounded in the distance.

"That came from the stairwell," I whispered. "He is somewhere downstairs. There are two sets of stairs, front and back. If we each take one, we can trap him between us."

Dixon brightened. "Brilliant! Now, send me toward my staircase with another sexy strategic gesture…one where you make a vee with your fingers and point toward your eyes first."

It was easier to comply than to waste time telling Dixon to stop playing games. Besides, I was counting on him to keep up the morale for both of us.

We split up, went downstairs, made another sweep of the second floor, then met in the middle. It was empty. But I did find a tiny, empty vodka bottle at the foot of my staircase that might not have been there before. Dixon took it from me and sniffed. "Maybe Quint is drinking his way down?"

But as he said so, a distant clink sounded—that of a small bottle hitting the floor. This time from above us.

I said, "Quint knows this place better than we do, and there are just too many hallways and rooms where he can hide."

"So…we need to corner him somewhere he can't slip away. Do you know of anyplace like that?"

I was about to say it was a fool's errand—too many hallways, to many exits—when I recalled the room I'd nearly stayed in back when I first arrived in Pinyin Bay. Luckily, I noticed the doorknob had been installed backwards, so it locked from the hallway, not the room. The owner resented the fact that I was not willing to sleep there, and put me in a room that reeked of cigar smoke and old cheese instead.

I made my way up the hallway, checking each door, until I found the backwards lock. "But with so many rooms, how can we get him to hide in this one?"

Dixon thought for a moment, then brightened. "Do you still have that fancy vodka in the truck?"

I slipped outside and retrieved it from under the seat—wishing I could avail myself of a few stout shots, but knowing I might be called upon to think on my feet. I brushed some lint off the bottle and gave it a regretful shake. It had not come cheap. But how much would I really enjoy a good vodka if I had no home in which to drink it?

I rejoined Dixon in the room with the backwards doorknob, where he was futzing around on the dresser with a pile of random objects. "Just in time," he said brightly. "Set that puppy down right here."

"Is that a…propeller?"

"The blade of a ceiling fan."

The long wooden slat stretched across the dresser top, balanced like a see-saw over a sideways coffee mug. Dixon held down one end, while the other, angled higher, had a billiard ball precariously balanced inside an old sock scrunched over the end of the blade.

"Whatever it is you think you're doing—"

"—will be totally awesome when the mousetrap is sprung! You probably didn't have that game in Russia, so I'd better fill you in. The vodka holds down one side of this tippy fan blade. And when Quint picks it up, the other side drops. Then, the pool ball rolls to the floor, banks off that wall, and smacks the door hard enough to shut it behind him. Bada-bing, bada-boom, we've got our guy."

He found a drinking glass in the bathroom, set it to one side of the contraption, and admired his handiwork. It was a ludicrous plan…but at the very least, it would make enough noise to alert us to Quint's presence.

"How do you intend to lure him to this particular room?"

"Good question! Let's see...how about a sign? Free vodka!"

There was no chance this ridiculous plan would work.

And yet, how could I resist helping Dixon?

"No, not free vodka. Quint thinks too highly of himself. Anything that strikes him as discount or bargain would only make him leery. Instead of *free*...use the word *exclusive*."

Dixon's eyes shone with delight as he walked up to me, snagged me by both lapels, and bumped up against me. "You've gotta admit, Yuri. You. Me. Even when we're not Crafting, we make a phenomenal team."

We took note of the room number, then went down to the office to pull paper from an old copy machine and dig up a marker. Even with such a clumsy instrument compared to his cockatoo quill, Dixon was nimble with the pen when he wrote, *Exclusive Vodka Tasting - Room 221.* Not only did the lettering look elegant, but the frame he drew around the border elevated the announcement even further. He worked rapidly, with quick strokes. But his hand was so sure, he dashed out the sign as quickly as if he was just jotting down a shopping list.

Dixon held up the finished product for inspection. "Too bad I don't have a fineliner to add a little fancy-work."

"It is perfect," I said simply, and he quelled a tiny smile as he turned to the photocopy machine to run off a stack of copies.

We hung a sign on the landing of every stairwell and all around the lobby. "Where else?" Dixon asked. "If Quint is three sheets to the wind already, he might not see the first one—or ten—he comes across. Front door, back door, the intersection of every hallway...."

We distributed the signs throughout the building. Even a very drunk man would not be able to miss them. I watched Dixon hang the final poster, and as I did, I felt a pang. Not pity, exactly. More like sympathy. Because he gave his heart so freely, it left him vulnerable to such disappointment. And there was no way his plan would work.

Once the paper was stuck firm, he turned an assessing look in my direction. In a deliberately bad imitation of my accent, he said, "Yuri, what is this face?"

I could have told him it was nothing, but he knew me all too well. So instead of pretending a confidence which I did not feel, I pulled him into a kiss. He could make of that what he wished. Given his baffling optimism, his interpretation would be much less of a killjoy than anything I could say.

He looped an arm around my neck and cradled the back of my head in his palm, smoothing his thumb over the shadow of stubble left on my scalp by the clippers. It never failed to surprise me—how intimate Dixon could be with the most unlikely of gestures. How confident. And tender.

But just as he pressed his mouth to mine and parted my lips with his tongue, something hit the floor above us. A sharp, percussive sound. Like that of a billiard ball dropping to the floor… and then rolling across it. And then a door slamming.

Dixon teetered back and mouthed the words, *It worked!* Though he was so beside himself with excitement that no sound came out.

The English language is full of nuance, and many words apply to only a very limited number of situations. Take, for instance, the word *cockamamie.* If ever there was a fitting time to use it, it was in regard to this vodka scheme. And yet, apparently, even the most cockamamie schemes had some chance of succeeding. "Come on," I said. "Let's go see what Quint has to say for himself."

We headed upstairs. The door to room 221 was now closed. I approached cautiously. Dixon, behind me, was vibrating with anticipation. I paused beside the door and listened so hard I could practically hear my own heartbeat. Eventually, I made out the sound of the glass clinking against the dresser, and then the hollow noise of the billiard ball rolling a few more inches.

Somehow, Dixon's plan had actually succeeded.

I rapped sharply on the door. "It is Yuri," I called out. "I am coming in."

I gave the lock a twist and flung the door wide, ready to tackle the obnoxious businessman as he tried to flee. But not only was the man in the room seated in the faded armchair with a full glass of vodka in his hand...but he was most definitely not Quint.

Dixon spilled into the room behind me. "Ladin Silver? What're you doing here?"

3

～

The portly Scrivener took a gulp of my good vodka, squinting at us the whole while, until he finally recognized us from the Hunting Party. "Ah, if it isn't the Penn boy and his grown man friend!" His nose was red and he was slurring his words, but only a bit. He struck me as a man who was no stranger to vodka. "The two of you were pretty good sports—hic—about losing that primo love nest over the popcorn shop to me. But now I'm wishing I hadn't—hic—jumped the gun in signing that lease."

"Why?" Dixon asked. "What happened?"

"When those big construction machines on the shore blew up the beach—hic—the explosion tipped over a kettle corn machine in the shop downstairs. Butter-flavored cooking oil went—hic— everywhere...and then it caught fire!"

"Oh no!"

"Oh yes! And it found—hic—every last sack of unpopped kernels. Talk about a blowout! There was so much popcorn—hic—it shattered the windows and shorted out the—hic—electricity." Ladin splashed more of my good vodka into the glass and filled it to the rim. He downed half of it in one gulp, smacked his lips, and declared, "The signs were right! This is the most *exclusive* booze I've ever tasted!"

While it galled me to watch him slug it down like that, at least the gulp quelled his hiccups…for the moment.

He declared, "The fire marshall says the building is uninhabitable until further notice, which leaves me with nowhere to go."

"What about your lady friend?" Dixon asked.

"She didn't take too kindly to the idea of serving me flapjacks in the bathtub. Can't imagine why. I guess there's just no pleasing some people."

I said, "So you have been at Pinyin Inn since the explosion?"

"I have. Figured since this old place was vacant, I might as well make use of it till I got back on my feet."

"And you are the only one here?"

"That's right," he said. "Just me." While I met Dixon's eyes and gave my head a shake, Ladin sighed wistfully and added, "If only I hadn't allowed myself to be seduced by a kitchen bathtub."

Maybe I should have been relieved the *volshebstvo* had moved him to sign that unfortunate lease before I did, but mostly I was annoyed to hear that Quint had gotten away. I snatched the half-empty bottled from the fan blade and turned toward the door. "Come on, Dixon. There is nothing more to learn here."

"Are you gonna be okay?" Dixon asked Ladin, but the Scrivener waved him off and settled onto a creaky old mattress to sleep off my good vodka.

We climbed into the truck, and I glared at my half-empty bottle for a moment, then tucked it under the seat where it belonged. It was silly of me to entertain hope, even for a moment, over such a ridiculous plan. Now, with no chance of forcing some answers out of Quint, I was out of ideas.

I could suggest we join Dixon's parents in their motel suite. We could tell Sabina we were going for ice cream. She might be suspicious of the fact that Meringue was with us…I supposed Dixon could concoct something about "bring your bird for a free cone day," a story which would hold together long enough to strap her down with a seatbelt and drive off.

As I considered how best to frame my suggestion, I realized Dixon had not said a word for several seconds. When he felt me watching him, he turned to me and said, "I can't imagine it was easy for Quint to live at Pinyin Inn, what with his fancy, big-city businessman ways. Maybe he's found someplace else to crash—after all, I wouldn't put it past an enterprising homeowner to make a few bucks renting out their empty place while they fled for unexploding pastures. It would take forever for us to check out all the recently vacated properties, and that's if we could even figure out which ones were up for grabs. But if he's got any gold body paint left, maybe we'll find him on the Boardwalk."

It was as good a plan as any.

We headed over to the Boardwalk and found it alarmingly empty. Not a tourist in sight. And the few performers who'd shown up were clustered around the single concession stand that remained open, stuffing cotton candy in their mouths while keeping a watchful eye on the large equipment visible beyond the tree line.

Unfortunately, the living statue was not among them. And no one had seen Quint since the explosion.

Dixon was not daunted. In fact, he was already moving on to his next idea. "Maybe while we're here I should make a wish on the Wishing Bell. The wishes still work, don't they? Or did the Re-crafting I did when we were looking for the vote nullify whatever it was that helped regular wishes come true? Or true-*ish*. Because Bell wishes were never anything as good as Spellcraft, but they did kinda-sorta work. I'd make extra sure to pat the bell—"

"Keep your eyes peeled for Loveland's Crafting. There will be no bell if the fracking starts again."

Dixon snerked. "You said *fracking*."

But before he lost his battle to quell a bout of adolescent laughter, a woman stepped neatly out from behind the Wishing Bell and pulled him into the shadows—the tour guide from the Barge of the Bay historical boat tour.

"Charlotte?" Dixon said. "I can't help you run a tour today. I'm trying to figure out how to stop a nasty corporation from drilling up our shoreline."

"I don't need an assistant—the Barge of the Bay won't launch if there's no one here to take the tour! But something's going on. Something big."

"I know! I saw Tiffany Tennant just this morning."

Charlotte rolled her eyes. "Tiffany should stick to her puff pieces about baking contests and makeup techniques. She asks all the wrong questions."

As much as I was leery of this woman's nervous energy, I had to admit…the reporter did ask ridiculous things.

"What are the right questions?" I asked.

Charlotte looked me up and down, then asked Dixon, "Can we trust this guy?"

"I'd trust Yuri with my life—and my family's cherished monkey bread recipe (contains no actual monkeys)."

"Well, if you vouch for him, I'll take a chance…." She narrowed her eyes. I held her gaze. "But if anything gets out that shouldn't, we'll all know where the leak is."

Dixon said, "Yuri is most definitely not leaky. In fact, he goes whole days without speaking to anyone. You can trust him one hundred percent."

"Then, it's settled. But I'm not saying one more word out here in the open." Charlotte cocked her head toward the parking lot. "Let's go somewhere private."

As we walked toward an old hatchback at the far end of the lot, Dixon tried to convey his excitement over whatever Charlotte might reveal with a meaningful wide-eyed look. As if I couldn't already tell he was beside himself with gleeful anticipation. Anything that smacked of intrigue practically sent him into orbit.

The woman's car was filled with stuff. Not as though she had neglected to clean it out—more like she'd been clearing out her office, only to find Pack in the Day had closed its doors and there was nowhere to dispose of her papers and records. She opened the back door, reached in among the boxes, and pulled out a roll of foil. She tore off a sheet and handed it to Dixon. He creased it into an inverted vee and placed it on his head.

Charlotte returned the roll to the pile, then pulled out a baseball cap with a shiny foil lining and put it on.

"What about Yuri?" Dixon asked.

"He doesn't need any shielding. No hair to pick up the signal."

I was already lost. But apparently, Dixon knew what was going on. "Listen," he told her, "there's some kind of loophole that's going to let the outsiders keep digging up Pinyin Bay. I need to Un...derstand what's going on. For my own peace of mind."

If the Handless woman noticed he'd very nearly blurted out a Spellcraft secret—the fact that spells could be Uncrafted—she didn't show it. She said, "You need to understand what's going on? I'll tell you *exactly* what's going on. There are secrets buried beneath Pinyin Bay."

I had to ask. "What secrets?"

"You'd never believe me."

"Try us," Dixon said. When she was not convinced, he added, "My mother always says the best way to cheer yourself up is to make someone else feel worse." Charlotte looked confused. "Which means that sharing your problems is always helpful! You know we make a good team, so do yourself a favor and confide in me."

One thing I can say about Dixon. For all that he's a formidable Scrivener with dubious morals and no sense of self-preservation, he always manages to come off as utterly harmless.

"All right." Charlotte nodded and took a deep breath. "Here goes. Something's buried under Pinyin Bay, and it's been there for generations. My grandmother knew what it was—she even wrote a book about it. I'm sure you've got a copy of *I've Been in Pinyin*."

"We sure do!" Dixon exclaimed. "Your grandmother wrote it?"

"That glorified doorstop? No way! Meemaw wrote a history of Pinyin Bay all right, but hers wasn't some whitewashed pabulum about bricks and fire hydrants. Meemaw's history cut straight to the heart of all the suspicious goings-on in Pinyin Bay that've been happening ever since the city became a city—things that just don't add up. Local taxes, for example. Did you know certain combinations of obscure deductions will earn you enough tax credits that the government ends up owing *you* money—and wealthy business owners aren't even taking advantage of them?"

But I would wager Pinyin Bay's Spellcrafters were. I cut my eyes to Dixon, and he gave me a smile and a shrug.

"And then there are the local noise ordinances. They're so convoluted that if your dog is barky, you could end up in a stockade. It's not one of those weird rules from the 1800's that never got taken off the books, either. It was passed thirty years ago!"

Dixon smiled wider and tried to look innocent. He failed.

"There are all kinds of absurd laws on the books. Did you know it's technically illegal in Pinyin Bay to whistle after midnight?"

And no doubt there was a nearby Scrivener no longer annoyed by someone's late-night serenade.

Spellcraft was not well suited to many things. It was notoriously unreliable around machinery, and it was not powerful enough to alter the mechanics of the natural world in any fundamental way.

But the law?

The *volshebstvo* loved nothing more than to take a complicated set of legalities and scramble them to the point of chaos.

Charlotte said, "I think it's pretty obvious what's going on."

Dixon laughed nervously. "Really? Because so often, a bunch of things that appear to have a common denominator are actually entirely unrelated. Take, for instance, the fact that the Pinyin Bay Annual Picnic was closed after someone stole all the grills from the park—"

Charlotte frowned. "But that's exactly why the picnic was canceled. I make it my business to keep an eye on local news. I was at that city council meeting, and I remember specifically what Mayor Dunce said: *This is why we can't have nice things. I hope that grill thief is happy!*"

"—and I'm sure that the special tax credits and touchy noise ordinance laws have absolutely nothing to do with each other."

If I didn't suspect it was all related to Spellcraft before, I certainly knew it was now.

"I understand your skepticism," Charlotte said. "But believe me. You haven't seen what I've seen. Everything is connected. Meemaw's book is proof—written proof. And when the Historical Society encouraged history buffs around town to put together a local history, she figured it was her big opportunity to shed some light on all the suspicious stuff that's been going on. It was a fascinating read—at least according to Meemaw—but as the book rolled off the printing press, in came Mildred Merriweather Block with her boring, whitewashed history. At the eleventh hour, production was called to a halt, and *I've Been in Pinyin* was printed instead."

"This is all…interesting," I said. "But what does it have to do with the fracking?"

"Fracking," Dixon murmured with a snort.

"The title of Meemaw's book is *Buried Secrets of Pinyin Bay.*"

"*Buried secrets* is a common expression in English," I said.

"True—but Meemaw didn't have a metaphorical bone in her body. And once you see the scope of what's going on, it'll be obvious why Loveland wants to dig up the shoreline."

Dixon clapped his hands together. "Well, I'm sold. Let's see the book."

"That's the thing," Charlotte said wistfully. "All those copies that rolled off the press were remaindered…which means that they tore off the covers and destroyed the rest."

Dixon said, "But don't you have the computer files?"

"This was all pre-computer. I've checked around, and even the printer's plates are long gone. Only a single copy of *Buried Secrets* wasn't destroyed—a galley proof—but Meemaw gave it away. Apparently, she had a best friend that no one knew about until her will was read. Her life's work passed on to this elderly woman, who was even older than her! I've tried getting in touch to plead my case for the book, but no matter what I do, I just can't seem to pin this woman down."

I did not need to see the *volshebstvo* bending reality to know it was in play.

"I'll bet I can get your book back," Dixon said. "Old ladies find me incredibly charming."

I was not so sure Charlotte believed him, but she seemed desperate to retrieve her grandmother's book. She mashed down her cap, squashed the foil more closely around Dixon's head, and made a few bizarre hand gestures beside my ears, as if she was batting away flies. Once her precautions were in place, she leaned in, fixed us each with a meaningful look, and whispered, "The old woman's name...is Morticia Shirque."

DIXON

4

I could barely contain my excitement as we headed over to the hospital where the head of Pinyin Bay's Spellcraft circuit was convalescing after an unfortunate black mold incident. "We'll sneak into the staff areas and steal face masks and scrubs," I told Yuri. "They're not exactly the most flattering of garments, but they're roomy enough that we can probably find something to fit even you. If not, I can put you on a gurney, cover you with a sheet, and act like I'm headed for the morgue. And if anyone questions me, I'll just say it's my first day. Acting incompetent is a great way to gain people's trust—"

"Or you could just *ask* to see Morticia."

"I dunno, Yuri. As plans go, that seems way too simple to actually work."

Yuri gave me the side-eye.

"All right. Fine. We'll try it your way." I supposed we could always sneak back in and do it my way if Yuri's idea didn't pan out.

As hospitals went, Bayside Mercy was not particularly impressive—though they did straighten out Uncle Fonzo's cursed hand without asking too many questions, so maybe their borderline incompetence wasn't all bad. The nurse at the front desk was working hard when we approached…or at least, she appeared to be. But then we got up close and saw she was doing a word search. Once she circled her word, she glanced up, bored, and said, "Can I help you?"

"We're here to see Morticia Shirque," I said. My mind was racing with various reasons we could give for the visit. We could say we were personal injury attorneys. Or out-of-town mold specialists. Or Jehovah's Witnesses. But before I could decide, the nurse took a better look at me and said, "Oh, are you one of her great-grandkids?"

"Yes," Yuri said quickly. "He is. And I…was adopted."

"I wouldn't have guessed about you, but I could totally tell the short one was part of the family. He looks just like all the others. But you all need to communicate better amongst yourselves. Ms. Shirque was released last night."

"I don't suppose she left a forwarding address," I said.

The nurse frowned. "Why don't you just ask your cousins?"

Before I could stammer out some patchy story about family rivalry, a long-buried feud, and a monkey bread recipe gone awry, a set of doors whooshed open and my actual cousin stepped out from the urgent care wing—followed by the tall, handsome geologist, who was now hobbling along with one foot encased in a gigantic orthopedic foot brace.

I hurried over and asked, "What happened?"

Dr. Stone gave a heavy sigh. "Twisted my leg. It was my own fault, really. I was so wrapped up in the protest, so pleased with the amount of public support we'd garnered, that I didn't look where I was going and found myself knee-deep in a gopher hole."

Sabina has been leery of gophers ever since we were kids. I was pretty sure they weren't the ones pooping in her sandbox and the more likely culprit was the neighbor's cat, but she was never quite convinced. "Someone oughta do something about those gophers. Now Skip is stuck in this dumb boot. At least the city council hasn't lifted that drilling ban…yet."

"That's a real shame about the gopher hole," I said. "And it's your driving foot."

"I'm fortunate to have such a caring nursemaid."

Sabina's cheeks went pink.

I can count the number of times my cousin has blushed on one hand and still have enough fingers left over to play tiddlywinks—so, the pink cheeks were a serious red flag. I took in the way they were standing, her with an arm linked through his, snuggling close, gazing up at him with limpid eyes.

Interesting development.

Usually Sabina couldn't go anywhere without tripping over a potential suitor. Ever since I could remember, I had to dress nice, practice my pickup lines and keep plenty of product in my hair. But Sabina could charm a guy by just standing there. (Like, seriously, she's met at least four boyfriends waiting at a crosswalk for the traffic light to change.)

This fancy geologist was a few layers above the typical Penn family social strata, so Sabina might need a little help to land him. And since my cousin has played wingperson to me many a time, steering all the gay guys my way, I was eager to return the favor. "Where are you staying, Dr. Stone? Hopefully not Pinyin Inn. Their vodka tastings really leave something to be desired. And besides that, they're closed."

"I've been putting the field cot in my van to good use."

"But you're all dirty," I said. "You should stay at our place. The water pressure's phenomenal, and our washing machine hardly ever shrinks anything. Sabina's on a daiquiri kick lately, so there's plenty of ice for your ankle. Never underestimate the healing power of a great night's sleep in a homey home. Why do you think hospitals discharge people so quickly these days?"

Dr. Stone's brow furrowed. "Their insurance runs out?"

"Besides that. It's the power of positive attention. Totally a thing—look it up!" Hopefully, he wouldn't. Or if he did, the search engine would lead him to something at least remotely plausible.

"I would hate to insert myself where I'd be unwelcome."

"Nonsense." If insertion occurred, I'm sure it would be entirely consensual. "My Uncle Fonzo's out of town, so we've got plenty of room."

"Sabina is good nurse," Yuri added.

His agreement totally fanned my flames. "Absolutely! She's the best darn amateur nurse in Pinyin Bay. She's kind, and nurturing, and conscientious."

Sabina was pretty much none of those things—in fact, most people described her as fierce, opinionated, and disarmingly prickly—but she'd kissed an awful lot of toads lately, and maybe this one had princely potential. As I sang her praises, a rousing soundtrack began to play behind me. Maybe it just turned out to be the crabby receptionist's ringtone—but even so. I don't think I'd ever heard anyone give such a persuasive argument.

Apparently, Dr. Stone agreed. "Very well. Miss Penn, I shall be forever in your debt."

While my cousin and her new geologist friend hobbled off, Yuri and I headed back to the truck. "Now what?" I asked.

"We do not know where Morticia Shirque is…but her great-grandson probably does."

"If we steal those scrubs and pretend to be doctors, we can look up Morticia's discharge records and find out where she went. I know the nurse literally just spoke to us, but maybe if I put on an accent—"

"We can see Vano's apartment from here. Literally." Yuri pointed toward Scrivener Village. "And his lights are on."

I groaned. "Vano is the last person I want to go crying to for help."

"Do you want to find out what that book can tell us or not?"

I supposed that with the fate of Pinyin Bay at stake, I could suck it up and go ask my old frienemy for help.

But that didn't mean I had to like it.

5

～

Vano Shirque has never done anything deliberately mean to me. In fact, I doubt he has any idea that his mere presence is so infuriating...which makes him even more insufferable.

See, Vano has this way of always coming up smelling like roses with no effort whatsoever on his part. In high school he was a trendsetter, even among the Handless. Our junior year, he had this one particular T-shirt that became the envy of Pinyin High. It was a dark burgundy knit with an incredible drape, and a somewhat disturbing Rorschach blot design front and center. Plenty of kids took their fashion cues from Vano—from the slouchy knit cap to the cheap necklace wrapped around his wrist to form a bracelet— but no one could figure out where this particular garment had originated. I knew this for a fact. Sabina and I hit every darn store in a twenty-mile radius trying to find one like it.

Turned out all our searching was in vain, because there wasn't another shirt like it to be had. He'd spilled India ink on himself and didn't care enough to throw the stained garment away.

I should have felt some small satisfaction over the fact that he was the one who'd ended up living in an apartment made of old doors, not us—especially since our attic was not only spacious, but upstairs from my family and incredibly cheap. And yet, it still stuck in my craw that he'd beaten me to the punch in signing that darn lease. Probably because while I'd been racing frantically toward the paperwork, he'd accidentally leaned into the table and a perfect signature just fell out of his Scribing hand.

Still, if anyone knew where Morticia Shirque might be, it was her beloved Vano.

Scrivener Village was just as deserted as the rest of Pinyin Bay. We can be a stubborn people, but without any Handless around, there was no one to Scribe for. If Vano was planning on joining in the great exodus, he hadn't gotten around to it just yet. Must've found some interesting lint in his bellybutton that required closer examination.

We trooped up the dingy stairs and I rapped on his door. It swung open slightly, and the heady scent of baking wafted out. I experienced a moment of cognitive dissonance—but no, this was the right apartment—followed by the elation that Morticia had been so easy to find. And here I was all tied up in knots about seeing Vano. Just goes to show how productive it can be to face your fears. Or your annoyances, as the case may be.

"Hello?" Yuri called through the semi-open door while I was patting myself on the back.

"It's open, c'mon in." Not Morticia. Vano.

Without the glamour of Spellcraft glitzing up the place, the empty apartment had been a real eyesore. Now, though, with Vano's stuff moved in, it looked like a magazine spread on boho chic. Each individual thing had obviously been rescued from the thrift store or the trash heap, and obnoxious seventies furniture brushed elbows with battered antiques. But together, it looked whimsically harmonious and breezily charming.

I rolled my eyes.

Vano was seated at the dining room table, which had a crocheted tablecloth that looked like a spider's web, and four mismatched chairs, each painted a different shade of turquoise. The table was covered from one end to the other in perfect little rectangles of shortbread. He piped a stunning dark chocolate flourish onto the piece he was holding, set it down, and then deigned to look up to see who he'd randomly invited into his apartment. "Oh, hey," he murmured casually, not as if he'd been expecting us, but like nothing particularly surprised him.

"Vano." I said his name coldly. Which I'm sure he didn't notice. "Can I see Morticia?"

"You could. If you were in Arizona."

"Arizona!"

"One of my uncles lives out there, so she went to visit. Said the dry air would clear out her lungs."

"If Morticia's in Arizona, then who baked all these cookies?"

"I did. For the Scrivener Village block party."

Where the heck had Vano learned to *bake* while I could barely make myself a piece of toast? (Like, seriously, they should warn you that flames will shoot out the top of the toaster if you let too many crumbs build up inside.)

He picked up another naked shortbread and piped on a perfect chocolate flourish. "The party got canceled, though, what with the explosion and all. So, help yourself. I've got plenty. Prob'ly end up feeding half of 'em to the seagulls."

I was about to tell him in no uncertain terms what he could do with his attractive and no doubt very buttery baked goods, though the sound of shortbread crunching between Yuri's molars distracted me from whatever point I'd hoped to make.

Vano added a few decorative dots to the flourish, which made it even better.

"Chocolate is really bad for birds," I informed him.

Vano set down the piping bag with a shrug, folded his arms and tipped back in his chair. "I guess that makes it easier for me. But since a lot of these are already decorated, if you wanna hang out and help me eat it, it'll be a lot easier than packing it up for the freezer...."

Yuri jammed another cookie into his mouth. They sounded delicious. Darn it all.

"Maybe *you* can help *me*," I forced myself to say. Because while I hated the thought of owing Vano any favors, it was preferable to sitting around stress-eating his perfect shortbread. Plus, he was a fellow Scrivener, so he knew full well how Spellcraft worked. "A *loophole* is keeping Mayor Dunce from putting an end to the drilling for good. There's a history of Pinyin Bay your grandmother owned that could help us close that loophole."

"The mold cleanup service dropped off a bunch of Nana's books. I think the one you're looking for was somewhere in the stack."

He oozed up out of his seat and led us deeper into the apartment. When we got to the room cobbled together from dozens of discarded doors, my heart sank. The "stack" of books was practically a library, jumbled up on the floor in waist-high, teetering piles. Vano considered one of the swaying towers of hardcovers. "If I remember right, there's a local history somewhere around...here."

One second, he was all listless ennui, and the next, he'd struck like a cobra to snatch a single book from the center of a pile. The stack wobbled momentarily, then settled. It was like a magician whisking a tablecloth out from under a three-course meal.

He held the book out to me. "Here ya go."

I was excited...but only until I recognized the title: *I've Been in Pinyin* by Mildred Merriweather Block.

Yuri swallowed his mouthful of shortbread and said, "This is not the one we are looking for. There is another history. A secret history. One of a kind. And Morticia had the only copy."

Vano whipped out his phone and said, "I'll ask her."

As plans went, that seemed awfully...simple.

He shot his great-grandmother a text. Which was kind of crazy, considering that while my parents were several generations younger than Morticia, my mother insists on yelling into her cell phone as if it can't hear her, and my father sends inscrutable texts via autocorrect.

I angled myself to watch—Yuri did, too—as the three little

reply-dots danced across the screen. And danced. And danced. But by the time I questioned whether or not Morticia Shirque was any better on her phone than my parents, a lengthy reply appeared.

I know exactly which book you're looking for, though I haven't thought about it in years. The Handless woman who wrote it was a friend of mine. A little too fond of conspiracy theories, maybe, but she shook a good martini. There's a secret attic over the secret study.

"Two levels of secrecy?" I gasped. Out loud. Then was annoyed with myself for letting on that I was impressed.

Look in the old steamer trunk and you'll find the key to your quandary. And don't forget to take your vitamins.

"Is that code for something?" Yuri asked as we followed Vano back into the kitchen.

"No, Nana's just overprotective." He grabbed a container of chewable kiddie vitamins off the shelf, the kind shaped like cartoon dinosaurs, and crunched through a stegosaurus and a triceratops. He held up the vitamins and rattled them in offering, but Yuri and I both declined.

Was it adorable how close the two of them were? Of course. But I wasn't about to let Vano lull me into a false sense of security. "How will we get into the mansion? I'm sure Loveland changed the locks."

Vano was, of course, unconcerned. "I know lots of ways in and out of that old place. I can't imagine they've found them all."

I said, "There's no need for you to come along. Just tell us about all the various obscure entrances. And the location of the secret room and its secret attic. And describe the trunk—"

"Dixon," Yuri said, in the tone of voice that hinted I was not being entirely reasonable in trying to leave Vano behind.

"I'd better come along," Vano said. "When Nana sold, she went on this minimalism kick and left most of her stuff behind. And when I was making cookies, I realized something that meant a lot to me was still in the mansion: my favorite wooden spoon. I know, it probably seems dumb to be sentimental about a spoon...."

Yuri cut his eyes to me. The look had *remember your lucky spatula* written all over it.

I quelled a sigh. "I suppose we could take a look...if you hand over what's left of that chocolate piping bag."

We were worried that someone from Loveland might be monitoring the Shirque Mansion, but that worry was unfounded. Even from the carriage house at the end of the drive, we could tell it was entirely abandoned.

"What architectural style is this?" Dixon asked through a mouthful of melted chocolate.

"That depends. Which part are you talking about?"

I took in the building's façade. It was complicated, with elaborately trimmed gables, fantastical posts and spindles, and even a turret. Definitely Victorian...until we walked around the side, and instead of shingle, we found beam and stucco.

Vano said, "The four faces of the building are Queen Anne, Tudor, Arts and Crafts, and Federalist." He pointed at the back of the carriage house, which looked more like a Grecian tomb, complete with caryatid columns shaped like scantily clad women. "The more avant-garde stuff is on the outbuildings. Most people don't know this, but my great-great-grandfather, Phineas Shirque, failed his Quilling Ceremony...and so he decided to become an architect. In fact, he designed a lot of the buildings that make up

Scrivener Village."

Why was I not surprised?

"The way Nana tells the story, her dad might not have been a Scrivener, but he still had a Spellcrafter's insight into the way people think. Back then, people sold their services by showing illustrated catalogs of various house designs. But Phineas knew that if customers had something physical, something tangible, to see, they'd part with more of their hard-earned cash. And so he built this mansion to be a showroom where he could really put his skills on display."

Dixon craned his neck to look at a waterspout shaped like a gargoyle. "This whole big place, and it was just you and your great-grandmother living here?"

"Ever since mom went to 'find herself' in India and was trampled by an elephant, and my dad took a header into the Ganges." Vano said this as casually as if they'd simply gone to the store and failed to return. Then again, they wouldn't be the first Scriveners who'd met with a baffling demise. Particularly if they were sloppy in their Crafting.

I convinced Dixon to leave the chocolate behind—he'd probably be up half the night as it was—and we approached the back of the building. Its doorway was flanked by a symmetrical line of tall classical columns. The wear and tear caused by the progression of time was much worse here. Unlike the Victorian front, which had been painted in a half-dozen bold colors, the Federalist back was entirely whitewashed. Once. But the old white paint was now peeling, and green with mildew where the tall trees cast perpetual shade. Freshly boarded windows were stark against a building that had been moldering for years. And a brand new lock shone from the door.

"This is no way in," I said.

"Not here," Vano agreed. He led us around the corner and pointed to an overgrown hatch set low to the ground. "But it looks like they missed the old coal chute."

Dixon blanched. "That doesn't look like it leads anywhere good.

In fact, it might not lead anywhere at all."

"Ask me how many times I found a raccoon rooting around in the pantry thanks to this door. It's a hop, skip and a jump to the kitchen from here."

"I dunno," Dixon said. "It looks awfully small."

Vano shrugged. "They were really big raccoons." He pried open the old coal chute and peered inside. "All clear! Let's go."

Fortunately, I am not claustrophobic. One by one, the three of us squeezed down the coal chute and into the basement. By the light of our phones, we picked our way through a warren of old washtubs and coal bins and even an old distiller until we came, finally, upon a set of stairs which led up to the kitchen.

Vano switched on a small light over the range, which was newer than the building itself, but still very old. "Power's still on. But I suppose we shouldn't light the place up too much, just in case anyone's watching."

While I was not afraid of the dark, the old mansion would have undoubtedly been eerie enough even with every light ablaze. "Where is attic?" I demanded.

But Vano was not easy to intimidate. "First things first. I go no farther without my favorite spoon in hand." He turned to the cabinets and began pulling out drawers. The sound of utensils clacking together filled the quiet room. Dixon and I stood by. Watching. Me with my arms crossed. Dixon rocking back and forth expectantly on his heels. But seconds went by. And minutes....

Until finally Dixon and I could bear it no longer, and then all three of us were searching for the spoon.

The drawers were a baffling array of shapes and sizes. Some shallow, some deep. Some tall, some wide. And every one of them had a different knob. Dixon's uncle has a "junk drawer" in his kitchen, one which is full of twist ties, odd bits of whatnot, old batteries and loose change. But every one of these drawers could be called a junk drawer. And they'd been accumulating that junk for well over a century.

By the time midnight came, we had been stabbed by myriad dull butter knives, found no fewer than thirty-eight wooden spoons, and still no luck. I slammed shut a drawer with a knob shaped like an acorn, turned to Vano, and said, "I am sure you have heard I am a Seer."

He gave me a cryptic almost-smile. "A new Seer is big news among the Scriveners of Pinyin Bay."

"Then let us find this spoon and be done here."

Dixon did not seem pleased I would offer a Seen to anyone other than him—but neither was he eager to continue searching.

"That's the thing about this old place." Vano took in the monstrosity of the mansion with a casual sweep of his hand. "Spellcraft goes wonky inside these walls. As far as we can figure, it's the fault of old Phineas. Whatever was in him that tanked his Quilling Ceremony must be woven into the fabric of this building. Crafting to find my spoon would be an exercise in futility."

When I shifted my vision and scanned the kitchen by the single small light, did the building feel different than a normal place? Impervious to the *volshebstvo* somehow? More quiet, or stable, or still? I could not say. It was difficult enough to see the subtle distortion of Spellcraft. Impossible to discern the total lack of it.

Dixon frowned in thought. "My mother always says, re-check the first place you looked. You probably weren't paying enough attention the first time around."

Vano considered Florica's advice. Then, he hauled open a deep, narrow drawer, thrust his arm in all the way to the back, and pulled out another half dozen wooden spoons. He tossed all but one on a growing spoon pile, but held up the final spoon to the tiny light. His expression turned poignant, but only for a moment. And then his unflappable demeanor returned. "Very cool. Now we can go grab that book."

We tested the flashlights that had been unearthed in the spoon search, found three of them which were still working, and followed Vano deeper into the mansion. The light beams bounced off hallways that changed every few meters, from paneling to wainscoting to wallpaper. The house he had grown up in was not unlike his current home. But while the apartment was crafted from stray bits due to necessity and thrift, the mansion was done for show—and in a time when everything was showy. The effect was both disturbing and captivating, as though with every few steps we took, we were shifting in and out of different realities.

There was a grand ballroom in the center of the house. As Vano's flashlight beam flitted across the far wall, I realized we were not alone. I recoiled with such force, I nearly flattened Dixon.

Good thing he is resilient. "They're just statues, Yuri."

"The mansion is full of 'em," Vano added.

Wonderful.

In addition to the still, pale figures lurking in every alcove, there was a fireplace on each of the ballroom's four walls, with a different mantle on each. Brick. Marble. Fieldstone. Wood. The wooden mantle was intricately carved with botanical designs. Vano strode over to it, took hold of a wooden pine cone, and gave it a twist. With a click, a single brick on the face of the mantle swung open. Dixon made a sound of annoyance—impressed despite himself.

"Oh, the mice were at it again." Vano flicked out a bit of insulation and fluff. He was surprisingly blasé for a Scrivener about thrusting his hand into a bed of rodents. But then his brow furrowed as he continued to grope.

"What's wrong?" Dixon asked.

"I could've sworn this was where Nana kept the key."

I was running out of patience. "The key to what?"

"The secret door."

I said, "Stop playing games. We have wasted enough precious time on coal chutes and spoons."

Vano was as unfazed by my tone as he was by the threat of a mouse bite. "It must be in one of the other secret compartments." He pulled out his phone and began texting. "Hopefully Nana's still awake."

"Why don't we just check them all?" Dixon suggested.

"Secret compartments were my great-great-granddad's specialty—they were a big hit back when Spellcraft could land you in the clink. Most of the hidden nooks and crannies in Scrivener Village were his doing. You know Scriveners—they're notoriously cheap, and they wouldn't part with their hard-earned money without good reason. Phineas had to demo his designs somewhere." Vano lifted a portrait of a dour-looking Scrivener with an impressive set of mutton chop sideburns and flashed a secret wall safe behind it. Then he twisted the top off a decorative finial to show us a pile of dominoes inside. "There are so many hidey holes in this house—heck, in this room alone—it would be faster to just wait for Nana's text." He shrugged. "At least she's an early riser."

"My cousin's got a Crafting that might help. I'll see if she can swing it by." Dixon called Sabina, but got no answer. "Maybe she's already...in bed."

I supposed she could do worse than the traveling geologist. Too bad we could not simply recreate the Spellcraft Fonzo had made her, *Persistence opens all doors*. But even if the mansion did not actively thwart Spellcraft, despite the fact that Dixon was a Scrivener and I a Seer, we could not simply copy the image and words. Spellcraft comes from the heart. True, there are only so many words in a language and not every Scribing would be entirely unique. But knowingly copying a painting or a phrase was the surest way to lose your grasp on the *volshebstvo*.

"Where is the door?" I said. "I do not need a Crafting to force it open."

"Actually...." Dixon caught me by the arm. "It really is late. And no one's drilling anytime soon. So why don't we get a little shut-eye and tackle this problem fresh?"

"Fine. But first thing in the morning, we get through that door. One way or another." I turned to leave. But as I did, I realized there was no obvious way out, unless I planned to crawl back up the coal chute.

"There's a couple dozen bedrooms," Vano said. "Stay wherever you like. But I'd avoid the woodland room if I were you. Unless you're into taxidermy."

Great.

Wallpaper changed styles so often I lost count as we made our way upstairs to the bedrooms. Some rooms were locked. Others disused, with furniture covered in sheets. Still others had been so neglected over time that the elements had encroached, crumbling the plaster ceilings and staining the walls with damp. But eventually we found a room far away from the taxidermy—a room that was not only still intact, but had seen use sometime in the current century. It would do...once I dragged the disturbing statues out into the hall.

Though it was hard to see by the light of the flashlights, clearly the decorating was overwrought, with fringes and tassels and an overabundance of silk moire. We were covered in coal dust. And even though the place would likely be razed to the ground by developers with all the furnishings still inside, we took care to wash up in the adjoining bathroom. We shed our soiled clothing before climbing into the musty bed. Both of us were too exhausted to be aroused, though our bodies had grown accustomed to one another these past few months. When we nestled together, even this strange bed could be made to feel somehow comfortable.

I woke the next morning with Dixon's head pillowed on my biceps and his knee wedged between my legs. When he saw my eyes open, he traced the tattoo on my collarbone with his fingertip, and despite the body heat we'd built up beneath the covers, I shivered.

I captured his hand and brought his knuckles to my lips, kissed them, then said, "What is the real reason you discouraged me from breaking down the door?"

"Who says I've got an ulterior...motive?"

Dixon's brow furrowed in puzzlement. I followed his gaze, and saw the entire ceiling was painted with cherubs. In *trompe l'oeil* fashion, it was made to appear as though the ceiling was open to the sky with a dozen grinning creatures leering down at us...which they had been doing all night long, and me none the wiser.

I hiked the covers up to our necks.

Unperturbed, Dixon rolled to face me and slid an arm across

my chest. "I suppose I always figured Vano had it all. Status. Looks. Talent. He got to live in a *turret*, for crying out loud! Everything came so easily to him—to his whole family—while the Penns had to scrape and struggle for even the most modest success. Worst of all, though, he made me feel...inadequate. Like no matter how hard I tried, he could outdo me by just standing around. But hearing about his parents? Knowing now that his grandfather failed a Quilling Ceremony, like me? And then seeing how the inside of the mansion is nowhere near as cushy as I always figured it would be? I never thought I'd say this...but I kind of feel sorry for him."

"It does a man no good to have things handed to him. If you did not know what it was to strive for something, would you have ever found your quill? You are clever and persistent—qualities you might not have had, if there was no need to work. But this hatred? It does not sit well on you. You are too soft."

"Well...not entirely." Dixon butted his groin into my thigh. "You know how I am first thing in the morning."

"Not *that*." I pulled him even closer and nestled his head into the crook of my shoulder. I spoke low, words that he felt in the vibration of our bare chests touching as much as he heard them. "Your heart is soft, nothing like mine, and the shard of hate is uncomfortable for you to carry."

We stayed that way, curled together, for a long, thoughtful moment. And then he said, "For someone with such an impossibly petrified heart, you've got a lot of insight when it comes to love."

I felt my cheeks grow warm. But luckily he could not see it with his face pressed into my neck.

"You are more than adequate," I said, and felt Dixon smile against my shoulder.

Eventually, with a reluctant sigh, he rolled away. "Vano's probably heard from Morticia by now, and we should deal with that secret door before Loveland blows up anything else...though I'm guessing the mansion will be even more spectacularly weird in the cold light of day. Plus, now we can get a better look at the funky statuary!"

DIXON

7

The word *mansion* dredges up all kinds of notions: excessive, baroque, larger than life. And yes, the house where Vano had grown up was all of these things...while being completely devoid of any sort of cohesion. I've never tried hallucinogens, but if I had, I'd imagine the experience would be a lot like walking the halls of the Shirque Mansion, albeit with less dust, fewer cobwebs, and more giggling.

My folks have a rec room in their basement. The ceiling is low, the paneling is drab, and every now and then, a truly bizarre insect will crawl out from a crack in the building's foundation. But since living space was at a premium in our house—especially back when I was a teenager who required extensive amounts of privacy to browse online pictures of naked men—we made good use of all available square footage. There also wasn't much disposable income in the Penn household, so we tended to make do with what we had.

This was how the rec room floor came to be covered in carpet samples.

"Can you believe they were just throwing these things away?" my father asked. Rhetorically, I presumed.

Mom looked like she certainly could believe it—and not only that, but if she had her druthers, she'd make him put those carpet squares right back where he found them. But since she only went downstairs to look for Halloween decorations (she got a real kick out of scaring the neighbor kids with her gruesome lawn tableaus) she let him keep his lucky find.

As Scriveners, we have a certain bent toward making things aesthetically pleasing whenever we can. And so, Dad laid out the carpet squares in the best pattern he could come up with. It was part checkerboard, part mandala. A kaleidoscope of carpet. But what he didn't consider was that while he'd managed to create a design with great visual appeal, thanks to the difference in pile and weave, the texture he'd ended up with was disconcertingly inconsistent. You could hardly walk across the floor without tripping.

And it turned out the construction adhesive he'd glued it all down with was literally impossible to pry off.

The Shirque Mansion was a lot like the rec room carpet. On steroids. Times a million. Plus statues. And it looked even more cringeworthy now that we could properly see it.

We found Vano in the kitchen crunching through a bowl of cereal with a cup of tepid instant coffee at his side. He shoved the cereal box in our direction without looking up. We ate it dry. The nuggets were soft and the marshmallows were kind of rubbery— and it definitely could have used some melted chocolate—but it settled my growling tummy.

"Nana should be up soon." Vano sighed. "Then we can grab your book and get out."

How had I failed to notice that his disaffected boredom was a thin veneer masking his sadness? Maybe it took the presence of so much actual veneer to clue me in. Seeing someone down in the dumps—even Vano Shirque—invariably made me up my game. "Once we do find that book, maybe we can help you liberate a few souvenirs. After all, it's not like Loveland will appreciate all the beautiful antiques and artwork in this mansion." Frankly, I doubted they'd even notice anything was gone…which made me realize I'd probably just made things worse by opening my big mouth.

Vano sighed again. "Nana always hated the artwork. Especially the statues. See, her dad decided if he couldn't Scribe, he would sculpt. Whenever he wasn't working on the mansion, he was making these sculptures, and now the whole place is full of 'em. All the local art dealers said they were a waste of good plaster. Nana says she couldn't get rid of those darn things even if she paid someone to take them off her hands. She actually tried, but no one wants 'em. They're too amateur. Too strange. And the proportions are all wrong. The heads are way too big for their bodies."

Yuri shuddered.

"I'm sure you'd find a taker online," I said.

"Nope. Not even there."

Clearly, they hadn't put forth enough effort, because for every yin there's a yang, and no doubt there was someone out there who'd think those statues were the bee's knees. But…not me.

And most definitely, not Yuri.

Vano went on. "Even the trash collectors wouldn't haul them away. It got to the point where Nana started pitching them down the dumbwaiter shaft…at least until they backed up so badly the dumbwaiter stopped working." He turned to the wall and opened a door set into the cabinetry to show us a plaster arm sticking up from the shaft. It looked like it was waving. "It's not the statues I miss. It's Nana."

Have I mentioned how flustered I get around other people's sadness?

"Listen, Vano. It's true that you live in an apartment made of old doors, and it's a real shame that you're not sleeping in a turret anymore. Plus, for all we know, you've grown accustomed to living under the blank white gaze of a bunch of misshapen plaster statues and their absence has resulted in a vague, yet discernible, feeling of nostalgia. But Morticia pulled through the whole black mold crisis—possibly because it wasn't weird enough to actually kill her—so you've still got your Nana, and that's what counts. When she comes back to Pinyin Bay, she shouldn't set foot in that moldy apartment ever again. Have her move in with you."

Morticia's ears must have been burning, because just as I finished my rousing speech of encouragement, Vano's phone dinged. Did it get under my skin that I could actually relate to Vano missing his family? Maybe a little. But spending as much time with him as I had lately, I'd become a lot better at picking up on his subtle cues. It might only be a quirk at the corner of his mouth and a subtle twinkle in his eye, but he lit up when his great-grandmother texted. And I could hardly take issue with a guy who was as attached to his family as I was.

That's what I told myself, anyhow, when it turned out the key had been tucked under the doormat all along.

A bajillion hidey-holes at their disposal, and *that's* where they hid the key? Not to mention the fact that no one puts a doormat in front of a secret door if they want it to remain a secret—and if it hadn't been so dark last night, I would've totally noticed how suspicious it looked.

Unfortunately, the secret study behind the poorly concealed secret door looked nothing like the mad-scientist haven of my imagination: filled with grand bookcases brimming with leather-bound volumes, and flanked by forbidding wing chairs where bespectacled men with weird mustaches could retire with their snuffboxes.

No, it was just a plain old office. Utilitarian shelving. A battered metal desk. A single orthopedic shoe. The shelves were full of books, all right, but not the fancy tomes of my imagination. Instead, there were manuals and instructions, blueprints and plans. The most interesting part of the collection was the leisure reading— midcentury adventure magazines with lurid covers, the kind that featured lantern-jawed heroes fending off various monsters from busty damsels in distress. But wood pulp makes for fragile paper, and when I picked one up to take home with me, it crumbled.

Vano poked through a few storage closets before he figured out which door had a staircase behind it. "Nana was never too keen on either of us exploring the attic. Nothing up there but bats."

Beside me, Yuri stiffened.

"Look at it this way," I told him. "At least you don't have any hair for them to get tangled up in."

Apparently, that reassurance didn't help.

But Vano wasn't particularly concerned. A thick sheet of cobweb hung in the doorway like a lacy curtain. He grabbed a rolled-up blueprint and used it to clear the way ahead, then trooped upstairs. I followed with Yuri close behind. Also armed with a blueprint, I noted. Since Yuri didn't play baseball growing up, I wasn't so sure how effectively he could use it as a bat against the bat...and I wondered how he made sense of the word "bat" having multiple meanings. Before I could ask, though, we emerged into the attic... and all vocabulary-based questions fled my mind. Because the whole attic was covered in stalagmites. Or was that stalactites? Tighty-toppy, mighty-moppy? No, that wasn't a real mnemonic.

Or was it?

If not, maybe it should be.

The three of us stared up at the massive icicle-shapes dripping down from above. Some were smaller, maybe a foot long, while others were easily as tall as Yuri, making the whole attic feel like the inside of a piranha's mouth...one with particularly challenging dentition. Vano gave a prod to one long, pointy tooth. "I don't *think* there's any risk of them falling."

I wasn't so sure. Not after hearing about his mother's final vacation.

I said, "I'll be the first to admit, I could've paid better attention in Earth Science...though I basically only took it because I heard it was an easy A. But how come your attic looks like a cave?"

Yuri scratched one of the stalag-ma-tites with his thumbnail. "This is not rock. It's plaster."

We all peered harder at the ceiling.

I said, "Maybe Phineas was working on some kind of avant-garde ceiling finish."

"This used to be his studio," Vano said. He wove through the dripping forms and hopped up onto a scaffolding to get a better look. "Maybe he was just storing all his plaster in this overhead loft. I can see daylight through the roof up above, so it must've been getting rained on for years. And when the boxes broke open, we ended up with...this."

The fact that the plaster formations were essentially natural somehow made them even weirder.

Vano hopped back down and unveiled the nearest sheet-covered form. The plaster-covered canvas crackled. When the dust settled, we saw it was no steamer trunk underneath, but a stack of wooden statue pedestals. Wind whistled through the holes in the ceiling, and the plaster danglies creaked alarmingly overhead. And as much as Vano was the closest thing I had to a nemesis, if I were to see him impaled by a plaster icicle, I knew I'd be scarred for life. "Maybe we should figure out an alternative way to access the chest. A lasso...or maybe a lariat."

"It's fine. See?" Vano gave a stalag-ma-tite a leisurely prod. "The bats are long gone. And the plaster icicles aren't going anywhere."

Good thing. He was moving slower than a sloth on valium right underneath them.

Yuri poked at one of the dangling plaster shards. It did seem pretty firm. And since there were no faces on the things (at least, I hope there weren't), Yuri wasn't particularly spooked by them. He waded impatiently into the fray and began dragging tarps and sheets off anything even remotely trunk-sized. Unfortunately, there were lots of things in the defunct workroom fitting that description.

When I got too antsy just standing by, I inched over toward the nearest object and pulled off a tarp. The fabric was surprisingly heavy with plaster drips and part of it was welded to the floor, but a good tug revealed...a Christmas tree. A really old Christmas tree, in sparkly silverish aluminum. I was about to ask Vano if his family had ever celebrated Christmas or if it was just for show when I noticed that Yuri now had a book in his hand. But before I could ask if he'd found what we were hoping he'd find, my question was cut off by the sound of an engine chugging to life outside.

A very loud engine.

Very nearby.

Not just any engine, but the sort that ran heavy equipment. But that couldn't be! What about the moratorium? Before I could express my outrage, there was a huge boom. Not an explosion. More like a crash...even bigger than the time Uncle Fonzo dropped his bowling ball on the floor and very nearly collapsed his own bedroom. I spun around to face one of the garret windows to see what was going on, and through a stand of scraggly trees, saw the claw of a massive digger coming down.

Loveland wasn't drilling. They were *digging*.

Evidently, Spellcraft wasn't the only thing that knew how to exploit a loophole.

I watched in horror as the giant claw swung down. It hit the rocky soil with a thud so massive it knocked my teeth together—and I wasn't the only one who felt it. The ceiling creaked as dozens of humongous plaster icicles were disturbed. Some big, and some bigger still—each of them creaking with its own pitch, which made the noise sound like a cross between a freakish harmony and a wail.

And then the stabby plaster came raining down.

Smaller hunks at first. Pieces with less plaster to anchor them to the ceiling. Yuri and Vano both looked up, startled. Vano eased away as a pointy icicle crashed into the spot where he'd been standing a nanosecond before. Yuri lunged toward the exit, but as he did, a wooden beam came down right in front of him. I might have veered around it and kept going, but not Yuri. He froze with the book clutched against his chest.

And a gigantic plaster hazard creaking directly above his head.

Through the window, the motor roared as the digger geared up for another strike.

I would have called out directions—if there'd been anywhere for me to steer him that wasn't a path of certain doom. Outside, the claw came down. Inside...so did a dozen more plaster shards.

But in a move so fast it was nearly a blur, Vano Shirque whirled a heavy, plaster-saturated tarp overhead, shielding both him and Yuri from a freakish demise. The plaster raining down was brittle, and when the extra-big stalactite hit the tarp, it shattered in a spray of harmless flakes and a cloud of white dust.

I held open the door as Yuri and Vano skittered out, shedding the tarp behind them, and the three of us barreled down the stairs, nearly tripping over each other on our way through the secret door. Yuri closed it behind us just as another boom sounded, and a crack fired through the silvered glass of a nearby mirror like lightning.

"Don't touch it," I cried as I hauled Yuri away from the crackling surface.

"Bad luck," Vano said...and as he agreed with me, I realized just how similar the two of us truly were. Something welled up inside me. Kinship? No, that was a bit extreme.

But tolerance? Definitely.

Would I have come to the same conclusion if he hadn't just saved Yuri from getting plastered to death?

I suppose I'd never know.

YURI

Only an idiot would continue to dig in an area where their drills had caused an explosion. But as Dixon's mother would say, if people had ink for brains, most of them couldn't write their own name before the pen gave out.

We piled into the truck and I kicked up gravel in my hurry to get as far away from the digging as possible. We were all so covered in plaster dust, we looked like a bunch of donuts dusted with powdered sugar. As did the book we'd found in the attic, which rested in Dixon's lap. "I hate to ask," I said, "but did I get the right book, or not?"

Dixon drew a deep breath…and blew.

Once all the coughing subsided, he said, "I can't open it."

Vano took a closer look. "Is that Spellcraft on the cover?"

Of course it was. I knew as much without even taking my eyes off the road. "*Protect this book from prying eyes*," Dixon read. "But I don't understand. Why write a book if you won't let anyone read it? And how is it prying if I just want to know what's been written?"

Good questions. But if the book had any answers, we could not read them. The pages were stuck firmly shut.

Dixon took the pocket square from his jacket and carefully cleaned off the Crafting. "Pull over, Yuri, I've got an idea."

Dixon's cockatoo quill was a delicate thing. He drew it from its protective case while I opened the ink and held it ready. Scriveners train for years before Crafting their own spells. Uncrafting was even more of a specialty, a skill that most of them never mastered. Dixon, however, had figured out his first Uncrafting only moments after receiving his beloved quill.

One can learn much with the proper motivation.

Even Vano was intrigued as Dixon took a deep breath, centered himself...and began to Scribe.

Protect this book from prying eyes...
But show it off when needs arise

Dixon finished the phrase. I could not tell if I felt the *volshebstvo* tugging at the small hairs on the backs of my hands or if it was just the plaster dust mixed with my sweat drying into a tightening crust. We all watched the book. Not that we expected it to fly open of its own accord, defying all laws of nature. But it certainly seemed as though something should happen.

Vano observed, "You didn't dot the 'i' in 'arise.'"

While it seemed that Dixon had been less prickly around Vano— though it was hard to tell if it was just because we were all fleeing a catastrophe in the making—he definitely bristled at the slight to his calligraphy.

"Just planning out my final flourish," he said loftily. He dipped his quill once more and topped the letter-i with something that started as a simple dot. But, like a seed, this dot was only the beginning. An elaborate stroke sprouted from it, whirling and looping to frame the Scrivening, weaving in and around the letters. It was bold and confident. And, yes, it was excessive. But even though it was clear Dixon was showing off, the flourish was so stunning, he had every right to be proud....

Until the pen nib hit the crease where the spine folded open.

It skittered clumsily, spattering ink. I was merely surprised. The Scriveners—who had spent entire lives learning to ink—each let out a startled gasp of dismay. But as the pen staggered across the surface, the quill caught on something: a hole so small, none of us had seen it. But the cockatoo quill was so slender, so fine, it slipped right in.

With a click, the cover opened.

"It wasn't the pages that were stuck," Vano said. "It was the spine."

The title page was simple. *Buried Secrets of Pinyin Bay*. And the author: Meemaw Jones.

"And here I thought it was Charlotte's cutesy grandma-name." Dixon put away his quill and traced the name with his fingertip. "Let's just hope that if anyone's dirty laundry is hung out in here, it doesn't belong to anyone we care about."

Vano said, "This thing is nearly half a century old, and even if there's a compromising story inside, whoever needs to feel embarrassed about it is long gone...unless there's anything in there about Nana. And I can guarantee, she's old enough not to give a rat's keister."

"Well then. Let's see what we can see." Dixon dusted his hands together briskly and turned the page. "Table of contents: *The dubious origins of Coral Beach*. That seems like a promising start. *How the Dunces bought their way to power*. Not quite as relevant, but sounds pretty juicy. *Pesticides and fluoride linked to tourism decline*. O...kay."

As Dixon listed the chapters, his enthusiasm quickly waned, until finally he fell silent. Vano and I followed his ink-stained finger as it trailed down the page. With each entry in the list, scenarios grew less promising, more unlikely, and even more paranoid. Accusations of foul play. Strange phenomena with perfectly logical explanations. And then, to top it all off....

"*A town founded on alien artifacts*. Great—now we're descended from little green men." Dixon thunked his head against the seatback in exasperation as the book slid from his lap. "I'm so sorry I dragged you both into this. My friend Charlotte is a little eccentric, but she's got a bird's eye view of Pinyin Bay from her tour boat, and she's a smart lady. I really did think this book of hers would pan out."

Vano retrieved the book and turned to the last section Dixon mentioned. He cleared his throat and read. "While a great many prestidigitators found fame and fortune causing things large and small to disappear, those vanishing acts of yore were but an illusion. Sleight of hand. There is a history, however, of an entirely different sort of disappearance in Pinyin Bay: one which can only be explained by alien abduction."

I could think of a great number of ways people might disappear that were much more plausible—mainly that they were now food for eels at the bottom of the bay. But the author clearly had a knack for zeroing in on the most convoluted explanation possible.

"In 1894, the founder of Central Plains Paper and Sundries Corporation disappeared without a trace from the wagon train between Kansas City and Pinyin Bay, leaving his brand new, state-of-the-art paper factory untouched. The property sat unused for several years." Vano looked up from the book. "Didn't it eventually become the massive Spellcraft shop that put the Strange family on the map during the Great Depression?"

Dixon sat up straight again. "I've heard of that place. The one that burned to the ground, despite being surrounded by fire hydrants. Faulty wiring." His tone clearly implied *faulty Spellcraft*.

Vano consulted the next passage. "During the second World War, GI Arbor Silver mysteriously vanished between basic training and his assigned battalion."

Silver...yet another familiar Spellcraft family. If Arbor was anything like Ladin, no doubt he decided going to war was far more effort than he was willing to expend, and used his quill to make himself disappear.

"But the greatest mystery of all was the disappearance of an entire cell block from the Bay County Prison, when twenty white-collar criminals, including bootleggers, counterfeiters and forgers, vanished from the prison yard without a trace." Vano glanced up. "I know all about that one. My grandpa was doing five years at the time for forging Englebert Humperdinck autographs."

"Five years seems awfully excessive," Dixon said.

Vano shrugged. "My grandmother was so sick of him she slipped a Crafting to the judge to make sure he didn't get out anytime soon. I'm not sure why they bothered getting married to begin with—maybe for a tax break—but I guess it was a real pain back then to get a divorce. Anyway, after four years, Grandma changed her mind. She hid his quill in a homemade Thanksgiving card among five other turkey feathers, and by the end of the week, he'd Scribed his way out of there. A seagull stole a guard's lunch, he left a gate open he shouldn't have, and everyone in the cellblock went for a little swim."

Dixon nodded. "Whoever built that jail put it way too close to the bay."

"And ten days later, Grandpa died of pneumonia. It was December, after all. Anyhow...too bad about the lack of aliens. That would've been pretty cool." We pulled up in front of Vano's apartment. He climbed out, gave us a lazy salute with his wooden spoon, then headed back to the room of doors where he seemed curiously at ease—which made a lot more sense now that I saw how he'd grown up.

Dixon watched him go. I would have expected Dixon to be relieved to get rid of his rival, but he must have made his peace, as he had no parting complaints.

A sound like thunder boomed in the distance, but the sun was high. It was not the weather we heard, but the heavy machinery along the bay. Dixon sagged in his seat, dejected. "What a waste of time. We spent all night looking for *Buried Secrets*, but it's useless. Now what?"

But before the words were even out of his mouth, a familiar van rounded the corner, hurtling toward the shore. A traveling geologist's van...with Dixon's cousin at the wheel.

DIXON

9

Yuri gunned the engine and we charged after Dr. Stone and Sabina. Normally, Yuri is a cautious driver. Even though he's got a green card, he's not a hundred percent sure he won't get himself deported for failing to heed the posted speed limit. And I'm fine with that. While I love letters and words as much as any Scrivener, I'd never want some disgruntled cop to throw the book at me.

Sabina was not nearly as careful.

She raced toward the beach like they were giving away free hot dogs—and she was starving. And they were made of gold. Edible gold? On baking shows, they sometimes decorate fancy pastries with gold leaf, so it must be edible. Still, ingesting copious amounts of metal, even gold, hardly seemed healthy for the digestive tract. But I'll bet if you found the right buyer, that golden hot dog could feed you for a year—or a few months, at least, depending on where you shopped....

"Dixon?" Yuri said.

Oh. We'd stopped. I hardly recognized the municipal lot with the heavy equipment all around. "Where are the hot dogs?"

"What hot dogs?"

"Never mind—there's two sets of footprints heading up the sand dune. Let's go!"

Judging by the tracks in the sand, Sabina was half-helping, half-dragging Dr. Stone and his orthopedic boot. But the sand was soft and tricky to navigate, and we caught up with the two of them at the top of the dune. Normally, other than the cries of the seagulls, there's not much to hear. But the air was thick with the revving of huge engines. "What's going on?" I called over the cacophony.

Sabina yelled back, "Tiffany Tennant is gearing up for another Pinyin Minute."

Dr. Stone said, "It's crucial we convince them to stop digging!"

I caught the geologist by his free arm, and together, Sabina and I managed to haul him to the top of the dune—but it was no mean feat.

Turned out we weren't the only ones that had difficulty navigating the sand. Once we reached the top, we saw that on one end of the dune, caution tape was looped all around like streamers at a particularly low-rent birthday party. That side of the dune butted up against the boardwalk, and The Fence was in sight just below. On the other side, a bulldozer struggled, nose-down, in the valley between the dune and the salt pile like a turtle flipped on its back. Its tank treads spun uselessly, spraying sand, while the construction workers from all the other big machines stood around looking perplexed.

Tiffany Tennant and her cameraman had planted themselves on high ground, with the panorama of heavy equipment spread out in the background. She brightened when she saw Dr. Stone was in tow, and motioned for us all to join her. "I wanted to interview someone on the construction crew, but they claim it would be a safety hazard." Behind her, the bulldozer flailed, and a guy in a hardhat looped more yellow caution tape around anything that would hold it. "I'd love your professional opinion of whether this was sabotage or something else."

Something like...Spellcraft? Yuri, Sabina and I all clammed up, but the Handless didn't seem to notice. Gingerly, Dr. Stone went down on one knee to scoop up a handful of sand while Tiffany motioned for her cameraman to make sure he got some good footage.

"Sand is notoriously hazardous for heavy machinery," the geologist announced knowledgeably. "The grains unconsolidated and unstable, which results in a lack of traction."

Tiffany was unconvinced—despite the fact that the bulldozer was throwing up a shower of sand in its struggle to right itself. "How can that be, when sand is spread on streets for traction in icy conditions?"

"That's different, of course, when you're providing friction on ice."

"And what is this so-called sand made of, anyhow?"

The geologist seemed confused, but he answered as best he could. "Sand is primarily silica. Some organic sediment. Of course, in this region, the bedrock is full of schist...."

"Doctor Stone!" Tiffany gasped. Yuri flashed me his phone. Apparently *schist* is not a swear word, but a type of rock. Huh. You learn something new every day.

Skip straightened up, brushed off his hands, and took in the machinery fiasco with a sweep of his arm. "Surely, in your extensive journalism career, you've covered all kinds of accidents. What is sabotage but the addition of the human animal to an already fragile system?"

Sabina tugged my sleeve and motioned for us to duck behind a nearby port-a-potty. It wasn't big enough to hide the three of us—not with Yuri—but it did put us out of earshot. "Extensive journalism career?" she complained. "Gimme a break!"

"Maybe he was being sarcastic," I suggested.

"Skip doesn't have a sarcastic bone in his body. In fact, he's painfully sincere. Do you think he's into her?"

Frankly, I doubted he could even see her through those thick lenses of his.

Yuri leaned out past the edge of the blue plastic outhouse and scrutinized the two of them as they spoke. "He does seem very focused on Tiffany. But he is doing an interview. So maybe this is to be expected."

"Why do you ask?" I poked my head around the side and had a look for myself. Hard to tell if he was ogling her, what with the glasses. "Didn't you two seal the deal yet?"

"Hardly! Once he organized my dad's magazine collection, he spent the rest of the night re-reading the Wikipedia geology page, then nodded off on the davenport."

"Maybe that's a good thing," I said. "If he saves us all from getting blown up, there's a better chance you'll have a future together." Yuri gave me the side-eye. "What? If Dr. Stone develops a sentimental attachment to Pinyin Bay, he could make it his base of operations." Plus, it was a lot easier to date someone who *wasn't* blown up.

Yuri crossed his arms. If it weren't for all the revving engines and the flailing bulldozer, I'm sure we would have heard threads snapping. "If he is more interested in the reporter than in you, then it does not matter how educated he might be. He is an idiot."

"You always say the sweetest things," my cousin grumbled, and reached up on tiptoe to give him a peck on the jaw.

"There you are!" Dr. Stone said, and all three of us jumped apart. But before I could fabricate a likely topic of conversation that was anything other than *What's the deal with you and my cousin?* he shoved his phone into Sabina's hand and said, "Would you mind snapping some pictures of Miss Tenant and me for my blog?"

"Uh...sure." Her face fell as he turned around and clomped away in his big plastic boot.

"Look at it this way," I told her. "You can insist he gives you credit as the photographer."

Once Sabina was out of earshot, Yuri said to me, "Is Wikipedia not the site you would visit if you knew nothing about a subject and needed a quick education? What reason would a geologist have to study it?"

"I dunno. Maybe he needed to double-check something. After all, these rocks all look pretty much the same."

Yuri watched with narrowed eyes as Dr. Stone posed for his

photo beside Tiffany Tenant in his orthopedic boot. "And how did he step in hole? A geologist should be more aware of the ground."

Okay. Here's the thing about Yuri. While he's never made me wear a tinfoil hat, he does tend to regard everyone with a healthy amount of suspicion. And while he'd deny it up and down, when push comes to shove, he's endearingly protective of my cousin. She needs protection like Pinyin Bay needs another explosion, but it doesn't matter. As far as Yuri's concerned, Sabina is the kid sister he never had.

He'd shown admirable restraint with her last couple of unfortunate romantic liaisons. But a guy who didn't appreciate Sabina's obvious charms?

Yuri was having none of it.

"Notice how eager he was to convince us that a nameless, faceless corporation was behind all the digging. How would he know?"

"Geology records? Look, I know you mean well, Yuri. But maybe it's healthy for Sabina to actually put forth some effort into catching someone's eye for a change. After all, look at what you and I overcame to be together. And it's only made us stronger."

I hadn't convinced Yuri, it was obvious, but when Sabina rejoined us, we tabled the discussion. She hates it when we talk about her, unless there's praise involved, in which case she gives us full permission to have at it. She planted herself beside us and looked daggers in the general direction of the reporter. "I get it," she said. "Being on camera is a lot more glamorous than working in some stuffy old Spellcraft shop. How can I compete with someone so famous?"

I patted my cousin on the shoulder. "She's only internet-famous."

"Still. I really like this guy. He's brilliant. He's ambitious. And he's incredibly passionate...about geology, anyhow. But I'm dying to tap into that passionate side myself."

Yuri caught my eye over the top of Sabina's head. "Then we must win him over."

"Uh...we?" I said. I could tell Yuri was up to something. I just wasn't sure what.

"It is obvious Spellcraft is at the root of this whole situation. We find the Crafting and stop the digging, and not only will this *Dr. Stone* see how resourceful Sabina is, but he will have no more reason to talk to the silly reporter."

Yuri had very nearly put air-quotes around the word *doctor*, but Sabina didn't notice, as she wasn't as well-versed in his particular flavor of sarcasm as I was. Obviously, Yuri just wanted to expose the guy as a phony. I watched as my cousin's potential love interest gesticulated at the camera with a small rock in his hand as he explained something science-y to the viewers of Pinyin Minute, and as he waved the thing just a little too emphatically, doubt crept in. Was he really a traveling geologist...or, like us, did he merely claim to be whatever it took to insinuate himself? After all, the flashy Nature World van, the lab coat...the *glasses*. Would a real geologist really need to try so hard to *look* like a science geek?

Even if the guy did turn out to be a fake scientist, I wasn't so sure I wanted to meet the problem head-on and expose him in a big, dramatic reveal. Don't get me wrong, I love it when Yuri is all bold and decisive. But Sabina's feelings were involved, so I thought the situation called for a bit more tact. "Are you really sure the two of you would be compatible? I mean, yeah, he's tall...and of course, he's handsome. And I'm sure scientists make more money than Spellcrafters—"

"Dixon," Yuri warned.

"But you're not particularly interested in geology. And if he hasn't noticed your obvious charms, even after spending all this time together, maybe his libido is on the fritz. And I'm sure a fritzy libido would get old pretty darn fast."

Sabina's brow furrowed. No doubt wriggling past this guy's resistance might seem like a fun challenge now, but the thought of having to work so hard for his affection each and every time she wanted some lovin' was not so appealing. But then the interview wrapped up and Dr. Stone realized Sabina was no longer at his side. He scanned the dune with the construction workers and protestors milling around, until finally his gaze fell on Sabina. He brightened, then clomped over in his ungainly plastic boot—handsome and tall, and weirdly adorkable—and I knew my attempt at subtly diverting Sabina's interest was all for naught.

As they clip-clopped over to a picnic table together, Yuri's piercing gaze followed. "Whatever it is you're thinking—" I said.

"We ask him questions only a true geologist would know, entrap him in a ludicrous response, and expose him for the fraud he is."

Well, then. I had to admit, as plans went…Yuri's idea was pretty darn solid.

10

We joined Sabina and her geologist—if that's what he truly was—where they rested in the shade of an off-duty auger. The massive drilling machine was sinister even in repose. But hopefully it could protect us from any flying debris that might come at us if the giant claw machines hit anything that was fixing to blow up. Meanwhile, on the other side of the dune, a couple of dump trucks were being chained up to the capsized bulldozer to try and drag it out of the ditch.

"Good thing you're both here," I said enthusiastically over the sound of all the massive revving engines. I'm pretty sure they bought it. "Because Yuri and I need an argument settled. A geology argument." That was really all I had, but since the science quiz was Yuri's idea, I figured he could take it from there.

Everyone looked to him expectantly. There was a momentary deer-in-headlights pause. Should I claim it was possible something had been lost in translation? Throwing around random Russian vocabulary had suited us well in the past. But before I could convey all of this to Yuri with a meaningful wag of my eyebrows, he snatched up a random rock from the sand, slammed it onto the picnic table, and said, "What kind of mineral is this?"

Dr. Stone held it up and squinted at it through his thick lenses. "It's granite. A common igneous rock. The grains are coarse. You can see flecks of quartz, and a hint of feldspar in the pinkish vein."

Yuri was not impressed. The confidence of the answer only made him more eager to prove it was all made up. He grabbed another nearby rock—the most boring gray rock I'd ever seen—smacked it down even harder, and demanded, "What about this?"

"Limestone. Typical of the lakes in this area, formed from the calcium carbonate in the sediment of the bay." When Yuri glared hard at the guy, daring him to flinch, Dr. Stone merely added, "If you're lucky, you'll find a fossil inside."

I was starting to think Dr. Stone might be an actual doctor after all—then again, Sabina had seen him browsing Wikipedia, so it was also possible he just had a really good memory. Yuri was positive there was something hinky going on, and wouldn't take an answer for an answer. He kicked angrily at the dune until he dislodged a small, blackish chunk, which he brandished in triumph right in Dr. Stone's face. "And this?"

Dr. Stone plucked it from Yuri's grasp. "It's a charcoal briquette that never caught fire. Likely from someone's picnic. See the edge, where it's dusted with gray? That's ash. And it even still smells a bit like lighter fluid...."

Before Yuri could tell him to shove that darn hunk of charcoal where the sun didn't shine, I said, "Those big, pointy things hanging down from the tops of caves—what are they called?"

The answer to that was clearly advanced geological knowledge. After all, I'd been puzzling over this question, off and on, since we escaped from Phineas Shirque's plastery attic, and I was still confused. But Skip answered without hesitation. "You're referring to stalactites. Fascinating things. Spleotherms are the most common type—what you'd find in limestone caves. But what most people don't know is that other things can mimic the spleotherm, such as the common icicle. And, of course, there's the so-called soda-straw formation that occurs on cement, which forms a calthemite—"

"But I'm sure it would be *totally* impossible for a stalactite to form out of plaster."

"Not at all. Plaster contains gypsum and lime. Prime candidates for calcite formation...."

While Dr. Stone continued to ramble on about minerals, I got a text—a text from Yuri, who was still standing right next to me. I love it when he texts me. In fact, his messages give me shivers all over, because I never fail to hear them in his sexy accent.

He will not slip up. We must try another way. Find Spellcraft.

Genius! If we found the construction loophole on Dr. Stone, we could just skip the part where we exposed his bogus credentials and go right to discrediting him for digging up the beach while he pretended to be on our side.

Was it possible to get him to turn out his pockets without making myself sound like a complete weirdo? Maybe Sabina would back me up if I told him it was a lucky Pinyin Bay tradition. But before I could launch into my suggestion, Yuri whipped out a piping bag full of chocolate and splooted it all over the front of the geologist's shirt.

"Oops," Yuri said blandly.

"What the heck?" Sabina cried.

"Sorry."

Yuri really needed to work on his delivery.

The geologist was completely unruffled. "That's quite all right. Accidents happen. Why, I've been dropping things left and right trying to get acclimated to my new glasses."

It seemed he didn't notice anything suspicious about the piping bag. What luck! Unfortunately, when he stripped down to his undershirt, shook out the chocolate-covered garment and set it aside, it was clear there was nothing Spellcrafty stowed away in the pockets.

The piping bag was not entirely empty...and Yuri now had his eye on our target's pants. But before he could christen them with chocolate, Tiffany Tenant leapt out from between the massive yellow earthmovers and got between the two of them. "Dr. Stone, there you are! I was hoping to do some fact-checking with you for the Pinyin Minute blog post."

It sounded perfectly reasonable. But something in the way she delivered the request pinged my alarms. Her voice was always a little too cutesy, but now she was practically simpering. And her eyelashes were fluttering so hard, she looked like she'd just come through a cloud of plaster dust.

If Tiffany planned to swoop in on Dr. Stone, that should come as a relief, so as to spare Sabina the chagrin of accidentally sleeping with the enemy. But I knew my cousin—and she's not one to back down from a challenge. If anything, knowing Tiffany was gunning for the same guy would only make Sabina double down on her efforts.

Tiffany slotted herself into the picnic table at the purported doctor's side, sandwiching him between her and Sabina. "There were a few things we didn't cover in our interview that my readers might be curious about." She pulled out a pocket notebook with a pink rhinestone cover and an adorable little matching pen. "How is it again you can tell whether a cave is natural or man-made?"

"It's the tool marks, of course...."

While Dr. Stone treated Tiffany to a lecture on Spelunking 101, Yuri stood up from the table and gestured with his eyes for me to follow. Once we were out of earshot, he said, "That reporter will have many questions. We should take this opportunity to search van."

Brilliant!

Unfortunately, Sabina had locked the doors behind her. Would she think it was weird if I asked for the car key? Or I could just have her cough up that piece of Spellcraft Uncle Fonzo had made her—though if she thought I was trespassing somewhere, she'd insist on coming along. As I considered my options, Yuri strode over to his truck and tore off the wire coat hanger he used as a radio antenna. He bent it into a hook, shoved down past the weatherstripping on the van's window, and popped the lock in fifteen seconds flat.

Wowsa. Gotta love a man with skills!

I took a furtive look around to make sure our little B&E had gone unnoticed. At the top of the dune, the construction workers nearby were all busy on their phones, my cousin and the reporter were both focused on Dr. Stone, and he couldn't see two feet in front of his own face.

"Good work," I told Yuri. "Now let's see what we can find."

There'd be something incriminating. I was sure of it. Yuri and I squeezed inside the back of the van. We had plenty of practice navigating small spaces together, thanks to the bathroom in his old cabin. Though we weren't naked here. And since we were in a hurry, I couldn't rub up against him quite as much as I might like.

I assessed the van's contents. There was the field cot Dr. Stone had mentioned. A laptop. Boxes of equipment with long, scientific names, all helpfully labeled. Even a small bin of various rocks. No helpful receipts from costume shops, or bulleted lists labeled *How I Will Scam a Small Town*. Nothing at all that marked him as an impostor.

How disappointing.

There was a pegboard partition that separated the cargo area from the driver seat. Not only was it hung with a variety of small tools—hammers and chisels and all kinds of electronic gauges and sensors—but the blank spots in between were filled in with a few framed certificates and photos. There was a picture of him with an older mom-type lady and a golden retriever. A framed certificate for the Arena Rock Award. And an old shot of him as a gawky teenager holding a science club trophy. If Skip Stone was conning us, it was a *really* long con. All signs pointed to him being exactly who he said he was...though I'm sure the science club photo could have been Photoshopped, and maybe that trophy had actually been for something else, like bowling.

Beside me, Yuri was scrutinizing the award. "It's real," I told him. "Not just some bogus thing he put together on the computer. You can tell by the paper the certificate is printed on and the quality of the engraved border. And that signature is real ink, not just printed. See there? The stroke had a wet edge that's really hard to mimic with printing. What's the award situation like in Russia? I'll bet there aren't quite as many to go around as there are over here. My mom always says that if the Handless could give their kids a prize for falling off a log, the world would be covered in lumber...."

Tiny hooks pinged to the floor of the van as Yuri grabbed the frame off the pegboard.

"It's real," I insisted. "I'm sure of it."

"Maybe so. But there is more here than just an award." Picture frames aren't exactly rocket science—or geology, for that matter—but there was no apparent way to slide off the backing. At least, not until Yuri bent the frame with his bare hands and pried off one of the sides.

So butch!

He tugged out the paper and turned it over. And on the back? Spellcraft sparkled to my inner eye like a burst of glittery confetti.

Unobserved
And well-preserved
A creature of routine
Expertise
Shall never cease
But labor sight unseen

I didn't recognize the calligraphy, so the Crafting must not be from my circuit. I read it once. Twice. Grudgingly admired the rhyme and meter. But once I read it yet again, I had to admit, "I have no idea what this is supposed to do."

"It is obvious," Yuri said—and I'm glad it was obvious to one of us. "Look at Seen. It is cave. This Crafting gives him access to the excavations 'sight unseen.' It allows him to infiltrate Pinyin Bay in a professional capacity with no one being the wiser to his presence." Yuri fixed me with a meaningful look. "You know what you must do."

I wasn't so sure. I could hardly Uncraft something I didn't

completely understand. But I couldn't just let this guy continue to run rampant, and so I did my best to dissect the Scrivening's meaning.

Unobserved and *routine* must mean Skip could dig up Pinyin Beach without anyone even noticing he was doing it. Ditto for *sight unseen. Well-preserved* must be the reason he looked so young and non-threatening. And after the little "name-this-rock" session, his expertise was definitely not in question.

Usually, when I Uncraft something, I need to sneak words and letters in and around the existing Crafting. But this? The certificate was nice and big. There was enough space for me to simply *append* to the narrative. I scanned the rhyme scheme—not my usual—and that old familiar tingle prickled through my Scribing hand when I added....

> *But then his stay*
> *In Pinyin Bay*
> *Made justice intervene*

Justice was entirely subjective, and as I finished the sentence with a big flourish that would stop a future Scrivener from changing the story by adding yet another paragraph, I worried that maybe I should have been more specific. But if there's anyone who's cultivated a healthy distrust of fairness, it's Yuri. When he gave a satisfied nod, I decided our problem was now in the Spellcraft's hands.

Yuri bent the frame back together and hung up our altered Crafting. Since it was face-down, it should have plenty of time to do its work.

Satisfied, the two of us slipped out of the van...only to find one of the construction guys off in the distance pointing us out to a very interested Officer Hotti.

Justice should have intervened with Skip, not us. After all, it was his name on the certificate.

I should not be so surprised the *volshebstvo* would take any opportunity to be capricious.

In a small town like Pinyin Bay, bribes were given in the form of compliments and baked goods. This Officer Hotti, however, had the air of a man who would not accept so much as a stale brownie without writing himself a citation. Hotti was trim and fit, but maybe we could outrun him, lose him in the maze of machinery and equipment. We were not far from the beach that was my home all winter long, and I knew the nearby woods well enough. We could evade him.

But Dixon was connected to an officially recognized Spellcraft shop. If they searched the van—if they gave Skip a reason to notice his Spellcraft had been altered—all blame would be placed squarely on Dixon's shoulders.

And so, instead of heading directly for the woods—for safety—I veered toward the picnic area and said, "We can't leave without Skip and Sabina."

"Good thinking—the last thing my cousin needs is to get caught with that dubious Crafting she carries around. I doubt it would unlock the jail cell she'd find herself in once the cops took it away. So, what are we going to tell them? There's a geology emergency on the other side of the dune? Or a hot dog eating contest? Ooh, wait I know—we say a rabid wolverine has been spotted in the parking lot! That'll flush 'em off the opposite side of the dune."

Dixon is capable of generating a baffling amount of ideas. I know, since I am so often on the receiving end. But I am a slow and deliberate thinker, and by the time we hurried over to the picnic table where Sabina was just helping Skip get up, I could think of no plausible reason to persuade them to head away from the van.

Then again, there is more than one way to persuade.

I jabbed my finger in the direction I wished them to head, and commanded, "Go. Now."

Strangely enough, they did. I was not surprised about Sabina. Ever since they were children, wherever Dixon might lead, Sabina was eager to follow. Whether Skip trusted us or simply wanted to keep an eye on us, I did not know.

Though perhaps he should have been keeping an eye on the ground.

His big plastic boot came down on a pointed rock at the edge of the dune. If it had been his other foot in a regular shoe, he would have twisted his good ankle. But the orthopedic cast was too rigid for that, and the stone acted as a fulcrum, just like Dixon's vodka trap back at Pinyin Inn. It was a fifty-fifty chance of Skip falling toward or away from the edge.

He fell toward it.

And Sabina's arm was looped through his.

Together, they tipped through a stretch of bright yellow caution tape, which parted for them like the finish line of a marathon and fluttered to either side in the wind. It was not a particularly terrifying fall. Not a bluff, but a slope, and a sandy one at that. At worst, there should be nothing more harmful than a few bruises to show for it.

Except that when I crested the top of the bluff with Dixon and looked down, I saw they were still rolling...straight for the curve of tall wooden fencing at the edge of the boardwalk.

Add some cuts and splinters to that assessment. But at least the fence would stop their fall.

Or so I thought.

Skip Stone burst through the old lumber like a cannonball, and Sabina tumbled through right after him.

Dixon clutched my arm frantically. "Yuri! You know what's behind that wolverine fence?"

Indeed, I did. "A tunnel."

We hurried after them, sliding most of the way.

"I'm sure it'll be fine," Dixon declared. "The entrance is sealed off by a very sturdy...gate."

We skidded to a stop at the broken wooden fence and peered through the gap. I remembered the tunnel well. It had been blocked off by not only the tall fence, but a stout metal gate...a gate which was now hanging cockeyed. The gate itself was perfectly intact, but the stone around it had crumbled like shortbread.

Sabina and Skip were nowhere to be seen.

The tunnel was man-made, a shaft which led into the sandstone bedrock beneath the dunes. Not toward the natural shoreline cavern beneath the Wishing Bell, but somewhere inland. Dixon took two flashlights from Shirque Mansion out of the messenger bag he carries, and together, we peered deeper into the tunnel.

The passage inside sloped downward. The angle was not terribly steep, and yet, no Sabina.

"Hello?" Dixon called. "Anybody there?"

"Hello?" At the sound of Sabina's voice, my heart did a painful flip of relief. I was unaccustomed to worry.

I did not care for it.

"What the heck happened?" she called out from a distance. In a different sort of tunnel, it might have echoed. But the sandstone was porous, which stunted the sound. Our flashlight beams played over the walls and floors, and something that appeared to be a shadow against the far wall resolved itself into a meter-wide crevasse.

Evidently, the worry was not through with me yet.

"You fell in a hole," Dixon called to her. "A hole inside a hole. But don't worry. We're on it. Or should that be, *in* it?"

We crept over to the edge of the fissure and shone our lights down. Sabina peered up at us, squinting into the flashlight beams. "Hey, Dixon—I finally beat you to The Fence!"

Skip was beside her crawling around on his hands and knees. "My glasses...I can't find my glasses."

He was so pathetic, I might have felt sorry for him—if it were not for the whole reason he was in Pinyin Bay to begin with. Sabina said, "Toss me a light. He's blind as a billiard ball without his glasses."

Dutifully, Dixon lobbed her the plastic flashlight. Its beam flashed wildly over the walls of the crevasse as it fell, but Sabina caught it neatly...though in taking a step back to do so, something gave off a distinctive crunch.

Sabina aimed the light toward her feet. "Skip? I think I found them."

It served him right. He should never have come here. But I could not enjoy reveling in his downfall until Sabina was safe and sound.

Rescuing Sabina was no problem. Skip gave her a boost, and I grabbed the collar of her jacket and hauled her up the rest of the way. But Skip?

"We need rope," I decided.

"No problem," Skip said. "There's some in my van."

Dixon leaned in and whispered in my ear, "Emember-ray the ake-in-bray."

"What??"

"We can't go back to the parking lot until Officer Hotti is gone."

True. But the policeman had not seen Sabina with us. While Dixon and I could not retrieve the rope, she certainly could. And better yet, it would give me the chance to confront this Skip person about his real reason for being here without Sabina feeling the need to jump in and defend him.

Skip called up, "The rope is in the cabinet under the centrifuge. And there's a pair of old glasses in the glovebox—bring those, too."

"You go," I told Sabina. "We will keep him company."

"Great idea! I'll be right back." Sabina did not even think to question me. The assessment Dixon's mother had about her being a follower and not a leader was no exaggeration.

Once she climbed out of the tunnel and scampered up the sand dune, I turned back to Skip. "Your time of hiding in plain sight is over. Pinyin Bay will no longer accept you at your word."

"About what? The drilling? It seems pretty self-evident that you shouldn't keep drilling something if it might blow up."

"That is true...if your actual intent was to stop the drilling, and not enable it."

"I have no idea what you're talking about!" When I shone my flashlight beam in the man's face, he squinted back helplessly. He was a good actor. If I did not know better, I would believe he truly was the harmless, myopic scientist he pretended to be.

Footfalls sounded behind us, and Sabina's shadow played along the cavern wall. She must have forgotten something and came back for it. "Stall your cousin," I told Dixon. "I must make him confess before she gets here."

"I'm on it!" Dixon hurried away to head off Sabina while I turned back to Skip.

"There is no use denying it," I told Skip. "We found your Spellcraft."

"Spellcraft? You must be joking! I'm a man of science. I wouldn't truck with Spellcraft any more than I'd consult with an astrologer or a Magic 8-Ball. Any evidence that Spellcraft does more than part gullible people from their money is purely anecdotal. If it were up to me, every Spellcraft customer should sign a waiver of informed consent that what they were purchasing was nothing more than an elaborate placebo."

"You'd be surprised how many people feel that way." It was a woman's voice—but not Sabina's. I swung around to find Tiffany Tennant was there, with Dixon at her side looking wide-eyed and panicked. His reaction seemed out of proportion to her presence. After all, what would she do but ask a bunch of ridiculous questions?

But then I saw she was aiming a gun at him.

Not a regular gun—a nail gun from one of the construction workers.

I narrowed my eyes. Tiffany gave me a sweet smile with a brittle edge.

"Who is that?" Skip called up. "What's going on?"

Tiffany spotted the crevasse with evident delight. She edged over, still holding the nail gun on Dixon, and assessed the depth of the fissure. "That's convenient! Then again, everything about this digging expedition has been convenient...at least until those stubborn Boardwalk people refused to sell and things started blowing up."

My heart sank as I realized that while our enemy had indeed been hiding in plain sight...that enemy was not Skip.

Tiffany gestured toward the crevasse with the nail gun. "Go on, baldy, hop down there and join Dr. Stone. I only need the Scrivener. Not his bodyguard."

"Yuri's not my bodyguard," Dixon protested. "He's my significant other. And he might look all big and scary and tattooed and musclebound, but looks can be deceiving. He's totally harmless. Unless you're a fly. In which case he's really accurate with a rolled-up Pinyin Bay Journal."

Tiffany looked me up and down. "I'll buy that there might be some hanky-panky going on between you...but if this guy is harmless, then I'm Barbara Walters. In the hole, Mr. Yuri. Now."

Over the years, I have been threatened by many people. And any one of them was more menacing than Tiffany. I puffed myself up to loom over the girl and said, "I refuse. And the nail gun might sting...if I felt it at all."

If I expected to intimidate her, I was in for a big disappointment. Instead of aiming at me, she grabbed Dixon by the wrist, gave his arm a solid yank, then pressed the gun directly into the palm of his hand.

His right hand.

His *Scribing* hand.

"Hands," she said conversationally. "Surprisingly delicate, what with all the nerves and muscles and teeny-tiny bones."

"Those would be the metacarpals," Skip called out.

Tiffany ignored him and said, "So whether you're his bodyguard or his boy-toy, I'm thinking you don't want to see what happens if I empty a whole strip of nails into his palm."

"Don't listen to her, Yuri," Dixon said. "She's bluffing."

Tiffany said, "Am I? This excavation has dragged on way too long already and my trust fund is nearly tapped out. If you know what's good for you, Yuri, you'll put your cell phone on the ground and go join the good doctor."

I fumed so hard it was a wonder the inflammable gasses around us did not ignite. But even a single, well-placed nail could cost Dixon not only his livelihood, but his vocation. The drop to the floor of the chasm was jarring. A shock jolted my bones and my teeth rattled together. But I cared little for myself with Dixon at the hands of that woman.

"Now the other phone," she said, and we tossed up Skip's phone as well. She considered us for a moment, then added, "I'll take the flashlight, too. I might need a backup, and it's not as if there's anything interesting down there for you to look at."

I shot her a look of such hatred I thought she must surely combust. But she simply smiled in return, then grabbed Dixon and headed deeper into the old mine.

"I'm not sure how much of Dr. Stone's diatribe you overheard," I told Tiffany, "but Spellcraft is just as much of a science as it is an art. We Spellcrafters can't scribble down just any old thing and have it come true. A very specific set of conditions is required for the Crafting to take shape—and even then, the effects tend to be subtle and gradual, not striking and sudden."

My dad had a similar spiel, and he trotted it out whenever a customer had "dissatisfaction" written all over them. Managing expectations, he called it.

"Don't worry, Dixon, I'm fully aware of the way Spellcraft works. You'd be surprised at the low opinion most Spellcrafters have of the Handless."

Not once had I met any non-Spellcrafter who knew how we referred to them amongst ourselves. As I was reeling from the fact that Tiffany Tennant was a much better investigative journalist than anyone ever imagined, she herded me into a big chamber that was shored up with old lumber. One side was open to the elements where her diggers had scooped out the sand dune to expose the old mine, and sunlight shone through the scoop, with sandstone particles dancing in the shaft of light. Rumbling engines were still audible, but they sounded far enough away that even if I called for help, it was doubtful anyone would hear me.

Tiffany watched me take it all in. "The quartz mines beneath Pinyin Bay were active throughout the first half of the twentieth century, but digging stopped when an explosion took out most of the mining equipment in the adjacent quarry. So-called experts claimed the blowup was caused by inflammable gases. But, was it?"

"I...have absolutely no idea."

"At that point, the mine was nearly tapped out, and digging was no longer worth the risk. So they said. And yet, mere days before the big explosion, someone snapped this picture."

She jammed a sheet of paper under my nose, one that looked like it'd been torn from a textbook. There was a photo printed on it, slightly grainy, black-and-white—and really tough to discern. "What's this supposed to be?"

"You've heard of sarcophagi found in ancient Egyptian tombs? Preserved bodies in Pompeii? That's what you're looking at now. Only this discovery will turn everything science thinks it knows on its ear...and who will be right there when the news breaks? Me, that's who."

She waved the picture emphatically. "I've had this photograph analyzed by leading experts. You're looking at the origins of an ancient civilization. And that origin is not terrestrial in nature."

I cut my eyes to the wrinkled page. "And where did you find this photo?"

"Packing material from a Christmas ornament I bought on Etsy—and it came from Pinyin Bay."

And I could guess exactly where it had shipped from. Pack in the Day must have moved on from girly magazines and onto...what, exactly, I wasn't sure. "May I?"

She handed me the photo, too proud of what she thought she'd discovered to resist showing it off.

Now that I knew the random jumble in the picture was actually the arms and legs of body stacked upon body in some bizarre mass burial, it was difficult to see anything else. But I made myself take stock of the whole page. When I did, I saw that I recognized the font, the kerning, the overall layout…and especially, the title in the footer. *Buried Secrets of Pinyin Bay* by Meemaw Jones.

Tiffany must have read admiration into my silence. "No more small-town internet spot for me," she preened. "This is my ticket to the big time."

Maybe. If by "big time" she was talking about utter humiliation and a professional demise.

Whatever was going on in that old photograph, I had no idea. But knowledge of its origins cast everything in a whole new—distinctly skeptical—light. The single page might've seemed somewhat more plausible out of context without all the other zany conspiracy theories, though, and I hated to think what Tiffany would do with that nail gun when she realized she'd emptied her trust fund based on the ravings of a delusional wannabe historian. "Sounds like you've got things all figured out," I said nervously.

"Not everything." Tiffany ran her fingers along the stony wall. "I've matched certain distinctive tool marks from the photo to this locale."

"Then why keep digging and risk blowing everyone up?"

"Do you hear any digging right now? Of course not. The equipment flailing around up there is just a ruse to keep the authorities busy while I strategize my next move. And that's where you come in."

"I'm not much of a strategist. In fact, I think the term 'winging it' was coined specifically for me."

"I don't care about your planning skills. I need you to Spellcraft."

You know I'm scared when it's tempting to admit I failed my Quilling Ceremony, if only to get out of Scribing. But while stating as much might make me seem like a less viable candidate for whatever she had planned, I couldn't expose such an integral secret to a Handless. "We're not exactly hurting for Spellcrafters in Pinyin Bay. In fact, you can hardly walk down Main Street without tripping over a Scrivener. And, frankly, I'm not even all that experienced.

I only started Spellcrafting earlier this year. I took a gap year after college…and somehow that gap just got wider and wider—"

"Fact: you come from a long line of Spellcrafters. Fact: Spellcrafters train their whole lives to do what they do. And, fact: you, Dixon Penn, are the go-to Scrivener when someone in Pinyin Bay needs a Crafting altered."

"Well, I uh…really? Where'd you hear that?"

"I have my sources."

That's the problem with trying to flim-flam an investigative journalist—they come equipped with all kinds of facts. But hopefully, my fellow Scriveners were vague when it came to the finer details of the Craft. "Okay, Tiffany, I'll look at your Spellcraft. But I make no guarantees that I can change it."

Tiffany cocked her head toward an old wooden crate marked *Coral Beach Quartz Company* and motioned with the nail gun toward the ground. "Kneel. Keep your hands clasped behind your back. And if you try anything funny, just remember: I've got a whole strip of nails."

She pulled her little pink notebook from her jacket and placed it on the crate in front of me. "Open it to the third page."

"But you told me to keep my hands behind my—"

"Just do it!"

She didn't have to be so testy. Carefully, I eased open the notebook. Page three was nearly as sparkly as the glittery cover…but for entirely different reasons. In the background, a pale watercolor skyline was painted. Once I blinked away the sparkles, I could make out the Ferris wheel, the power plant, and roofline of Shirque Mansion. The Scrivening read:

> *Pinyin Bay has*
> *No way*
> *To stop me*

"So, you see the problem," Tiffany said. "The Crafting created a loophole that allowed me to dig despite the clear and obvious danger of explosion. And yet, that same loophole is also stopping me from actually finding anything, because if I found something, they could order me to permanently stop. Good thing there's plenty of room to add more words."

"How...fortunate...for us." I reached into my bag and pulled out the chisel-tipped marker I'd used to advertise Ladin Silver's vodka tasting.

Tiffany gave me a long-suffering look. "With your *quill*." Boy. All those dumb little questions she was continually asking really added up. "Unless you'd like me to nail that marker to your hand."

And this is why the Handless shouldn't know our secrets. It was tempting to tell Tiffany that I didn't carry my quill around with me...but if she upended my bag and found a long cockatoo feather in a fancy protective case, I could hardly convince her it was just the quirky souvenir of an avid bird enthusiast.

I couldn't hide my quill—but maybe I could sabotage my own ink. As I dug through my bag, I said, "Uh oh, something's wet in here. I think I spilled my ink."

"Let's hope not." Tiffany hefted the nail gun. "I'm sure this thing can easily open up a vein."

"False alarm...heh. My water bottle must've been sweating."

And that wasn't the only thing all a-sweat. It was really hard to figure out how to re-craft the spell to my advantage while appearing to be helping the reporter.

The most elegant solution would be to add some letters to *Pinyin Bay has no way to stop me* so that instead it read, *Pinyin Bay has another way to stop me*—and then hoping that the cavalry would charge in before Tiffany realized what I was up to and ventilated my Scrivening hand. Unfortunately, the spacing between the words was way too tight for four more letters, even with my superfine quill.

"Just need to warm up," I said, doing my best to buy time. I pulled out some scratch paper and penned a delicate line of loops. It was way too simple to be called a flourish—more like a precursor to cursive I'd learned, back when I was still too young to use a toilet without a special potty seat to stop me from falling in.

I could watch someone loop-de-loop for ages—but the Handless get bored with such things pretty quick. Tiffany was vigilant, but only for a few moments. And eventually she began sighing and yawning and rolling kinks out of her neck. And when she inhaled at the cusp of a long and hearty yawn, I dipped my quill.

As her eyelids fluttered shut, I swung my hand toward her Crafting with my arm suddenly ablaze with tingles. Lightning fast, I added a cascade of words to the far end of each line.

> *Pinyin Bay has / great beaches*
> *No way / would I want anything*
> *To stop me / from enjoying them*

Yuri always says the *voshibbyshibby* has a will of its own. I couldn't tell if I was still basking in the Spellcraft sparkles, or Tiffany's startled reaction to my Uncrafting just kicked up a bunch of dust. At least not until we were both seized by a racking fit of sneezes that caused the nail gun to leap from Tiffany's hand and begin spraying nails everywhere in a startling burst of *ca-chunks*.

YURI

13

Of all men for me to be trapped with alone in the dark...did it have to be the one I had falsely accused of exploiting Pinyin Bay?

Long after Dixon's nervous babbling faded into the distance, we sat quietly, the geologist and me. I supposed I would need to apologize, though such words are always awkward on my tongue. But before I could figure out what to say, Skip filled the silence. "Well, I suppose I really stepped in it this time."

"What do you mean?"

"Those things Tiffany said about your partner Dixon being a Spellcrafter? Now I realize what a nincompoop I've been. He and his cousin welcomed me into your home, dropped everything to help me in my time of need—me, a total stranger—and here I go, spouting off and debunking their livelihood. Sabina told me her family was in the stationery business. I had no idea it was a euphemism for Spellcraft."

Skip's regret easily eclipsed mine. What a relief.

"It does no good to sit here feeling sorry for yourself," I told him. "We must get out of here and help Dixon before that woman nails him to the wall."

Unfortunately, that was easier said than done. I tried to give the man a "leg up" as he had done with Sabina, but only ended up getting kicked in the head with a big plastic boot. Luckily, my skull is very hard. And Skip did his best to boost me, but it was no use. He was an academic, not an athlete.

"It's no use," he said. "We'll never get out of here."

I glared in the direction of his voice, considering whether I should have given him more of a fling than a boost, when he slumped to one side and revealed a thin sliver of light in the stone wall. "Turn around," I said. "What is that?"

Thankfully, his vision was not so poor as to stop him from seeing the single thread of light in the darkness. I could make him out faintly now by the meager illumination. He pressed his ear to the wall and knocked. "There's a thin spot, right here. In fact, it feels like this wall was formed by a cave in. Now, if only I had my excavation gear—"

I leveled a solid kick to the wall, and though it jarred my very bones, I felt something give—something other than my foot. A pebble fell from the wall, and though it let in only the faintest bit of light, to our sensitized eyes, it was enough.

With a shriek of Velcro, Skip tore off his orthopedic boot and beat it against the thin spot. I took off one of my own shoes and followed suit. Once a bigger chunk came free, another soon followed, and within minutes we widened the hole large enough for Skip to squeeze through. He crawled across a set of metal tracks on the floor and declared, "It's an old mine shaft! What luck!"

I was not so sure I believed in luck, but I had no desire to return to a discussion about the validity of Spellcraft. He found a rusted prybar and hammer in a jumble of discarded tools, and together, we widened the hole enough for me to squeeze into the shaft as well.

A few holes in the ceiling let in daylight…enough for me to see a massive handcart just a few meters away. One end of the shaft was lost to collapse, but the other burrowed deep into the dune. It curved away into the darkness, and there was no reason for us to think it led anywhere useful...until we heard a burst of sneezing. Followed by a burst of nailing.

"Quickly," I told Skip. "The handcart."

He swung around to squint at a random wall. "Where?"

I grabbed him by the shoulders and pushed him onto the cart, then hurried around the other side, kicking debris off the tracks. The propulsion was a two-person lever. No doubt it would be stiff with age, if it even moved at all. But when I pushed down on my end of the lever, the opposite end smacked upward, catching Skip by the jaw. He somersaulted off the back of the handcart. The momentum launched me forward and sent me hurtling down the tunnel into darkness.

DIXON

14

On my eighth birthday—which would've made Sabina barely six—an overabundance of balloons and an unseasonably warm Spring saw us gearing up for the water balloon war of the decade. We were filling up at the garden hose. The nozzle was busted and leaky, but Uncle Fonzo had helpfully shown me how to pause the flow of water by simply stepping on the hose.

What I hadn't realized was how much pressure would build up in the amount of time it took my cousin and me to argue about whether the next balloon we filled should be red or blue. When I took my foot off the hose, the nozzle shot up out of my hand like a bottle rocket.

Good thing Sabina's front tooth was already somewhat loose.

Anyway, that's what popped into my head as the nail gun leapt from Tiffany's hand and my life flashed before my eyes. Nails shot everywhere—*Pew! Pew! Pew!* And while the sandstone ceiling was able to absorb them, the century-old wooden walls were not. Most bounced off and dropped to the stony floor. But one ricocheted and sank into a knotted rope high above Tiffany's head.

A knot that appeared to be holding shut a really thick wooden hatch in the wall.

Like the surrounding wood, the knot was old—but unlike the wood, the rope fibers had grown brittle and more fragile with age. The rope was as thick as my wrist, but at the impact of the nail, a single twist of fibers popped free with a dusty twang. Followed by another...and another....

Until finally, the massive hatch behind Tiffany was held up by only a single strand of ancient rope. It quivered menacingly as she edged one way, then the other, scrambling for an escape route. And just when it seemed that she was in the clear, a mighty squeal of metal on metal filled the chamber, and the opposite wall burst open in a spray of sandstone crumbs and old lumber.

Explosion?

No—even better!

It was Yuri, soaring through the air on one of those old-timey prospector's see-saw carts. And neither one was particularly aero-dynamic—though luckily, I was there to break Yuri's fall.

Once I was through seeing stars, I realized the old crate I'd been Scribing on was now flattened, and Tiffany's little pink journal was totally black with spilled ink. Wow. Talk about an indelible way of setting the Spellcraft. Lucky for us it happened *after* I Uncrafted the magic.

And then the final, quivering rope fiber snapped, and the big wooden hatch behind Tiffany dropped open like a drawbridge, flattening her...but also revealing a tangle of bone-white petrified bodies.

First thought? Death cooties. Second thought? Yuri won't be able to sleep for the rest of the year...possibly the rest of his life. But as I inserted myself like a human shield between him and the nightmarish remains, I realized the pale bodies looked strangely familiar.

Especially the big, misshapen heads.

If that wasn't evidence enough that I was looking at Phineas Shirque's cast-off statuary, the broken dumbwaiter car would have tipped me off for sure.

Everything in Pinyin Bay is connected. The beach gave way to the Boardwalk. The Fence surrounded the hole. And the hole led to a mine shaft that burrowed below Shirque Mansion.

Maybe everything is connected everywhere, if you're creative enough to find the connections. And maybe those six infamous degrees of separation are the channels through which the Spellcraft flows.

Unlike Pinyin Bay, in which the landmarks are all physically connected through mysterious tunnels that burrow through the bedrock like the maze of a giant ant farm, Spellcraft connections were esoteric, not limited by time or space, or even plausibility. They'd brought Yuri and me together across an ocean, after all, from hundreds of miles away. Wait, no. Thousands? Hundreds of thousands.

Yuri would know. But he'd tell me in furlongs or liters or hectares, which made even less sense than the circuitous route of Spellcraft.

I made a mental note to look it up later.

The big wooden hatch had knocked Tiffany out cold, but Yuri disarmed the nail gun anyhow, just to be safe. We were retrieving our phones from her pockets when my cousin called out, "Dixon? Can you hear me?"

"Over here!"

Her head poked through a portion of the ceiling that was partially collapsed. She was so backlit, it looked like she was calling down from heaven. "You need to get out of there—Skip says it's not safe."

Another head silhouette joined hers. "Where is Tiffany Tennant?" Not Skip's voice. Not at all. "What's going on down there?"

With an eye-roll in her voice, Sabina said, "Officer Hotti saw me hustling over here and insisted on tagging along. In fact, he wouldn't take no for an answer."

"Tiffany just had a little run-in with this trap door," I explained—and how I managed to sound completely guilty of something even though I was telling the unvarnished truth was beyond me!

"Everything is fine." Yuri sounded even guiltier than me.

Officer Hotti swung through the gap and made his way down the pile of rubble with the footing of a mountain goat and the speed of a cheetah, which left no time for me to make it look like I was doing anything other than going through Tiffany's handbag.

"I'll need you to put your hands where I can see them," the cop told me. While he'd looked pretty striking from a distance, he was even more intimidating in person. Almost as tall as Yuri, with an even deeper frown and a bulletproof vest.

"Wow! Talk about stern! Those bridesmaids must've been pretty tipsy to mistake you for a stripper, whether you were carrying a boombox or not. Not that you're not attractive enough to be a stripper. Heck, I'll bet you could pose for one of those local fund-raising calendars. You know the ones—shirtless guys and their dogs? Though I guess you'd need a dog for that. Have you got a dog? If not, maybe you could rent one, though I'm not exactly sure where one would go about renting a dog. But if you can settle for a leopard gecko, my parents are looking to unload one cheap—"

"Sir?" Officer Hotti snapped, and whatever train of thought was running rampant in my head screeched to a precarious halt.

"Forget about my cousin," Sabina cried. "He's obviously not at fault. It couldn't possibly be more clear that this woman was attacked by a door. And everyone knows there's only one possible reason that might happen." Before I could say *nail gun run amok*, she answered her own question—very forcefully, at that. "Spellcraft!"

Now she had the cop's attention.

When he turned to her, I frantically gestured "time out" behind his back. But other than dodgeball, which gave her a gym-sanctioned opportunity to nail the mean kids with a red rubber ball, Sabina was not much into sports. She said, "This was no freak accident. Tiffany Tennant was carrying around a dangerous piece of Spellcraft. I'll bet it's even illegal!"

Where was Sabina getting all this? Yuri was gesticulating now too, something Russian that looked like he was threatening to cut her throat, while I time-outed so hard I nearly jammed my own finger. When Officer Hotti turned back around to see why my hand-flapping was fanning the back of his neck, I quickly flailed into an innocent hands-up while Yuri succumbed to the sudden urge to scratch his jaw. The cop gave us each a very stern look, then said, "Don't move. And remember—the evidence will speak for itself. If you've got nothing to hide, then there's nothing for you to worry about."

I was considering whether or not I should entrust my quill to Sabina while I got sent to the big house, when Officer Hotti plucked something out of Tiffany's unconscious grasp and said, "What's this?" He held up a sheet of stiff watercolor paper that was the perfect size to hold a bit of Spellcraft, and read, "Persistence opens all doors."

"No wonder that door fell on her," Sabina declared. "What with that extra super illegal piece of Spellcraft she was walking around with right in her hand. Arrest her."

Officer Hotti leveled a look at Sabina while I practically squirmed out of my skin. And just as I decided that while Sabina's heart was in the right place, she couldn't act herself out of a paper bag, he reached for the little radio thingie on his shoulder and said, "Obviously, I can't arrest an unconscious woman. I'll call some paramedics to revive her first."

I decided not to mention the little pink notebook—after all, there might be more Spellcraft in there that needed undoing. Besides, I didn't want to take the spotlight off the one that would land Tiffany in jail. Even if it wasn't technically hers.

Once the paramedics carted the reporter away—thankfully, with the intimidating Officer Hotti in tow—Sabina, Yuri and I could all breathe a sigh of relief...at least until I realized we were missing someone. "What happened to Skip?"

"He's waiting for us in the crack. He told me all about what Tiffany did and insisted I go help you guys and come back for him later."

"Skip turned out to be a pretty good guy after all," I said.

Sabina gave me the side-eye. "What's that supposed to mean?"

Oops. She hadn't been privy to our suspicions. I exchanged a glance with Yuri, then said, "Well...er...just that you never can tell with traveling geologists."

Sabina let it slide. "When I got to the science van, I realized I didn't have the first clue what a centrifuge looked like. And when I tried to look it up, I found out I'd fallen on my phone and smashed the screen. How the heck did people survive before Google, anyway?"

Yuri said, "It is fortunate it took you as long as it did. Otherwise, you would be stuck back there with Skip. Or worse, Tiffany could have made an example of you."

Still.... "Too bad you sacrificed your Crafting to get us out of hot water."

Sabina shrugged. "Officer Hotti was distracted by you rambling about dogs, and I had to do *something* before you ran out of steam. You were on a pretty good roll, but I figured even you would need to come up for air at some point."

"But it was your favorite." And while Craftings were easy enough to come by when everyone in your social circle is a Scrivener, each instance of Spellcraft has got to be unique. Otherwise, it wouldn't be a craft, but an industry.

Good thing. Nobody in my circuit would last more than five minutes on an assembly line.

"I'll survive," my cousin said. "And at least now I can stop worrying about getting caught."

It turned out that Skip could see a heck of a lot better with his old prescription than he could with the glasses that met their demise beneath the heel of Sabina's combat boot. And that observation made me re-think the Crafting on the back of his Arena Rock Award. Since he didn't even believe in Spellcraft, he clearly hadn't commissioned the piece. We figured one of his rivals had been trying to keep him from rising up any farther in the traveling geology ranks.

Whatever the Crafting's intent, as was so often the case, the

Spellcraft had a mind of its own. Laboring "sight unseen" not only left Skip working away in obscurity—it rendered him practically blind. I'd done him a huge favor by Uncrafting it. But given his hardcore, science-driven disbelief in Spellcraft, my chances of collecting any financial recompense were slim.

A good deed is its own reward. Now, there's something no one in my family would ever say. But I will admit, my loved ones and I all benefited from Skip's restored vision. He spotted a squashed blueprint in Yuri's truck—the one we'd used to clear the cob-web-covered way to Phineas Shirque's attic. With those plans, he determined that the explosions rocking Pinyin Bay were not due to some random naturally-occurring flammably inflammable substance, but a series of long-forgotten septic tanks.

Even so, when Mayor Dunce rolled back into town and ordered Tiffany's construction crew to fill in the collapsing tunnels beneath the sand dunes, we thought it best not to second-guess him.

Skip's restored vision had another unexpected consequence: now that he'd had a good look at Sabina, he no longer saw her as just a helpful friend. His libido hadn't been on the fritz after all. He just hadn't realized how cute my cousin was! And yet, the next day, he packed up his Nature World van, gave Sabina a stilted hug, slipped off his orthopedic boot, and drove gingerly off into the sunset toward his next geological adventure.

We stood on the sidewalk in a loose cluster—Sabina, Yuri and me. My cousin and I waved goodbye. Yuri glared at the van's receding taillights. Even though it turned out Skip wasn't the secret master-mind behind the Loveland Corporation after all, Yuri never took a shine to him. So, I was surprised when he asked Sabina, "Why was he so eager to leave?"

"Oh, that was my doing. I told him my dad was on his way home with a sawed-off shotgun."

"As if Uncle Fonzo would know which end was which!" I chortled.

Yuri was puzzled. "I thought you were interested in Skip."

"I was...but ever since he started wearing that old prescription, he's been staring at my chest. Never trust a guy who's fixated on your boobs—unless you're trying to pickpocket him, in which case, have at it."

That sounded a lot more like my family.

"Did you ever figure out why he spent so much time on Wikipedia?" I asked.

"Apparently, one of his favorite hobbies was to fact-check other people's entries. I guess he found it soothing."

Yuri seemed grudgingly satisfied by that explanation. "And what about all the properties Loveland bought?"

"According to Pinyin Minute," I said, "the financing is all in default and the bank will be unloading them cheap."

"Tiffany Tennant is still reporting?" Sabina asked.

"Not at all. Remember my friend Charlotte, the one with all the conspiracy theories? She took over Tiffany's job. I'm guessing the local news is about to get a *lot* more interesting."

"That reminds me...." Yuri went to his truck and pulled out a familiar book. The cover no longer stuck together. "I am curious to see what other secrets are buried in Pinyin Bay...even if they are all elaborate ruses meant to throw the Handless off the scent of the local Spellcrafters."

"Hold on," I said. "You think the whackadoo was deliberate? How do you know the author wasn't just as paranoid as her granddaughter?"

"I took a better look at the history. Not only was Meemaw Jones old friends with Morticia Shirque, but her husband was the illustrator of this book. And his original paintings were more than just pretty pictures."

"How about that?" Sabina remarked—it really takes a lot to impress her sometimes. "You never know where you're gonna run into a Seer." And with that, she headed to the backyard to watch the fireflies.

I carried *Buried Secrets* upstairs (very gingerly, I might add) while Yuri retrieved the cedar panel from the back of his truck—the hunk of wood sent airborne by the most recent explosion—and brought it up to our bedroom. Only one side of the panel was splintery.

Yuri hid that part behind our mattress when he bolted it to the wall. It made for a handsome headboard, but even better, it filled the bedroom we shared with the comforting scent of cedar.

We got Meringue settled in her cage with a blanket over the top to encourage her to stop singing the Banana Splits theme song and finally get some sleep. Once the attic was all quiet, it was almost like being in the cabin again. Except the mattress was cushier. And there were no wayward drafts whistling through the crack beneath the door. And Yuri didn't bonk his elbows on the walls when he stripped me down and had his Russian way with me.

Afterward, I stroked our new headboard as we lay together in a tangle of limbs, feeling sentimental about the fact that our tiny love shack was no more…but only a little. Because while we'd made some great memories in the cabin, the attic apartment was truly ours—Yuri's and mine.

Yuri captured my hand and brought it to his lips, brushed a kiss across my knuckles, then said, "You are very quiet. What are you thinking?"

"Oh, just the normal sorts of stuff you'd think after a studly tattooed guy well and truly rocked your world."

"Such as?"

"Such as, I'm relieved none of my other childhood memories will be exploding anytime soon. And I'm thrilled it's safe enough for my parents to come back once they're done enjoying their suite. And…" dare I say it? "After all that we've seen together and all that we've done, I've never been more sure that…*Yahtzee blah you-blue.*"

No doubt I'd really mangled the sentiment. The urge to fill the silence with something—*anything*—was strong, but I couldn't think of anything else to say.

Yuri's expression? Unreadable.

But only for a moment.

And then his gaze went soft as he gathered my hand in his…and warmed my ink-stained knuckles with a kiss.

ABOUT THE AUTHOR

Jordan Castillo Price would love to live in Scrivener Village, but the closest she can find is a century-old house in which none of the doors work.

She has spent time in an orthopedic boot. It was not fun.

www.jordancastilloprice.com